YOURS

German First Edition December 2014

© Don Both: bethy86@hotmail.de

https://www.Facebook.com/pages/DonBoth/248891035138778

All rights reserved!

*Reproduction, even excerpts, requires written permission from the publisher. Persons and events are fictitious. Any resemblance to real people is purely coincidental and not intentional.*

English translation/editing/proofreading:

buchuebersetzer.webs.com

Cover: Babels

Published by: A.P.P. Publishing House

Peter Neuhäußer

Gemeindegässle 05

89150 Laichingen

Mobi: 978-3-96115-433-3

Epub: 978-3-96115-434-0

Print: 978-3-96115-435-7

*This novel is translated, proofread, and edited according to American-English grammar.*

# DON BOTH

# YOURS

A.P.P

# Already published by Don Both:

The Unholy Books of Tristan Wrangler,
Book 1

My Girl

MINE

# 1. The Merger

*Tristan 'Helpful' Wrangler*

H'm, today my slut looked delicious enough to bite as she came toward me. Her long legs were in tight black jeans and her small feet were in sneakers, which did not bother me. A dark blue V-neck pullover flattered her upper body, immediately captivating my attention. I liked it when she wore it because I loved her cleavage.

Her hair, as so often, was again in a ponytail, but nevertheless, it hung down below her shoulder blades. Her face was lightly made up, the mascara making her eyelashes appear even longer. The delicate lipstick that matched her pink cheeks tempted me and did not deliver me from evil.

She was not styled, wore no designer clothing, high heels, or push-up bra.

Yet, she was divine.

Her curves always made me think nasty thoughts.

Then there was her pretty face with flawless complexion. Those expressive big eyes...the delicate neck...those beautiful small hands, which always instinctively touched me. I could have continued like that forever because there was not one single fragrant inch of her that I didn't enjoy. Fuck, I already wanted her again and here she had just arrived in my office.

"Hi," she softly murmured and hung up the coat she had peeled herself out of on the hook next to my door. I immediately noticed how unenthusiastically she greeted me and I didn't like it.

"Hi?" I replied suspiciously, raised an eyebrow, turned completely around in my office chair, put my outstretched fingertips together, and looked over them.

She remained near the entrance as her gaze slid back and forth between my face and body. Her cheeks reddened. Oh, yes, Mia wanted me as badly as I did her. Maybe she also recalled our last time, which turned her on even more and made me even hotter for her.

Of course, I also looked hot in my plain white shirt and low riding jeans.

"What do you have planned for me for today?" she asked. I could tell by the tone of her voice that she was already quite excited. Naturally. She never knew what I had planned for her, whether I would send her to hell again by fucking her in front of strangers, or if I would just fuck her in private and send her to seventh heaven.

Today...it would be seventh heaven.

Because, honestly, I had a somewhat pretty guilty conscience about the Eva thing. I should have known Mia would not forgive me for teaming up with her worst enemy.

That she was still around was all the proof I needed: Mia Angel truly loved me. And that changed a lot...

Granted, Eva Eber also loved me in her own way, but oftentimes her feelings were quite pathological and nothing compared to Mia's unquestioning nature. Eva's tenacity alone was scary. During my jail stint, she had continuously bombarded me with letters even though I had not answered even one of them. Once I was released, she found out about my club and one evening showed up, facing me with tears streaming down her face. I had sent her away night after night. Still, she had not given up. That was about the time the first rumors of me being gay started circulating because the fucker had not been in the mood for broads and vehemently refused to do its duty — oh, yes, I, Tristan Wrangler, was impotent with all other women but *her*! She had literally turned me into a limp dick! So, I had decided, partly out of spite, but also to finally escape all those homophobic wisecracks, to take Eva Eber as an alibi girlfriend. For no other reason. Eva was happy to be seen with me in public and bragged about it. Everyone who knew us was also aware that we had some kind of relationship and she wallowed in my reputation like a pig in mud, which was enough for her. Otherwise, she left me alone, at least for the most part.

But as if she sensed that Mia had entered my life again, she suddenly became obtrusive, always calling unannounced, even suggesting in her madness that she *come over* and using every opportunity to touch me!

What was that overly skinny bimbo thinking?

I was so sick of her scheming. Already back then. Even today, she almost drove a wedge between Mia and me. But I would no longer allow it. Never again. Slowly, we fell back into our old rhythm, including our strong bond...

Because Eva's subconscious attempt to separate us was anything but successful. Mia Marena was finally here — with me.

The relief that she was not gone for good hung thick in the air yesterday. Just because of that, she was able to make me promise not to be like *that* anymore. Both of us knew what that meant... No humiliation and degradation... At least nothing that would destroy her.

I stood up, walked over to my closet where I grabbed a prepared basket and again felt like Little Red Riding Hood as I wordlessly offered Mia my arm. She linked her arm without hesitation and grinned. Amused, I rolled my eyes and led her through the gallery to the rear of the property – also called *The Garden of Eden* – a part of the outside grounds of my special club. During the summer, you could enjoy the fresh air out here, which was why large four-poster rattan beds and other fucking sites (for example *in* a tree, a cave, etc.) were plentiful. There were various scavenger stations with love swings and bulls with dildos sticking out their backs, especially good for a women's rodeo. An amusement park for adults. For the more daring, you could even try it on a small roller coaster. Numerous paths snaked along the spacious grounds, benches hid behind huge tree trunks, and kinky statues lined the avenues. Everything was beautifully equipped with floodlights and fog machines, reminiscent of a mystically wicked place.

Mia stared wide-eyed at me as I led her outside. Although it was not raining, it was rather cold and the air full of moisture. At the end of the garden, we reached the planned destination.

She did not immediately realize where we were because dense fog surrounded us. Only when we were closer did she notice the hot thermal spring I led her to. Her gasp betrayed how impressed she was. I had forked out a couple grand for the installation, but then it was also a hit, especially with the play of color underwater.

The bubbling source lay somewhat hidden under the far-reaching branches of a large willow tree. Everything was made of smooth volcanic rock with no sharp corners or edges and it was gently illuminated. The colors alternated between red, yellow, orange, and purple. There was nothing cold, nothing hard (except my fucker), only warmth and heat.

"Wow!" was Mia's first comment, which made me grin. Of course, it certainly was *wow*. At least my world offered a few benefits.

"M'm-m'm." Unable to resist, I approached her from behind and wrapped my arms around her flat belly. Immediately, I undid the button of her pants and ran my nose over her neck. Inhaled...felt... smiled... Intoxicating!

She shuddered and squirmed somewhat, whereby her soft ass cheeks rubbed against my fucker. Oh-oh, I had to get in there now... Obviously in the hot water because out in the open we might freeze vital body parts.

Fog still wafted around us when she turned to face me and carefully undressed me. Button by button, she timidly opened my shirt, looked me in the eyes, and kissed every inch of exposed skin. I allowed it... She was particularly thoroughly with my left breast, caressing every inch below the tattoo before wrapping her full lips around my nipple and gently sucking on it. With a harsh growl, I pulled the scrunchy out her hair so it would spill over her delicate shoulders and pert breasts. Then I rolled my head back as I gleefully buried my hands in her velvety soft brown-blonde curls and disheveled it.

I loved grabbing it in my fist and pulling her head back to show her the desired direction. I did that now too because if she were to continue sucking and licking so thoroughly, I would want her to do it further down. But we weren't that far yet. All in good time. After all, I wanted to undress her first, see her before me in all her glory. Urgently so!

I wasted no time and stopped the little minx. She gasped, but I released her hair, grinned at her, pulled the sweater plus undershirt over her head so that she stood topless and freezing before me.

"Are you cold?" I teased her because her nipples were as stiff as whipped cream. Before she could reply, I leaned down and paid her back.

"Yummy..." I hummed gleefully against her soft skin as I sucked on a nipple while kneading the other tit with my whole hand. Gently, not roughly.

"Oh God, Tristan! What is going on with you today?"

"I am merely sticking to our latest agreement..." I mumbled innocently, "...why, are you complaining?" and glared at her provocatively from down below. I could also do it differently — if she wanted...

"*No!*" she immediately cried and arched her back. I laughed passionately against her increasingly cold skin and abruptly moved away from her upper body. Hastily, I squatted before her and released her from the rest of her clothes. As promised, she wore no underwear, which I happily noted.

As soon as I stood up, she relieved me of my pants following my subtle command to free my, as usual, impatient fucker from the confines of the fabric. I grinned as she forced the denim down my legs and almost fell over. Eventually, she succeeded and both of us stood there naked, albeit unusually quiet. I had never spoken so little since I began fucking Mia. But today I only wanted... Yes, what exactly?

To silently enjoy... To let the past be the past...

I grinned down at her, unexpectedly threw my arms around her, and grabbed her smooth bare buttocks. Trembling, she grinned at me and leaned against my shoulder as I lifted her up. Absolutely instinctively, her legs wrapped around my hips and I carried her into the hot tub.

I leaned my back against the round stone behind me, sighed, rolled my head back, and watched her intently as she sat on my thighs. I sat comfortably as if in a chair because the hot tub was built so you could sit on the edge and swim in the center. It could accommodate at least 15 people and the other end lay shrouded in fog and could not be seen. Colored lights danced softly across Mia's pale skin and her hair darkened as it floated on the surface of the water. She was a sexy little mermaid...

Luckily, she was not an actual mermaid; otherwise, she would not have the appropriate orifices apart from maybe her mouth.

Slowly, I wrapped a wet strand around my fist. Puzzled, she snorted as I pulled her nearer. So close that the tips of our noses almost touched. Oh, fuck! Why was I torturing myself? Now *I* wanted to kiss her! Yet it was prohibited. Even her eyes betrayed her longing for the same. But I didn't, I merely held her until I felt her vibrating with excitement because I enjoyed toying with her even though I knew it was wrong to give her false hope. Nevertheless, I loved it when she looked at me like she did at that moment.

"Mia," I whispered against her little face.

"Yes?" She sounded so fragile, so uncertain, gentle and, above all else, devoted as always... The sound went straight to my fucker.

"You may ride me now," I announced magnanimously, releasing the strand of hair and grabbing her hips with both hands.

Her wet upper body popped out of the water briefly as I easily lifted her up. She gasped when the cold air hit her heated skin and she closed her eyes when I positioned her over me. I held it in position with one hand as I slowly lowered her. Divinely, she threw her head back, even rolled her eyes. She arched her back as I entered her fully, thrusting her nipples toward me, and I could not resist, sat up, wrapped her firmly in both arms, and sucked extensively on them while she, without prompting or guidance, started rotating her hips. She clung to my shoulders and made small gentle moans mixed with delicate whimpers each time I mimicked her movements.

Steam surrounded us, the water splashed softly. The night was otherwise silent and dark except for the hot tub's dancing lights and absolutely soothing noises. It really seemed heavenly ... How had I ever gone without it for so long? How was I ever supposed to do without it?

I sucked harder on her nipple. She shocked me by contracting tighter around me and moaning louder, only to push me back by my shoulders.

"Stop, Tristan! Or else I'll come at any moment!" she explained unsteadily.

*Oh, fuck!*

I could no longer look at her or *I* would come!

So, I rolled my head back, put my hands on her thighs, happily closed my eyes, and simply felt her...as well as listened. Because I loved the desperate noises she made, loved how she grew increasingly demanding in her movements, and idolized the way her fingertips dug hard in my chest while she forcefully bit her lip and frowned. Her legs were shaking and she was trembling on the inside, nearly triggering a premature orgasm.

Now *I* had to grit my teeth as I clawed at her pliable flesh because I wanted her to come first.

"Mia!" I growled because she was intentionally holding back. I opened my eyes so I could glare at her indignantly.

What did she do? She smiled at me naughtily, knowing perfectly well what she was doing to me as I restrained myself for her and how it tormented me.

"You little bitch!" I managed to snap, half-laughing, half-moaning in torment because she fucking again contracted around me.

Okay...she asked for it! I could easily bring her to climax despite her resistance. Gently, I took my fingers from her thigh and stroked her clit.

Shocked, she panted and grabbed my hand, but it was already too late. The timer had been activated, the bomb would go off. Any moment now... Just a little gentle friction while she continued gripping my wrist and...

"WHO… lives in a pineapple deep in the sea? Sponge Bob Square Pants! Sponge Bob Square Pants!"

It was a ringtone!

What was that crap?

And then she did something I would never forgive her for. *Never!*

She got off me!

"*What the fuck?*" I cursed and tried to stop her, but she evaded my grasp!

Meanwhile, she was rummaging in her pants pocket while the song continuously trilled on, riling me up even more. It wasn't until shortly before the grand finale when she finally answered.

"Hello?" Breathless, she listened while I stared at her. She was kneeling at the edge of the hot tub, naked and shivering and not making any move to return to me!

I had been *so* close, just as she had been!

"What?" she screamed and jumped up, her expression panicked. Searching, she looked for and gathered up her clothes. "Yes, I'll be there in 20 minutes. Tell him I'll be right there!" she cried desperately and actually started to pull on her pants with one hand. I was speechless! "Okay, see you soon!" She hung up, totally ignored me, and forced her wet body into her clothes. I still hated it when Mia dressed. It was downright depressing.

With a jolt, I jumped out of the hot tub.

WOW! It was cold! But it didn't matter. Freezing, I stood in front of her as she tugged her undershirt and sweater, both at the same time, over her wet head.

"Hey, hey, hey... Stop!" I helped pull the items down because by herself she was unsuccessful. "What the hell is going on?" I asked as soon as her face poked through the neckline, unable to do anything for my shivering because it really was fucking cold.

Then, for the first time, I noticed her expression. She truly seemed concerned.

"Tristan, I have to go! I'm sorry, but it's an emergency!" She searched for her shoes to slip on without bothering with socks, but only found one. "I have to... I have to go to the home..."

"What happened?" I handed her the missing one. When she was finally good to go, she eyed me with drooping shoulders and a fearful expression.

"It's Robbie..." Which explained her panic. He was her favorite child at the home where she worked — with whom she had a special relationship.

"I need to call a cab!" She tapped her phone as if her life depended on it and I barely kept my eyes from rolling as I took it away from her. Not waiting for her protest, I threw on my clothes while at the same time, I managed to ward off her small hands that were trying to grab the cell phone.

"I'll give you a ride!" I announced and marched off. She seemed confused and hesitated for a moment before she followed me across the grounds, past the side of the house to my Audi.

\*\*\*

During the drive, she seemed restless. I could tell she was literally cursing every red traffic light and wishing I'd use all the horsepower my baby number... I was not sure anymore... had.

Mia was excessively nervous and I was worried she might collapse, so I did something I had planned to never to do again! I calmed her, spoke to her, once again risked everything and perhaps even making a fool out of myself — okay, nothing new when it came to her...

"Mia..." Unintentionally, I sounded soft and calm as I lightly squeezed her leg. "What's wrong with him?" Distressed, she glanced at me and I noticed the smooth skin of her cheeks was covered in tears. Great!

"He's been throwing up for the past four hours. He won't stop crying and no one can calm him!"

"Oh." That didn't sound good.

"I'm sure I can calm him. I have to be there for him. He trusts no one but me!"

Well, if that's not a mistake...

"We are almost there," I replied because her last sentence conjured up too many negative memories.

I rounded the last corner and as soon as I came to a stop across the street from the home, she jumped out and ran full speed to the entrance. I was tempted to leave and pretend I didn't care, but a small part of me that was already not so small anymore whispered to me that my girl needed me and that I should not waste time and get my damn ass up there! So, I got out swearing and actually followed her.

When I entered the hallway of the huge converted farmhouse with its colorful shutters, I saw her sprint around a corner and heard her rushing upstairs. The floor beneath my feet creaked like the door did when I closed it behind me. The wooden staircase also protested under my feet and although I had misgivings, I followed her up to the second floor and down the corridor to the end, where she ripped open a door to disappear once more from view.

By the time I entered the room, she was already sitting on the edge of a small old bed wiping the forehead of a pallid Robbie.

"Mirti?" he asked in a fragile voice and his tiny hand reached for hers.

"Yes, my darling. I am here," she whispered and bent down to put her full red lips on his sweaty temple. I swallowed hard. Tears were running down his cheeks as he closed his eyes and breathed deeply.

"I feel so sick... I must have eaten something bad..." the little one muttered and snuggled against her palm. Oh...fuck!

The way he looked at her as if she was his queen. And the way she was looking at him...as if he was her personal little prince for whom she would lay the world at his feet.

"What exactly did you eat?" Mia asked softly, a slight trace of a smile on her beautiful face.

"Grass. Johann and Stefan said it would be good for me," Robbie replied and I huffed. Surprised, both glanced at me. Apparently, they just noticed me. I felt awkward as I shifted my weight from foot to foot.

"Um... I..." I had no idea what to say. I felt like I was sticking my nose where it didn't belong, but then the corners of Robbie's pale lips turned upward before he briefly closed his eyes.

"I'm glad your friend is here too...Mirti... Just don't start fighting again!" Mia stared at Robbie. Then me. Then Robbie. Then me. And I smiled devilishly. *Let's see how you dig yourself out of this one, baby...*

"I did not tell him you're my friend," she said defensively and right then, she was my girl again, the one who had won my heart with her uncertainty. I released the doorframe and sauntered over to her. Before I could reply, the boy continued.

"It's so obvious. It's yucky the way he looks at you with his lovesick gaze. I hope you are not going to kiss now!" He certainly was on to us. I was about to sit down in the old rocking chair next to the bed when I stumbled the last step. Mia was completely overwhelmed; probably scared I might become angry. But even I was a bit taken aback.

How did the little shit arrive at that? I may find her seductive, sometimes even charming, and occasionally even sweet, but I did not love her! Hadn't in a long time!

"That I can promise you, boss," I laughed and finally sat down. Robbie smiled a bit more contently as he glanced back and forth between the still-shocked beet-red Mia and me. "So, you aren't going to kiss?"

"We sure will," I countered immediately without batting an eye. I don't know why...well, okay...I felt like teasing him a little. It sparked his spirit, which was better than wallowing in self-pity whining about nausea.

Mia merely raised an eyebrow. "Is that so?"

Oh, yeah! It's not like we kiss! Oh, fuck! What was wrong with me today? How could I have forgotten?

"Argh!" Robbie cried out soulfully and I chuckled as he buried his face in the pillow. "I feel sick again..." he mumbled suddenly and Mia jumped up.

"Do you have to throw up?' she asked and I rolled my eyes because she was creating panic when she picked up the boy in her shaky arms even though he was fine to walk by himself...

"I believe so," he announced and she ran with him into the bathroom. I felt sorry for him, especially when I heard him cough and choke... And still, I didn't move. Instead, I scanned the dimly lit room while they were gone.

It was quite tiny, but for a children's home, it was probably quite luxurious to have a private haven. Under the window was a small table made from a partially splintering light wood. The chair in front of it looked as if it would break at any moment. Above the desk hung quite a few pictures. Most featured boxing gloves or two drawn stick figures beating each other up. For such a little guy, I thought he drew quite well... In addition to the work area in the corner, there was a wardrobe — without little bear knobs... On the wall above the bed hung a giant poster of Ukrainian boxers, who I knew personally because they sponsored the gym.

The wall was plastered with friendly yellow wallpaper that, unfortunately, was already quite faded and flaking in many places.

Mia returned with Robbie, who had a bit more color in his face. However, he seemed weaker than before.

As soon as she put him to bed, covered him, and sat next to it, his big eyes closed and he promptly fell asleep. Mia continued stroking his bright thin child hair and I realized it was exactly what he needed. Her touch. To know she would not disappear again, to know that even though he was dreaming, someone he could rely on was there in his little world, no matter what time. To know someone who would drop everything at a moments' notice when he needed that person, regardless of where that person was or what they were doing.

I could tell by her gestures and facial expressions that Mia loved the child unconditionally. It was exactly the way she looked and touched me too. So why the betrayal? Back then, did she truly no longer want to be with me? Was she capable of getting rid of me in such a vile way? Could she do something like that to Robbie? No! Definitely not. Because she loved him...

Truly... With all her heart.

"Do you love me?" As soon as I uttered the words, I wanted to take them back...but it was too late. Mia's head whipped around. Calmly, I returned her stare while on the inside the fiercest battle of a lifetime raged. An all-decisive battle or had I already lost? *Won?* Depending on...

"I love you more than life itself, Tristan," she replied, feigning calmness. However, her eyes betrayed that she felt like I did.

Robbie turned on his side and sighed blissfully. He pulled Mia's hand along so she had to bend over him as he held it tightly against his little chest like a stuffed animal.

Gently, she smiled down at him before looking up at me again. I stared back — focusing on those caramel colored depths...

"So, why did you do it then?" I whispered, barely audible. The question had plagued me for years until I arrived at the conclusion that the *why* didn't matter. The only thing that mattered was that *it had* happened.

Her eyes took on a suspicious glint, which I didn't like one bit, but I would still insist on an answer. I could see she had a guilty conscience, felt remorse, regret...but had no intention in redeeming herself.

"I was a trap. My father set me up." She was quiet and calm, voice trembling minimally like she had prepared herself for this conversation about a million times.

"How?' She swallowed hard and tried to sit up somewhat, but Robbie grumbled restlessly and she froze.

"He threatened to put you in jail and destroy your career if I did not testify against you... The statement was supposed to be his leverage...and I stupidly believed him..."

I laughed humorlessly because if it was actually the truth, then yes, that was precisely what happened...

"Tell me, how was he supposed to make sure I went to jail? Did he have evidence against me," I asked pointedly.

She squared her chin in response to my caustic tone. "He had evidence that pointed to you. He had an ally..."

"Is that so?" My brow shot up.

"Yes." Mia looked me squarely in the eyes.

"Who?"

Now one of Mia's eyebrows raised in such an obvious way that a verbal response was no longer required. Immediately, I knew who she was talking about. EVA!

Promptly, I started to laugh.

The woman who had played my alibi girlfriend, who had always been Mia's pussy rival, who acted like a complete lunatic, who, compared to Mia, *would* not be able to do such... Besides, what evidence could she supposedly have against me? She had always been too clueless as well as stupid.

"Forget it!" I had to laugh and when Robbie rolled over I abruptly stopped. "Now you've given yourself away! Tell that fairy tale to someone else!"

"But it is the truth!" she said defensively a few octaves too high, just like I had. Robbie groaned.

"You know what, Mia Marena?" I snarled contemptuously, "I'm in no mood for your bullshit!" I forced myself to talk softer and stood up. Mia stared at me, shocked. She probably didn't expect me to react so harshly to her lie. "Eight years ago, for whatever fucking reason, you had enough of me...but I don't get why you are now going through all the trouble to dish out such fucked up crap!"

I ran a hand through my hair as I walked to the door.

"Tristan, no!" In the next moment, she hugged me from behind. I had no idea how she had managed to catch up to me so quickly, but her arms wrapped tightly around my stomach. Her face pressed between my shoulder blades. My shirt became soaking wet and she shivered all over as she kept a tight grip on me. Frantically.

With my hand already on the knob, I stopped and stared straight ahead at the door.

"Let go of me," I demanded softly.

"Never!" she immediately swore and tightened her grip on me.

"What more do you want from me, Mia?" I hissed between clenched teeth and almost crushed the doorknob in my fist.

"You!" I rolled my eyes hearing her sobbing reply. *Why* did I even ask?

"Why would you want me the way I am now?"

"I've always wanted you! No matter which you!"

Unnerved, I huffed because we simply weren't making progress.

"Okay, so be it. I'm not good enough for you." Somehow, I had to keep her at bay, dammit! All this was already way too intimate.

Dangerously so!

Now, she snorted wryly, rubbed her nose across my back, and deeply inhaled my scent.

"I know I hurt you. But you really have to come to terms with the fact that not everything happened the way you pieced it together over the years... If only you had a little more confidence in us...then...you would have seen it. But I understand what happened; even I fell for it... No woman has ever given you a reason to trust her, but you can trust me! I've learned from my mistakes," she suddenly whispered. "I know you are purposefully keeping me at a distance, Tristan, but you will not succeed! Never!"

FUCK! Why did the little slut see right through me?

"Don't you realize it was fate that brought us back together again? Can't you see we still have the same feelings for each other that we had eight years ago? They won't stop simply because you want them to! Don't you realize what we could give each other? Why make it difficult on ourselves? How many times in recent weeks have I tried to get rid of you? How many times did you send me away? And yet, here we are, together again!"

"All I know right now is that you should stop drooling on my shirt..." And with that, I removed my hand from the doorknob...and grinding my teeth, hung my head. She was right — dammit...

"I need you... Please..." she whispered hoarsely and I sighed resignedly... As usual, I had no chance when she acted like that... Oh, damn old tactics... "Yes, okay," I waved her off, and only then did she wordlessly, but clearly relieved, let go of me, and turn back to Robbie's bed. She smiled at me and self-consciously wiped the tears away as I sat back down in the rocking chair and watched how she stroked the little boy.

"Thank you, Tristan," she said and I leaned toward her, supporting myself with my hands on the mattress on either side of her ass so I was again oh-too-close to her and her scent.

"Don't thank me yet. I demand retribution, Miss Angel," I murmured. She bit her lip hard and again drew my attention to that damn cherry mouth. "Stop. Chewing. Your. Lip!" I hissed and with a silent *Oh!* she released her lower lip from her teeth.

"Good girl." I patted her cheek, leaned back again, and let my gaze travel around the room once more and dryly noted, "Quite a fucked up place." Naturally, Mia was immediately defensive.

"We have no money to renovate."

"Honestly?" Too bad for the little guy...

"Yes." She looked at Robbie, who was still sleeping peacefully. "The house needs lots of work. Windows and doors need to be insulated, the heating system needs a complete overhaul, everything could use a fresh coat of paint, and new flooring. We are actually in ruins. And we are no longer receiving state funds; this home belongs to Sister Carmen. She founded it with four other nuns, all of whom have already passed on... She is broke and struggling every month to pay the bills. I don't think she can keep this place open much longer..."

"Then what?" I asked because I didn't like the thought of it.

Mia shrugged. "Then all of us lose our jobs and I'll probably never see Robbie again..." Her pain did not escape me although she suppressed it immediately because she was a fighter. Always to the extreme — which was typical for Mia when she loved something.

"We are organizing an Oktoberfest with a beer tent to raise money. It was the older children's idea..." Crap, she was so attractive when her eyes shined full of hope.

"Oktoberfest? With beer? Lederhosen and dirndls?" I inquired quite excitedly with a raised eyebrow — I had dirndls on my mind.

Mia laughed softly. "Yes, with dirndl and lederhosen, but with lemonade."

"Crap!" I pumped the air with one fist, which she accompanied with a slight chuckle before chewing on her lip again — brooding.

"We still have no idea how we'll manage it in two weeks because, as usual, we lack funds and equipment, but we have no choice since the advertising is sponsored and we've already distributed it. So, it will happen... No matter how... We need every penny the visitors are willing to part with."

"It'll work out." I winked at her and before she could reply, I voiced my next question. "What exactly did you have in mind?"

"Well..." Now she was all fired up. Typical! When she cared about something, she literally embodied passion.

Oh, yesss...

"We'll definitely have bratwursts and pretzels, which are a must. Then we want to set up a few booths where the kids can throw balls at cans, paint each other's faces, bow and arrow shooting, handcrafts, and a booth selling handmade pottery, an egg-spoon race or sack races, a petting zoo would be nice... and something for the kids to roughhouse on because they like it so much ..."

"A boxing ring..." I added grinning, and her eyes widened.

"YES!" She clapped her hands and grinned at me euphorically, which made me laugh because she was too cute... "Will you help us?" Now she was clinging to my sleeve, lightly tugging on it. And then there were her joyful wide eyes. How was I supposed to resist her when she was like that? How was I supposed to *even* resist her? I sighed resignedly when I realized I would never be able to do it.

"Yessss..." I said reluctantly.

"YESSSSSSSSSSSSSS!" she screamed so loud she woke up Robbie. Mia quickly went to the bathroom with him while I used the time to go outside for a smoke and stared senselessly at the moon to clear my head.

\*\*\*

By the time I came back upstairs, Mia had fallen asleep next to the boy in his tiny bed. She was spooning him with one arm wrapped over his hip. Her lips were pulled into a slight smile and his smile was just as sweet. Both looked completely relaxed, obviously comfortable with each other... My heart knotted up.

Robbie embodied part of the future that we had always envisioned for us but had never achieved. It was as if he had existed all these years as a part of us both... It was crazy, but that was how I felt when I looked at him — as if he actually was a part of me and the link that would somehow always bond Mia and me together.

A small descendant of my being, who was saving the space next to her that the universe had chosen for me for as long as it took for me to be ready again to command it. But he did not fade into the background and disappear...not at all...

I caught myself picturing them as *my* family.

They would sleep in my home, in their beds, in my secluded wood cabin with the knowledge that I was watching over them so nothing would ever happen to them. All the while, I sat there smiling down on them, well aware I would never be alone again.

In the life that Mia and I had imagined eons ago, it would have been possible. It had represented reality — our future.

But over the last few years, I lost faith in our imaginary life, probably due to my own doing because ultimately, one alone was responsible for how one turned out. Thanks to Mia, I found my way again. As always, she brought out the good in me because she was always the only one who saw something positive in me no matter how nasty I behaved. She always believed in good for it was what she embodied. A human being always projects onto others...

And so, I caught myself as I bent over her and just one damn time, carefully and gently pressed my lips against her smooth forehead.

Somehow, I could no longer suppress feeling that she was really mine... That strange – albeit utopian – certainty steadily grew within me the longer I stared at her...

During that night as I watched over her as she slept, took Robbie to throw up so Mia could continue resting, and after he eventually fell back asleep on my lap, it happened...

I stepped out of the darkness and back into the light because no one else would do it for me. Suddenly, I was facing the 18-year-old grinning prick I once was.

And Mia Angel belonged to old Tristan like the fucker. She was his girl; she was everything that made life worth living, everything he ever needed in order to know who he was, where he stood, and where he was supposed to go. And it felt unusually great to embrace the feelings that had always been dormant. That younger carefree playful version — the side no person should ever lose.

I probably never stood a chance because you cannot go against your nature without breaking at some point — I was on the rebound.

But first, I still had to learn to make peace with the past. I was still a little resistant to letting it go completely. For that, I saw too many inconsistencies that threatened my insight. Mia and I had to expel our demons if we ever wanted to make headway. And we would, a fact I was irrevocably certain of.

I accepted all of that in those minutes, which possibly transformed me into a new/old person, although I never made the mistake of thinking about the event further.

In fact, only one thing mattered: Mia Angel was here with me after eight damn years and still embodied everything I needed.

We had already wasted far too much time on absurdities as if we had eons to live instead of just a short crappy life.

One that I wanted to spend with her...

... and would.

# 2. His Defense

*Mia Marena 'Back to the Past' Angel*

When I opened my eyes, I was disoriented at first.

Where was I? Why did I feel so hot? And why did it smell so unusual...?

However, after a few seconds, my confusion cleared.

I lay in Robbie's bed in the children's home where I worked. Buried under two thick blankets, I was offered the cutest image ever: Tristan Wrangler – my personal sex god ever since I could remember – was still sitting on the tattered white rocking chair in the corner of the room. A small blanket lay over the top of him...which was basically useless as it only reached his belly. I immediately knew that only Robbie could come up with such a lovable but useless idea.

The six-year-old angel was enthroned on a tiny stool before Tristan with his elbows resting on his knees and chin cradled in his cute tiny hands while the two were deeply engrossed in conversation.

Tristan was chuckling softly and my heart warmed because unfortunately, I heard the sound far too seldom. He tousled Robbie's fine light hair before holding his big hand out to him.

"That's a deal, boss!"

"Really?" I knew how Robbie's eyes sparkled when he sounded like that.

"Yes, really," Tristan reassured him, still chuckling and shaking the little hand.

"YESSS!" Robbie exclaimed and both immediately glanced at me, alarmed.

I smiled at them in a way so they'd know they didn't wake me.

"What are you two up to?" I asked, stretching leisurely knowing that Tristan was ogling my breasts before giving me an innocent look and shrugging.

"Nothing."

"It's a secret!" Robbie added, whose cheeks already had a much healthier glow than yesterday evening.

Last night, when I had been so scared.

One, for Robbie, who apparently suffered from the stomach flu or food poisoning, and two, if Tristan would actually leave…

But in regard to Tristan Wrangler, much had changed! We definitely made progress because more and more of the old Tristan, who eight years ago had been my personal hero with his bright red Audi and dirty thoughts, came to the forefront…

And he didn't seem to mind.

\*\*\*

As he drove me home, I thought extensively about the events of the last few weeks.

Our first meeting at his photo exhibition; our first sex — so brutal and uncaring and yet, somehow exhilarating; the agreement, which really was never fully observed; his cool and distant behavior, but also the moments when he had softened and allowed me closer to him. Ending with the trip to Prague and our clearing the air on Petřín Lookout Tower.

EVA EBER!

And his confession that during all that time I was his only one, not to mention his promise to no longer ACT like that toward me.

For some reason, he stayed silent and seemed introverted as he focused on the road — which made getting through to him impossible. However, it was not unusual and gave me the opportunity to continue my own ruminations.

I recalled yesterday evening in more detail and remembered that Tristan had allowed me to kiss him in the hot tub even though it actually violated the rules of our agreement, which he had presented to me at the beginning of our *relationship*. My lips had actually been permitted to touch those perfect muscles under his fragrant skin! And he didn't seem to notice that I directly violated his holiness' laws. He might have been too intoxicated with pleasure to give a damn about anything else — just as it so often happened to me when we were intimate.

But that was not everything!

Yesterday, he had been so different, so gentle — a bit like in the past! He joked with me, laughed, and toyed with me, yet it had not intimidated me.

However, it might only have been his guilty conscience regarding Eva Eber!

But maybe also because I almost left him, thereby making it clear to him that he could actually lose me. And he didn't want that because the old Tristan still loved me and fought for us. Deep inside, hidden beneath all the hatred...from which I kept pulling him out from underneath.

Maybe that was why he tended to Robbie for the remainder of the night, which definitely was why I felt so unspeakably happy this morning.

Longingly, I turned my head and studied his distinctive profile and pronounced jaw, which looked so sexy and always magically attracted my fingertips or mouth to brush over it. And his full lips...which could kiss so unspeakably well, his beautiful hands, one of which was grabbing the stick shift and the other, loosely holding the steering wheel.

As usual, Tristan knew I was staring at him because he glanced at me.

"What?" he asked curtly, but not unfriendly.

"Nothing," I replied shyly, blushing because he had caught me yearning for him — once again!

Naturally, it wasn't enough for him. "Nothing?"

I rolled my eyes. "I was merely admiring your hard earned looks again," I admitted, knowing he wouldn't leave it alone.

"Oh that," he made a dismissive gesture and chuckled. "Do you like me now better than in the past, as a strong mature man?" He was teasing me — most definitely. "Now I can hold you effortlessly in any position imaginable. Are you already familiar with the hanging variation of position 69?" I grew beet red.

"Oh man, Tristan... Your appearance might be more mature, which, by the way, I find extremely sexy, but you have the same dirty mouth as when you were eighteen..."

"And you don't find that sexy, Miss Angel?" he inquired.

"Actually, I do," I replied sheepishly and slid around on my seat because the erotic sound of his velvety voice made me unspeakably hot. Besides, he once again called me *Miss Angel*! Not *Mia Marena*!

"Am I causing your panties to flood?" he continued inquiring with great pleasure.

"No!" I stopped squirming and crossed my arms in front of my chest defiantly. "I'm no longer as easily aroused like in the old days. Simply snapping your fingers is no longer enough to make me orgasm!" Oh man...I really laid it on thick, but he was so damn self-assured and arrogant! Granted, he had every right to…ah…whatever.

"No, I really don't have to snap my fingers for that, although that's also not quite true. I know a few spots on your body where it would be enough. But, for the most part, it's enough when I implant certain images in your dirty mind. Shall I?"

"NO! I might still have to work to do today! Maybe I'll have to operate heavy machinery; I'll most definitely have to use a knife!"

Now he really laughed.

"Oh be quiet!" And I actually pouted!

"So, I'm also not allowed to tell you that I find you sexy as hell you when operating heavy machinery? Like an excavator or crane...best when wearing overalls and nothing else," he whispered.

I snorted. "Actually, I was talking about the lawnmower..." whereupon he laughed louder. But before our liberating banter could escalate, which made it seem like the old days – simply happy – we had arrived! And, unfortunately... I had to go home now and separate from him...

As if he also didn't want to part, he actually prolonged our time for a few minutes by escorting me to the door. Before walking upstairs, I almost stumbled over the three bright pink suitcases on the floor in front of the mailboxes. Shaking his head, he caught and steadied me with one arm — once again.

We stopped in front of my apartment door. "So..." I gnawed my lower lip while staring at the pectoral muscles not covered by his black shirt.

"Yes?" He put a finger under my chin and lifted my face so that I sunk into his green-brown bottomless depths.

"Yes," I whispered.

"I'll be going now..." His thumb brushed over my lower lip and I fancied he was struggling not to kiss me.

"Ahem..." I unobtrusively pushed my lips out a bit because I knew they looked fuller that way.

"I'll be seeing you..." He stared at my lips as if mesmerized — I did the same.

"Ahem…" I hummed again and purposefully got up on my tiptoes.

Tristan lowered his face. Extremely slowly as if hypnotized.

"Now what did you do to me again that I cannot think of anything but you..." he whispered.

OH MY, TRISTAN!

I felt and tasted his minty breath on my mouth and sighed.

"The same thing you're doing to me..."

Only a few inches separated me from paradise. Only one more breath... I closed my eyes and clung tightly to his forearms. Suddenly his hands were on my cheeks, holding me as if I was made of expensive fragile porcelain...

"Tristan..." I breathed, expecting it to finally happen.

But I was wrong...

Someone in high heels came up the stairs and we jumped apart. When I saw *who* was interrupting us, I froze.

"OHHHH, WOW!" the bright voice cried out and before I knew it, a hand which was not mine and therefore did not belong there, expertly touched Tristan's biceps.

"HE HAS MUSCLES OF STEEL!" Long red fingernails burned my vision. "OH... an eight-pack, right?!" she trilled deafeningly loud. That first moment, I could only stare at her, just like Tristan.

"Why didn't you tell me you're dating such an Adonis? He's better than Ian Somerhalder and Channing Tatum. And looks even better than Robert Pattinson! Oh, and those broad shoulders... probably get a daily workout..."

"Mother, stop touching him!" Simultaneously, I grabbed her hands, which were about to grab his ass, and pulled her out of reach of Tristan.

"Mother?" he repeated hollowly.

"Yes, Mom!" I burst out and took a closer look at her. It had been about seven years since we'd last seen each other and yet, I still could not get used to her appearance, for in all this time she had not changed a bit.

In addition to a light blue top, she wore an incredibly pink short jeans skirt. Thousands of necklaces hung around her neck, rings in her ears, and bracelets around her wrists. She had dyed her hair light brown with various blonde strands, and somehow, teased the whole thing into some strange hairdo, which must have taken a can of hair spray to hold together. In short, my mother looked like a chipmunk. Now, years later, her overly painted eyes bore tiny crow's feet, but they didn't make her less attractive. Her dark black lashes were obviously fake and her lips were painted red. The teeth in the background were bleached. Her high cheeks glimmered with strong rouge... by and large, it immediately stood out that my producer was still into her looks — too much so! Although I disliked thinking it, she operated like the personified bitch and thus resembled, very much so, Eva Eber, whose image must be assigned the term *super slut* as an explanation.

By now, even though I planned to meet whoever without prejudice, I had developed a deep aversion to such women, but whatever!

Everything about her was wrong whether it was her character, breasts, or nose, which made me wonder how she had financed it all.

Her figure was slim but well proportioned, which the solarium tan only emphasized. Her legs were in white boots with murderous heels. Her get-up easily took off 10 years, yet the outcome was still far from lovable.

I no longer wanted to be associated with her and even though it was hard, all I felt for her was contempt.

"What are you doing here?" I asked, unable to keep the revulsion out of my voice. I did not want her here!

She smiled mockingly without taking her intrusive gaze off Tristan for even a second, who in turn, gave her a pretty presumptuous if not slightly disgusted and somewhat distraught gaze.

"Martin Schmitt opened a new account in a downtown bank and guess who his clerk is? This hot guy here!" She attempted to touch Tristan again, but he stepped back out of reach.

"Keep your hands off me, woman!"

After she laughed, she continued to speak as if nothing happened. In fact, she babbled on without period and comma. "When they talked about their girlfriends, your name came up. Naturally, Martin called me immediately to tell me where I could find you... So, I thought I'd look up my baby... I still cannot believe that YOU and your average looks managed to get your hands on an actual bank administrator...and now that I SEE HIM... I believe it even less. How did you do it? Oh well...at least you're not such a fatty like in the old days anymore... That's probably why! Then again... I see your tits suffered greatly from all that dieting. Maybe your jackpot will spring for breast implants so you finally look like a decent woman...and what have you done to your hair? It's all dry! Aren't you protecting it from the heat? Apparently not because it looks rather like..."

"Stop it!" Now I had tears in my eyes because I was no longer used to being so humiliated and at that, in front of Tristan, who stood there seemingly speechless for the first time in his life.

Unimpressed, my mother turned to him, lowered her eyelids, licked her lips, thrust out her breasts – cougar mode – and pulled a business card from her purse, which she held under his nose while lasciviously leaning against him.

"Call me if you're ever in the mood for *real* fun."

"No, thank you!" Tristan emphasized each word and shoved her hand away in disgust. She was not discouraged...

"I'm open to *anything*."

Tristan pretended to vomit. She continued her sales pitch.

"I'm also experienced, sweetie. Experience she can only dream of... I can do things to you this little mouse here has never heard of! Mia, you don't mind me borrowing your man once, do you?"

"SHE DOES!" Tristan burst out. I was so overwhelmed by her utter boldness I could not say or do anything to come to his defense. Worst of all... she was probably right... No, she *was* right and she always managed to destroy my self-confidence. She had been doing it since I was a kid and it worked just as well now. I felt small and worthless, wanting to dig a hole to disappear into or something else, but I couldn't move. Panic started flowing inside me. I was running out of air, everything felt tight...

"Mia baby..." Tristan suddenly whispered in his best I'll-soak-your-panties-off-you manner. Without warning, he again took my face in his hands, thrust my mother out of the way, pushed me against the wall behind me, and pressed himself against me. I immediately felt the demanding twitch in his pants. Demanding ME!

"Knock it off!" Unexpectedly, he leaned down and gave me a tiny kiss on the lips. This tentative touch sent an electric surge coursing through my body. I gasped, clawed at his hips, and snuggled up close to him. Where raw chaos raged within me a moment ago, longing and even happiness emerged. Wordlessly, he turned and marched away. While he was walking, he tore up my mother's card and tossed it uncaringly on the floor. Light-headed, I stared after him and slowly touched my lips, unable to believe Tristan Wrangler had just placed his lips on mine.

*He had kissed me. And he initiated it!*

Realizing this made me smile despite his sudden departure and a warm feeling spread throughout my body, which not even my mother with her cruel cold nature could destroy.

"You really have to tell me everything about Francesco," she continued babbling as if nothing had happened. "You guys go nicely together again, although I'm sure he's fucking around on you..."

I rolled my eyes. "Mom, what are you doing here? I'm serious!"

Cumbersomely, I took a step, unlocked my apartment, and entered. She followed like a Dachshund.

"So...um..." She stalled for time as I stared at her, annoyed and expectant as I took off my shoes.

"I'd also like to move to the city. The situation with your father has become too much... I'm two weeks clean now, you know...and my therapist advised me to change my environment. Then I heard about you and that rich banker and I thought to myself... you could pay for my stay at a rehab clinic. There I might also find a wealthy man and the mouse will have found its cheese!"

"The stay is free!"

She laughed.

"I'm not going to just *any* clinic!"

"Merely because my friend has money doesn't mean I spend it as if it were mine, Mother."

"Well, your father was quite happy when I told him about you and Francesco." She pulled me to the couch. Just mentioning Harald Angel's name caused sweat to form on my forehead and she knew that!

"You told Dad?"

"Yes, of course! He doesn't want you ending up with a guy like that Drustan."

"Tristan, Mother..." Crap! Crap! Crap! Okay...for now I'll pretend Tristan was Francesco... Telling her the truth would alert my father much faster than I like...and he would come here quicker than I could warn Tristan.

"Whatever. Anyway, Francesco is the best thing that could have happened to you..."

"Uh, um..."

"When shall we all go out to dinner? I want to get to know him properly!"

"THAT'S impossible!" I stated resolutely.

"Why? Is he not interested in getting to know his future mother-in-law? Or do I have to get your father to teach him manners?'

"NO!" Not my father! Just not him! He had already destroyed everything once before. And it was enough with one parent here!

"Well, tomorrow evening works for me," she smugly announced. "And then we can also talk about my stay at the clinic. Or maybe I'll simply stay here with you forever. Your apartment might be ugly, but I can easily remedy that..." *Yes, your input will make this place look like a dump in which I'll suffocate...*I thought sarcastically. My mother touched up her lips as I sat next to her on the couch and dug the phone out of my pocket.

I texted Tristan.

*Need your help* and sent it off before I could change my mind.

*I expected as much ;)* was his immediate reply and even before I had time to enjoy the atypical smiley, my mother abruptly reached for my phone.

"Who are you texting?"

"None of your business!" I quickly raised my arm and went to the kitchen to put on a kettle for tea.

*I have to get rid of her again, Tristan!* I felt sick as I texted him. But, at the same time, I knew he was the one person who could understand me in this respect, after all, he knew my past all too well.

*I know.*

*Will you help me?* I peeked into the living room and saw she had made herself comfortable on the couch with the remote control. Her long red-painted toenails glistened in the glow of the TV. I had to turn away... As a child, I had hated her feet...for whatever reason.

*What would you like me to do?* came his reply. THANK GOD!

*First, you have to pretend to be Francesco...* I gnawed my fingernails as I waited for his reply.

*I'm no damn teeny weenie!*

*Tristan, please! Or else she will find out who you really are and tell my father who will also come!* I knew he did not want that to happen as much as I did.

*Anything else? Should I dance and strip for her or just go ahead and fuck her?* Oh, okay... NOW Tristan was pissed off.

*No...you just have to take us to dinner tomorrow evening! Please, Tristan... You are the only one who can help me get rid of her. If we succeed, I'll do anything you ask of me...* I felt bad asking him for help...especially considering our past, but I knew he wouldn't let me down. Tristan was a generous and helpful person. Besides, I would pay him back in kind. No matter how. He knew it and certainly would take advantage of it. Nevertheless, I did not receive back an instant text and grew increasingly more nervous as I prepared two cups of green tea. I might not want my mother here, but it was not like I could show her the door... And I was hospitable, no matter my distaste for whatever guest.

Would he let me down, after all?

When I received his text, I was so happy tears came to my eyes.

*Oh, the things I do for my goddamn girl, who has a psycho for a mother.* HIS GODDAMN GIRL!

He might not have noticed it, but he addressed me more and more often as Mia, baby, or better yet, MIA baby. Now I was his girl again and no longer his slut. Now I felt like dancing on the table for joy!

Such news only required one response from me.

*I love you so much, Tristan Wrangler*! His answer arrived promptly and was typical for him.

*Yes, yes.*

# 3. Strong Words

*Mia 'No-fucking-clue' Angel*

"Francesco... Sweetie..." I approached the grim looking Tristan and didn't stop until I embraced him even though seeing his murderous expression, my legs shook.

We were outside *T & P*. Once again, Mista Wrangler looked stunning as well as dangerous in his tailored black suit, yet he didn't seem thrilled to be dining with my procreator. He was not used to women making such fearless advances as she had done. Usually, he was the brazen and unscrupulous one, albeit, with my mother, he seemed to have found his equal.

I didn't know which one of us would first start thinking about killing her. It certainly promised to be an interesting evening where we would struggle with our self-control!

"You'll pay for this," he whispered in my ear, then greeted me with a quick peck on the lips. I shuddered.

*Yes... I thought as much...*

"And there he is again, the winning lottery ticket!" I tried to lighten the situation, but even I had to roll my eyes when I heard my mother's much too shrill and boisterous voice as she raved about the layout of the restaurant.

"You'll pay GREATLY." Smiling charmingly, Tristan broke away from me and kept his arm around my waist as we turned to face my mother, who wore a frighteningly short black dress.

Then again, it could very well have been a negligee. It was truly hard to tell. High heels and tons of makeup accompanied her outfit. I felt terribly embarrassed and her dirty grin, with which she had recently leered at my Tristan, almost transformed my already existing aversion for her into hatred.

"How I have looked forward to being able to do this here!" She absolutely didn't care that I was standing right next to him, that this man belonged *solely* to me, so I shot her a warning look. Nevertheless, one of her arms snaked around his body and I fervently hoped she wasn't about to pinch his bottom.

"Lady, don't you dare!" Tristan held her wrist in sure fingers before she could carry out what she had in mind. He managed to remain courteous only because the woman, although mentally ill, was my mother, of that I was convinced. Besides, he still did not slap females — at least not in anger. Otherwise, he made an exception when it came to my nipples, probably in order to drive me crazy.

Grumpily, I studied his long skillful fingers as they touched the skin of another.

Tristan looked at me out of the corner of an eye as I tried not to show my displeasure that he was touching someone else...no matter the reason.

"This body is only at your daughter's disposal," he added charmingly as he released her and reached for me. He firmly linked our fingers and ran his thumb over my knuckles.

OH my, Tristan! He held me by my hand, NOT THE WRIST! He stroked me and acted as if we were a couple...a happy couple...

I smiled shyly at him, noticing the telltale heat in my cheeks as he led us to a slightly secluded table, relieved us of our coats, and pulled out our chairs for us. AHA! So he had refined manners after all. Well, he was certainly a polished gentleman now for he had the necessary maturity WHEN he wanted it!

His face was watchful as he sat down between us and winked at me conspiratorially. I grinned back — simply unable to resist. I had waited far too long for that charming expression and felt a deep connection between us because none of his usual coldness was present...

What happened?

Mom snorted and aggressively grabbed the menu from the nice handsome waiter. I reached for mine and hid behind it because Tristan's warm friendliness, which he radiated since the incident with the incarnate bitch Eva

Eber, greatly unsettled me. His behavior made it even harder to read him. Was it his new way of playing games with me?

"So, how long have you two been together? It can't be that long, considering the way you still adore her, huh?" my mother inquired provocatively and I stared at her through narrowed eyes. Without knowing what to order, I tossed my menu on the table. I wouldn't be able to tolerate such behavior much longer!

"We've been together for two years now!" I proclaimed icily and out of habit ordered a glass of water from the waiter...

"She'll have a Spezi," Tristan immediately interjected knowing it was my favorite drink. Stunned, I stared at him, but he grabbed my hand from the table and gave it a brief squeeze while continuing to utterly ignore me. "I'll have the same."

My mother ordered water.

"And the Italian veggie plate, please," I added. I didn't want to bother with an appetizer so the situation would not be prolonged unnecessarily.

"She'll have the Bavarian pot roast with potatoes, green beans, and lots of gravy," Tristan corrected me again without being asked. Not that I didn't like beef... I even craved it on special occasions, especially pot roast with potatoes, green beans, and lots of gravy... but dammit! I rather had the fuck enough of our agreement!

"I'll have the VEGETABLES! Tristan!" I whispered reproachfully.

"What?" my mother asked suspiciously across the table and I immediately realized my mistake because she believed he was Francesco Cavalli.

"Um... I mean, you see..." I squinted innocently at her. Tristan chuckled.

My mother raised a pencil-thin plucked eyebrow.

"...I usually don't eat anything that used to have hair on its body..." I defended myself.

Tristan was almost choking now from laughing so hard, he grew beet red in the face and finally ordered the same thing.

"Aha..." My mother still seemed slightly suspicious, but eventually she turned to the waiter. "I'll have the salmon on fettuccine. No pepper. No cream!" she ordered snootily, closing her menu and eyeing Tristan intently. It bothered me how obviously she was undressing him with her eyes.

"Well, your ex, the one you grieved over for so long, certainly didn't look as good as Francesco..." She addressed the ultimate UNMENTIONABLE. Sure, she had never laid eyes on Tristan even though in such a small cow town where we grew up that was an actual impossibility. The one time she could have seen him she was intoxicated and passed out.

I gasped for air because I had the feeling it was going to get worse. Tristan tensed noticeably.

"What was his name again...Romeo?"

"NO!"

"Dante?"

"Mom, his name was Tristan! Tristan, like *Tristan and Isolde*!" The other guests raised their heads and stared at me disapprovingly because of my loud voice. Lately, it had become a habit. Embarrassed, I shrank somewhat in my seat and tried to calm down.

"Whatever..." My procreator took another sip of water. "I've never understood why you tortured yourself so greatly over one man! Especially considering how he had finished the thing with you!"

I literally felt Tristan's piercing stare. "You only heard Dad's side of the story..." I hissed.

"Well, you did stop talking to me once you moved in with your uncle. But Patrick told me you looked like the living dead! You never even bothered to call me..." She shrugged her thin shoulders and tossed her long hair back, which, today, was not teased but fell smoothly down her back.

"Did it ever occur to you that you are to blame for your only daughter not wanting to talk to you?" It must have been Tristan's presence that allowed me to find the courage to throw that in her face or maybe it was because I hadn't seen her in so long or a little of both.

She snickered.

"All those years you had a roof over your head and food in the fridge. Why are you complaining to me?"

"What about consideration and respect? Or love?" I whispered oh-so-softly while staring at the empty plate in front of me and felt tears burning behind my eyes. Suddenly, Tristan's hand grabbed mine under the table. He pried open my tight fist and caressed the palm.

"Bah! No one can survive on love alone!"

"But, not without it..." Tristan intervened coolly and I thought I misheard.

"Well, love would be your department, wouldn't it?" She raised her glass to him and Tristan snorted. *Love* ... Presently, he must be miles away from loving me, right? "And from what I can tell, you're doing a good job..." my mother added bitterly when she noticed the look I was giving him.

I whipped my head around because I did not expect such a comment. Was he giving the impression he had feelings for me?

"Perhaps..." Tristan shrugged and released my hand under the table. It was like he had confirmed my thoughts. He didn't love me — probably would never be able to again...

"Well, it can't be her looks that does it for you..." Thankfully, the waiter appeared at that moment; otherwise, I was sure Tristan would have exploded. Now I had lost my appetite — completely.

"Eat..." his velvet voice demanded decisively and I obliged, grumbling, even though my stomach was starting to rebel.

Honestly, it was delicious. The veggies were lightly fried with spicy seasoning and the pasta homemade. My mother dug in as if her previous meal had been a year ago. She smacked, gravy dripped from her chin, and in general, made no attempt to show any manners. At least she was quiet...focused only on her food. I, however, was shrinking in my chair, hoping the nightmare would soon end...

Watching her utterly embarrassed me. I wondered whether I had inherited some traits from the woman, praying that if that was the case — then only a few, and right then, decided to only watch Tristan.

A wise choice. And quite stimulating because he looked quite sexy chewing... Those jaw muscles... My stomach knotted.

As always, Tristan noticed me staring and abruptly turned his face to me. When he saw me doting on him again because I could not avert my face quickly enough and to make matters worse, blushed beet red, he gave me a lopsided grin and out of nowhere, placed his hand on my knee...

On my *bare* knee...

Now my insides were an inferno. I immediately recalled our last visit to this restaurant and almost choked on my beans.

Not wanting to be upstaged by my mother, I had donned a purple dress, the sluttiest my wardrobe had to offer. Tristan seemed to like it because his fingers gently traced circles on my skin, slowly inching up my thigh. I didn't know how to react. So, I bit my lower lip. Tristan growled quietly. I sighed. Oh, NO...

"Go to the restroom in five minutes!" He had leaned toward me... and now his lips were on my ear. Feeling his hot breath on my neck made me shudder.

"Not here." I shook my head even though the idea of obliging his order was incredibly tempting, but my mother was here too!

"Am I hearing you say no?" His nose slowly brushed over my cheek and his fingers continued slowly upward. "If you weren't planning to seduce me, why wear SUCH A dress?"

"I didn't say no!" I exclaimed and almost gasped because his hand was close to arriving at my, naturally, no longer dry panties.

"Five minutes! But first, finish your meal...or there won't be dessert, Miss Angel," he hummed in my ear and briefly, quite tenderly, nibbled my earlobe. I suppressed a comforting groan and he leaned back.

His face was smooth and unemotional, while my state of agitation could be seen from miles away.

Obviously, I obeyed because I honestly felt like having dessert!

Unfortunately, I had no watch.

Tristan rolled his eyes when I grabbed his wrist after what felt like five minutes to gaze at his Rolex. Nevertheless, it did me no good because I didn't know what time it was when he said it. I looked at him questioningly.

He was annoyed although he was only pretending for his underlying amusement was unmistakable.

"Go!" he whispered and I glanced at my smacking mother again, who was still busy with her salmon.

"Excuse me," I announced and almost ran to the restroom...

However, I never made it...because I collided with a broad male chest. Large hands caught me by my upper arms before I could land on my butt and booming laughter burst out above me.

"Sorry!" I briefly froze when I recognized the voice and looked up at Phillip Wrangler, who noisily sucked air into his lungs when he saw my face.

"Mia!"

"Phil!" we said in unison and then stared at one another. He was still holding my upper arms... Then he quickly released me as if he had burned himself.

"What are you doing here?" we again asked as if from one mouth. Tristan's brother fuming — I, excited. We stopped simultaneously and peered at each other. He looked grim — I, scared.

"Does Tristan know you are here?"

"I'm here *with* Tristan!" Even these two sentences came in unison.

"YES!"

"WHAT?"

God...we couldn't continue in this manner for it makes decent conversation impossible. I made way for him, but he unexpectedly grabbed and dragged me behind him into the stainless steel kitchen.

"Why are you here with my brother?" he hissed. "How do you even have the nerve to come near him?" Oh man... his big blue eyes looked rather angry. I had never seen him like that before. He would have looked quite scary if it weren't for the oversized chef hat wiggling around on his head.

I sighed. "It was just a...misunderstanding..." How could I instantly explain everything to him?

"What?!" he yelled. His three kitchen helpers cringed and gave us a wide berth. But I too recoiled — seeing his muscles straining...

"Whoa, whoa, whoa... Phil...take it down a notch..." Tristan's athletic body pushed like a brick wall into the narrow space between his choleric brother and me.

His tone was icy... Never before had I heard him talk to one of his brothers in that manner. "If someone yells at her, it'll be me — *and only me!*"

"Tell me, have you lost it, you damn idiot?" Obviously, Phillip couldn't believe it, but it didn't keep him from pushing Tristan. Fortunately, the latter also had considerable muscles and was able to withstand it, otherwise, he would have most likely smacked into me. Yet here I was, merely pressed against the sideboard behind me.

Afraid, I peeked over his shoulder. I had no idea why I did. Maybe because the sight of me cringing and clinging to his little brother caused Phil to have another fit. Well...he already had a problem with me in the old days...which now seemed to have grown.

"You really are a dumbass! You want this slut to use you again? And end up experiencing a broken heart again? DAMN, TRIS! She is a little manipulative snake who used her doe eyes to wrap you around her little finger. She doesn't give a CRAP about you!"

I winced...

"That's enough!" Tristan was shaking. Phil appeared not to have heard him.

"I would spit in her face if I could! Then she would know what she deserved!"

NOW I was honestly frightened!

"PHIL. STOP. IT!" Tristan stated doggedly.

"Why stop? It *has* to be said! She's WORTHLESS! She's a piece of trash! She's a — Dumb. Ugly. TURKEY!"

Tristan took a step forward. Even before irascible Phil knew what hit him, he had him in a headlock and I knew he was mustering all his self-control to avoid professionally rearranging his brother's face.

"Tristan!" I shouted in shock.

"She's *my* fucking Turkey!" Tristan growled oh-so-softly.

"REGARDLESS!" Suddenly, Phil swung around and in the next moment, had Tristan over the kitchen counter with his massive forearm on his throat. Just a few inches away from the hot stove top.

"Phil! Be careful!" I squealed in alarm.

Both merely stared at me. The cook hateful, Tristan calculatingly. He promptly used the distraction to get rid of his opponent by kicking him in the belly... OUCH!

Phillip staggered backward...right into a cupboard. The pots and pans inside upended and rattled — I quickly took a few steps toward safety, at the other end of the kitchen.

My heart was racing... What had I gotten myself into again? AND WHY was Tristan fighting his brother about me? Couldn't he have found another way? Talking or something?

Even before Phil had time to steady himself, Tristan pinned him by grabbing his arm and twisting it around his back. The larger of the two groaned in pain.

"Don't ever talk about her that way!" Tristan repeated a bit out of breath. His brother merely growled...

"Please, let go of him now! He wasn't so bad..." I tried to reassure him.

Both truly intimidating men were looking at me. Of course, Tristan didn't listen, as if ever... until a laugh rang out behind me.

"OHHH... Now you have two hot guys fighting about you! My mother was obviously pleased with the show the Wrangler brothers unintentionally put on.

Reluctantly, Tristan released his brother and patted him on the shoulder. Phillip slapped him on the back. So hard Tristan stumbled forward.

"Fucking prick!" he grumbled, rubbing the sore spot. Then he walked over to me and put his arm possessively around my shoulder.

"We're going now!" We turned around and were about to disappear when Phil called after us.

"Tomorrow at one. Here! With her!" Tristan merely snorted.

"Come on, Mom!" I grabbed her arm and pulled her along because I figured Tristan was not going to stop.

"I call shotgun!" my mother said as soon as she saw the beautiful, shiny, polished, cherry red Audi A7 right out front at the end of the carpet leading to the entrance.

"No!" Tristan said at the same moment I muttered "Okay..."

He sighed and opened the passenger door for her.

She slid onto the seat, happy as a little kid at Christmas. Yes...luxury...was something that made my mother truly happy. Nothing else was required... Sad but true!

Then Tristan opened my door – the rear one – and helped me in. With a quick glance, he assured himself I was fine, slipped gracefully behind the wheel, and immediately pulled away, angering a few people who had to jump out of the way so as not to get run over.

Exhausted, I leaned my forehead against the glass and thought about the likelihood of encountering the rest of his family tomorrow. How would they react? Would they immediately rip my head off? Would they chase me out of the country with pitchforks and torches?

I was so lost in my reverie that I did not directly notice my mother leaning over to Tristan and whispering something in his ear.

I was about to interfere and protest because I clearly saw where her hand was touching him, when out of nowhere, he slammed so hard on the brakes, I was thrown face forward against the back of the seat in front of me.

"Ouch!" Trembling, I braced myself with both hands and was about to let her have it when Tristan beat me to it.

And much better than I ever could: "YOUR DAUGHTER is in the back seat! I am YOUR DAUGHTER'S friend! *Your daughter,* the one for which you should only want what's best! Your daughter, who is so fucking adorable, you should love and worship her, dammit! I have no idea how someone like you, someone who has no conscience, could create such a being! But, I'm glad she managed to fight your fucked-up influence! And you would be wise not to touch me again!"

My mother just stared at him — as I did. Tristan glared at her as he reached for his checkbook in the glove compartment.

"You are here for money — well, it's money you shall have! Then, you and your brain-handicapped husband will stay away from her, UNDERSTAND? Fucking crap, I really have had enough of your miserable clan! And this time you won't fuck with me!" Meanwhile, he scribbled wildly in his checkbook.

"Why else would I be here?" she hissed back and something in her expression looked petrified. "You can't believe I'm here because of this piece of shi..." She didn't get to finish because Tristan grabbed her throat and pulled her head close to his. She fell silent and panted as he leaned in so their noses almost touched.

I sat there frozen.

"Don't you dare!" He emphasized every single word. She shuddered visibly and nodded frantically. Tears ran down her cheeks. "Don't you ever dare insult her again. The only piece of shit here is *you*!"

Now her eyes flashed...Defiantly... "I'll sic my husband on you!"

I burst out laughing rather hysterically. Tristan abruptly let go of her but not without smiling — icily.

"Well, I can't wait to see him!" Now his eyes glittered so longingly, similar to when he looked at my pussy.

"Tell him, Tristan Wrangler sends his regards..." He continued to scribble in his checkbook as he spoke. Her eyes widened as he said his name. "And also tell him, Mia Marena is mine! For fucking forever!" He tore a page from his checkbook and tossed it at her chest. "I'm looking forward to seeing him, after all, I still have a score to settle. But *you,* I never again want to see you around Mia. YOU have done enough damage. Now get the fuck out of my car before I forget my damn manners!"

"B...but my things are..."

"GET OUT!" Tristan annunciated these two words in such a soft but threatening way that she immediately seized the small piece of paper and literally jumped out of the car.

I did not believe getting rid of her would be so easy... Well, easy... for me! I merely sat quietly and felt three things.

First: Fascination.

Second: Satisfaction.

Third: Guilt.

Fascination because Tristan was so incredibly sexy when he came across strong and authoritative and let everyone know he didn't give a fuck about what they thought of him... Simply sure of himself...and with reason!

Satisfaction because she finally got what she deserved... From a person she tried to impress.

And guilt because I felt pleasure when it was my mother's turn to be humiliated.

I couldn't believe she didn't look at me when she slipped out of the car and slammed the door shut behind her. Quite fittingly, it was now coming down in buckets and she and I exchanged one last look as we left her standing in the cold night like a wet poodle.

Tristan floored it and sped off. The way he clutched the steering wheel and was grinding his teeth told me he was still angry.

"I simply can't stand her talking to you like that... Fucking crap... Next time I'll kill her..." he muttered to himself utterly furious and I had no idea what to do... I knew it was best to leave him alone when he was in such a state. So, I sat back in my seat and tried to relax. Exhausted, I closed my eyes and breathed deeply and evenly while I processed what just happened and tried to figure out the consequences...

"Mia!" he suddenly yelled at me and I sat up so abruptly that I almost hit my head on the roof of the car

"Yes?" I replied hurriedly.

His eyes flashed gloomily at me in the rearview mirror. "Are you all right?"

I smiled weakly. Right now, I had not expected a question like that. Really not...

"Yes, Tristan..." *My radiant hero with the bright red Audi and dirty thoughts,* I added in my head and smile dreamily. Because he had proven, quite impressively, that he had now reverted to exactly that. "It was really nice of you to stand up for me like that, but now you basically sent my father an invitation..." occurred to me and my smile instantly disappeared from my face.

"I know," he answered calmly.

"But, Tristan..."

"Stop that ridiculous way of spreading panic, Mia. I know what I'm doing."

"But..."

"I don't give a shit about BUT!" he snapped. "He'll get what he deserves! And this time I won't act so amateurish as I did eight years ago!" he added grumbling so quietly that I almost didn't understand him.

Again, I closed my eyes and fell back in the seat. "I don't think that's a good idea..."

"You have nothing to worry about. I'll have your apartment watched. And, I'll also have a security lock installed that cannot be easily cracked. He won't be able to get to you. NEVER AGAIN! That prick will pay for what he did to us..."

"So, you believe me?" My heart seemed to be ablaze with hope.

"No!" Tristan immediately shouted and extinguished the flames. "But he's still a sadistic prick and I know I'd be doing the rest of the people on this planet a favor if I make him disappear once and for all.

"Tristan..."

"Oh, yes..." He made a dismissive hand gesture and then turned right. To my disappointment, I realized we already were at my place.

CRAP! I had hoped...he would still drive a little crazy. In the good old Tristan sex-god kind-of-way... But that didn't happen.

He double-parked, got out, and opened my door.

Wordlessly, I got out and stood before him. I glanced up at him and admired the flawlessness of his face, which was, at that moment, looking down at me reservedly.

"What exactly is this between us, Tristan?" I asked...it was less than a whisper because I was a deathly afraid of his answer.

Something flashed in Tristan's eyes and then it was gone. It was some of his old look and it again filled me with hope. He stared at me for a few seconds, unreadable, then he sighed deeply and suddenly his hand was on the side of my neck and his thumb was stroking the spot where my pulse raced. I shuddered even though his skin was warm and soft.

"I don't know," he whispered just as brokenly.

"What will you tell your family?"

"I have no idea..."

"Do you believe me, Tristan?" I sounded insistent.

He shrugged.

Okay... I guess tonight he won't give me a concrete answer, but at least he didn't say *no*!

Sighing, I closed my eyes and enjoyed his touch because I knew it was all I would get. After a perceived eternity and a few shudders on my part, he spoke again.

"Go inside!"

I opened my eyes again and was annoyed that I hadn't kept them open the entire time. How could I spend even one second not looking at him? At times, I really was a stupid cow!

He removed his hand, but not before sliding the strap of my dress back in place that had slipped from my shoulder. I smiled at him because it was such a sweet gesture.

He rolled his eyes and gallantly stepped aside to make way for me.

I left...heavy hearted. But I went...

When I arrived in my apartment and sat down on my couch, which still reeked of my mother's disgustingly sweet perfume, something occurred to me. I ran to the window just in time to see the Audi speeding off.

Crap!

So, I grabbed my cell phone and typed. *How much did you actually pay my mother for her to leave me alone?* With clammy hands, I petted my chihuahua Stanley, who welcomed me by waggling his tail. His answer came quickly and shocked me so much that I almost didn't sleep for the rest of the night.

*50,000... Have a pleasant wet dream!*

OH. MY. Tristan!

# 4. Forgiveness

*Narrator, alias Don 'Fucking' Both (Oh God, I've been meaning to do this for so long!)*

*Renée Angel* stepped into the hotel of her choice a week later with a big smile on her face. It was expensive and luxurious — just to her liking. She had played for high stakes and got lucky, which was why she could afford her new lifestyle.

In her bag was a cashier's check that could fulfill all her immediate wishes and there was a man she had her eye on who would take care of the rest.

He was fat and old, so to speak, in his dying days — the perfect candidate!

Yes! Finally, she was completely free!

Fact was, Harald Angel, the man who had oppressed and terrorized her all those years, had died two days ago under mysterious circumstances, drowning while fishing... Briefly, she wondered whether the stunning conquest of her dull-witted daughter had a hand in it. One thing was for certain, he had no scruples.

Recalling how relieved she had felt when she received word of Harald's death, her smile widened...

Now, she could finally leave her past behind and start living. In secret, she wished the same for her daughter.

Tristan Wrangler would give her what she never had: Security. He had proven as much.

## Tristan 'Little' Wrangler

What should I tell them? How am I supposed to explain it to them? And would they even understand? After all, they were still convinced Mia Marena had betrayed me, that much was clear — however, that was not my main problem.

What about my feelings?

Did I still believe she destroyed my life solely out of spite?

I glanced at the seat to my right, which usually was always empty. Now it was occupied by her. She nervously inspected her fingers, pushed the nail skin back, and dug a little around under her nails. Her thoughtful gaze was directed out the side window. She definitely was excited — seemingly so *innocent... and beautiful*. She had fashioned her long hair into a ponytail, her cheeks were pale, skin still flawless. Her little body was clad in a thick black sweater and tight-fitting jeans, which nicely emphasized her small but nice ass, as I noted earlier.

She was so...*beguiling* in her simplicity.

And she slid around her seat.

As I sighed quietly, she looked at me questioningly — her big brown doll-eyes, which were so damn open, they immediately betrayed her every lie. And so, I allowed myself...to think about it...

Then why... had I not noticed it at the time? Why had she been so shocked when the door rang that dreadful morning? The night before, she was quite distraught — therefore she must have had a hunch. At least, *to some extent*. Why hadn't she talked to me about it openly and honestly? Why hadn't she trusted me? We would have found a solution. I would have done whatever damn *thing* to protect her!

Anyway, I would do so now.

She bit her lip, smiling shyly, with a slightly cocked head... I raised a brow.

"Your lip," I reminded her and, visibly unnerved, she released it from her fangs.

"You..." she replied cheekily.

My eyes must have grown quite large when suddenly she reached out a hand to brush an exceedingly long strand of hair from my forehead. As her fingers caringly slid over my skin, I should have stopped her gesture, but every touch, regardless how subtle, represented a little absolution. I simply couldn't continue...being...so cold...

Yet I still tried, one last rebellious act, so to speak...

"We agreed on a few rules, Miss Angel..."

"YOU did..." she proclaimed off-handedly and was bold enough to keep her fingers where they were, namely, on my neck, caressing me. I directed my eyes back to the road and frustrated, snorted while I ignored the pleasant shudder.

Dammit! She was already getting too much under my skin, NOT just my fucker.

"Lately I have been neglectful, but it does not mean we'll completely ignore our agreement! You still recall how I feel about you, correct?" At that moment, I felt I was fighting an already lost battle because I once again pushed her away from me.

"Yeah, you consider me a slut!" she grumbled as I moved her fingers back onto her lap.

I smiled to myself because it was too funny how easily she became upset. At the exact moment I looked at her, she restrainedly wiped her eyes with her sleeve. The sight made me sick.

"ARE YOU CRYING?" Now I was shocked because I *hated* seeing her crying like I did the clap.

"No!" she snapped defiantly even though I heard her voice tremble. She turned her face from me. However, she was out of luck because we had just arrived.

I parked in my space right next to the restaurant and unbuckled. I leaned over, gently grabbed her chin, and turned her face to me.

YES, SHE WAS CRYING! And she glared defiantly at me as she sniffed. The hands in her lap were now balled into small fists. Broodingly, I gazed into her eyes. I almost did not want to ask because her reply scared the shit out of me, but I had to know.

"Why are you crying?"

"Because every time I think we've taken a step in the right direction, you destroy my illusions by making me realize we have no common goals to achieve and despite everything, you still regard me as a cheap little slut... THAT'S WHY. Now, let go of me, Tristan!" she hissed in good old/new Mia manner.

I was a bit perplexed, which was why she managed to break free of my hold and get out. But I recovered quickly and went after her. Naturally, it was again raining buckets.

"Mia!" Why was I constantly chasing her since her reappearance in my life? And why did she never listen to me when I asked her to stop?

I finally caught her by the arm as we reached cover under the wide, glassed marquee of the restaurant and spun her around to me.

"No!" She actually tried to squirm out of my grip, but I wouldn't allow it. "Let go of me! Please... I can't right now..."

My heart pounded two beats, which fought against each other. One became more prominent... increasingly so...

"HEY, calm down!" I decided to distract her with my most effective weapon: my body, using it to press that little wet thing in front of me against the wall next to the door. Mia gasped and frantically wiped a few damp strands from her forehead. Now her look of defiance gave way to anger.

"You knew right from the start what you were getting into! I never promised you anything other than sex!"

"It's not enough, Tristan!" exploded in my face. "I LOVE YOU! Don't you get it? It hurts to hear I'm merely some slut to you! And, it pains me to hear we will never have the future we once envisioned! I thought I could bear anything as long as I was near you. But I was wrong! I can..."

That was as far she got for with the next breath she had to gasp because my lips touched her. Even I was somewhat taken aback. But first, I would not see her cry – not anymore – especially not because of me! And second, her lips were wet... inviting and I simply could no longer resist.

So, I broke the agreement. For both of us.

I was not gentle and careful but passionate and hungry, running my hands through her hair and pressing her against me as my tongue entered her sweet mouth. I emitted a strange noise, not a moan or growl, rather something in between.

Because she was MY GIRL and she was the best I ever tasted. So sweet yet at the same time, so soft and velvety...

I loved how her little tongue met mine.

I loved the way her fingers dug into the sweater at my chest and how she clung to me as if there was no tomorrow.

But it was not enough — not by a long shot. One hand moved from her hair. When it brushed her shoulder and down the side of her ribcage to her thigh, she sighed quietly in my mouth, causing me to become even wilder because the sounds she made were amazing.

I firmly grabbed her knee and wrapped her leg around my hip. I needed her — as close as possible...urgently!

Unequivocally, I rubbed my crotch against her — which REALLY made her groan. Before I knew it, she had wrapped her other leg around me and we gasped in each other's mouth when I grabbed her ass with both hands and pulled her even closer to me.

This here...was goddamn heaven...

I wanted her... RIGHT THERE... RIGHT THEN! Yet my mouth could not break contact with her soft, full cherry red lips, not even for a second.

"Trisi?" The shrill, stunned voice screaming directly in my ear, snapped me out of my primal urge.

"No!" Mia moaned, frustrated as I breathlessly detached my lips from her. The interruption made my fucker twitch violently, protesting as much as she did.

As soon as I looked to the right, I was unable to suppress my curse. There stood my former alibi slut. FUCK!

"Not again..." Mia continued as her fingers clawed at my sweater more urgently. Even her legs around my waist tightened... She buried her face in my neck...and I neither could nor wanted to let go of her. So I held onto her as I looked at Eva, raised a brow, grinned, and shrugged. She closed her red painted mouth again and narrowed her eyes. Before her lame brain came up with an apt response, I seized my chance. With ten fingers, I dug into Mia's buttocks, whereupon she gasped against my neck. Then she giggled...which sounded so much better than hearing her cry.

"Eva, your skills as an alibi slut are no longer required. You're fired!"

"Yes!" I heard Mia whisper against my neck and felt her smile against my skin.

Eve's mouth opened again — her eyes narrowing even more.

"You can't do that!" she hissed.

"I can do whatever I want. Now, get lost! Can't you see I'm busy?"

"O...kay," she suddenly said quietly, then her gaze went to Mia, who still had not acknowledged her with a look. "As you wish..."

"Eva..." I growled warningly.

"NO!" she exclaimed and as she took a few steps back, grinning mischievously, I grew suspicious. "Go, be happy... with your... *Mia baby!"* Before I had a chance to reply, she had already turned around and with quick steps, marched off through the rain.

"She's gone."

"I wondered where that penetrating unnerving tone disappeared to." As she looked up, I was taken aback and almost stumbled backward.

SHE GLOWED! Her eyes glowed! Her cheeks glowed! I wondered if she was emitting radioactivity and frowned.

"THAT surely was a sign," she said with a satisfied grin. "You can set me down before your arms get tired."

"OH!" Frankly, I had forgotten I was still holding her, but she weighed next to nothing.

I set her down and pulled her sweater down, which had ridden up because I didn't want her to catch a cold. She laughed as she stared at my lips and before I could ask what was so amusing, she lifted a hand and a bit roughly wiped over them.

"OUCH!" I complained.

"They were smeared with lipstick," she giggled happily and I sighed resignedly. Since hers looked the same, I followed her example.

"What can I say, I'm a tranny. HA, HA," I joked feebly. She laughed louder.

When my lips were smudge-free and she looked presentable again, we quickly entered the restaurant because we were drenched and it was anything but warm outside.

However, as soon as we were in the warm room, she tensed.

I glance at our regulars' table right next to the kitchen door. Everyone sat there waiting like a lion about to devour its prey — the prey being Mia Angel. OH MAN...

One appeared more pissed off than the next. I felt her desire to turn around and leave as soon as their gazes fell on her.

*No, baby... you stay put...* I placed my arm protectively around her dainty shoulders and led her to the table. Luckily, the restaurant was closed – at lunchtime, we were always closed for two hours – because I knew it could get loud, all depending on what happened next. We were quite a temperamental family, which Mia knew. That was probably why she hesitated and why I had to push her in the right direction.

By the time we arrived at the table, everyone had already taken a deep breath only to let us have it.

"STOP!" I first pulled a chair out from the table on which Mia settled insecurely and then one for me, which I turned around and straddled.

"Everyone, shut up, okay?" My family closed their mouths. Everyone glared at me with hate in their eyes. Well, except for Katha, who was happily spooning her soup — she simply ignored the situation. She had never been involved in family events like the rest of us.

"Maybe we should let Mia speak first before you all pounce on her." She grew even paler and I realized it was exactly the wrong way to proceed. "Or you start, Vivi!" I could count on her not to put Mia through the wringer.

She sat across from us on the bench next to Tom in her dark blue wool dress with high neckline, looking like an elf, and was already eying Mia compassionately. Her gaze traveled over her thin contours and on over her unhealthy complexion... Then she sighed before gently starting.

"Hi, Mia..." who suddenly had tears in her eyes. The friendly welcome must have been unexpected. "We have not invited you here to dump on you...we're past that phase. We will remain civil and settle this like adults!" Vivi cast a stern look at everyone. Annoyed, Phil snorted. Tom rolled his eyes. Katha snickered quietly, probably due to the term *adults*. I glared at every one of them. Except Vivi...she was doing well.

"Yesterday, when Phil told us that it seemed you and Tristan were back together, we were quite shocked...as I'm sure you can understand, right?" Mia nodded and looked shyly at Vivi from under her long lashes.

"I don't know how it came about, but it seems it's what Tristan wants and it's his decision. It doesn't matter whether some of us cannot fathom it!" Another stab...

"Especially me! She's a traitor!" unexpectedly burst out of Phil and Mia winced in her chair.

"Philip!" Katha butted in before I could read him the riot act.

"I. DID. NOT. BETRAY. HIM. DAMMIT!" Mia said firmly and loudly, leaving the impression she had had enough of constantly repeating herself.

Now they all stared at her with skeptical expressions. The feelings I was currently experiencing were more than two-fold. I simply didn't know what to think anymore.

Finally, I decided we had to talk about a few things and that it had been unfair of me not to listen to her side of the story. I looked at her.

"Okay! Spill!" It sounded cold because my insides were churning again.

Mia's shocked gaze moved from Vivi to me. Then she swallowed loudly...and glanced at the napkin in front of her.

Her forehead bore deep wrinkles.

I too – like her – had a hard time, but not because I couldn't remember, rather because every time I allowed those memories to surface they almost tore me up.

Luckily, Mia sought no eye contact when she hesitantly began.

"I think it's best to start at the point when everything...got out of hand... When you went to boxing training, I decided to take Stanley for a walk..." Her gaze seemed far away, seeing the events from eight years ago. "In the woods, my father ambushed me..."

We all inhaled sharply. My quickly raised hand stopped Vivi from remarking.

"He threatened me..." Now she sounded tormented. "He threatened to destroy your career and have you thrown in prison if I didn't do as he asked. He told me he would get you transferred to the worst prison in all of Germany and destroy your reputation forever. That alone would have been bad enough, but then there was Eva Eber!"

Meanwhile, all eyes were directed at her again while I sat there with my hands balled into fists, staring at the expensive wooden table.

"She wanted to accuse you of raping her."

Now my family eyed me suspiciously – those idiots! – I laughed contemptuously. "You all seriously believe I had to resort to raping her?"

"Of course not!" my family almost said in unison — the relief in their voices quelled the lies. Although they immediately focused on Mia again.

The situation was too funny. The only thing missing was popcorn. Well, not quite…

She gulped, grabbed the napkin, and began shredding it into small pieces as she continued talking in that absent, slightly pained, delicate voice.

"She had seen my father and made a statement. He told me he could protect you as long as I cooperated... What could I do, Tristan? Should I have let him ruin everything you were and wanted to be?" Now she looked at me and I met her gaze. Her eyes were glassy — desperate. At that moment, I had no idea what to say without sounding completely sarcastic and hurtful, so I chose to stay silent, besides, I was breaking apart from the inside out.

As soon as she removed her despondent burning gaze off me, it seemed as if a great weight had been lifted from my chest.

Mia continued her piecemeal account.

"At the time, I had no idea what he was up to... Other than keeping me away from you, I had no idea he was pursuing a greater plan. I agreed to leave you in order to protect you even if it broke my heart, but I couldn't see you destroyed, after all, you were my one and all..." By now she was near tears...but she was brave. "I agreed and had to sign my own death sentence, so to speak. I told him I would cooperate, but he wanted to have something in his hand as a means of leverage in case I was thinking of running away with you... You know... back then it sounded logical to me..."

She paused briefly and took a deep breath. "So I gave him a statement...assuming he would *never* use it against you... My childish stupidity told me I could trust him — that was the biggest mistake of my life... the biggest mistake *of our* lives... It was the end of our life." Mia fell silent and let her head droop.

Then she scared everyone who was anxiously listening by shooting her hands upward, burying her face in them, and sobbing loudly.

"E...exuse me..." In no time, she was up, hurrying to the restrooms. I stared after her, not knowing what to think. All this was a bit much. Way too much...

Perplexed, I looked at my siblings, who returned my gaze and looked just as bewildered. Except for Katha.

"Well, I sure could go for a cookie right now!" Her statement interrupted the tense silence; she stood up and headed for the kitchen to make a mess. Tom and Vivi sat there dumbfounded, Phil stared after her ass...and I sincerely wished my father was here to give his two cents!

"I'll go check on Mia," Vivi announced after a few seconds and disappeared in the direction of the restrooms, leaving us three brothers alone.

"Anyone care to say something?" I asked when the situation grew too annoying.

"I'm going to join Katha!" Phil said, the ass! I rolled my eyes. What a GREAT family!

UNREAL!

Shortly afterward, Tommy and I had the whole table to ourselves.

"Are you planning to take off too?" I asked dramatically.

Tom grinned wider and whistled. "I wouldn't dream of it."

I smiled, glad the tense mood had lightened up a bit.

"So... What do you say? In your professional opinion as a lawyer..." I eventually began somewhat surly.

Tom took a sip of his damn organic ginger tea and adjusted the seat of his stylish rectangular glasses on his nose before replying.

"My opinion about it doesn't matter. What is important is how *you* feel about it, Tris..."

"Well, you're no damn help either!"

"That's just how it is, Tristan. Besides, what could I say? It was only yesterday that I learned you fiercely defended one of your sworn enemies to the extent that you attacked your big brother and now she tells such a heart-wrenching and logical-sounding story... That's her... acting rather dimwitted... Mia is the most gullible person I've ever met."

"Yes, but Tom... is it merely that, a story?"

Suddenly he leaned forward. His gray-blue eyes pierced mine. "Just look at her with open eyes, then you'll know!"

"Oh man..." I grabbed my other brother's glass of water and almost downed it in one gulp.

"Besides, what does it matter what happened in the past if you love her now?" I swallowed the wrong way and in a wide arc, spit everything out on the table as Phil and Katha came back from the kitchen and appalled, stared at me.

"I don't love Mia!" I cried as Tom made a show of looking disgusted as he dabbed water from his damn wool sweater. Katha carried a bowl of chocolate cookies and was busy nibbling as Phil sat next to me, pulled her onto his lap, and again slapped me on the goddamn back.

"You'd seriously take me on for a woman you don't love? And in my kitchen? With MY knives?"

Tommy laughed and helped himself to one of the blonde slut's cookies, which immediately earned the notorious look that could kill. And with her, it came *really* close to being fatal!

"You truly are no help!"

"I could tell you what I think after I've slept on it with Katharina," Phil offered while also snagging a cookie. Katha grabbed the bowl from the table into the safety of her lap and hissed at him.

"Let me have one too!" I demanded and Phil quickly sneaked one for me.

"Sorry, baby! He paid his share for this crap," he rationalized to his grumpy woman, who was castrating him with her eyes as he handed it to me.

"And I can do without your opinion! I know all too well that you always focus on the negative!" I muttered and bit into the fluffy chocolate cookie.

Naturally, he ignored my wish and continued, surprising me.

"You know, Tristan... I don't think she has the talent to be that good of an actress... Not when it concerns you," Phil suddenly said. "At the time, I did wonder how, especially a girl like her, one who adored you, could do something like THAT to you. I guess I was too angry at her to listen to reason. I mean, come on, you are my little brother! Besides, she never wrote to you! And she even testified in court. She was to blame for your shitty situation... And yes... I knew you'd disapprove, but when you were in jail, I went to confront her. I couldn't find her. It was as if she had disappeared from the face of the earth. Not a soul in that damn cow town had any idea her whereabouts. And now I see she had it as bad and is totally broken. I mean, look at her! She's a wreck! Just like you! Yet put you two together... dammit... and you're whole! As soon as she stands next to you your entire expression changes. It's incredible! You immediately snap out of your constantly pissed off, bitter mood. And she too can be herself because she knows no one is going to hurt her as long as you're there. Now, united, you are the people you were turning into eight years ago... Now, I finally recognize *you,* my old brother again."

Sighing, I rubbed a hand over my face. It was typical of Phil, ignoring my wish for no one to go looking for her.

"Besides..." Tom continued musing, "...I could never think of a reason why she would get rid of you. I mean, she's worshipped you since the first grade, so to speak, and you've been crazy about her ever since your first fuck. You liberated her from her fucked-up family... Oh, yeah, Vivi and I also searched for her — ta-da, surprise! What can I say, I'm sorry, but when Vivi sets her mind on something, well, she'd crawl over corpses and she really wanted to know what had gotten into Mia...but no such luck."

"Miserable traitors!" I grumbled to myself, although I should have known! Tom continued. "You've given her all the things she had obviously always longed for. She benefited from you, and when it came to sex, she also seemed...um...more than satisfied judging from the sounds that, for countless nights, tormented me... So the story Chief Dickhead had convinced you of that morning had been just too illogical. But leaving you believing was better for you. It gave you the strength to endure your new reality, the situation you had no chance of changing." Tom shrugged, took off his glasses, breathed on them, and cleaned them with the corner of his sweater.

"So, what? You believe her?" I wanted a definite confirmation.

"Tris..." Sighing, Tom shook his head as if I was a *total* moron. "I already told you my opinion does not matter. Actually, what happened eight years ago is also insignificant! People can change after such a period of time. Today, tomorrow, *anytime!* All that matters is the here and now. So, tell me this: NOWADAYS, what do you feel when you look at her? What does she MEAN to you?"

Now even Katha stopped nibbling on her cookies and stared at me as expectantly as the other two.

I had no difficulty imagining Mia in my mind because she was always there. I saw her, when she was asleep – with Robbie in her arms – in the hot tub as a sexy mermaid, in a quite vulnerable position on a massage table in a hotel in Prague, looking unspeakable sexy on stage at my club while *Sex is on Fire* boomed in the background, while looking out at my boxing gym. Or totally vulnerable in my room on our last night eight years ago, happy by the clearing by the stream, even happier in the school shower stall, uncertain in the gym... There are thousands of images and if I was honest, she represented one thing in every single one...

"She's my girl..." I replied feebly with sagging shoulders.

Tommy placed the glasses back on his nose.

"There's your answer!" Satisfied, he leaned back as Vivi and the object of my desire and the reason for countless sleepless nights were returning.

I threw a brief questioning look at Vivi and almost peed my pants when I saw the angry look in her eyes. OH, GREAT! Now she had switched sides. Which was foreseeable! After all, I was the ass here!

Mia sat down in the chair next to me, her eyes rather red yet she seemed more composed, although she wouldn't look at me and instead, stared intently at her hands in her lap.

Vivi sat on Tom's lap and once again, all eyes were on me, except for Mia.

I, on the other hand, looked at — *my damn girl*. When I regarded her in the light the new facts cast on her, a completely new world of emotions opened up for me. A complete *liberated* world of emotions. Not stifling, gloomy...

"Mia?" She bit her lower lip when I softly addressed her. It took her a few seconds to raise her head and look me directly in the eyes. Once again, she saw right through all the layers and walls I had erected *again* straight to the core of my damn heart.

Her gaze ate through my being, my soul, stealing my breath.

She looked at me oh-so...devotedly, as if her entire world depended on my next words. The tension she conveyed was almost unbearable.

FUCK!

What had I put her through? Why, dammit, had I not believed in us — in her! It was the only thought I could ponder at the moment. Assuming everything she said was true — as it made more sense from one minute to the next... then *I* too was faced with only one important question: WHAT. HAD. I. DONE. TO. HER?

I wanted to sink into my chair and hide my face behind my hands and never look up again, but I couldn't.

Apparently, it was high time for me to make amends before she might actually decide to leave me, the sadistic bastard, of all...

And to make matters worse, now I could also see the pain in her eyes. The severity seemed to increase the longer I hesitated.

That fact gave me the necessary push.

I noticed how the image I had created of her over the last eight years from the knowledge I had, fell apart. Only one thing remained... It shined inside me with new intensity. Right where my goddamn HEART was. Because her love for me was rock solid, no matter what and she was here... had endured and put up with everything just so she could sit next to me now... and so it was actually perfect! I was whole again. I had not been able to feel my heart due to her absence and not because she had cruelly ripped it out and destroyed it. After all, she was my damn heart.

In all these years, all I ever needed to be happy was her.

My... Mia baby.

"Mia...baby..." Oh fuck... I was such a loser... My voice sounded thick and raw and just those two words... oh my... initially, she appeared shocked followed by experiencing such unbridled joy, I was afraid she might overdo it. But I had to say it, it was important I liberate her guilt, which her caramel eyes betrayed every time she looked at me. I had to give her the opportunity to live again.

Free. Happy. Together with me.

And so, I said three words... The only ones she wanted to hear from me.

No... not those words! The other ones!

"I believe you."

A silent fart could have been heard had someone let one rip. Apart from the ticking of the expensive wall clock and subdued street noise that penetrated the windows and doors, NOTHING could be heard.

No one breathed — especially Mia.

Instead, she grew pale. I wanted to jump up and revitalize her, but unfortunately, like everyone else, I couldn't move...

As I was using whatever strength available to me to eliminate my state of shock so I could come to her rescue, she startled all of us with a bloodcurdling scream, which made ALL of us cry out at once. In the next moment, she was straddling me, wrapping her arms around my neck, and clinging to me, flooding my face before gently cradling it in her small hands, showering it with little soft kisses.

I was so shocked and hearing impaired I needed a moment to comprehend before I could react. I was grinning from ear to ear when I wrapped my arms around her waist and pulled her firmly against me.

The others took a deep breath and started complaining about being startled by the scream, but then fell silent and decided to give us a little privacy, scattering to fuck-who-knows-where.

Nothing mattered to me.

Because just then, her damn lips were kissing the corners of my mouth and I knew what she wanted... However, what about the DAMN FUCKING RULES!

FUCK'EM!

The only thing that mattered was her! And to tell the truth, it was not only now!

"M'hm, baby..." She giggled happily as I once again addressed her by it. "I know what you want..." And with that, I grabbed the back of her head and turned it toward me, my mouth capturing her lips for a long intense kiss. It was the most intense kiss we had ever shared.

THAT was pure redemption.

Relieved, we groaned as are our tongues touched and devoutly tasted each other. My hands brushed over her back, which made her shiver, but I had to FEEL her. Every single square inch of my girl!

I noticed the salty pearls running down her face, but I knew they were tears of pure happiness, so, no reason to interfere. I felt her fingers digging into my shoulders, her hot pussy, which rubbed against me, her ample bosom, her velvety tongue, her lips, her hair in my fist.

But even the most beautiful kiss eventually ends, at the latest, when both parties threatened to suffocate.

We were breathless and panting frantically when we broke apart. I leaned my forehead against her. She licked her lips and had closed her eyes dreamily as her fingertips ventured forward and started playing with the hair on my neck. It unleashed a tingling sensation down my entire back and I quickly leaned in to start the counterattack. Gently, I brushed my lips over her neck.

"Tristan..." I ignored her rebuke, but certainly not her lower body – also called a pussy – which rubbed against me again.

Groaning, I slid further down.

"Tristan!" She sounded reproachful, yet on the verge of melting.

"Quiet!" I ordered as she was about to say something else and made a strangling noise as soon as she started to dry fuck me. Her body was helpless against me, regardless of her mind's momentary reluctance.

"Tristan... THERE ARE PEOPLE OUTSIDE WATCHING US!"

"OH!" Bewildered, I peered over her shoulder at a family of three standing at the door. They had almost flattened their noses on the glass, especially the, around, twelve-year-old little girl with braces and glasses.

I laughed loudly and rose together with Mia, setting her immediately down on a chair with reddened cheeks and bright eyes, leaving her alone with the cookies Katha had strangely forgotten, to tell the people outside we weren't open for another hour.

Why was I so happy? Oh, yes...I stopped being a grump and instead, started living.

\*\*\*

Unfortunately, for now, I had to send my new life and Vivi home because work called. Apparently, Lena was pretty upset because last night she had been thoroughly worked over. Thus, she would not be able to work tonight, maybe not even the entire week, even if she had been made of steel. The perpetrator, a highly respected Italian Mafiosi who had snuck into Germany from Sicily and who obviously had no idea how to behave at my place, had to be taught a lesson.

Mia was not thrilled that our paths were already parting, but I promised to call her as soon as I had time.

"Maybe later we can talk about everything again?" she asked shyly at the open window as I got behind the wheel of my car. Appropriately, it had stopped raining and the sun peeked out between the dark clouds, illuminating her as the saint that she was.

"Yep!" I brushed a strand from her face and was happy to do so again without doubt nagging me.

"And you won't change your mind later on?"

"About?" I asked playfully clueless.

She smiled shrewdly and leaned forward, keeping her hand on the upper doorframe, offering me a phenomenal view.

"That..." Abruptly, she kissed me.

Delicately… Gently... *Promisingly... Enticingly...*

I growled against her lips. The desire that took an uncontrollable hold of me when she kissed me like that was almost stronger than when she was passionate.

Laughing, she broke away from me and her eyes sparkled so promisingly, I would have preferred to grab hold of her never to let go again. But, despite new insights, we each needed some time to process it. Besides, she had to take Stanley for a walk... Yes, she still had him, which made me incredibly happy. It somehow provided the impression that we had not wasted eight years and that we actually could continue where we had left off. And without the four-legged pooper, it would not have been the same...

"See you, baby!" Her glow grew more radiant. I gave her one last little peck on the forehead and once she had stepped away from the car, forced myself to drive off...

FUCK!

I was such a lucky motherfucker.

Even I no longer recognized myself.

*** 

All joy abruptly flew out of my chest as I entered my office and switched on the monitor in the cabinet next to my desk, which allowed me to monitor Mia's apartment.

My previously reanimated damn heart instantly stopped functioning because Francesco was sitting on her bed, seemingly bored! Next to him was a brown envelope and he was gesturing wildly with a DAMN GUN! A plastic tarp covered the floor like a damn slasher film!

"No!" I shouted through my office, grabbed baby number three out of the drawer, and shoved it under my waistband, then I RAN FOR MY LIFE while dialing her number.

ONLY THE MAILBOX! The same with Vivi.

FUCK!

# 5. His Protection

*Mia 'In danger' Angel*

At first, I thought the day would end in a complete disaster — I definitely had not expected anything like that!

Tristan was mine again! My Tristan! I could tell by the soft expression in his beautiful eyes. I could tell by the way his tongue touched mine and heard it in his words...

I was his Mia baby again... His girl... His one and only.

I was so happy I cried the entire drive home in Vivi's yellow Porsche. She had been the first to believe me and comforted me when I ran off to the restrooms as if the last eight years never took place. Like nothing had ever stood between us. Vivi told me that she and Tom had been looking for me despite Tristan forbidding the whole family from doing so. She never believed I could have done such a thing to him. Yet I had difficulties to come to terms with the fact that Vivian Müller... that the whole Wrangler family was back in my life.

And Tristan and I had a future.

Ultimately, their eyes no longer bore distrust. I had no idea whether it was because of what I had said, my collapse, or Tristan forgiving me. In any case, they seemed to believe me... not just FORGAVE me — but actually believed. That was the most important step in this story!

And they had gone looking for me, had not forgotten me, I had always been important to them.

It was so heartwarming. I was so happy and I still felt the tingling sensation Tristan's lips had left on mine when Vivi dropped me off in front of my home but not without making a date with me. She wanted to visit me at work and I couldn't wait to learn how she had been these last few years.

Slowly but surely, my life was returning to normal again. I no longer felt dead.

Everything was colorful and cheerful. I waved wildly at Vivi, then danced inside the house and hummed as I climbed the stairs. I sang the song from the Alfred Jodocus Kwak series, *Why am I so happy? So happy? So happy?* Yes, a children's song! At that moment, it seemed fitting...

I thought about Tristan. His glowing eyes...his warm hands...his gentle smile, which came close to causing me to faint every time.

I thought of him being mine again and started to worry I might burst with love...

UNTIL...

I unlocked my front door...

The first thing I noticed was Stanley not there to greet me. That was unusual — he always did.

"Stanley?" I called down the hallway, but no sign of him.

Panic overwhelmed me and a lump formed in my throat. My chest began to burn because he was up there in age and I was afraid I might find him dead in his doggie bed. Regardless, I ventured down the hall and with an outstretched shaky hand, opened the slightly open door to the bedroom.

But everything proceeded completely different...

I found Francesco on the bed. He wore a dark-green casual shirt and black jogging pants like he had come straight from the gym. He seemed relaxed and didn't glance up when I stepped through the doorway.

He alone was not all that intimidating — but what he turned back and forth in his hands was... incredibly so...

A weapon. A big silver one. I had no idea he owned such an item, but then he must, given he was the nephew of the Italian drug lord in this not so small town.

"Hi, MOUSE..." he greeted me in a strange faraway voice, but it was still as loving as if he had waited for me at a set table with a self-cooked meal and glasses of champagne.

"Francesco?" I felt my heart beating far too fiercely in my chest. The scene did not bode well... I also saw a tarp covering the floor and gasped.

Only now did he look up and grin, his eyes gleaming with madness...

I took a step back and considered if I could make it to the front door because it was not a friendly house call, this here was something entirely different.

Something terrible.

"If you try to run, I'll shoot you in the leg. Better come over here and sit with me. I merely want to chat a little with you." Francesco placed the gun beside him on my gray bedspread and patted the other side invitingly. Shakily and with sweaty hands, I obeyed his request.

"Where's Stanley?" I asked and scanned the room, close to tears. *Oh, please, please, dear God please, if you exist, don't let him have hurt Stanley! Please!*

"Over there!" He pointed to my wardrobe and shrugged. "I did not want him interfering and ruining it, like biting my calf... Be happy I didn't kill the smelly turd, one blow would have sufficed.

I swallowed loudly and hoped he was telling the truth as I carefully settled next to him. My butt touched paper and I immediately jumped. Francesco laughed as he grabbed the big envelope on which I had briefly sat. Tense, I lowered myself again and tried to get comfortable while making sure to leave as much distance as possible between us. My nerves were as taut as piano wire.

While I was staring at Francesco, he fussed with the envelope while giving it the evil eye. The silence made the whole situation increasingly more unpleasant. The blood coursing through my body caused my ears to experience an ever-increasing rushing noise while a sickening feeling that threatened to close my throat, settled in my stomach.

Then he said...icily and unforgivingly, "I presumed much of you, you know..." He opened the envelope and pulled out a couple of photos. He showed me the first and looking at it, I froze... "BUT I DO NOT WANT TO BELIEVE YOU'RE HIS SLUT! Wasn't it nice of Ms. Eber to send me pictures?" The picture showed Tristan and I...at the pole...in the club... It was poor quality — but everything relevant could be seen.

Before I could comprehend everything, he had yanked my head back by the hair and leaned over me. Stricken, I groaned. He was deranged... very much so. YES! OKAY! I had betrayed him, but it did not justify his actions here. He tugged harder!

"When did you start fucking him?"

Fear stopped my breathing, which was why I couldn't answer him. Then again, I wouldn't have known what to tell him. He struck me in the face...with his fist no less! Pain shot through me like a cannonball, spreading to every fiber of my being. Blood gushed from my nostrils and dripped onto my sweater, Francesco, and the bed.

"AHHHRGH!" I reflexively covered the throbbing area with both hands. As tears welled up in my eyes, he pulled me up by my hair only to force me down on my knees — directly in the center of the tarp. I collapsed onto my hands.

Blood dripped from my nose onto the plastic. *Drip. Drip. Drip. Drip.*

Unintentionally, tears mixed with it and I started to tremble incessantly. Everything happened so quickly it was hard to comprehend. Panic dug its claws into me and I barely managed an explanation.

"I... I'm sorry Francesco... I... I love him... but I should have..." Before I could say another word, he stepped on my fingers. First, I heard the terrible cracking and then the pain started. I screamed. He kept the weight of one heel on my hand and twisted his foot back and forth. I groaned.

"Pleeeeaaaassseee... stop...!" I pleaded. Sobbing, I used the other hand to grab my wrist, trying to wrestle it free, bobbing back and forth. The pain was unbearable!

"Oh, how I love it when they whine, cry, and beg for mercy..." He no longer sounded like the man I knew, but a madman.

I simply could not comprehend. How could I have read him so wrong?

He inhaled and exhaled deeply. "M'hm..."

He obviously enjoyed me being weaker than him, but I did not want to give him the satisfaction. Instead, I had to find a way to stall for time and remain strong. I recalled the cameras Tristan had installed everywhere and placed my hope in him. If he didn't come to my rescue, I probably wouldn't make it out alive.

Francesco took his foot off my abused hand and squatted in front of me as I straightened up a bit and with my good hand, gently grabbed my aching, quivering fingers, lightly pressing them against my chest.

"At first, you were only for show…a distraction from my actual leisure activity." Now he was talking to me as sweet as could be.

*What was he talking about?*

He laughed softly. "I love it when they bleed out like pigs as soon as I'm done with them…!"

My eyes widened and my breathing grew more frantic. A horrible notion overwhelmed me and at first, my stomach protested before I was overcome with infinite peace and the certainty I had ignored my stupidity all these years. "You are a murderer," I noted.

"I prefer the term slasher…" he replied nonchalantly. "Actually, I'm pretty good at it…" Casually, he got up and walked over to my bed. "Now it's your turn…" He must have thought I didn't have it in me to flee; however, I decided I could not sit idly by and surrender to my fate like a fair maiden waiting for her prince. So, I pulled myself together, jumped up, and ran with a loudly pounding heart toward the living room and front door.

Unfortunately, I had no damn chance. As I reached my couch, he silently overtook me and tripped me so that my upper body smashed forcefully onto the coffee table. The impact expelled whatever air I had left in my lungs.

I automatically rolled off the table and came to rest on the floor on my back, laboring for air. Francesco leaned over me, grinning, with the gun in his hand.

"Go!" He pointed to the bedroom. I couldn't move... Suffocation was imminent.

"ARRRRRRRRRRGGG!" he roared and kicked me in the side. Before he could pull his leg back, I quickly pulled myself together and, panting and crying, crawled toward the other room.

As soon as I returned to the terrible, now blood-spattered tarp, he ripped my upper body into an upright position and stood before me.

I barely suppressed a panicked cry when I felt something cold pressing against my temple. It was his weapon.

My heart froze. I was thinking that any moment now he might pull the trigger and squeezed my eyes shut.

I was only thinking: *Tristan... Tristan... Tristan...*

He didn't pull the trigger.

I carefully opened my eyes and saw him looking down at me with a satisfied grin. Oh yes, he was enjoying himself... *Very much so.*

"I won't kill you until you have done everything with me that you did with him. And when I'm done with you, I'll take care of him..."

"Don't worry, he'll take care of you!" I hissed, with no idea where the sudden courage came from. When I saw pure hatred flash in his eyes, I immediately regretted my big lip.

"We'll see about that." Francesco actually began to open his pants. "I did ask when he started fucking you. Before the meeting in the gallery?"

I owed him an answer because nothing I said would matter, besides, his gun still frightened me.

"Or was it when you visited him alone... Did he fuck you on his desk...? In his club?" Then he remembered something. "WAS THAT YOU AT DINNER?"

Oh no! My eyes must have betrayed me because he increased the pressure of his gun against my skull. I could tell his hand shook by the barrel. We were caught and I was sure there was nothing that could defuse the situation. Basically, now would be a good time for Tristan to show up and save me. Just as I finally had him back again, someone seals my fate!

"HE DARED TOUCH YOU IN FRONT OF ME?"

"Actually, he fucked me right in front of you! He was quite deep inside me while you were eating, not suspecting a thing!" I would die either way, besides, it felt so damn good...

"JUST FOR THAT, my dear, your ordeal will be prolonged by a few hours..." he finally proclaimed, trembling all over, and then he took his penis out. "Open your mouth!"

I pressed my lips together and stubbornly, looked him in the eyes. No way would I willingly pleasure him. All the while, tears were streaming down my cheeks.

"OPEN UP!" He pressed the gun even more firmly against my head. Regardless, I refused to obey and instead, stared at the fired up lunatic.

Suddenly, his gun moved from my temple and ended up point blank against one of my breasts.

"Then I blow your tit away!" I closed my eyes in anguish and wished he would just shoot me already. I had no strength left to pray for a miracle.

To distract myself, I tried to think about Tristan... about the last wistful look he had given me once our lips had parted. However, my brain would not cooperate because I was a complete mess and too scared to concentrate.

I wanted to die. Just like that... NOW!

Tristan was the only man who was ever in my mouth and it should remain that way. I was not about to be soiled, I belonged solely to him... Especially now, where we had found each other again. Now, when we were hopeful again... it was supposed to end?

For some reason, there was always someone standing in the way of our happiness!

Overcome with all these gloomy thoughts, I merely kept sobbing, waiting for the cruel end, because there was no way I would willingly open my mouth for another man! Never!

Suddenly, a deafening bang that made my ears ring echoed through the room, and I was certain I would die now. Instead, I felt something warm splashing me, especially in the face. Then Francesco started to scream, no, he was roaring...

I ripped open my eyes and saw him desperately covering his privates with both hands. He fell onto his knees in front of me. I was shocked to see so much blood gushing out from under his fingers. His weapon lay off to the side on the floor.

Francesco cursed and whimpered in Italian. I was dazed, just staring at him, when two legs stepped into view. Without seeing the face, I knew to whom they belonged. At once, I felt utterly relieved and calm. No more panic. I glanced up, straight at his divine butt and broad back — he had placed himself between us in order to hit Francesco over the head with his weapon, who then collapsed...

He was unconscious... yet still bleeding from his crotch.

I refused to look closer for, instinctively, I knew he had shot his thingy off, which the madman had been about to stick in my mouth.

Finally, it was dead silent, but as before, I still did not dare move. Completely motionless, I knelt on the bloodstained tarp and stared down.

Then Tristan's face appeared. He covered my cheeks with both hands and all I could see in his eyes was deep concern... and ANGER.

Sheer, brutal rage.

"Can you hear me? Mia!" I blinked a couple of times, still unable to believe that my rescuer was squatting in front of me. To reassure myself, I raised my good hand and touched his cheek. He closed his eyes, placed his hand over my fingers, and pressed them against his face. Hastily, I jumped up and threw myself into his arms.

"Tristan..." I gasped.

"Yes, baby, I'm here now... I'm sorry I didn't get here sooner... I'm so sorry! FUCK..."

"Shhh... You are here now." How could I be so calm in such a situation? It was incredible how secure this man could make me feel. For a moment, he held me even tighter before breaking away and turning my face for a better look.

"The nose isn't broken," he noted dryly. Then he raised my left hand and gently inspected my fingers. They no longer hurt as bad, merely throbbed a bit, but seeing anger flash anew in his eyes, I knew Francesco should write his last will.

"Thankfully, THEY are not broken either... Now, I'd like you to go into the living room and lie down on the couch. I'll be there momentarily."

I clung to his sweater, wildly shaking my head. No...he couldn't leave me alone. He shouldn't leave me alone!

"Only for a moment. I'll be right here. No one can hurt you anymore. Please. Go. Into. The. Living room!

"No!" Desperate, I managed the strength to hold him even tighter. Tristan inhaled and exhaled deeply into my hair.

"Then stay! But he is going to suffer... He touched you, Mia, dammit, *he goddamn fucking touched you...*" he whispered in a low and trembling voice.

I merely nodded, still in a haze...

He released me and probably wondered where I should sit. I used the opportunity to crawl to the cabinet and free Stanley, who was motionless. He breathed, fortunately. I crouched with him in a corner and watched Tristan get up, looking equally dangerous and beautiful, and then disappear into the bathroom.

With an extremely determined expression, his lips pressed thinly, eyes icy cold, I knew I wouldn't want to be in Francesco's shoes, who was still lying unconscious on the floor, no longer bleeding.

Tristan returned with a bowl of water and as I wondered what it might be for, he flung it in Francesco's face.

He came to, panting and, although still dazed, still in pain, immediately went for his crotch. As before, I chose not to look closer.

"Hey, teeny-weenie!" Tristan tapped him with a foot. "You know who I am?" and in the next moment, he kicked him full force in the kidneys. "Your worst nightmare!"

Francesco's eyes threatened to pop out of their sockets as he writhed around on the ground in pain.

Satisfied, Tristan grinned. Although we were quite far apart, at that moment, he could not have been closer to me. As agile as a predator, he squatted before the sadist and waited patiently until Francesco was calm, and with difficulty, looked at him.

"You touched my girl," he noted dryly and Francesco's eyes widened. Confused, he looked around the room until he saw me squatting in the corner. I stared at him.

"Hey, man...it was an...accident... I didn't mean...to..."

"Wow, wow, wow..." Tristan chided calmly. "Considering the tarp, I don't believe it was an accident that you hit her in the face, almost broke her fingers, and were about to stick your dick in her mouth... Was it...?" He took hold of Francesco's blood smeared hand and with his other, grabbed a finger — the pinkie... Then his vigilant gaze slid to me...

"I would look away if I were you!"

Since my stomach was already queasy, I hurriedly did as advised and Tristan whispered in the man's ear, "Does this feel like an accident?" and then a terrible cracking was heard, followed by Francesco roaring...

"Or this?" *Crack. Scream.*

"Or this?" *Crack. Scream.*

"Or this?" *Crack. Scream.*

"Or this?" *Crack. Scream.*

Now, I honestly felt sick...

I tried to breathe deeply through my nose, which helped a bit... Maybe I should have gone into the living room. Tristan looked as if he was just warming up...and he seemed to enjoy it... However, I was not shocked because I too *would* enjoy tormenting whatever person if they did to him what Francesco had done to me.

"You may look again," he announced cheerfully, but I could not!

"Baby?"

"Yes," I replied bitterly.

Then I felt his fingers gently brushing my cheek.

"Go into the living room," he ordered gently. "I don't want you to see me like this!"

Huh? Now I glanced up. "You cannot seriously think that it would change how I feel about you?"

Now, Tristan was puzzled.

"Nothing can do that, besides, he deserves it! I was not his first or last victim," I stated matter-of-factly.

Tristan grinned. "That's my girl."

Then, he leaned forward and his soft lips gave me a brief gentle kiss. And I... I smiled...

\*\*\*

Eventually, I couldn't handle it anymore and gave up...

Seeing Tristan force Francesco's head onto the cool tarp became too much.

"You broke my girl's nose..." To which he put his heel on Francesco's nose and...hearing THAT crack sent me running.

# 6. Revenge

*Tristan 'Hunting' Wrangler*

I was no longer sane when I arrived at Mia's door. I rather resembled a spree killer than a rational thinking person.

The image in my head of Mia kneeling before him, in PAIN because he had INJURED her, brought out a side of me I had never felt so intensely before.

That was exactly what happened NOW, what she used to be afraid of: I mutated into an insane madman.

Definitely!

I was no longer rational!

Or I would have thought of screwing a silencer on before pointing my weapon at some guy's wiener in an apartment in some shitty row house. AND FIRED!

Those who had never heard a shot would have no idea how loud that shit was. It was not like in the movies where a gunfight takes place in a 12-family apartment complex and no one calls the damn police because no one HEARD it.

*It* was heard! Throughout the whole BUILDING! And that was when the police were called! It happens not only in Germany! Everywhere! Even in a big rat-infested city like this...

Had my brain functioned normally, I probably would have assumed the neighbors would hear the shot and set my damn weapon aside and instead, beat the fucker to death. Unfortunately, all reason had recently vacated my brain.

All I saw was his goddamn dick in front of her face and I held a suitable device in my hand to stop what he had planned for my girl.

I mean, hey... you could pretty much shoot a man anywhere and he'll survive if he doesn't die accidentally. However, if you shoot a guy's cock...

Oh, oh, oh...

For such action, that probably fell under the death penalty in the law books.

That was why I gave him a Tristan style circumcision, wounding him only superficially so he would not bleed to death from THAT wound. I was not going to make it too easy for the sick pig. Oftentimes, a person's life could be crueler than death itself, especially when bad things happened to that person.

So, a short time later, Francesco lay on the floor, writhing in pain and panting.

My girl had just lost unconscious when the doorbell rang. Not once, but twice in a row, sounding quite insistent.

Instantly, a bad feeling overcame me and I didn't even want to know who was coming to interfere.

Naturally, I first took care of the most important thing. I went over to Mia baby and picked her up off the ground. I could not leave her cowering in the corner even though she was unconscious.

"Baby...wake up..." I placed her on the bed when the doorbell rang again. Shortly thereafter, someone pounded on the door and shouted,

"POLICE! OPEN THE DOOR!"

FANTASTIC!

... I wanted to shout a greeting, but I thought better of it and went over to Francesco to knock the little shit out again before he could call for help. Besides, I could not concentrate with all that moaning.

I was in fight mode ever since I had entered the damn apartment, which was why I gave him a well-aimed uppercut that put him out of his misery for a while. In the middle ages, it was the way to knock out people before pulling a tooth. So, that prick had no reason to complain, I was treating him humanely.

He collapsed like a boulder onto the goddamn floor and I glanced at Mia, who had just opened her eyes while someone continued pounding their fist against the door.

"If you do not open the door this instant, you give us no choice but to enter the premises by force!" were the first words she heard since coming to and she gasped.

"Tristan...what's going on?" she whispered weakly and blinked as she glanced at me when I squatted next to the bed.

"Francesco is unconscious and the cops are at the door. How are you doing, baby?" Concerned, I felt her forehead.

"The police are here?" she gasped, then focused on the incessant pounding, shouting, and ringing. "Tristan! Shit!" She abruptly got up and tried to study my face, but I pushed her back onto the pillow.

"I'll handle it... But perhaps you could strip down to your underwear and then come to the door." She stared at me in disbelief as soon as I charmingly expressed my idea. NO! For once, I wasn't thinking about THAT! A smile crept across my face.

"You know, under normal circumstances, I'd kill anyone who dared ogle you, but in this instance, it could be beneficial, okay? And wash your face, baby!"

"We are breaking down the door now!" I kept looking into Mia's eyes for as long as it took her to scramble up and storm the adjacent bathroom. Rushing, she pulled off her clothes, groaning painfully. In the meantime, I tucked the blood-spattered blanket under her bed and quickly disrobed, leaving only my shorts on as I walked to the door.

I ruffled my hair with one hand while the other opened the door.

This was every professional criminal's worst nightmare. Just when you are about to torture your victim, the cops show up at the front door...

I was confronted by two male officers — unfortunately. Dealing with two broads would have been so much easier. One guy was built and only as old as Mia, the other a little taller than me. They were in uniform and both wore a stern yet bored look.

No Hello. No nothing. Ill-mannered bunch!

"Is everything all right here?" Their hands were close to their belts, which were fastened way too tight under their beer bellies as they tried to look around nonchalantly considering my almost naked appearance.

"Everything is actually fine and dandy..." I was as loose as a goose.

"We received a call that a loud bang like a gunshot was heard coming from your apartment..." one guy rattled off monotonously, while the other peered over my shoulder into the hallway. No problem, nothing to see there.

Skeptical, I frowned.

"Aha."

They stared at me encouragingly and I returned the same look. Nice information – so meaningful – now what did they want from me?

Finally, the light bulb went off in their heads and they flashed their badges — visibly annoyed. I took my time staring at them until I sensed a renewed state of nervousness. Then I grinned.

"I was a bit...*preoccupied*, so I might not have heard it..."

An unmistakable groan came from the bedroom. *WELL, GREAT, teeny-weenie better shut up!* I stared at the cops admonishingly, whose ears immediately pricked up. "Now she is continuing without me!"

Now they seemed *slightly* irritated.

"May we take a look around?" FUCK! Why did the damn fucking cops always play it by the book?

"I don't know if my girlfriend would consent to that... She might consider it sexual harassment if you were to barge in while she's in such a state..." Now, my tone was more assertive.

"I'm sorry, but we insist." And my dear fellow men in puke blue uniforms (it seemed green was out of date, nowadays, they prefer to look like underpaid ticket collectors) pushed past me.

Dammit! In actuality, they needed a search warrant to enter and search someone's premises except when they had a *strong suspicion*.

And these idiots would consider a fart a *strong suspicion*, fuck!

They carefully examined the living room and found nothing seemingly controversial about my scattered clothes. It seemed to confuse them because one...the taller cop...KEPT staring at me skeptically with one eyebrow raised as if it was frozen in place. I would not be intimidated by those idiots and leaned against the wall with my arms crossed.

I didn't mind them looking around in here, but I would stop them before they set foot in the bedroom.

"So, you haven't seen or heard anything suspicious, Mr…" the smaller of the two, who had already stumbled twice even though nothing was in the way, eyed me questioningly. It seemed they were still leery of me because their hands were still close to their nightsticks… It seemed they could smell one of the top villains in town.

"As I said, I've been busy with my girlfriend for the last hour. The only thing I've seen is her womanly attributes!"

I decided to shock them a little to distract them from inquiring about my name. *That* would cause unrest.

Now the klutz REALLY stumbled, almost falling on his crooked nose while the other with the permanently raised eyebrow regarded the discarded clothes with disgust.

Ignoring my apprehension and the goose bumps running down my back, I leaned in conspiratorially. "You know how it is as a man… Once you're in you never want back out, no matter what happens… Even if the bed collapses."

He refrained from replying and instead, took a step away from me — obviously in a hurry to leave. Wonderful.

The little guy snorted and opened the door to the bedroom without giving me the slightest opportunity to prevent it.

Fuck!

I expected to see Francesco laying in a pool of his own blood, slowly wasting away with naturally, lots of hyperbole, the wimp! But that was not the case. Instead, there was no sign of the tarp or Francesco, only Mia on the bed, seemingly worked up, a flushed face and drenched in sweat as if she had schlepped bags of cement at a construction site. With difficulty, I restrained the laughter threatening to erupt as the Smurfs stopped in the doorway with shocked expressions on their faces.

"Oh my God! THIS IS YOUR SURPRISE?" she immediately yelled and my eyes widened. What was the woman up to? "TWO STRIPPERS? Honey, you're the best!" Lustful, she licked her full lips. ARGH! SHE WAS KILLING ME! AND I WAS USED TO HER!

How would the other two fare? She was divine as she lay on her side without an ounce of inhibition, just like I taught her. HA! I knew that shit would come in handy one day.

Considering teeny-weenie had wanted to fucking kill her, the normal response would have been for her to be completely out of her mind. But my girl would not allow herself to show weakness, oh no, especially when it came to me. She always surprised me, which made me proud of her.

Her underwear was white and innocent, covering a flawless shapely body, not to mention, how lasciviously she eyeballed the cops, making me completely randy again, regardless that her little show wasn't meant for me. One of her fingers ran invitingly down her curves on one side. Yes...if she wanted, she definitely knew how to use her womanly charms.

The cops stood there, literally salivating, unable to stop staring. The little one looked turned on, the bigger one shocked.

Well...I was the lucky guy who could call this little sexy nymph his. The sight of her immediately made the blood rush from my brain into my pants and I was hard again, just like evolution had in mind for us.

Slowly, she assumed an upright position...and then she did something that really made my knees weak. She sat on the corner of the bed with her beautiful smooth legs SPREAD. I watched her expectantly as her fingers uninhibitedly slid down over her flat stomach and into her panties.

"I enjoy pleasuring myself while watching two hot guys undress..." she remarked naughtily. "Come on guys, get a move on!"

"E-e-excuse the intrusion." The big cop stormed out of the room. The small guy, albeit reluctantly, followed his embarrassed colleague.

Mia gave me a cute wink and I mouthed WOW before seeing the policemen out.

"There's no need to bother you any longer... Call us if you remember anything. Have a nice day!" And with that, the big cop handed me his business card.

As they started to leave, the little one cast one last wistful look toward the bedroom.

*That's...right...it's not every day you get to see such a treat*, I thought smugly.

And then they were gone. I stood there a while longer, still somewhat flabbergasted before closing the door and ripping up the business card...

Once I locked the door, I went to my pocket and pulled out a smoke and lighter. It wasn't until I took my first drag that my adrenalin finally diminished.

The sight of Mia had placed me in another mode other than combat. First, it was time to learn what she had done it with Francesco. I hoped she hadn't lost it and tossed him out the window, gangster style.

Unfortunately, when I entered the bedroom, she was no longer sitting on the corner of the bed but immediately flung herself around my neck.

"Oh my God! Tristan!" I caught her and quietly groaned in discomfort because she was pushing against my fucker. I used one hand to hold her hip.

"That was so crazy!" she gasped, in shock and her whole body shaking.

"One moment..." I carried her into the adjacent bathroom and threw my just lit cig in the sink. Mia was trembling far too much.

"Are you okay?" Gently, I raised her face and read her widened eyes. She nodded.

"You were fucking fabulous, baby! You saved our butts," earning me a shy smile and a slight blush to her cheeks. Clearly, she was no longer used to compliments.

"When your ass is on the line, I'll do anything..." and she hugged me again and I held her for as long as it took her to stop to shaking... I gently caressed her back while imagining everything that could have happened if I had not made it in time. I mean, we had just found each other again...

Fuck... I felt like crying, but the longer her body pressed against me, the more my mood changed. My need for melancholy was replaced with other cravings that required attention. Like, for example, my addiction to the drug called Mia's pussy.

At least that was decided by the owner because at some point she pulled my head down and kissed me.

She would not waste an opportunity after such a long period of deprivation. Not even now for she grew increasingly more passionate. Her ass landed on the sink and I quickly pushed her bra up so I could feel her soft tits pressed against my naked chest. Her nipples were excited. She too was stimulated by the whole situation.

I groaned in her mouth as she hectically used her legs to pull me closer to her lower body, which I immediately rubbed against her hot spot with my hips.

"Where is he?" I asked as my lips moved down to her nipples, which were already standing at attention for me. Her nails dug into my neck and she arched her back as I firmly sucked on one and circled its tip with my tongue. She tasted so damn sweet...

"In the closet," she gasped.

I laughed against her damp skin and she shivered.

"That's where the prick belongs!"

"And the tarp is tightly wrapped around him." My laughter grew more boisterous and I raised my hand to rub her clit a little through the panties. OH FUCK! Her intimate area was hot to the touch and soaking wet. My cock twitched violently.

"You remember the last time I came in your pussy?" I whispered in her ear and made her moan helplessly. My lips brushed over her cheek and I licked her lip.

"It has been way too long..." I gently bit the delicate meat as I released my fucker and slid her panties aside...

Just then, apparently our baked potato had regained consciousness because he started to scream, which pissed me off a bit. NOBODY BOTHERS TRISTAN WRANGLER WHEN HE'S ABOUT TO FUCK HIS GIRL!

"Should we annoy Francesco a little?" I asked mischievously and helped her down to the ground.

"Even more so?" she replied, sounding a bit skeptical, but I was already dragging her behind me into the bedroom. Since the closet somewhat muffled his screams, I grabbed a pair of rolled up socks from the dresser drawer and stuffed them into his big mouth as soon as I slid the door aside.

"Shut up!" was my first command as I kicked him in the ribs and laughed when I studied him more closely. He looked like a poorly wrapped mummy, only his pale head was sticking out. "Watch," was my second command before I positioned Mia right in front of him so that he *had to* look at her.

My presence must have given my baby her strength and self-confidence back because as I was slowly circling her, Mia eyed him with one raised eyebrow and, dressed in her white lacy lingerie, she looked like the goddess of death.

"Watch and learn how to treat such a heavenly being, how to adore her...because only then will it make you experience the greatest possible pleasures." Mia shuddered as I brushed my fingers over her chest, arms, and finally her back, while still circling her.

When I was partially behind her, I stopped so I was in the prick's line of vision. My fingers effortlessly opened her bra clasp while I leaned forward and showered her elegant neck with a few well-placed kisses. She trustingly lowered her head to my shoulder and offered me access.

"M'm...you see? She trusts me...totally... She gives herself to me. She knows my hands would never seriously harm her... I can do anything with her. I can touch her everywhere," I whispered against her skin while never taking my eyes off him and his horrified, yet almost mad with lust expression. My hands came up and slowly removed her bra, which I tossed in Francesco's direction. It came to a stop close to him, but his eyes were glued to her long erect nipples.

"Only I can elicit such sounds from her." Gently, I took both nipples between my fingers and lightly tugged on them. She moaned softly and pushed her plump ass cheeks against my fucker.

"Only I can drive her to the point where she almost goes insane with lust, isn't that so, baby?" I whispered smoothly and the sound of my voice alone made her shudder.

Like a good girl, she immediately moaned "Yes!" when I cupped her mounds and started kneading. My breathing conveyed how much it turned me on and how she too, drove me insane with her strong reactions to my charms.

I loved our sex. More than anything!

"Can you tell how she enjoys my voice? How it makes her body shudder? She will never shy away from me... Even when my hands go astray..." Agonizingly slow, I slid my long fingers down her stomach.

"ARGH!"

I chuckled softly at her complaint as she urgently rubbed her ass against me. She knew that was how she could make me lose control. But it was not only that...at the same time, it was torture...and looking at Francesco, obviously pretty effective... Therefore, I unceremoniously put a stop to her wriggling with a whip-like slap.

"Don't move!" She grumbled impatiently to herself and I grinned.

"Can you hear her longing because I won't touch HER most intimate spot? Right now, she would kill just so I would stroke her clit once."

"OH, YES!" Mia hissed between clenched teeth, which again made me chuckle, followed by showering her temple with a few soothing kisses.

"Patience, baby... You're my torture tool...so behave like one."

She giggled breathlessly, no longer complaining because my hand slid under her panties and one finger accidentally brushed between her folds...

"Tristan..."

Francesco made a strange choking noise.

*Yes, it makes your dick hurt, doesn't it?* If I aimed right, he would NEVER have the pleasure again!

"You want to see it, huh? Well, you may and bleed to death." I squatted behind her and pulled her panties down.

At that moment, various groans erupted in unison from three throats.

Francesco sounded distressed, Mia excited, and mine... *fascinated!*

Now I was kneeling behind her, brushing my index finger between her shapely lips. She pushed back against it and moaned deeply. Restrained, I ground my teeth and obliged her wish by sliding my finger effortlessly into her.

"You will never know how it feels when she gives herself like this..." I rubbed his nose in it and when my movements created smacking noises, Francesco moans sounded even more tormented.

"H'm, once again, my girl is dripping wet... BECAUSE OF ME... Because only I am her sex god. Tell him, baby!" For emphasis, I added a second finger.

"YES!" she gasped sharply. Her legs began to tremble and I realized it would be better for her to lie down if I continued. Otherwise, she would collapse from too much lust.

With a heavy heart, I pulled my fingers out, moved around to face her, and smiled because I didn't want her to feel I was using her. She smiled back conspiratorially and pulled my face down to kiss me while I was pushing her backward to her bed.

I purposefully positioned her on the edge and spread her shapely legs far apart so that ALL was in plain view for him before I knelt between them. I didn't stop kissing her as my hand brushed along her thigh and my fingers slid into her again.

"So tight," I muttered against her lips. My other hand freed my rock hard fucker and started rubbing it to relieve the excruciating pressure. "You're so wet..." Mia moaned in my mouth and scratched my back. "So perfect ... *Mine*." With this word, I pulled my fingers out of her silky softness and gazed deep into her eyes.

She was close. Her cheeks were flushed, hair wildly disheveled, all in all... simply a beautiful vision. I leaned my forehead against hers while continuing to rub my fucker.

"Can you put your legs over my shoulders, baby?" She obliged me while looking at me expectantly as she let herself fall back onto the sheets. Suddenly, she turned to face Francesco and stared at him. "Francesco, is this what you had in mind when you mentioned the desk?"

Upon entering her ALL THE WAY, I laughed when he grunted as if on cue. Her muscles contracted tightly around me and my eyes rolled back. I held her silky smooth legs firmly because I didn't want her to exhaust herself while my hips followed the rhythm for which they were made.

"You see?" I gasped in Francesco's direction. "She does ANYTHING I tell her, even if I demanded she give me her asshole!" Mia watched me warily through narrowed eyes between hearty moans, which she made every time I sank into her. It was a clear NO! — Thus, ass fucking was deleted from my still to do with Mia sex acts list. I didn't mind, there were plenty of other things to do.

"H'm, baby...it's like in the clearing. Do you remember? Am I as deep now?" I gritted my teeth and thrust even more forcefully into her.

"OH, GOD," she cried and I hoped the two horny cops had already left the house.

"That was not an answer!" Francesco appeared flabbergasted when I mentioned the clearing — despite having amazing sex, I was still alert enough to increase the torture. And they say men cannot multitask!

"Yeah, I was and will be her only fucker, Francesco. I was her teacher eight years ago. But even without me, she already was the BEST ... AHHH... fuck Mia!" Groaning, I threw my head back when she started her game of I-contract-around-Tristan-and-drive-him-wild,                thus confirming my harsh words.

"She likes it hard...and deep... she can withstand any kind of thrust and no matter how wild you get...she always wants more." I moved more urgently, thrusting harder and harder into her wet slit.

"When you think you've reached heaven, she will show you that there are always new heights!" She grabbed my free hand and moved it to her jiggling tits. To feel the soft warm flesh was almost too much and I had to clench my jaw so as not to come right then.

She did not fare any differently. Granted, she didn't threaten to squirt wherever, but she almost came when I started to massage her tit.

"AHHHH... Tristan... GOD!"

I fucked her even harder.

"And once you have come inside her," I managed to say with whatever brain cells still worked...you instantly are addicted...and you no longer have the urge to fuck anyone else for the rest of your life other than...*this...pussy* ... Come for me, baby!

Mia came... LOUDLY. Screaming. Twitching violently. Pulling me along...

The end!

***

When we returned somewhat to the here and now, I let go of her legs. They slid down my hips and came to rest on the bed, partially hanging off, which allowed me to collapse on her naked torso. Sweat freely poured from our pores.

I breathed heavily and took great delight in Mia's typical after sex aroma. Slowly, I brushed the tip of my nose over her stomach and up between her breasts, here and there, showering her with kisses as well as licking a few drops of salty sweat from her clean heated skin.

"M'm, that was madness," she hummed satisfied and already somewhat sleepy, stroking her hands over my forearms, which lay on either side of her.

"That it was. Thanks to you," I said with a smile, stretching further up as she leaned on her elbows so we could kiss. I could not get enough of her and almost lost myself in her sweet caresses when wheezing reminded me of the present situation.

Teeny-weenie was also here.

Grinning lightly against her lips, I separated from her.

When I glanced at Francesco, he seemed to have completely lost his mind. Ha! Wrapped like he was, aroused, in pain, and no free hands to relieve himself, our performance did more than breaking any bone in his body would have accomplished.

I promptly kissed my girl again.

Simply because we were awesome...

# 7. Having Arrived

*Mia 'Confused' Angel*

Tristan had just fucked me in front of my tormented ex-boyfriend. Deeply, forcefully, mercilessly... and yet so full of feeling. Now I lay there and blankly stared into the empty eyes of the man who had been at my side for the past several years. The eyes of the man who first intended to rape, then kill me.

Tristan had not been the psycho-lover!

It was funny how one could misread a person because, come to think of it, it had always been Francesco who came across as the real psycho, it was only that it eluded me. Never in my life, would I have thought him capable of doing something so dreadful. I was lucky Tristan's surveillance cameras were set up...

Otherwise, no one would have come to my rescue, no one would know what had happened to me today. Otherwise, I might have been done in already and buried under tons of freshly poured concrete. I would have been lost forever unless some archaeologist discovered me thousands of years later. The only thing left would be my skeleton... No, I did not want to speculate what conclusion they would have arrived at about me.

Francesco watched me through narrowed eyes as I slowly stroked Tristan's muscular back. I raised an eyebrow. Did he think he was in a position to say something, perhaps, complain? Tristan followed my gaze and growled deep in his throat.

H'M, the sound was so sexy... I instantly shuddered.

"No..." I muttered and turned his face back to me. I didn't want him freaking out again. In my opinion, Francesco had received just punishment even though Tristan probably didn't think it was sufficient.

"We should go." His green-brown eyes inspected me closely. His features were now completely relaxed again — free of all the resentment and hatred of the recent weeks. He simply appeared open and lovingly looked down at me, my reddened cheeks, and still disheveled hair.

"I'm so glad I made it in time." His voice trembled suspiciously.

Shocked, I ripped open my eyes, but he had his head already buried against my chest, hugging me tightly, only to let go of me the next moment and sit up.

"EWWWW." I grimaced disgustedly as cum ran down my legs.

Tristan chuckled against my skin and I felt him kiss one of my nipples.

"Look at the mess you're making, really!' he playfully scolded. "We could have Francesco lick it up."

I almost puked, which made him laugh again. Then he went to get a roll of toilet paper, spread my legs again and cleaned me. Déjà vu! The situation was so intimate, tears came to my eyes, and I couldn't help but pull him close to give him a brief but quite passionate kiss on his full lips. He grinned slyly and silently gathered up my underwear. Once he handed them to me, he put his shorts on properly and strolled over to Francesco.

"If you yell or call attention to yourself in some other way, I will let you rot in this cabinet. I believe you are aware of that fact, right?" As soon as Tristan had relieved Francesco of the rolled up socks, he spit out some fluff and nodded. "First, you're coming with Uncle Wrangler to the house..." OH NO! I would not do THAT to myself because Tristan's eyes gleamed ominously and animalistic again...

Roughly, he grabbed his hostage by the shoulders and hauled him effortlessly out of the closet.

Francesco was barely able to stand upright and managed not to fall over as Tristan had his fun unwrapping him. Next, Tristan put on his jeans, then shot Francesco a warning look as he shoved his gun under the waistband of his pants, followed by pulling his shirt down and hiding it.

I too, quickly slipped into a pair of fresh jeans and pulled on a sweater, then sat on the bed with Stanley, who was just waking up, to examine him. At first glance, he seemed fine – thank God – and started to lick my hands. I really don't know what I would have done had anything actually happened to him! As I fantasized various murderous scenarios, I stared gloomily at Francesco, who had sat down in the corner across the room and was watching me in a similar way. My hatred far superseded his. To me, he was nothing more than a piece of dirt; after all, he had laid a hand on Stanley!

I wanted Tristan to take him along!

When he was fully dressed, he unceremoniously grabbed and pulled Francesco to his feet by the upper arm. Groaning, the creep covered his crotch and stumbled after Tristan. Out of politeness, I stood with Stanley in my arms and accompanied them to the front door.

"Call me later, yes? Okay...so...bye..." I said in lieu of limited alternatives. I was about to close the door when Tristan quickly put one foot between it and the frame.

"Bye?" he repeated incredulously and pushed the door open with one hand. "Tell me..." he stared at me, stunned as if it was obvious why he was now upset and looked at me like I was from a different planet.

"What?" I inquired rather belligerently because I was tired and exhausted. All I wanted was to take a hot bath and FORGET...

A hot bath would be great!

"Put on a coat and shoes, grab your bag and Stanley, and get moving, WOMAN! I'm not in the mood to drag him around if he loses consciousness.

WHAT? He wanted me to come to his place? Okay! LOVE TO!

I did as instructed and followed Tristan, who was still propping up Francesco, down the stairs. Luckily, it was quite late and we didn't run into anyone. My mind was going a mile a minute.

What did he have planned for my ex? Would he kill him? Did I want Tristan to become a murderer on my behalf? Would Francesco leave us alone if Tristan let him go? As it turned out, my questions proved unnecessary as soon as we reached Tristan's car in the large parking lot. As soon as I touched the door handle on the passenger side, I felt something cold against my temple and froze.

"FUCK, ALEC!" Tristan exclaimed, swiftly pulling the gun from his waistband and aiming it at the man threatening me. "Take your piece out of her face! IMMEDIATELY!" he growled, while still holding Francesco upright with his other hand. The man continued moaning and looked like he would collapse at any moment now. He was as pale as a sheet and shaking. Stanley growled at him from the safety of my arms.

"Let go of him, man! If you kill him, Leo will tear you and anyone connected to you a new asshole!" Alec replied, seemingly calm and I saw Tristan grinding his teeth. He didn't like what he heard and immediately repeated himself.

"Take. Your. Piece. Out. Of. Her. Face!" His eyes flashed a warning and after a few seconds, during which I couldn't breathe, Alec finally lowered his weapon.

"Get in, Mia!" Tristan ordered and once he walked around the car with Francesco, he pushed the man into Alec's arms and opened the door for Stanley and me. All the while, he never took his eyes off Alec and Francesco, not even when he got behind the wheel and started the engine.

I could tell he was REALLY pissed off now that little Alec had snatched his entertainment. So, I kept quiet as he sped off with squealing tires.

To me, it seemed as if he was relieving his aggression by racing aimlessly around like a madman, so I leaned back, exhausted and rested my temple on the passenger window. However, eventually, I couldn't stand it any longer and asked because my biggest fear was being separated from him again — one day!

"Are you dropping me back at my home?"

At first, I received no reply whatsoever as he continued driving the car to who-knows-where, obviously lost deep in thought. By the time he actually spoke, I had long since given up on receiving a reply. "Remember years eight ago, when you finally confided in me and took me home to your place?" I winced, and then nodded when he looked at me with a raised eyebrow.

"Have I ever left you behind in a place where I knew you felt uncomfortable?"

"No!" I whispered.

"And, what did I end up doing?" My eyes grew increasingly bigger... Now I must have looked like an anime character, at least regarding the size of my eyes.

"You took me to your place," I whispered and could not – no, WOULD NOT – believe it. For me to get my hopes up now, thinking we were already at that point and then it turned out it to be merely wishful thinking on my part, would have devastated me. So, I made an effort not to daydream as he continued to talk.

"Correct... I took you to my place. So, don't you ever again think of asking me if I'm taking you home, not now, not tomorrow, or even days from now." That concluded the issue for him. He returned his attention to the road, sat back in his seat comfortably, and began to whistle. Every now and then, he patted Stanley's head, who was nestled in my lap and let him lick his hand.

Oh my Tristan ... I was overjoyed and felt like poking my head out of the moving car and screaming at the neighborhood, but given the time of day, I didn't want to be rude and instead,   was content staring at him.

***

Okay...he did not take me to his bedroom, but instead, moved me into the enormous white bedroom next to his club office. In passing, he informed me the entire level was a residential floor and that I should not think about entering Garrett's or Georgi's room, who also lived here, as did Mary and Lena.

At the moment, everyone was gathered in the large living room-kitchen area, cooking and once they were over their shock at seeing Tristan's arm around my shoulder, they offered me burnt pancakes.

I had a hard time ignoring their sex outfits, especially Georgi's, who was (perhaps for timely reasons?) buck-naked. At dinner, he informed me he was born a nudist and that I should just accept it. Tristan merely rolled his eyes and pulled me possessively onto his lap. Then he kept me distracted from the others by feeding me. He even let me feed him, whereby my finger did not enter his mouth accidentally. All the while, his eyes sparkled.

It was actually heavenly to be this close to him again.

Yet despite my apparent overstimulation, I almost fell asleep on his lap. And so, soon after, Tristan carried me to my new room and unabashedly watched me undress. All the while, he did not say a word, but stood in the corner with Stanley in his arms, watching. As soon as my beet red cheeks touched the pillow, he strolled over to me, handed me Stanley, and kissed my forehead... No, he did not lie next to me in bed. No, he did not make love to me... No...instead, he left and I ignored the pain in my heart when he quietly closed the door behind him. Old Tristan would not have left me alone; however, new Tristan would have never taken me to his home.

I had to accept his rejection because I could sympathize with his behavior. He might believe me now, but he still needed time to digest everything. As long as I had reason to hope for a common future, which I had, I would wait patiently...

I ignored the burning sensation in my chest and, well aware I was still somehow with him, I closed my eyes. No matter what I had experienced today, I would not allow anyone to ruin what I had. Never again...

# 8. Vivian Müller and her Plans

## *Mia 'Marathon Runner' Angel*

The next morning, I was running late for work since I had nothing appropriate to wear. I easily spent an hour in the walk-in closet of the friendly, quiet, and beautiful Lena, where I almost got lost as I tried to find an outfit that would not make me look like a streetwalker... I saw latex, leather, the nurse, a sexy waitress, the doctor, the farmer's wife, even an Indian, but more than anything, there were thousands of outfit variations for the serious dominatrix. I did not come across anything normal like an employee at a children's home would wear...

I ended up wearing a black jogging suit from Tristan's boxing gym, which fit superbly. Tristan's eyes almost popped out when he sauntered past the kitchen at the crack of dawn and saw me sitting on the bench drinking coffee. He had come to an abrupt stop, peeked through the doorway, grinned, then approached me and professionally kissed my mind blank for the rest of the day. (Actually, he skulked through the corridors regularly, probably because of the naked Georgi. Tristan's motto: trust is good, control is better.)

Now, I stood in the kitchen of the children's home, taking care of all the preparations for Vivi's visit. I inhaled deeply the aromatic smell of coffee and peered out the window where the kids and Eric were raking leaves, getting the garden ready for winter.

Coincidentally, I was wondering whether the house could even survive another winter, no matter how thick the walls seemed. I immediately suppressed those thoughts because, at the moment, it made absolutely no sense to worry about that too. I alone could not change the situation...

The door creaked as it swung open and Vivi came sauntering in with a briefcase, interrupting my thoughts.

Her long dark red curls had been pulled into a stern ponytail. She wore a beige wool coat, high boots, which I was sure were environmentally friendly and vegan, together with a sweater from the organic brand *Waschbär*, which only she could make look like it was from Dolce. After setting her coat on the chair, she greeted me.

"Hi, sweetie!" I received a peck on the left and right cheek, then she shot past me. She stood in the middle of the room armed with a notebook and pen and closed her eyes. Breathing slowly, she stretched out her hands.

"Vivi?" I asked, eyeing her skeptically as I heard her mumble something about *good vibrations* followed by scribbling in her moleskin notebook. Without bothering with a reply, she scurried over to the almost ceiling-high windows.

"This really is an old building," she determined as she opened the window and inspected the hinges. Next, she gauged the thickness of the wall while scribbling in her notebook.

"Vivi, what are you doing? I thought we were having coffee..."

"Psssst, you're disturbing my inspiration." Suddenly, she crossed the kitchen, leaned under the counter, opened the cupboard, and looked at the water connections. Again, she scribbled. Curious, I peeked over her shoulder and jumped as Vivi, without warning, spun around, and scurried to the other corner of the kitchen where she scrutinized the wallpaper thoroughly. I had to follow the slight scent of her perfume to find where she had flitted to because she was almost too fast for the human eye.

For 10 minutes, she crawled across the floor examining the scuffed wooden floors.

Finally, I was drafted to help her measure the size of the room.

Here too, the results were meticulously noted while any information on what the little witch was up to was withheld. Then again, as I know Vivi, she must be following one of her more or less ingenious plans.

"Now off to the facilities!" she announced happily and ran ahead...

I followed obediently and as soon as we reached the washrooms, she repeated her game of measuring, crawling, sniffing, and scribbling.

The planned for a nice and especially cozy afternoon coffee that would have included the oh-so-important exchange of information among women had turned into an I-run-around-like-idiot-without-knowing-why afternoon.

When we finally returned to the kitchen, the coffee was cold and my feet ached. She had even dragged me down into the hateful cellar and then up into the cobwebbed attic, where she had inspected everything like a lunatic.

We sat and, exhausted, I let my head drop onto the tabletop.

"So!" Now, for the first time, Vivi actually closed her notebook.

"Care to enlighten me why we took a trip around the world?" I asked, a bit short of breath and slowly peered up at her. Vivi let out a clear-as-a-bell laugh.

"I'm an architect, you ninny. Katha and I have our own office."

"Huh?"

"Tristan commissioned me to renovate this castle! So, can I now get a cup of coffee?"

"HE DID WHAT?" Now I sat upright and my pain was blown away.

Vivi flashed her eyes at me and then rolled them. "Obviously, he didn't warn you."

"Really?" Hectically, I fished for my phone in my tight pants pocket.

"Have I ever lied to you?" she replied dryly, as usual, answering my question with a question. "As friendly as always, he told me he wants this crap taken care of by next summer, at the latest... and I wasn't to spare any expense." She shrugged, sighed, and stood up to make new coffee as I continued fumbling for my cell phone. Always such narrow pockets... "It's too wet to work on the exterior, but I think we can manage to get it all done by early summer as long as we begin in February or March. And that depends on whether there is still snow on the ground. Anyway, I've already organized a place, an old country home...where everyone can stay for the few months the renovations take...but we definitely have to..." she continued babbling as I dialed Tristan's number and her words faded into a confused barrage. "The outer walls are stable and well-built...they will stay...I can already tell there is no threat of it collapsing! But I have doubts about the floors."

"That's reassuring..." I muttered ironically, growing impatient waiting for Tristan to answer.

"Definitely new windows and doors and the floor plan will be changed. There should be coed restrooms on the first and second floor. The attic could be expanded to provide lots of storage space... I imagine the kids would be thrilled to have a big recreational room...maybe even a small adjoining gym...and a proper kitchen..." She gave the outdated Grandma-green kitchen, which had been here before the war, a reproving glance. I was about to tell her not to go to any trouble when he finally answered.

*"Baby?"*

"Tristan!" I cried accusingly and Vivi chuckled.

He laughed too. *"I take it Vivi is there?"*

"YES, she certainly is... She just ran me through the whole house for an hour!" Tristan laughed louder. "THAT'S not funny! My feet are killing me!"

*"That's why you're calling? I guess now you want to hear an offer to massage them..."* I faltered.

"Would you?"

*"Yes."*

"Oh!" Now my train of thought faltered because I literally could feel his talented fingers spoiling the soles of my feet — with oil!

*"Stop daydreaming. Right now, I don't have time for phone sex."* His remark made me blush, which quickly reminded me of why I called.

"Tristan, this is the most generous thing you've ever done, but you cannot go through with it."

*"How do you know it's the most generous thing I've ever done? I've done many generous deeds, I simply don't brag about them... You are deeply offending me..."* I rolled my eyes because I knew it was almost impossible to offend the man.

"I know you're only doing this because of me. It would make me feel obliged to you forever."

*"And?"* he asked nonchalantly. *"I don't mind you owing me and you don't mind showing your gratitude in bed. Besides, I am not only doing it for you, but also for Robbie, so stop annoying me. I'm conducting interviews."* Instantly, raging jealousy flared, outshining everything he had just said.

"Interviews? What kind?"

*"For strippers,"* he informed me straight out and I could tell he was smirking.

"Are they working the poles professionally, huh? Do you already have a boner?" It was impossible for me to keep the venom from my voice. Vivi looked at me wide-eyed and visibly struggled not to burst out laughing.

*"Those are some question! For any man, no matter how old, no matter his origin, no matter the situation, there is nothing better than a woman with a perfect body to show it ANY WHICH WAY. At the moment, Monique is doing a fine job, in case you're interested. Hey...let me see how you can shake your ass, enough already with the titty shimmying! I feel like I'm getting seasick!"* he shouted at MONIQUE and I saw red, ready to explode and puffing out my cheeks.

*"Mia?"* he inquired, chuckling quietly. *"Have you exploded yet?"*

"NO!" I croaked and quickly hung up before I could voice my objections. With trembling fingers, I turned off my phone and cradled my head in my hands.

"It's like steam is coming out of your ears." Vivi's small hand patted my forearm. "Now what happened?'

"He's hiring new strippers, busy watching how they can dance! Including shaking their tits!" I replied bitchily.

"That's part of his job."

"I don't care!" On that, I would not budge. "I don't want him looking at other women like that, besides, will he try out the new hookers too? Did he ever have sex with a hooker?"

"If so, I'm sure he used a condom," she remarked off-handedly, which was typical for Vivi. Was that supposed to reassure me? Too late, she noticed my expression and quickly continued talking. "You don't actually believe the great Tristan Sexy has had to resort to a prostitute?"

"I don't know!" I was still too furious for her attempt at conciliation. Besides, my guilty conscious was slowly gaining the upper hand. I had made a date with her to spend a relaxing afternoon talking about old times, not bother her with my current stress. But Vivi was not finished yet and I almost flung myself around her neck when she uttered her next words that transported me back eight years...

"Considering you get so worked up when he watches other women strip, I have a plan... YOU become his stripper."

From that moment on, everything revolved around adult topics and stimulating suggestions.

Most of our conversation regarded the present. Even though Vivi and I both had questions about the past, talking about it was too painful for me. After Tristan had been sent to prison, the clique had scattered throughout the country, pursuing their studies and making something of their lives, with always the thought of helping Tristan once he was released. But he had declined their help, opting to go into solitude for a few years. However, none of them had allowed contact to break off completely. They all loved him and always took his side even though, according to him, he could have done without all the sympathy. And each of them had been searching for me!

I was *so* grateful!

It was only shortly before I made an appearance again that had he seemed to open up a bit to them. Then he and Phil created the restaurant chain. Tommy became his lawyer and invested in the club. The brothers were a family again. Katha was four months pregnant and secretly damn proud. Vivi also wished for a kid, but even though they tried for a year, it was unsuccessful. That was the reason they switched to an organic lifestyle because she was afraid that drugs (during his youth) and unhealthy food (always) had messed with Tom's sperm. Vivi and Katha ran their architecture agency in the same tower where Tom had his law firm. All in all, they led a happy life and I was glad for them.

Vivi liked my job, but that was about it.

Her conscience plagued her because we had not seen each other in so long. But she was afraid Tristan might harm me if she had tracked me down and unnecessarily drawn his attention to me. That was why she had searched in secret.

However, the past was the past and now she was overjoyed that we had found each other without outside help. Supposedly, she always suspected fate would bring us together again because those who knew us knew we belonged together.

Overall, it was still a relaxing afternoon where I regained my girlfriend. By the time Vivi finally left, it was late evening.

We had cooked together and eaten with the children. She was quite smitten with Robbie, as he her. He considered her an elf disguised as a human and Vivi naturally let him. Throughout the afternoon, he ogled her with his beautiful green eyes, did everything for her, poured her drinks, and even proposed taking care of the vegetables for her! I guess my little man had his first crush, just as she also lost her heart.

Robbie simply had a way of wrapping everyone around his finger simply by being himself.

# 9. His Submission

*Mia 'The Sexbomb' Angel*

Around nine, when I entered the club's common kitchen, Lena and Georgi sat there drinking coffee, probably filling their tanks with caffeine for their upcoming shift. Stanley was perched on Georgi's lap, obviously loving the attention.

"How many dog biscuits have you stuffed in him? He looks like he swallowed a basketball!" Both laughed as I picked up my dog and critically inspected his belly. He honestly looked like he would burst.

"One or two..." Georgi admitted innocently, smiling.

"Or ten..." Lena muttered dryly.

"H'm." I poured myself a cup of coffee. "Where's Tristan?" With the hot aromatic drink in my hands, I leaned against the sideboard.

"In the studio. He wants to open one in the next town, which he is talking over with his associates."

"So, in essence, it might be a while," I noted and horrified, realized I was turning beet red.

Lena rose and washed her cup. "Definitely... Why are you blushing?" she inquired, amused in her gentle way, which made me turn a shade darker.

"Well...that's...because...um..." In obvious curiosity, Georgi leaned back in his chair, where to my surprise, I noticed he was wearing sweatpants. Lena too, looked at me expectantly from the side as I gnawed my lower lip while staring indecisively at the floor. Okay... it was now or never...

"Can you guys teach me to strip?" I felt so naughty!

Everything was quiet for a few seconds before Lena laughed, grabbed my hand, and pulled me up. Her light brown hair bounced as she led me to the stairwell.

"Ha-ha, THIS is going to be something!" Georgi was obviously already turned on. He followed us down the steps and through the back entrance to the basement area.

"Where are you taking me?' I asked Lena, who still did not stop. Without further ado, she suddenly stepped right and pulled me through a red-painted door.

"AHA!" We definitely were in a stripping room, of sorts. Each wall was mirrored, making the room visually larger, and emphasized the pole in the middle. At the other end stood a black executive chair made of leather. As I imagined Tristan sitting in it, watching whatever girl, I was overcome with jealousy again. A metal framework snaked upward behind the leather armchair, which must have been for tying up the man of his choice. Diffused lighting set the right mood, yet you still saw everything. Just like in Tristan's bedroom, where the aurora borealis was mimicked. All possible shades of red danced like splashes of paint across the room that ricocheted each time they hit a mirror. It was a fascinating sight from which I could barely tear myself away.

"I like working in here," Lena announced with a grin. Georgi sat effortlessly cross-legged on the armchair. Anticipation shone in his big green eyes as Lena led me onto the fluffy red carpet in the middle of the room.

Unsure, I looked at her because, at that moment, she was so beautiful with a natural charisma, appearing virtually noble, that she came across as downright classy — like a graceful Egyptian feline. Was I supposed to perform the stripping turkey right in front of her? God...why did I ask?

"Tristan will freak out!" I was thinking the same thing, but her conspiratorial grin instantly dispelled my concerns.

"Me too!" Georgi shouted and I tried to ignore him.

"So, the most important thing is for YOU to know what you have to offer. Because that is the only way you will have sex appeal. While dancing and with many other things, it is all about charisma. You are a beautiful young woman, perfectly proportioned. Everything is in the right place and your face is simply ADORABLE. That's a big advantage because no one can acquire a pretty face simply by working out at the gym. Tristan Wrangler, the most beautiful man on this planet, is crazy about you. He will always find you beautiful, always adore you, and always love you. No matter what you do, even if you stumble or bungle something else up. Never forget that, okay?"

"Is he really that crazy about me?" I asked, full of hope.

"You have no idea!" Both confirmed it simultaneously. "He's a changed man since you hooked back up," Georgi added.

"So," Lena took my hips in her soft hands, "This is the most important area. If you cannot move your hips, frankly, you cannot dance. Can you shake them?" OH, YES! I certainly can! I do it every time I ride Tristan. As proof, I shook my hips.

"WOW!" Lena and Georgi seemed thrilled.

"She could perform professionally!" Georgi promptly said and I rolled my eyes.

"You will really blow his mind!" Lena laughed brightly.

Then she started to strip right there in front of me while giving instructions. She moved as fluidly as water. Nothing appeared unsure or clumsy. She was a dream woman, completely in tune with her body and great at showing it off. Besides, it immediately became noticeable that she had basic ballet lessons and I knew exactly why Tristan had hired her.

When it was my turn, what had looked so easy was rather difficult. Both of them were really sweet and kept encouraging me. However, I simply couldn't pull it off the way Lena had, besides, the entire time I was self-conscious, thinking about my mismatched underwear while Lena showed her body off with a breathtaking set of satin and lace.

In the end, despite my inappropriate underwear, the basics were clear to me — but not much more. The two assured me I could move my body quite well, that, without question, they had seen when I pole-danced... OH, MAN!

"So, Mia...this move here will kill him." Georgi got up and moved behind me. Pretty close behind me, but for now, I pushed it out of my mind.

"Arch your back, stick your ass out, and throw your head back." He grabbed my hair and showed me what he had in mind... "Then rub your ass against his crotch as you assume an upright position, which will definitely drive him crazy right then and there. YES, JUST LIKE THAT!" I did him the favor and rubbed a little against Georgi and I blushed even more. Seeing Georgi's expression of anguish, Lena laughed.

"And you're sure I can't poke the boss' girlfriend? Just once? Just briefly stick my cock in her? LOOK AT WHAT SHE'S DOING TO ME!" Georgi whined to Lena as I rested my head on his shoulder and lightly moved my body against him.

Lena laughed louder and whacked his head. "You volunteered to be the training subject, so suck it up!"

"ARGH ... SHE'S KILLING ME!"

I had turned around and was pressing my breasts against him as I crouched down. Obviously, my uninhibited behavior was thanks to the glass of vodka those two had given me to loosen up... At least, that was what I used as an excuse.

"You like this move, Georgi?" I continued teasing him, to which he snorted wryly.

"I DON'T LIKE IT AT ALL!" Out of nowhere, an icy voice blasted through the room, separating us instantly.

"OH, CRAP!" Georgi cursed quietly in Russian, then louder, "HEY, BOSS!"

"Out!" he thundered and Lena quickly gathered up her things before hastily departing the room with Georgi.

I turned around and faced the door. There he stood: Tristan, in all his glory!

His beautiful body was clad in black dress pants, a matching shirt, narrow tie, his dark hair tousled, and a tense expression — the psycho-look. As usual, when he glared at me like that, I grew scared and turned on at the same time.

"Hi," I mumbled and literally felt his glowing gaze sliding over my body in the most possessive way. After all, I was only wearing underwear. Despite sweating profusely, I forced myself to approach him because his expression was anything but inviting. He folded his arms across his broad chest as he leaned back against the door and arrogantly and divinely raised an eyebrow.

"Suddenly shy?" he asked coolly. I could not tell whether he was still angry or if the sight of my body had somewhat calmed him.

"It's not what it looks like," I whispered and stopped in front of him, gnawing my lower lip.

Now he looked amused and pissed off at the same time. "Is that so?" His eyebrow shot up even higher. "How do you think it looks to me?"

He knew perfectly well that he was intimidating me right now. AND HERE IT HAD BEEN HIM WHO HAD SPENT THE DAY WATCHING OTHER WOMEN STRIP! Maybe even in the very same room! Now everything was corrupted again!

As I had apparently forgotten.

"Yes, Mista Wrangler... And you're as innocent as a lamb, aren't you? I hope you had enough singles to stuff into the *ladies'* cheap underwear..." I hissed unexpectedly. Surprised, Tristan peered at me for a moment and then burst out laughing, which I did not find amusing at all.

"Tristan!" I hissed between clenched teeth.

"Mia!" Instantly, he pulled me close. His scent enveloped me, as did his hard muscles. I couldn't help but sigh soothingly.

"Stop being jealous. You're no longer 17 and this here is my job! I make a living with stripping, fucking, and other things related to sex. I'm not watching to get off simply because I HAVE TO, okay? If it were up to me, I'd only watch one girl undress for me." He gently kissed my temple while his large hands ran over my back and unexpectedly grabbed my ass. "Got that?"

"Ahh," I panted indignantly, but couldn't help my giggles when he picked me up and hugged me as I wrapped my legs around his waist. We really were a well-rehearsed team.

"Just a moment ago, you were anything but shy when you crouched in front of Georgi." He kneaded my buttocks. "And now you look at me like sex is new to you..." His curious fingertips slid under my panties.

Um, was it always so hot in here?

"I practiced," I whispered against his neck and inhaled his scent. "For you."

"For me?" Now his bad mood was gone.

Swallowing hard, I hid my glowing face against his chest. "Yes, for you... Can I have five minutes of your time?"

"H'm, let me see," he teased and raised my chin with two fingers so I had to look at him. He held me loosely in one arm. "I guess so," he said, finally taking pity on me and gave me a brief, tender kiss on the lips.

"M'm," I hummed, trying to prolong the kiss, but he had already let go of me, lost in thought, and calmly sat down in the chair.

I stared at his hot worldly appearance and succumbed to daydreaming again. "Your time starts now, Miss Angel. Five minutes!" For emphasis, he tapped the glass of his watch.

OH, YES, always a time restriction! I rushed out the door and was glad to see Lena and Georgi standing there waiting for me.

"Phew...her head is still attached!" Georgi said, relieved.

"Of course it's still attached, you idiot! How would she blow him without a head! Let's go quickly!"

"Uh? Have you been eavesdropping?"

"YES!" Lena dragged me into her room, straight into the walk-in closet where without hesitation, she retrieved a black see-through nothing set for me to put on.

OH, GOD! Blinking, I looked at myself in the huge mirror.

I looked damn sexy in it! Like an actual professional stripper. Before I could admire myself longer, a white blouse and a short black skirt were pressed into my hands...along with boots...or should I say two-inch suicide heels.

Time wise, I was still good with one minute remaining.

For the finishing touch, Lena pulled a few strands loose after I tied my hair into a ponytail, which I would release at the appropriate time.

When I stepped out of Lena's room, Georgi gave me the thumbs up to let me know what he thought of my outfit.

"Oh, wait!" she muttered, remembering something and quickly flitted back into her room, returning a brief moment later to hand me a pair of silver handcuffs.

"Cuff him or else you won't be able to finish your dance. Here's the key..." She gave me a dirty grin and slipped it between my pushed up breasts. I hoped my blush would disappear by the time I reached Tristan below.

\*\*\*

Obviously, that wasn't the case.

I was so excited and tense as I stood at the red door, knowing I'd soon be stripping for Tristan, it almost took my breath!

Vivi and her plans...might eventually end up killing me. After a few deep breaths, I overcame my apprehension, pushed the handle, and entered. Insecure, I kept the handcuffs hidden behind my back as I closed and locked the door because I did not want an uninvited visitor. For an unnecessarily long time, I made sure the peephole was closed too before I turned and shyly glanced at him.

Tristan was still sitting comfortably in the chair, his long legs stretched out before him, his hands interlinked and resting on his flat stomach with his head rolled back. His eyebrow rose again before his gaze slowly and leisurely traveled over the blouse, the short skirt...and over the shoes, then back up seeking eye contact.

He stared at me like a hungry lion, the electricity between us could literally be heard. Eventually, a nasty grin played with the corners of his mouth, causing my pulse to race.

"I have a premonition...hopefully it's not too good to be true," he said smoothly and sensually.

My knees weakened, but when he straightened up, about to rise, I took a quick few steps toward him. I had to overcome my inhibition and slip into my role, otherwise, he might take over, and my little performance would never happen.

"No, Mista Wrangler!" Before he could get up, I jumped on his lap with my legs spread. He looked at me in surprise. "Today, you will obey me!" Tristan used his SUPER INTIMIDATING LOOK, including narrowed eyes and mocking snort. Nevertheless, he was not serious because a hint of amusement flickered in his eyes...as well as lust. Pure, unbridled lust. It burned hotter as I brought out the cuffs from behind my back and playfully dangled them from my index finger so they twinkled directly in his arrogant handsome face.

"Can't you restrain me some other way?" he asked provokingly, yet at the same time, willingly reached up and grabbed the scaffolding so I could cuff his hands to it. Was he for real? Surely not. I certainly could not do it! Honestly? In this pose, he was absolutely hot!

"M'm," he mumbled dreamily in my décolleté as I leaned forward and, with trembling fingers, snapped the cuffs close.

"Is it okay?" My heart raced as I straightened up on his lap and peered down at his helpless male form... I was overcome with a sense of hot power when I noticed how he was already staring at me. Like a predator does with prey that it craves more than anything. However, right now, he was out of commission...

All he could do was rub his crotch against my skimpy panties and show me how much he liked his predicament. He bit his soft shiny lip...

OHHHHH!

Now I knew why gnawing my lip turned him on so much. Now I felt like nibbling on him.

"You can easily feel that everything is fine, Miss Angel." He circled his hips and nearly succeeded, cuffed and helpless as he was, to regain the upper hand again by intoxicating me.

HECK NO!

"Okay, so all is well!" And with that, I lightly slapped his cheek with my palm. As he sharply drew in a breath, I quickly hopped off his lap, hoping the handcuffs would resist actual pressure.

"Wait until I get rid of these things..." I heard him grumbling behind me as I stalked over to the music system with my head up, back straight, hips swaying, and played the CD I had preselected with Lena and Georgi.

The music played softly and I waited for it to move me into another world of feelings... The heavy rhythm could be felt in my stomach. It enchanted me...aroused me...even more than I already felt.

I could already hear his laborious breathing, which betrayed his torment. And all I was doing was standing with my back to him, lightly swaying my hips...while I lasciviously peered over my shoulder at him and winked.

Then I turned around.

Slowly and with animalistic moves, I approached him, placing each step deliberately, without even stumbling once! I was so proud of myself! My fingers glided over the blouse and one by one easily released the buttons.

I stopped right between his spread knees as I let the piece of white cloth slide off my shoulders to the floor. His jaw was clenched as he subconsciously tugged at the handcuffs and at that moment, I was convinced he longed to squeeze my nipples. I merely shook my head teasingly and ran my hands down my body, hoping he imagined they were his...right down to the zipper of my skirt. The slight tremble of my hand as I turned and pulled the fabric SLOWLY down must have been impossible for him to miss.

Yet all I heard was the grinding of his teeth. I stooped right in front of him as my skirt fell to the ground. At the same time, I thought about sticking out my butt and arching my back when I changed my mind, deciding instead to shock him. At which point, I simply dropped onto his hard lap.

He gasped in my ear. I used my arm to prop myself up on the armrests of the chair, then kicked my skirt off with a foot, leaned my head against his shoulder, and teasingly circled my hips on top of him.

"Okay... UNCUFF me!" he growled in my ear and I felt him licking my earlobe...

The hell I would. Instead, I countered by shocking him again. He gasped again as I plunged headfirst off his lap so that my knees straddled his thighs, as I braced my upper body on the floor with outstretched arms so he could enjoy a wonderful view of my butt and his paradise.

"ARE YOU CRAZY?"

I could not help but chuckle softly as I offered him an unobstructed view of my see-through panties. I circled my hips a little, squirmed, showing him how I usually move under him.

"I swear by my fucker if you do not take the cuffs off this instant, then... Mia!"

With one hand, I had opened my bra snap and slowly lowered my feet to the floor so that I ended up kneeling with my back to him. I stretched out one hand in the air while the other tossed the lacey fabric aside and I once again winked at him over my shoulder.

Meanwhile, he looked somewhat tormented... With a faint satisfied grin, I turned to him and grabbed his knees with both hands.

Tristan's eyes were glued to my breasts. I rubbed my bare skin against his pants as I crawled up him and brought my arms together to offer him an exquisite view of my cleavage.

"You'll pay for this," he hissed. The telling beads of sweat on his forehead were not lost on me as I sat down on his lap again. With one jerk, I yanked him forward by his tie to one of my breasts.

"Suck on it!" I commanded. Tristan groaned hoarsely for whatever reason but immediately obeyed. He urgently circled my nipple with his warm wet tongue while moaning in torment.

Panting, I threw my head back. I thought about his tongue elsewhere and right then decided to get what I needed.

"Enough!" I pulled his head back by grabbing a fistful of hair and in the next moment, was frightened because it was taboo...wasn't it? My mask of self-assurance withered away as I stared at him.

But to my utter astonishment, he rolled his burning eyes. "GO ON!"

OKAY! I WAS ALLOWED TO TOUCH HIS HAIR AGAIN! I was overcome with joy and my insides warmed, my stomach fluttered, and my heart beat even more fiercely.

However, I forced myself to remain professional.

"Why so impatient?' I asked angelically and hopped off his lap. "Should I take these off?" I teased him by hooking my fingers into the waistband of my panties.

"Mia ..." he warned and rattled his chains like a caged hungry sex monster.

"Y-e-s?" Happily, I turned around and simply pulled down my hot pants...

Tristan made a strangulated noise like he was close to death. I smiled to myself and leaned a bit forward while I ran both hands up the inside of my smooth legs. It felt like velvet and silk...like drenched silk.

"ARGH!" Tristan gasped as he watched me slide one of my fingers inside me. When I turned to face him, he definitely came closer to looking like an obsessed vampire than a sane person. Then I sat with my heat right on his knee while I held out my wet finger directly under his nose.

"Would you like to taste?" He eagerly leaned his head forward and tried to grab my finger, but I quickly moved it out of his reach and smiled. "You better be a good boy!" I stated mischievously. Tristan raised his dark gaze and growled at me with glowing eyes. I shuddered but decided to torture him a little longer because he was not acting like a good boy at all. Without further ado, I raised my left foot and placed it on the back of the armchair, providing him with an excellent view.

"Okay...if you do not want to be nice to me, I'll simply have to treat myself." So, I ran two fingers through my wet lips.

Tristan groaned in frustration while impatiently jerking his hips. I put my hand on his excitement, which twitched in his pants, rock hard. "Oh...poor little Tristan...does it hurt?" He rubbed his crotch against my hand and threw his head back in agony when I did not give him the salvation he truly needed!

"Baby, please..." he hissed through his teeth and for a moment, I thought my ears had played a trick on me. However, it had actually happened. Tristan Wrangler had begged me!

"Please what?" I slowly opened the button of his pants...

"Mia!" A very unhappy sound followed my name.

"Yes, baby?" I pulled the zipper down.

"You're driving me crazy!" He looked accusingly at me, so I happily smiled at him.

"Is that so? Well, now you know what I always have to go through!" And with that, I hopped onto the armrests in one smooth motion with my legs spread so that my snail was right in front of his face.

I grabbed him by the hair again and pressed his face against my crotch.

"Lick!" I demanded and shuddered violently as soon as his tongue brushed over my clit. It was impossible to hide my excitement, I was that swollen and wet. But then I did not have to because Tristan was licking me as if his life depended on it. I held onto his head with both hands as his tongue danced over my mound.

Without mercy. Without restraint. Without shame.

He was like a wild animal and within minutes, had me trembling all over, which made me afraid I might collapse. All the while, he made hoarse noises that vibrated over my pulsing flesh, which also contributed to bringing me closer to the edge. The sounds clearly indicated how much he liked my taste.

"OH...God!" I was convinced I would come at any moment and squeezed my eyes closed. At the same time, I secured my stance on the armrests because I did not want to mime a falling turkey during orgasm.

A few more well-placed licks of his tongue made me come – intensely – but not loudly because I kept him pressed close against me. I heard his tortured groan as his tongue felt my pulsing...

WOW! That was the ultimate climax!

I slumped down on his lap, rested my face in the crook of his neck, and sniffed dreamily. The song was on auto-repeat so the sexy tune continued to envelop us. It was then I realized that Tristan was ready to burst. His breathing was laboriously and he almost SHIVERED!

OH! OH!

"Uncuff. Me. Now. THIS INSTANT!" he growled in my hair and his demanding and threatening tone of voice made me shudder.

"Of course...hold on..." I avoided eye contact as I jumped at the bra to search for the key.

Carefully, for I was still naked and sweaty, I sat astride his lap and reached over him to open the cuffs. I felt his hot breath on my nipple and decided to make light of the situation.

"Do I have to run away once I released you?"

Click...one handcuff...

His free arm instantly encircled my waist like a steel girder and held me tight... Okay... so much for running away.

I swallowed hard and opened the other cuff... In one smooth easy move, he had his fucker freed from his pants... Now there truly was no more chance to escape. He caught my eye and smiled demonically.

One thrust of his hips, he entered me fully, eliciting a hoarse sound, and my fingernails dug into his shoulders. As soon as he was inside me, he held me upright since my legs were still weak from my orgasm, and pushed slowly in and out.

"Do you feel that, baby? How deep I'm fucking you? How I stretch you? Did you want to do without it?" he moaned roughly in my ear and I sighed loudly as my lips touched his, which tasted of me, and our tongues became fiercely entwined. His movements started to get out of control growing arrhythmic, and I knew he would come at any moment now even though he took me extremely cautiously.

His fucker began to pulsate inside me when his finger pushed on my clit and thus, one more time, the right button so that for a second, everything grew black before my eyes because I had not expected such a sudden orgasm.

Then I actually collapsed, breathless, completely spent, and happy with the world on top of my personal sex god...

"You're the hottest stripper ever who shamelessly drove me mad." Yes, yes...he was onto my plan. The way he held me in his arms and how his lips smirked against my hair told me I had outshined everyone else by miles... Yeah!

"I want you to only watch me like this!" I mumbled against his neck.

"Baby ..." I could literally feel him rolling his eyes, "I own a sex club! I have to look at girls to see whether they're good or not before I can hire them!"

"Am I good?" I stiffened briefly as soon as the question left my mouth.

"No. You're not good..." he answered calmly and I thought I misheard.

"What!" I exploded and sat up, glaring angrily at him, when I saw his mischievous smile. He carefully took my face in his hands.

"You're not good, you're the best, dammit. Any man would love to have sat in my place." Then he pulled me close and kissed me. I simply could not stop smiling against his full lips.

\*\*\*

Half an hour later, we were on our way back upstairs. Tristan escorted me to my room again.

"Why can't I sleep with you?" I simply could not hold back the defiant tone.

Tristan raised an eyebrow and in part, looked amused, part admonishing, as soon as I turned to face him.

"Because, my dear Mia, I'm not yet prepared for that step." He gently stroked my sex-tousled hair.

Disgusted, I plopped down on my bed. You are...but Tristan..."

He did not let me finish and instead, squatted between my legs. "I need more time."

"For what?" I lost myself in his green-brown pools and at the same time, peered into heaven.

"Contemplation, to think about us," Tristan whispered as I had. "It has been eight years, Mia. Eight YEARS WITHOUT YOU... EIGHT YEARS alone with my hatred. I do not know how or if I'll ever be completely over it. Or when I'll get a complete handle on myself again...but when the time comes, you'll be first to know." Winking at me, he forced himself to keep the conversation light without upsetting me. He was so compassionate and although he rejected me, his words filled me with renewed hope.

"So, will there be a happily ever after and they still fuck to this day?" I asked, then raised a hand to stroke his straight nose...then along his prominent jawline. I made him smile and, at the moment, knew he found me cute. The soft look in his eyes told me as much. Without saying a word, he leaned forward and gently kissed me.

"H'm," he muttered. He made no reply other than the noncommittal *h'm*! As he pulled back, he grinned mischievously. I loved the sparkle in his eyes.

"What's with *h'm*?" I asked and managed to stop myself from slapping him on the shoulder. "What am I supposed to understand by *h'm*? *H'm*, yes? *H'm*, no? *H'm*, maybe?" Now he chuckled softly and I raised one eyebrow, appearing stern.

He stood up gracefully and brushed a strand of hair from my face as he glanced down at me.

"Tristan!" I complained and tugged at his shirt. He caught my fingers, leaned over, and pressed a soft kiss onto the back of my hand.

"H'm, definitely," he added before turning and leaving the room.

Dumbfounded, I stared at the door for a few seconds…

*Definitely!*

With a shout, I fell back onto the pillows, hugged one, and thrashed about.

There would definitely be a happily ever after and they still fuck to this day!

# 10. Fuck

*Tristan 'Totally FUCKED' Wrangler*

The next few days were slow and lethargic. However, considering recent events, I was grateful for a little quiet. Teeny-weenie had escaped because I was reluctant to see a bullet enter my girl's pretty head, so now I could expect retribution. In addition, I had to plan something appropriate for Eva, something at least as tingling as Mia's and my absolutely incredibly GRATIFYING torture of Francesco. But that could wait...

I knew the storm was far from over, regardless, I would not let it faze me. Should the shit hit the fan, well then, the shit hit the fan...it simply was inevitable! Therefore, it made absolutely no sense to worry about possible shitty situations before they even happened; all that mattered was how one handled the situation when suddenly confronted by it.

Mia was the only person I was concerned about, which was why I assigned two of my security guards as her personal protection. They followed her at every turn, naturally, without her knowing about them. Or I was sure I would have gotten an ear full. In addition, I ordered Georgi to wear damn pants!

I spent two hours in my office, during which I smoked a thousand cigarettes, drank about five cups of coffee, and did the bookkeeping, which I hated more than anything else, while I mulled over the last few days.

Only one meaningful thing had changed: Mia was my girl again.

She was *the* woman in my life. I could deceive or lie to myself regarding everything else, but that fact would forever remain. For as long as I lived. Like black on white.

We belonged together. We *fit* together because we were bound together on a higher plane, one only a few ever reach. One that got under the skin...

How pointless it was for me to think I could ever resist her.

My heart might beat in my chest, but in a very frightening way, it still belonged to her, at least since I started believing her because nobody could pull off such an elaborate performance.

So much had changed! Ever since her hot-teary confession, I lived without the constant feeling of resentment because I knew she had fared as bad as I had. She had suffered and atoned enough. Like me, she was a victim and as in the old days, fought by my side.

And now...when the sun was illuminating my gloomy hole a bit, it was absolutely unclear how I had been so wrong — deceived by demons of the past.

How could I have thought her capable of all that? My girl? Why had I let my own insecurities and prejudices eat away at me, especially considering how much I hated prejudice myself? Why had I chosen the path of least resistance again and with it, thrown away eight years with that wonderful woman?

Why had I willingly given up her laughter, her kisses, and her touch?

How could I have treated her, my Mia baby, like that?

I was such a dumbass moron...

And I was not good enough for her.

I would have loved to run away, far far away. But this time to protect her from me.

Such precious things did not belong in the world where I dwelled. Although she was a sex goddess, she had nothing in common with the fucked up business I was operating. Mia was only my sex goddess — pure and unspoiled! I had to make sure to keep her away from the bad influences that had ruined me so she was not pulled under. After all, I knew perfectly well I no longer wanted to be without her. I COULD not. Not again.

If I lost her again, I might as well put a bullet in my head!

Of course, considering the situation, I should have made her stay with my brothers. She definitely would have been safer, but I wanted her by my side every minute — for we had been separated too long. In that regard, I was too selfish. I even acquired stalking tendencies because night after night, I had to watch and guard her as she slept. I had to know she was near, had to wake my girl with kisses, had to fuck her damn slowly and gently, and in the evening, fall asleep with her in the arms, as it should have been all these years. My personal needs were more important to me than her safety, which, once again, proved what an ass I was — but then that was nothing new.

Regardless, I still had to perform a daring tightrope walk. I had to make sure no harm came to Mia baby and see her as little as I could bear.

\*\*\*

At eight o'clock that evening, when I exited the boxing gym after watching a *words, not fists*, class that was new to our program, I received an unpleasant text message that immediately shattered the tranquility of the last days.

*We need to talk. At once. And bring your new slut along.*
*L.*

"Fuck ... Fuck ... Fuck ... Fuck!" I cursed as I entered the classy kitchen of my club in my designer shoes.

"What?" Five chewing mouths asked in unison.

It smelled delicious and I immediately thought I must be dreaming, but sure enough, my girl had cooked her legendary Czech pepper chicken for which I would have willingly died, even eight years ago. However, my exuberance was short lived because as soon as I looked at her, I caught her worried gaze.

Sitting on the bench with her legs pulled up, she wore a simple red knit sweater that was too big for her with black skintight leggings. It looked like a nice position to fu...

OH, FUCK!

And she had that ponytail, which I liked to use to direct her. And her big *I-know-your-fucker's-every-wish-from-its-glans-down* eyes and those soft shiny red lips. The slightly flushed, high cheeks, the shimmering light brown curls. She was seduction personified. And, I WOULD DEFINITELY NOT TAKE HER TO LEO!

"It's nothing!" I snapped, agitated by the idea of bringing something as precious as her to the lion's den and silently cursed for having been dumb enough to bring her to that dinner. Great, so much for having proven she did not mean anything to me...

Sullenly, I dropped onto the bench next to Mia and stooped to pet Stanley, who, as always, came running up to me, wagging his tail. Then I texted the Italian pissant back.

*Be there in half an hour. Alone.*

Clenching my teeth, I pressed *Send*, leaned back, and closed my eyes to avoid Mary, Georgi, Lena, Garrett's, and MOST OF ALL, her curious stare.

"Care for a bite to eat?" she asked gently and carefully touched my hand that rested on my thigh. I opened one eye and glanced skeptically at her. She was gnawing her lip to shit again! DAMMIT!

"Since you're asking, sure," I announced with slight merriment, yet still quite aggressive, to which I pulled her head back by her ponytail. In the next moment, my lips captured hers.

She gave off a startled gasp as I overpowered her with all my passion.

HEY! I had not seen her all day and still was unable to think of anything but touching her again. I was SEX-STARVED!

To demonstrate, I bit her lower lip — lightly, not hard. She winced but groaned the next moment when I nibbled it the way I did her clit.

Her little hand slipped off my hand and onto my thigh, which was clad in white dress pants, and as she helped herself by OH-SO-ACCIDENTALLY brushing over my ever-growing bulge, I moaned hoarsely and unceremoniously lifted her with one arm onto my lap.

Startled, she gasped, but then pressed against my body and ravished me.

Good! I did not care if she wanted to give those other two a show! I grabbed her pliable wonderful ass cheeks and enjoyed her little moans as I started to knead them. I knew she loved it when I touched her in such a primal way and showed her how crazy she drove me, but ONLY when my girl beguiled me with her charms.

At some point, we ran out of air, but Mia decided not to let go of me during the kissing free time but continued breathlessly pampering my neck. Satisfied, I leaned my head back, simply stroked her back while keeping my eyes closed and enjoying.

Of course, by then the others had fled. Although...I was sure Georgi and Garrett had appreciated her little performance, I was not so convinced about Mary because I had often noticed many times she did not interact well with Mia. I hoped her antipathy for my girl wouldn't become a problem someday for then I would have to fire her. Right now, we had no time to deal with new crap.

Meanwhile, Mia was sucking on my Adam's apple as she spoiled my neck with kisses, I groaned.

"Baby..." She giggled happily when I called her that and her breath tickled my neck. I shuddered and pulled her away from me by her ponytail. Oh...that thing was so damn fucking versatile!

"You have to stop now because, whether I want to or not, I honestly have to go!"

"No!" She licked along my jawline as her hands caressed my upper arms, feeling my muscles while she pressed her thinly covered hot crotch against me. Her pussy touched my fucker...and I no longer thought with my head.

I snorted. "Okay!" In the next moment, I swept all plates and whatnot off the table with one hand – some things even clanked – and raised her up by her hips.

"As you wish!" She laughed excitedly as I placed myself between her legs, which encircled me, and spoiled her neck. My fingers had already strayed to her wetlands where they urgently rubbed circles.

"Oh, God... I've missed you!" Spellbound, her head lolled backward as she relaxed under my lips and tongue, turning her face so I could easily reach her. Meanwhile, her hands effortlessly unbuttoned my shirt.

"I've missed you too," I murmured against her fragrant skin and pulled her hips firmly against my lower body so she could feel the proof of my longing.

"Ahhh..." She rotated her pelvis against my fucker and for a second, I was scared SHITLESS I might ejaculate prematurely because her damn leggings were so thin. However, Leo apparently decided to text back because his incoming message interrupted us.

"Wait!" I straightened up a little and braced one hand next to her on the table as I fished with the other for the smartphone.

Annoyed, I read. *Bellisimo. And do not forget Mia Angel.*

"Fuck!" OH! I became aware I had cursed loudly, quickly got up, and looked down at her. She was still under me, but now her lips were swollen, cheeks wonderfully red, and that trusting yet oh-so-veiled lustful expression, just like my little sex goddess, and I was supposed to deliver her to him? NEVER!

"What is it, Tristan?" she asked, probably alarmed by my outburst.

"Nothing..." I had to distract her, so I leaned down and kissed her again, but she pushed my chest away and I sighed, annoyed because I knew she had already seen through me. I assumed it would not matter how persuasive I was, I probably still wouldn't get her off my back. Damn, stubborn, sexy bitch!

"Who texted you?" she inquired softly and ran both hands over my chest.

"Leo," I growled and straightened my clothes.

"What did he want?" She sat up and readjusted her clothes.

I was more than reluctant to be interrogated. "He wants to see me..."

"Crap!"

"Crap?"

"Yeah, crap! I don't like that you must hang out with those people!" she explained immediately as if she had been waiting for this opportunity. "They are not a good influence on you, Tristan. For them, all that matters is money, drugs, and power. Besides, they are dangerous..."

"Oh!"

"Don't go, stay here with me," she suggested, hopeful. "I am such a better influence on you..." Her pleading look and promising smile immediately got the attention of my fucker, to which it energetically demanded I obey her instantly. Theoretically, I would have given it free rein any time, but I could not because I had to see Leo so as not to completely screw up things with him...

"Baby... I know you're worried, but I'm a big boy now — I can take care of myself. Besides, I cannot stay away when summoned since I'm dependent on Leo. My business can't run without him!" She had to understand that.

Pondering, she gnawed her lower lip again.

"Then I'll come with you!" she finally announced as if it was the idea of the century.

"No!" I yelled instantly, making her flinch.

"How am I supposed to not worry when you're so nervous? What did his text say?" FUCK! Why did this devil of a woman know me so well?

"He received a new shipment of Parma ham, which you have never heard of! This is my business!" Pissed, I took a step back and went to the sideboard to pour another coffee. Naturally, the idiot that I was, I carelessly left my cell phone on the table! When I turned back to her with my cup in hand, my eyes almost pooped out of their sockets.

"Mia!" She had not moved and stood there with my smartphone in her hand, looking intently at it while frowning with her lower lip extended.

"Are you for real? Do you have any regard for a person's privacy?" In three steps, I was at her side and about to grab my phone, when she easily jumped from the table out of reach onto the opposite bench.

"Then don't lie to me!" As I was about to grab her, she climbed over the table to the other side.

"AAAARGGHHH, Mia!" I screamed.

"I'm supposed to accompany you to see Leo?" Fucking perfect! She actually read it. My shoulders sagged as she glared at me. It only took two steps to get to her and I grabbed my cell phone roughly from her hand.

"Fucking crap!" I swore again and closed the text message. "Be happy I am not going to put you over my knee!" However, Mia was no longer listening and instead, headed for the door, which she demonstratively held open for me.

"Forget it, baby!" was all I managed to say.

"He demanded I come, so I will come. I don't want anything happening to you because you disregarded his order. Besides, we're a great team, it's not like I have never helped you out of an awkward situation...think of us wrapping up Francesco!" When I was next to her, she glared at me DEFIANTLY with the doorknob still in her hand. DAMMIT! When had she wrapped me around her little finger again? And when did she become so combative and unyielding?

I sighed...and decided not to give in, regardless if she got pissed off, it couldn't be helped.

"Come on, then," I whispered angrily and offered her my hand, which she reluctantly grabbed.

"Come on then? That's it? No ten-round macho fight?" she needled skeptically as I pulled her through the door.

"Nope," I said lightly and grinned inwardly at my sneakiness.

As soon as we had our coats on and sat in the warm car, I drove to a fast-food joint. After all, I wouldn't want to risk my girl starving to death because I did not let her finish her plate earlier. She was too thin anyway. I bought two colas, but not DIET because DIET tasted like shit and two orders of nuggets. In the meantime, she watched me through narrowed eyes.

"What?" I asked. "I haven't eaten yet!"

"You could have had a good meal!" Mia grumbled as she fiddled with the car radio. "But no, you were too busy chasing me through the kitchen..."

"What can I say, I'm the born predator!"

\*\*\*

Naturally, Leo's club was located in the middle of the red light district. It was the biggest in the city although it was greatly lacking in class compared to mine. I parked on a secluded side street and unbuckled my seatbelt. Mia hectically followed suit, unable to hide her excitement. But when she was about to get out, I held her back by the upper arm.

"Stay here for a moment! First, I want to make sure everything is kosher." I distracted her with my smile, cracked both windows a bit, and got out. Then I immediately locked all doors and circled the car.

Her mouth dropped open.

As I put my hands in my pockets, I looked at her feigning deep regret as if I actually was sorry. It was then that it dawned on her what I was up to and her eyes widened.

"Tristan, no!" She jerked on the door handle. In vain.

"You have a drink, food, and music. In case of an emergency, there is even a second cell phone in the glove compartment, but you can only dial my number. Should you have to go to the bathroom, well, you're shit out of luck. But I believe I have a gas can in the trunk..." I explained with a grin.

"You cannot be serious! This is downright deprivation of my freedom!" She pulled so hard on the door, her hair bounced around, making her look like a lunatic. I had to laugh. "Sorry, baby. But, it is actually dangerous — for you. Surely, you didn't actually think I'd take you along! I have not finally accepted that you mean everything to me only to see you shot or turned into Leo's personal whore. So, stay put, end of discussion!"

She rolled her eyes and angrily, sat back in her seat, pouting like a teenager with her arms crossed. Her cheeks were puffed up, making her look like an indignant hamster.

"See you later, baby." As a parting gesture, I tapped the car roof twice with my palm and started marching across the street. IT would haunt me for a VERY LONG time! However, the alternative would have been worse.

At the back entrance, Claus the doorman let me in without a word, yet he showed obvious respect.

I figured the lousy feeling in the pit of my stomach was because I restricted my girl's freedom. As usual, a little later, once I made it to the second floor, I knocked on Leo's office door and entered without waiting for the *Come in*!

I was greeted with a punch to the face while simultaneously kneed in the stomach.

FUCK!

For a second, I was out of air and touched my stomach. As soon as I raised my eyes, I knew why I had received such an unpleasant welcome. Next to Leo's desk sat teeny-weenie with broken fingers resting in his lap and his good hand waving at me. Half his face was black and blue and swollen, probably thanks to my treatment of his nose. I was about to pull my weapon out of my waistband when something cool touched my temple...

OKAAAY!

I looked left and froze for the eyes I was staring at seemed familiar even though I had never seen them before. They were big and an unnaturally bright blue. Nevertheless, I knew their round shape, just like I knew those lips. Considering I was not into men, I had no idea why I was thinking about damn cherries right now.

"Hi, Tristan ..." Francesco greeted me nonchalantly while leaning comfortably back in his chair.

I took my gaze off the icy eyes and directed it at the wimp.

At that moment, I put two and two together. "*You* sent those text messages!"

"Yep! It was not hard to hack my uncle's phone...and lure you into a trap." I felt like laughing. Did he really believe I could not handle two guys even if one was holding a gun to my head? "Where is the little girl? Have you fucked her to death yet?" Although he tried to hide it, I could see his disappointment.

"I don't know any little girl..." With that, I straightened up and threw blue eyes a warning for he was still pressing his gun against my temple. Francesco rose from behind his massive desk and strolled toward me. "Ever since I found out about you two, I've been wondering how long it has been going on..."

"For a very long time," I answered calmly. He stopped right in front of me and looked down at me because he was a head taller. However, I was much faster and more skilled...

"Well, it doesn't matter now because it's over anyway."

I raised an eyebrow. "I don't think so... By the way...would you mind taking that damn gun out of my face?" I spun around to the man with the icy eyes and long dark blond hair that was pulled into a ponytail. He smirked and increased the pressure of the gun. Annoyed, I rolled my eyes because I hated repeating myself.

"What about YOUR gun?" the guy with the ponytail asked instead and I gave him a crooked grin. Then, I pulled my baby number three out of my waistband and enjoyed – as usual – the feel of the smooth, cool, heavy and so masterfully crafted steel in my hands.

"You mean this one here?" Provocatively, I held it up close to his nose, deftly twirled it on my finger, and spun it in the air a few times. The pressure on my temple increased. I obviously made him nervous — beginner!

"Give it to me!" he hissed in my ear.

"Sure...you should have said so to begin with!" I countered, feigning resignation and handed it to him handle first. He watched me skeptically as he cautiously took it. I kept my expression neutral. But as his fingers touched my baby's slim curves, I slammed my knee into his kidney and at the same time, broke the wrist of the hand that was holding the gun to my head. He had not been prepared for it, dropped his pistol, and howled in pain.

Out of the corner of an eye, I saw Francesco coming at me. He was about to reach for the weapon on the ground when I kicked it to the nearest wall and energetically stomped on his groping fingers. I remained standing on them while grabbing the blond guy's forearm.

"AAAHH!" I ignored Francesco's screams as I increased the pressure of my heel and crushed his bones one at a time. He was taken out of commission for now!

In one fluid motion, I got behind the blue-eyed man while at the same time twisting and breaking his arm so that now I was pressing my gun against his temple, which I'd damn well never willingly hand over.

"So now what?" I whispered in his ear, savoring the visible chill that ran down his back as I swiped the gun barrel down his face and pressed it against the side of his neck.

"DAMMIT, Wrangler!" Francesco cried, who now held his freshly mauled hand with his already-damaged fingers since I decided I no longer wanted not to stain my shoe. I could not help laughing because it was funny.

Now I was the one with the only GUN and a hostage to boot. So much for luring me into a trap!

"So, Francesco...to make certain I understand you correctly...you wanted to be a little pussy and kill Mia and me without orders? That's not the fine Italian way... What would the family say about that? I think I'd better call Luca right away," I remarked politely and he paled instantly. I pulled the blond away from the door and felt my way into the corner with the black leather chair. It put a little distance between me and Francesco because I had no idea if he had a weapon hidden on his body. Most likely I was mistaken, otherwise, he would have tried to use it by now — somehow, even with a broken right hand.

Francesco stood there, staring stupidly at me through narrowed eyes. The hatred in them was unmistakable. Presumably, he was wishing I'd contract whatever painful disease or be crushed to death by a meteorite... But nothing happened... Thus his fate was sealed: I would rip him a new asshole.

I might not have an idea as to what the blond wanted from me, but I was sure I would find that out too...obviously, before ripping him a new one.

"Well, I think we'll keep this short. I can't wait to get back to my girl... So, who goes first?" I mused. "Ah, I know! Shall we do rock, paper, scissors?"

That was as far as I got before the door flung open and the aforementioned girl stumbled headlong in the room.

She looked quite pissed off, but when she saw Francesco, all the color drained from her cheeks. Before I could scream, he was next to her, grabbing and twisting her delicate arm around her back. Broken fingers or not! Adrenaline worked wonders — unfortunately!

"Hi, little mouse!" He pressed his disgusting lips against the fragrant skin of her temple. Shocked, she looked at me and I rolled my eyes. "Baby...this is a primo example of bad fucking timing."

However, she was no longer paying any attention to me because now she had discovered the blond. Her expression signaled sheer panic as she managed to whisper one single word.

"Patrick!" Her gaze alternated between him and Francesco as if watching them play tennis before it finally landed on me again. She started to tremble.

"Yes, your uncle was kind enough to come. I asked him to lend me a hand so I could keep what I had paid for..." Francesco led her to the big desk and my heart started to beat faster when he knocked off whatever documents, folders, and phone with a sweeping gesture of his arm. I felt a lump in the back of my throat as I watched how he set her on the desk. She kicked at him, but he skillfully dodged her attempt, opened the desk drawer, and pulled out a knife. I could not help but hiss when he held it up against her elegant neck, preventing her from resisting.

YOURS

He applied too much pressure.

He almost cut the tender skin and for the first time in my life, I experienced the shitty feeling that my legs might give out on me at any moment.

"No..." Fuck... I sounded like a desperate schoolboy.

"Let him go!" Francesco demanded dryly and I released my cramped grip on UNCLE Patrick's forearm. Holy shit! That was why he seemed so familiar! He immediately turned to me and ripped the gun from my shaking hand. Next, his fist crashed into my jaw and I involuntarily moaned. A good right jab, I had to give him that much.

"Stop!" Mia screamed shrilly and attempted to jump off the desk, but Francesco pressed even harder and her burning eyes shot up to him. "Do not move or your throat gets sliced..." he whispered. Her forehead broke out in sweat.

The sight of the knife against her throat literally paralyzed me. Patrick shoved me onto the stool, where I immediately rested my elbows on my knees and rubbed my face with both palms. If I saw that blade pressed against her neck for another second, I might throw up. When she whimpered, I pulled myself together and glanced up at them.

"TAKE. YOUR. HANDS. OFF. HER!" My voice sounded deadly and I wanted to go berserk right then. I was about there because Francesco was kneading her soft warm tits over the sweater. MY TITS!

"Tie him up..." he demanded coolly.

"Do you think I'll simply let you tie me up like that, pissant?" Full of hate, I glared at the dear uncle and bared my teeth as he came at me with handcuffs.

At that moment, my girl moaned again and captured my attention. The scumbag with the damaged teeny-weenie had dared to lightly cut her neck! Deep red blood ran in fine rivulets down her pale flawless skin and literally screamed at me.

"I'll rip anyone who KNOWS you a new fucking asshole!" Uttering those emotionless words, I held out my hand to the dear uncle while suppressing the feeling of nausea in the pit of my stomach, trying to reassure my girl with my gaze, but she merely stared back at me in a panic. Her chest rose and fell too quickly — she was scared shitless. And I could not let her see I was feeling the same.

"Baby...calm down!" I mouthed when the handcuffs clicked closed as the fucker of an uncle shackled me to the heater. He grinned at me before taking up a position next to me with his arms crossed. His eyes had a greedy glow to them. His death was sealed, end of discussion, just like Francesco... who had turned to Mia and was caressing her cheek with his bandaged broken fingers.

"By the way, did your great lover tell you how he manipulated me into letting you come to him?" DAMMIT! Defeated, I closed my eyes when Mia's reproachful gaze met mine. I rather expected the bum to mention that now. "Well...he offered to work you in for me so you would meet my requirements, as he did with lots of women before you.

You know, so you'd be nicely stretched out and, above all, obedient... For your sake, we pretended it was about some crap shoot. No fucker could have guessed you guys mimicked Romeo and Juliet!" I opened my eyes and looked at my girl.

"Do you know he can't get hard in the presence of a strong woman?"

"SILENCE HIM!" Francesco hissed and I was hit in the face with the handle of my own damn gun. This time my head actually whipped to the side. I used my free hand to wipe the blood from the corner of my mouth and as my cheek started to throb, I gave the fucker of an uncle a deadly stare. Then again, I was used to such and could handle it well for as a boxer, you had to be able to take punches.

"*Please* stop all this!" Mia was sobbing wholeheartedly and looked pain stricken at my cracked lip. GREAT! Now she was even crying!

"It's not that bad for fuck's sake! Calm yourself!" I reassured her and spat out a lump of blood on the floor. Her fear got him excited. He got off on tormenting her... He loved to see her that way.

"Let him go, please... I'll do whatever you want. But please..." She turned to Francesco and clawed at him. Annoyed, I could only huff — now she was even BEGGING!

"DON'T ACCOMMODATE THEM AT ALL, DAMMIT!" I snapped at her coldly. No more MR. NICE

GUY. How dare she suggest sacrificing herself for me! Mia swallowed her next sob and tears, pulling herself together because she knew when I used that tone I was damn serious.

That was more like it!

"What are you doing here?" she asked her uncle and her voice now barely trembled.

Patrick, who was actually her uncle, snorted ironically.

"Francesco paid your father and me handsomely for you! Meaning, he should have you! After all, we've put so much effort into educating... even though in the end, you didn't turn out the way we wanted you... All thanks to him!" He nodded derisively in my direction. She stared at him horror-stricken. If I wasn't mistaken, she paled even more as she hoarsely whispered, "You spent my childhood preparing me to be sold off and then abused for the rest of my life? THOSE were my father's plans?"

"Do you recall all those customers who came to our house every evening? They came to check you out. There were quite a few who were interested in you, but Francesco here placed the highest bid. So, I arranged to make it look like he saved you. I knew you would do anything out of gratitude...in that respect, Harald was good... I've never laid eyes on such a vulnerable, submissive, stupid woman such as yourself!" The fucker of an uncle, dressed in a black shirt, shrugged and regarded his niece as if she was some common slut.

Francesco grinned stupidly as he continued nodding.

"I realized right away that *you'd* make the perfect victim."

Mia shook her head. "No... That... NO!" she shouted and tried to push Francesco away, but that was exactly the wrong thing to do. I gnashed my teeth as he stiffened and yanked her backward by MY beloved ponytail.

"Oh, yes! You are mine. I even have the purchase contract! And now I will use you like I should have done way earlier. However, since I had other sluts to satisfy my special needs and I wanted to maintain your all-is-well illusion and heighten the anticipation, I spared you the first two years... BUT THOSE DAYS ARE NOW OVER!" He leaned down to her.

"Tristan!" Mia yelled in a panic. Then she whimpered in torment because he had pressed his mouth against hers. He forced her lips apart and raped her with his tongue while holding her hair.

"TAKE YOUR MONKEY LIPS OFF HER!" Francesco knew *that* was the perfect way to torture me. I flung myself around and furiously yanked at the cuffs, my face a mask of pure rage. All I could see were the hot tears running down her cheeks, the trembling of her body, and her little fists beating against his broad chest. Francesco broke away from her, laughing. He completely ignored my antics.

"Oh, you taste sweet. Now I understand why he's so crazy about you... Let's see if you taste everywhere the same. What do you think, Wrangler?" Now he set his knife on the side of the desk and smiled down at her. She shook her head and used her wildly shaking hands to cover her breasts.

"Francesco... man..." I hung my head in resignation for I had no idea what to say or do. "Please, don't do it." YES! Goddammit, I even groveled — like some fucking wimp. At the moment, I felt emasculated and had a hard time breathing because my girl was in the clutches of someone else and I was powerless to help. If he harmed her in front of my eyes, well, THAT would be my end... My worst nightmare! Simply thinking about the possibility ripped me apart and I had to clench my jaw to keep from screaming in frustration.

He grabbed her sweater at the waist and pushed it up. Presumably to save me further blows, she instantly obeyed his silent urging by raising her arms like a submissive doll. "I see Tristan Wrangler can beg after all... Interesting..." With those words, he pulled the garment over her head and exposed her creamy skin. Mia gasped as her soft curvaceous body was bared. Now I really clenched my jaw for her trembling became even more obvious. Meanwhile, teeny-weenie had picked up his knife again and tentatively moved it to the fabric of her innocent white bra, all the while staring provocatively at me. I gave him a look that could kill and hissed, "DONT'T DO IT!" Instead of listening, he smirked nastily and I heard ripping. Mia sobbed and shook.

"I swear you will regret this..." I breathed without conviction for I was still coping with being completely helpless. The disgust I felt was almost unbearable. As he was about to touch her, Mia automatically cringed, so he set the knife aside and unexpectedly grabbed her throat. Without any mercy, he pushed her down on the table and with his other hand, pawed her breast.

"You sly broad worked your spell on me... I have no idea why I treated you all this time with kid gloves," he gasped frantically.

"Please, don't..." Her quiet sobs sounded stifled as she tried to get his hands off her. I could understand her pleading, for I too would go down on my knees before him to end this.

"H'M... I'm sure they taste as good as they feel." I was a damn coward for I had to close my eyes as he lowered his head. Embarrassingly, I could not keep from gagging. Again, Mia sobbed and whimpered my name. It only made me feel worse. Much worse... Tormented, I pinched my eyes closed. My girl was being raped right before my eyes and I was unable to do a damn thing to stop it! It was killing me — oh-so-slowly. Over and over again... My forehead broke out in sweat and I wished I were somewhere else. I prayed it was a cruel nightmare, not reality...

"Tristan, don't..." she breathed softly and brought me back to the present.

Suddenly, Francesco gasped in shock. When I finally ventured a look, I caught her little hand grabbing his hair and pulling his head up. She looked him squarely in the eyes. He seemed utterly surprised — as I was.

"So, Francesco, you want to fuck me? In a rough and lecherous way like he does?" DAMN! Why did she suddenly sound so self-assured? So determined? Teeny-weenie was completely flabbergasted and could only nod stupidly. "THEN, let's do it just like I said!" In the next moment, she jumped off the table and pushed him on it. Francesco squirmed and groaned as she climbed on top of him to squat over him with her legs spread apart.

I had forgotten how to shut my mouth and was drooling, but I could not even concentrate on it. At some point, I finally found my speech again.

"Mia?" The sidelong glance she gave me said more than a thousand words. *PULL YOURSELF together!* How the fuck was I supposed to pull myself together? HOW? Had that woman finally lost her mind? Then again, it was not like I had a choice.

When she smiled at him and stroked his crotch, I wanted to yell at her but kept quiet.

"You want me to make you feel good, Francesco?" Irritated, I wondered what she was up to. His twig and berries were bandaged and out of commission, thus of no use to her. Disgusted, I eyed that fucker of an uncle, who stood a step away from me. He was so fixated on Mia's ass clad in thin leggings that he wasn't paying any attention to me anymore. His grip on my gun was too loose.

Francesco must have nodded stupidly again, for when I turned back to the horror show, Mia was in the process of unbuttoning his shirt. I suppressed my rage and disgust and waited for my chance. For once, I did not give in to my emotions and shout at Mia...no matter how difficult it was for me.

I was tense, even the roots of my hair, so I ignored the sounds coming from those two. I gnashed my teeth and listened to the uncle's gasps as she began to cover Francesco's upper body with kisses. I knew too well, how that drove a man crazy. Then she even spoke in a soft sexy voice, which was more appropriate for a telephone sex worker than my Mia baby...

"Oh, Francesco... oh, Francesco... you cannot wrap your head around how lucky you are right now, can you?" As she circled her little tongue around his navel, I had to repress the acute urge to puke and quickly focused all my attention so I would react at the right moment. Again, I peeked at the fucker of an uncle, who seemed as mesmerized as Francesco and I could not decide who disgusted me more!

"So now what?" she suddenly asked coolly and unable to resist my curiosity, I glanced back at the two of them. Shortly after, I almost laughed when I saw her holding the knife and what she was pushing it against.

Patrick was about to react, but since I had expected something to happen, I was faster. As soon as he raised the weapon, I kicked him forcefully on the back of the knee. He obligingly sagged and I placed another well-placed kick to his jaw, which made him loosen his grip on my gun. Then a deafening shot erupted that hit the wall behind Francesco.

As Patrick's head slammed against the wall behind him, I quickly bent down and reached for my gun, but it was an inch out of reach. FUCK! Instead, I fished for it with my foot.

By the time I raised my eyes and gun, Mia still had control of Francesco. He made no attempt to move... merely stared in shock at the cool blade pressing against the root of his weenie, his mouth seemingly too dry for him to swallow.

Clearly, she was in charge of the situation. Yet, at the same time, I was well aware that she could collapse at any moment. So, first I aimed the gun at the fucker of an uncle, who was writhing in pain on the floor while holding his head.

"Uncuff me!" I commanded and more than roughly nudged him with the tip of my shoe. Obviously, I never took my eyes off my girl, who kept staring at Francesco and he right back at her. Her hand started to tremble more and more, so much so, she risked losing her grip on the knife. "UNCUFF ME NOW!" I bellowed again because the blond fucker moved too slowly. We had to get out of *here*!

Now Patrick hurried and frantically fumbled with the lock. As the cuffs clicked open, I quickly grabbed his wrist and chained his ass to the heater.

Three steps and I was next to Francesco, unable to resist pistol-whipping him in the face with my gun. Hard enough to assure his lip burst open and blood slowly oozed down his chin. It took all my resolve to keep from losing it — and instead, grabbed the hand of my girl. Francesco writhed in pain on the table and spat out white pebbles, which seconds ago had been two of his teeth.

"Let go of it, baby!" I demanded softly and Mia stared at me with red, tear-filled eyes like I was the Holy Ghost. It took a few seconds for her cramped fist to open and release the knife that landed on the floor with a clatter.

I would have loved to kill Francesco right then and there, but as it sometimes happens in life, the shot had not gone unnoticed. Just then, the door burst open and two security men rushed into the room, so I immediately aimed my gun at them. Since they knew me and I was considered family, they refrained from peppering me with bullets and instead, took in the situation with somber faces.

I had to get Mia out of here. *Now!* So, I bent down and picked up her sweater and slipped it over her head as she raised her arms in that disgusting lethargic way.

"You won't make it out of here!" Francesco had straightened up a bit.

"You're a dead man walking!" I merely said as I backed out the door while keeping her body safely tucked behind me until we were out of sight.

Then I grabbed her upper arm and started to run.

We followed the brightly lit corridor, which I was familiar with from previous visits. Before we could turn the corner, I heard the frantic voices of the security guards and quickly pushed Mia through the nearest door. We found ourselves in a gloomy stairwell that led to the club.

"Come on, baby!" I linked our fingers more firmly, jammed the gun into the waistband of my pants, and pulled her down the steps. I ignored her tremors, her hectic breathing, even her because otherwise, I would have to worry about her and become distracted. It was imperative I keep a clear head now.

"Tristan," she asked breathlessly when we reached the ground floor.

"What?" I opened the door to the club and peered in to see if the coast was clear. The only thing that greeted us was a rich beat and nothing but partying half-naked people.

"Did he hurt you badly?" OH, MAN! I spun around, unable to hide the pain from my face. SHE ASKED ME THAT? It was not me who, against her will, was groped by a perverted sadist! My expression must have looked pretty wild because she backed away from me, looking horrified. I quickly made sure not to look like a maniac. Then, sighing, I cupped her still-pale face with one hand and brushed my thumb over her cheekbone...

"Are you okay, Mia baby? Just hold on until we are out of here, then I'll take care of you, okay?" I tried to smile at her and did not fail. She nodded weakly, then the corner of her mouth trembled slightly and her eyes lost a little of that haunted expression. Much better!

Sighing, I leaned down and lightly brushed my lips over hers. But I could not enjoy it, especially because, first, there was no time, and second, because my split lip burned like hell.

I pulled her through the door and pressed us against the wall as two burly security guards stormed by. "Wait!" I leaned with one arm on the wall next to her shoulder and lightly kissed her below the ear where I let my lips rest on the velvety soft skin. Mia dug her nails into my back and I was convinced it would only be seconds now before she finally collapsed. I felt her frantic beating heart at the jugular in her neck and listened to her faltering breath. Every fiber of my being wanted to calm, protect, and free her from this dangerous situation.

FUCK!

"Baby ..." I mumbled against her skin. "Untie your hair!" Without hesitation, she did as asked. "Now put your legs around my hips!" She looked at me as if I had lost it and I grinned.

"No...for once, I actually don't want to fuck you. All I want is for us to get out of here undetected and, above all, IN ONE PIECE!" As I spoke, I hurriedly took off my shirt. "Meaning, we have to blend in with everyone else and look ABSOLUTELY HOT FOR EACH OTHER!" Luckily, I managed to brighten her mood for I was rewarded with a sweet smile playing around the edge of her lips. She followed suit and wrapped her legs around my waist. I had a tight grip on both her ass cheeks so she barely had to hold on and then plunged into the crowd.

Damn, it was busy here! I had to fight through the dancing couples because it was the shortest path and we were less likely to run into those fucking security guards and their shitty suits.

"I kind of expected you would not listen and stay in the fucking car!" I cursed indignantly as I headed for the exit as quickly as possible. Mia's fingernails clawed my bare back while her hot panting breaths tickled my neck.

"I'm sorry..." she whispered over and over.

I rolled my eyes. "Stop with the apologies, dammit, and hold on tight!"

"But your gun," she wailed.

"What about it?" The flashing exit sign came within view. Now we had to make it pass the corpulent heavily made-up cashier without incident.

"It's pushing..."

"It's pushing?" We were almost at the cash register. In that dark area, only the rich bass of the music could be heard.

"It is pushing!"

"Where?"

"Against my...pussy!" AHH! I had to chuckle when I understood.

"Suck it up for now! Grab my wallet out of my pocket!" She did as told. "Take out 200!" Again, she obeyed, albeit while frowning.

Soon after, with a "You haven't seen anything," I handed the bills to the bored gum-smacking cashier, who merely nodded, disinterested.

As soon as I opened the door and the cold night air assaulted us, I felt much better.

I did not set Mia down until we had crossed the street. Then we dashed past the whorehouse located across from the club and zipped into the next side street where my car was parked.

"Okay...baby...we'll be home soon..." I whispered and brushed a few strands out of her still pale face as soon as she leaned unsteadily against the car. She nodded bravely and managed a weak smile.

I smiled back, took her hands in mine, and pressed a kiss on each wrist before opening the door for her. She was about to get in when suddenly her eyes widened and she focused on something behind me.

"What the fuck?" I whirled around to a very battered Francesco. In the next moment, I felt a thump on my head and the ground rushed at me at an alarming speed.

"Tristan!" I barely heard my girl's scream before everything went fucking black before my eyes...

# 11. Just One Thing: FUCK-ING SHIT

*Tristan 'Dying' Wrangler*

DAMMIT!

My damn skull... It hurt.

It was the first thing I registered as I came to and, still dazed, realized I must be lying in a bed because it felt soft and warm. Also, the damned whispering around me gradually penetrated my consciousness, seemingly growing louder and more obtrusive. Phil's voice was especially jarring, which grated on my nerves... What was he doing here in the middle of the night? Or Katha, Vivi, and Tom for that matter? *Dammit!*

I squeezed my eyes shut and tried to recall the events that caused me to wake up in this bed with my family gathered around me. Was I dead? Was this my funeral? Was I in a coffin? Why was nobody shedding any tears?

There I lay with all these stupid ideas in my head...when I was suddenly thoroughly shocked. I saw teeny-weenie's lips on my girl's tit, the mean eyes of the uncle, her fear, her quaking...our escape... Then everything came rushing back like a hammer blow and I straightened up.

"Mia!" Panicked, my gaze darted around the room and I realized I was in my fucking bedroom. Three times, I glanced at the figures assembled around my bed, but there were only four, not five.

"WHERE IS SHE?" I did not give a shit and jumped out of bed wearing only shorts. Nor did I give a shit that my brain was threatening to explode in my skull. I quickly held onto the nearest ass available, which was Tom — otherwise, I would have landed on my ass.

"TELL ME WHERE SHE IS! SAY IT!" I could not help but grab the collar of his crappy eco-shirt and shake him properly for I was freaking out! I could only think of one conclusion; I was here and she was still there!

"Stop it! Giving yourself a heart attack won't do anyone any good!" Patiently, he loosened my cramped fingers from his collar, which he then straightened as I determinedly reached under my bed and pulled out my big suitcase.

"Tristan, relax!"

"He's shaking all over..."

"Man, bro... let's get a cup of coffee into you!" I roughly knocked away the hands reaching for my shoulders to pull me close. Then I whipped open the suitcase, happy to find it still stuffed with 500 Euro notes.

"Don't you have a safe?" Phil inquired reprovingly.

"YES! But it's crammed full! I have cash stashed everywhere! Even in the bathroom cabinet! Anyway, who gives a shit?" And with that, I closed it again.

"Tristan...what are you up to?" I also flicked Katha's hand away.

"WHAT DOES IT LOOK LIKE? I'm not going to sit casually here, drinking crappy coffee while MY FUCKING GIRL is with that sadistic prick! Why haven't you done something by now? Why are you here and not with her? Why did you let me sleep in my bed like I'm fucking SNOWHITE! DAMMIT!" I couldn't believe it!

I was overcome with images. Images of my girl! Helpless...defenseless...in hell...with that sick bastard! Maybe she was already... *FUCK!*

The turmoil I felt was intolerable to my stomach and I actually started choking. I cursed silently as I ran into the bathroom, barely making it in time to the porcelain throne. Although I did not upchuck much, it still made me sweat.

Once finished, I rose unsteadily and glanced briefly at myself in the mirror before rinsing my mouth.

"How did you find me?" I yelled into the bedroom and Phil answered.

"Security interfered. Apparently, Leo does look after you...but since Francesco was not alone...had three of his apes...they could not do anything for Mia... She is not on the personal protection list... Vinc was one of the security guards, he brought you home," Phil stated. "You really need to calm down! BREATHE!" He must have noticed I was having a difficult time staying on my feet when he appeared in the doorway.

My family was right. For once, I should keep a cool head, even when my girl's life was at stake. I could not think about what he might be doing to her right now. Or that it might already be too late to save her... Those thoughts made me break out in cold sweat again and my stomach churned.

I squeezed my eyes shut and pinched the bridge of my nose. I took a few deep breaths and held on to the edge of the tub to steady myself.

My panic increased and ate through my skull...

*RELAX, Tristan...relax... Ignore your emotions, you can do it, dammit! Even when it comes to your girl! Because if you don't, who will?!*

I increased my grip on the tub. My knuckles turned white, my hair stuck to my sweaty forehead, my eyes looked wild and haunted, but slowly the cool veil returned and left behind a certainty as I looked in the mirror. I would get her out of there or die trying!

I was her fucking hero, her protector, the one who would shower her with everything and much more. I was the only one she could trust *and* love. She was counting on me!

I took another deep breath and used both hands to brush the damp strands back.

Once I felt somewhat collected, I walked slowly back into my bedroom. The others were sitting on the bed and concerned, stared at me. Tom seemed to be already working on a plan. Phil beamed with dark anticipation. Katha was nibbling on...cookies...and Vivi sat there in her poppy-patterned dress with her head in her hands looking forlorn as she stared blankly at the floor.

It was then when I realized that she hadn't said so much as a word, which was quite unusual. However, it wasn't long before I learned the reason. When I entered the room, she straightened up and looked at me with such a HATEFUL expression it stopped me dead in my tracks.

"Why, Tristan?" she whispered as a tear trickled from the corner of her eye down her smooth cheek to her chin before dripping on the ground.

"You know I didn't want any of this..." I sounded just as devastated as I feebly slipped into my jeans without looking at her. I was too ashamed.

"YES YOU DID!" she suddenly screamed. Considering there was already plenty of tension in the air I wasn't the only one who cringed, everyone else did too. Instinctively, I took a step back as she approached me. Her eyes were fiery and her hands were clenched into tiny fists. Basically, her overall attitude told me to watch myself.

"THIS IS EXACTLY WHAT YOU WANTED! YOU SICK ASSHOLE! YOU WANTED TO PAY HER BACK! TO DEMEAN HER! INSTEAD OF LISTENING TO HER!" And then her little fist slammed against my chest.

"Wow...calm down, sweetie..." When Tommy tried to pull her away from me, she shoved his hands aside as if he was partially to blame for the nightmare. Her face was now full of tears and reading the despair, she let me have it.

"YOU got her into this shit! It is your fault she is THERE! Yours alone! She doesn't mean anything to you! You don't care about her! All you care about is your DAMN FUCKER! Her life means nothing to you or you would never have introduced her to these people! That was the only reason you let her get close again, you sick perverted psycho! You're probably glad when she's dead and you're rid of her!"

"Vivi!" I could not bear to hear her talk about Mia's death. The pain caused by her statement, which was partially correct, was too much. I was unable to move let alone stop her little fists that pounded me relentlessly. Tommy unceremoniously picked her up by the waist and reigned in his little woman. She was so caught up in her anger, she scratched his arms while wildly kicking her feet and with red hair falling over her face, she screamed.

"SHE DID NOT DESERVE THIS! ANYONE ELSE, BUT NOT HER!"

With sagging shoulders and a blank expression, I studied her for a while as her words echoed in my head and drilled ever deeper into my heart.

If Mia died because of me...

"Let her down, Tommy!" He did, albeit, giving me an at-your-own-risk look! Eaten up by tormenting guilt no one else could imagine unless they'd been in my shoes, I dropped to my knees before Vivian, who froze in shock.

She was no longer the only one crying.

"I love her..." There was nothing more to say in my defense and I sounded as tormented as I felt.

First, her eyes grew big, then imperceptibly, the harshness left them, leaving behind endless mourning... grief, sorrow, and compassion...

She sobbed, then out of nowhere, dropped to the floor, and flung her trembling small body into my arms. She cried against my chest and I embraced her tightly. For the first time in my life, I let someone other than Mia give me strength...and shared my feelings.

"Then bring her back, Tristan...bring back our Mia baby..."

I buried my face in her soft red hair. "I will, Vivi... I swear." My eyes were closed when I squeezed her a little harder.

"And then...you never again let her go."

I nodded, as it was my intention all along. So, to make sure we would have a damn happy ending, I pulled myself together instead of letting the prospect that it may be too late petrify me. Still, I felt as if each step was one too many.

What would I do without her?

What would Robbie do without her? It was that thought that abruptly lit a fire within me, ripping me out of my despair, making me square my shoulders and straighten up as well.

Not on my watch...

"I cannot bring her back as long as you, little witch, are hanging around my neck, sobbing all over me... so..." With a tired smile, I pushed her away and was glad to see her humoring me by rolling her eyes and smiling despite the awful situation. I rose in one swift move and pulled her up by the hand.

I turned to Tommy — we looked at each other silently and he nodded wordlessly while he hugged Vivi instead of me. Then I felt Phil's huge paw squeeze my shoulder.

"Don't even ask..." he said and I managed a half-smile before we headed off...

\*\*\*

It was a blessing in disguise because tonight there would be a costume party at Leo's club, which, incidentally, was called *Glamor*. And as fortune would have it, I had all the necessary disguises for it was standard equipment in my job. So, Lena, Katha, and Vivi busied themselves dressing us up.

Phil ended up as a werewolf including a mask, furry shirt, and similar pants. Tom, on the other hand, mimicked a corporal of the Southern Army, wearing the hat and typical blue soldier uniform. And I played a damned vampire...thirsty for blood...complete with a long black leather coat over a see-through sleeveless dark shirt, plus lots of leather straps around the wrists as well as several belts around the tight leather pants... For the finishing touch, Katha saturated my hair with gel and combed it straight back, hurriedly fastened evil-looking eyebrow rings, and applied chalk-white makeup to my face even though I already looked like death warmed over.

In all likelihood, we wouldn't be recognized straightaway — provided our luck held out. I begged damn fate to show mercy, at least this once!

We made sure to leave early for the club. The line in front was still short and the bouncer admitted us without a problem. Obviously! Three sexy guys like us, most likely loaded with a bunch of cash, were the target group...

We looked like crazy strippers and I felt like hissing stupidly at the hoity-toity sluts who offered their necks to me as I walked by.

The main room was garishly decorated in a wide range of colors and the music was already blaring. We stopped on the top landing to survey the scene.

Considering the short line we encountered outside, it was rather busy inside. Security guards had positioned themselves here and there in the background, appearing bored because they knew it would not be until later when unpleasant incidents happened. In the middle of the dance floor, two sluts were already pole dancing. The light reflecting off their glittery costumes was reminiscent of disco balls. That was noteworthy.

Then again, all I was interested in was finding...my girl...in the crowd. I did not see her or teeny-weenie.

So, we decided to first hang out at the bar and order drinks. Preferably, I would have downed my whiskey in one gulp, but it was not advisable. Granted, my nerves were taut, but I had to keep a clear head and my senses sharp. I was prepared to react instantly to the slightest detail and do WHATEVER, even walk over dead bodies to get her out of here.

"Tristan...relax..." Tommy released my fingers – which were already white – from the heavy glass. "We will get her out of here, so calm the fuck down! We are the Wrangler brothers, man! No one has ever gotten the best of us, only temporarily, for we always hit back twice as hard."

"Yeah, that's right, we're the damn Wrangler brothers and Mia is our sister!" Phil toasted and sipped his damn cocktail as if we were here to have fun.

I snorted ironically and emptied the contents of my glass in one gulp after all. "She is not my sister, that's simply disgusting, Phil!"

Phil laughed, just like Tom. "Stop patting my fucking cheek!" I knocked away his hand that was pawing my face.

"Oh, sorry, but you have such soft skin...like a baby's bottom — thanks to ass cream..." Tom grinned and amused, eyed Phil, who was standing on my other side, sweating like a pig because he was far too hot in his furry costume. I ALMOST laughed... Then again, my brother's stupid banter was intentional... They were trying to lighten my mood...

"By any chance, are you hot?" Tom teased.

"Shut up... this shitty fur is so annoying! Katharina did this on purpose, although I have no idea why!" Phil wiped the sweat from his forehead. I rolled my eyes because my brother was pissed off at his unflattering costume, not to mention the embarrassing wolf mask...

I was about to make a stinky mutt comment when Leo, the self-proclaimed prince of the sex scene, stepped onto the stage. Meanwhile, the place was quite crowded and lots of heads turned to face him. Regulars began to cheer while the others stood there with stupid expressions on their faces. A growl escaped me as I gave my brothers the evil eye for both had their hands on my arms to hold me back.

"Stop that shit!" I whispered as I glanced up at Leo, who stood there in a bright white suit like innocence personified. His thinning hair was tightly pulled back, but the spotlights illuminated him so unfavorable, it made his wrinkles look like deep furrows. His not so unattractive face revealed many experiences that would drive most normal people insane. The shoes were crocodile leather, a wristwatch — pure big shot, and gold chains hung around his neck. So, basically, normal for a pimp, drug lord, and criminal. Unintentionally, I wondered whether I would look like that 10 years from now.

"Good evening, dear male and female fuckers..." He plagiarized that from me! I hated when someone stole intellectual property! Actually, something so uncreative should receive the death penalty! However, instead of growing more upset, I simply snorted, ordered another whiskey, and leaned back against the bar with my legs crossed. Two women in medieval costumes moved closer and I rolled my eyes at their attempt to flirt with me. Didn't they have anything better to do? After all, I wasn't here for my fucker's sake; this was a goddamn rescue mission!

My girl!

Fucking sluts!

"Tonight, I have a special treat, one I have been waiting to get from my dear nephew for a long..." I clenched my teeth.

FUCK!

Now she belonged to Leo? FUCKING CRAP!

"Damn!" Tommy cursed at the same moment. This was an entirely different scenario because Leo was not to be taken lightly. I simply did not have enough clout to put him in his place or pressure him with some means, let alone eliminate him for good. Which I would love to do to that pisser, Francesco – slowly bleeding him – but in his case too my hands were fucking tied. After all, he was still Leo's nephew and you simply didn't mess with family. Unless you were suicidal. It was an unwritten rule: whoever fucked with the family also fucked with Leo — and Luca. And fucking with Luca was an incredibly bad idea.

But I didn't give a shit! If Leo did not give her up voluntarily, his head would be introduced to a nice little bullet. And Francesco would be hung up by his scrotum — most definitely. When I realized he might have already had his sick fun with her, it was like a blow to the abdomen and stoked my murderous disposition. I bared my teeth, promising myself to make him bleed!

"Hi...evil vampire... the way you bare your teeth is so sexy..." Out of nowhere, medieval girl appeared next to me. She had long red hair and big tits that threaten to burst out of her dress. I ignored her.

"This is my latest acquisition...and the best part, she makes the perfect slave for a masochist!" Thankfully, I had makeup on so nobody could see I had grown deathly pale when one of Leo's enormous staff strolled up the stairs with a limp body over his shoulder while a red spotlight shone dramatically on them.

"FUCK!" Phil and Tom's hands simultaneously shot forward again as I made an attempt to rush the stage, ready to kill whoever dared stand between me and my unconscious girl.

She wore a skin-tight black catsuit and as the bare-chested employee set her down on her feet, he had to hold her so she would not collapse. Her eyes were barely open, her long hair plastered over her face, and her head hung limply forward. She seemed more dead than alive... Even though her body was obviously unharmed...to the extent of what was visible...I didn't want to know how she looked under the latex suit into which she had been forced.

The crowd began to yell as Leo showed off her attributes, starting with her long legs up to her *perfect tits*, which he slapped. Now Phil had to use all his strength to hold me back.

Once more, Leo riled up the crowd and made them horny for MY girl. His employee tossed her back onto his shoulder like a sack of potatoes or else she simply would have crumpled. I would never allow such a thing in my club! Hookers or not!

I was too far in the background to get a good look at her, but what little bit I saw was enough.

"Yuhoo? Wanna go to the darkroom and drink some of my blood?" Oh yeah, I completely forgot about the cunt.

"I'm a vegetarian!" I fibbed as Leo announced he would hold an auction for the brown-haired beauty for one night.

Fortunately, I carried enough money and we were lucky that everything worked out.

I might have had competition, especially from two men who were extremely persistent; one Chinese man was dressed in a Pokémon costume, the other was disguised as a barbarian although he was not as intimidating as the Asian. I actually had to go as high as 10,000 even though it was not even that much! MERE CHUMP CHANGE!

By now, I could no longer wait to be near her. I had to go to her. I had to see how she was doing. I had to reassure her that I would not let her die here. NO WAY!

A big man whose body was oiled and dressed only in black tight shorts came to get me. Tom and Phil wanted to accompany us, but I told them to stay behind since I was afraid we would draw too much attention. Besides, my baby number three, which was tucked in the back of my pants, reassured me. Not to mention, I always had my fists. So, it was better that my brothers observed from a safe distance, ready to intervene if needed.

"You won't have much fun with that little snail... I've never heard anyone scream *so loud*!" The oiled guy grinned lasciviously as he led me down one floor to the only extra room — the SM basement.

I felt like telling him her pain filled screams were incomparable to her cries of pleasure and that he was a fucked-up scumbag who would not survive the day because of that remark, but I refrained. I mean, he probably assumed I was as sick as Francesco and all the other fuckers who could only feel aroused while hurting a helpless person. It disgusted me that not too long ago I was exactly like those men. Luckily, I never really gave in to that urge because too much of the old Tristan remained deep inside me and he had not allowed me to destroy her...for it would have spelled my demise as well.

When we stopped in front of the pitch-black door, the oily asshole grinned at me again. He needed a shave, I thought, such beard growth would not be tolerated at my place.

"You might have to throw cold water in her face first." With that, he opened the door. "Have fun..."

With my teeth and fists clenched, I quickly entered the room before the urge to ram his nose right up into his damned skull could win. As soon as he shut the door, I locked it from the inside.

Hurriedly, I looked around. The room was big, cold, and stocked with the usual equipment. Various torture devices hung from the walls. There even was a rack, a St. Andrew's

Cross, an armchair, and a huge bed. Each item had handcuffs affixed to it. Bars were suspended from the ceiling, perfect for tying up your sub. Although the floor was tiled with expensive red marble, all in all, the room was not in the same league as my SM basement... not to mention, I had nine additional rooms.

I spotted her on the bed. My girl lay curled up in the fetal position, presumably asleep... albeit she was restless and moaning and her long hair plastered over her far too pale face looked dark. Suddenly she whimpered in despair. "Tristan..." and hastily rolled onto her back.

FUCK!

I was at her side in two steps and sat on the edge of the bed.

"Baby, I'm here," I whispered as I brushed damp strands from her forehead, knowing she could hear me in her sleep, as always...

"Please...I'm scared... Please...don't leave me..." Panting, she retreated to the fetal position and clung to my thigh. She was still dazed. It almost shredded my heart and with trembling fingers, I wiped away her tears.

"Mia baby... I'm here. Wake up!" I whispered, then kneeled beside the bed to lean my forehead against hers and stroked her again. Mia instantly relaxed. As I leaned forward a little more, I noticed she smelled of sour sweat. FUCK, FUCK, FUCKING, FUCK!

My simmering rage boiled again as I ran my fingers through her hair and felt dried blood. As soon as I carefully parted the wet strands, I saw a laceration. Mia whimpered as I gently examined her wound.

"FUCK, baby... Fuck!" I swore and looked at her distressed pretty face, her pinched eyes... wrinkled forehead...and compressed cracked lips.

Fuck...

She responded to my soft curse by pulling the corners of her mouth into a smile. I was well- aware of my influence on her dreams like the night when I had licked her in bed as Francesco slept beside her. Luckily, or should I say, regrettably, back then, she had not actually been aware of my softly whispered words.

I didn't want to know what she had endured. How could I have let it get so out of hand?

"Tristan...you're here...you did not forget me," she whispered hoarsely...

"I would never forget you." Again, I pressed my forehead against hers and stroked her cheek — intending to let her sleep for a few more minutes before rousing her.

"You're my knight in shining red Audi with naughty thoughts..." She smiled wider and the sun came up. I sighed.

"No... I'm a conscienceless vampire who will sink his teeth into your neck when you least expect it and leave whatever is left for the lions to feed on," I whispered in reply and she frowned angrily... My words must have upset her present state of delirium.

Shortly after, her eyelids began to flutter and her long eyelashes cast shadows on her pale cheeks. Her breathing too became more hurried and she quickly squeezed her eyes shut again. I knew she was resisting the urge to wake up as well as why. She was scared — as I was. I was afraid of the expression she would look at me with considering all she had endured.

She fought her consciousness...only to lose the battle...when suddenly, she was wide-awake and stared directly into my eyes. Only a few inches separated us. Her gaze struck me like lightning and I hissed when I could not recognize any of her former liveliness, no emotion whatsoever, reflecting in her caramel eyes. It was like looking into a corpse's eyes. They were... empty... COMPLETELY.

"Baby?" I asked after a few seconds once I had recovered from the initial shock.

She did not react but continued staring at me blankly, which immediately concerned me. I abruptly straightened up, but she remained lying on her side. The only reaction from her was that her body began to shake. She must have suffered quite a shock.

"Mia!" I turned her on her back and looked down at her in a panic. "BABY? Do you recognize me?"

*Nothing...*

"Fuck!" I frantically ran my fingers through my hair and closed my eyes for a moment because I could not stand the unresponsive glare.

I had difficulty maintaining a clear head. Hopefully it was only shock. Who could blame her after everything she had been through...

As soon as I realized it, I eyed her sternly.

"Listen, baby, I am here now. And Phil and Tom are not far away. We will make sure nothing else happens to you. I'd rather die before I let someone else touch you! And don't worry... it won't come to that. We'll make sure the others die first. I will never ever let anyone harm you again..." I waited for some kind of a reaction — a flash in her eyes, a gesture, a sound. Instead, nothing. She just kept staring at me.

OH, FUCK! Her behavior made me unusually nervous, although I made sure not to show it. Her mental state would have to wait for now it was more important to ESCAPE!

"We're leaving now, baby." Carefully, I raised her familiar delicate body and ignored her look as she watched me maneuver her into my leather coat. It was too big, but it covered her and kept her warm. Her face relaxed for a millisecond. Gently, I picked her up and carried her in my arms. Trembling, she clenched her jaw and clung to me.

If I were to act on my emotions, I would run shouting through the club and put a bullet in everyone who had taken part in harming her. However, she came first, my revenge...my bloodthirsty revenge, unfortunately, had to wait...

Perhaps it was an advantage that she now belonged to Leo. Francesco was too emotionally attached in his sick twisted way. Yet with Leo, it was all about money and I would pay whatever goddamn sum to get her out of here. That would be the proper way and worth a try. But if he did not agree to sell her to me, I'd end up a dead man. DAMMIT! Once again, I wondered why I had not seen it coming sooner. Why had I underestimated the actual danger the man represented? How could I have been so dense?

I had no more time to waste. As I opened the basement door, I almost had a heart attack when I saw something furry coming, but then realized it was Phil and Tom was close behind him. The oiled-up shit lay motionless in front of my feet.

"SHIT!" they shouted simultaneously as soon as they saw Mia, who still clung to my shirt with her face buried against my chest, shivering and crying softly. Meanwhile, I anxiously wondered whether she would ever stop, let alone recuperate. I quickly informed my brothers about the current situation.

"You guys take her out of here. I have to talk to Leo. Tom, take Mia! Phil, be ready with your gun. Shoot anyone who tries to stop you..." I was about to say more when I saw HOW SWEATY Phil was. Sweat was now trickling into his eyes, which was bad for aiming in the event of a shootout. Still, I could not resist a smart remark. "Or make them run for the hills with your odor, I don't care. Just make sure to get her out SAFELY and call Dr. Banner on your way home. Tell him to meet you at the club!"

Tom held out his arms and I hesitated, not yet ready to release her from my personal protection. "Tomas, I'm handing you my damn life."

"I know, Tristan," he replied firmly and with conviction, with no hint of ridicule in his voice. Sighing, I was about to hand her to him, but despite the hardships she had gone through, she was still very strong. She simply would not let go of me and kept her face pressed against my shirt.

"Fuck... Mia... nothing will happen to you. These are my brothers. You are in safe hands with them! Please, baby, let go..." As I desperately tried talking sense to her, I had my lips against her temple, but she refused to let go. Instead, she started sobbing louder and her trembling increased. It broke my heart doing it, but since it was unavoidable, I forced open her fists because I wanted her out of here as quickly as possible!

"Take her now!"

He literally pulled her off me and thankfully, they were smart enough to move immediately. I knew they would get her out. Phil, the yeti, would simply bulldoze anyone who dared stand in their way. Hopefully, it wouldn't come to that and if someone accused the two of theft, I was sure Tom had already concocted a plausible story for ANY possible scenario. He was incredible when he wanted to convince someone of something.

I stepped over the bouncer's unconscious body (Phil or Tom had taken all the fun from me, then again, there was no fun in shooting an unconscious man), who obviously hadn't done a good job guarding the door to the SM basement, pulled out my gun anyway, and headed down the shortest route to Leo's office.

I dispensed with knocking, ripped open the door, and stormed in with my gun drawn. At the moment, I was in no mood for antics.

Leo was alone and in the process of doing a line on a mirror that lay on his desk, the one on which Francesco had fondled my girl yesterday. As I stood there pointing baby number three at him while kicking the door closed with my heel, he looked up briefly and calmly finished snorting. Only then did he sit back and smile at me like a nice grandpa who was being visited by his grandson. There was only one thing for me to say.

"She belongs to me!"

"Oh, Tristan...put your Smith & Wesson down and check out this shit, it's from Colombia..."

"I'll pass!" He was about to make a line for me but then thought better of it. Since no one else was present and Leo seemed relaxed and not in a combative mood, I lowered my gun, squared my shoulders and pulled out my checkbook.

"How much?" Leo, always the businessman, flashed his eyes and smiled weakly.

"That depends on how much she's worth to you." Usually, I put on my poker face while doing business, which I was good at, but this deal was too personal and it immediately shot out me — shame on my pussy-whipped ass.

"EVERYTHING!" Leo's smile widened, almost sincere, then he leaned back in his chair, pressed his fingertips together, and eyed me like a snake does its prey.

"Dammit, spit it out already!"

"You love her, huh?" Unexpected, the question weakened my legs. I had to sit down.

"Isn't it obvious?" I asked resignedly and ran a hand over my face.

"What's so special about this *ragazza*?" he mused. I merely chuckled dryly because that was what I found out eight years ago.

"She's the best!" *And she's mine!*

"Francesco had the same sentiment..." Leo said thoughtfully. I noticed my cheek twitching nervously...and my trigger finger growing antsy.

"You knew about the sick shit he put her through?"

"No!" he replied, almost sounding outraged. "I had no idea about that. I was at Mama's... She made some great spaghetti with pesto..." Even though his eyes confirmed his sincerity, right then, I was in no mood to listen to his endless stories. One always got the impression Leo was 200 and once he found a victim who'd listen, there was no stopping him. The only thing I wanted here was to get to my girl. That was it! Dammit!

"Name your price," I repeated calmly and picked up the checkbook that I had thrown onto the table.

Leo looked at me for a few seconds, then his dark bloodshot eyes flashed, accompanied by a smug grin before he countered...

"Your club."

I swallowed. "My club?"

"Si, your club," he simply repeated and calmly started to make another line.

FUCK! MY CLUB! My empire, which I had established with my own hands? My pride and joy for which I had busted my ass and endured so many hardships?

"Considering you said you'd give EVERYTHING for her, well then, your club should not be a big deal, right?' he added with a slight smirk before returning to his line.

I swallowed — hard...

# 12. Dead eyes

*Tristan 'Caring' Wrangler*

By the time I arrived at the club, it was almost morning. The sun was already rising and starting to burn the layer of fog from the city, of which I had the perfect view of from up here. For three minutes, I leaned against my car with a lit cigarette and enjoyed the soothing smoke filling my lungs.

I was exhausted and my head drooped forward as I took a deep breath...

Phil's white Mercedes, which my brothers had used, stood in the parking lot with a written note that they had arrived safely. My conversation with Leo had taken only 10 minutes...so it hadn't taken long before I also arrived.

Mia was safe...my adrenaline rush had ebbed so the only thing I felt was...exhaustion.

Quite frankly, I was a little scared to go inside and peer into those dead eyes again. However, I was well aware there was no escaping it because she was my girl and I was the only one who could do ANYTHING for her.

I had no idea if she hated me now. Maybe our roles had reversed. Maybe now she knew I was no good for her and would only end up dragging her down the shithole. I guess the fact that she had met Francesco the psychopath without me had no bearing... But then, I couldn't blame her for holding me responsible for everything that had happened. I did. At once, gloomy thoughts overwhelmed me, carrying me in all kinds of devastating directions.

Every time I thought about almost losing her, my insides knotted up tightly in protest. However, if she wanted to leave, I would let her go even though it meant she would again rip out my heart.

Somehow, I would survive the loss — as long as I knew she was safe and I was convinced it would take her miles away from all this filth...where there was nothing dangerous and no reason to be afraid.

Aggressively, I flicked away my half-smoked cigarette and ran both hands through my greasy hair before abruptly turning and walking into the club. I really needed a shower. I had sweated, I had cried, I stank, I simply felt disgusting.

Tom, Vivi, Katha, Phil, Georgi, Garrett, Lena, and even Mary were assembled at the kitchen table. No one spoke, everyone remained silent, each holding a steaming cup.

"Where is she?" I immediately asked because now I couldn't wait to be with her.

"Upstairs." Vivi glanced up from her cup, the thick puffy bags under her eyes made her look like a zombie.

"Has the doctor seen her?"

"Yes...but she refused to be examined," she replied and continued an octave lower. "I tried talking to her, but she simply would not speak, let alone look at me. It was like I wasn't there... She didn't let me help her change either... Nothing..." It seemed the memory of it made her melancholic, which rather reflected my emotional turmoil. Just not as intense.

"I'm going to see her now!" I was about to turn when Tommy stopped me.

"She locked herself in and hasn't opened the door for anyone."

"Do you think a wooden door can stop me?" Again, I wanted to leave the room when Phil called me back.

"HEY! What happened at Leo's?"

I sighed heavily, "Don't ask," before I finally left the kitchen to go upstairs via the steps in my office. The others were right, it was indeed locked.

"Mia?" I called out and was not surprised when there was no answer. "Baby, please open the door!" She did not move. I snorted, stomped down the steps, and rummaged in my desk for the spare key. Once I found it, I went back upstairs and let myself in.

I discovered her immediately. She sat wrapped in a blanket with her knees pulled up to her chin, arms around her legs, in an armchair in front of the window. One cheek rested on her knee and her haunted gaze was...killing me. Yet again. Sitting there slumped together, looking indifferently at the radiant city with the rising sun in the background, she resembled a fallen angel illuminated by the golden light of the early morning sun.

My insides were eating me up as I watched her sitting there all broken. But now was not the time for me to lose it because I was the only one who could make things right.

"Baby?" Once I slid off my shoes, I slowly walked toward her and received no response as I quietly announced myself. I stopped behind her for a moment because I had no idea what to do. Recalling the dried blood in her hair, I knew I HAD to take care of her physical injuries first!

Therefore, I circled her, making sure not to touch her and ended up squatting in front of her. Mia seemed not to notice me and continued staring straight ahead as if I wasn't there. It was by far the worst thing I'd experienced. Unthinkable and devastating.

Mia Angel DID NOT SEE ME!

"Mia, I need to know if you sustained serious injuries..." I explained and took her ice-cold hands in mine. There was no reaction from her as I pressed them to my lips and face...but she did not pull them back either. I lingered for a few minutes to smell her fragrant skin and feel the familiar softness, just to reassure myself she was still alive because that was the most important issue right now. Nevertheless, she was not dead...at least not physically...

Unfortunately, there was no indication she was aware of my presence. As her small hands lay limply in mine, I noticed that my vision blurred from the moisture collecting in my eyes. However, before things could get out of hand and I really burst into tears, I quickly pulled myself together and cleared my throat.

"I'm going to carry you to bed now." She did not resist as I picked her up and carried her over to the mattress. All the while, she did not move in my arms, nor was there any sign of recognition or involvement. Damn, I would be even grateful for a hysterical scream now.

Although I was still in control of myself, I had to force my hands not to tremble when I grabbed the fucking zipper on her shit cat outfit.

Fuck! As long as my name was Tristan, she never again would wear latex!

Her whole body trembled as I opened the zipper. She even squeezed her eyes shut and turned her face away from me.

"I'm going to take off your clothes now, Mia. I'm not going to touch you sexually. I won't hurt you... You can always tell me to keep my hands to myself. I will DO SO IMMEDIATELY... It's me — you can trust me," I whispered with a damn quiver in my voice – which, unfortunately, I had no control over – and pulled the zipper down to her crotch. She flinched as my knuckles accidentally grazed her private area and I clamped my teeth together...

*You have to stay strong now! Absolutely! You goddamn ass, KEEP IT TOGETHER!* — my inner voice said over and over as the first tears started streaming down my cheeks. I was HELPLESS to do anything about it.

I shuddered as I breathed deeply and forced myself not to look straight at her face, instead, I breathed calmly and examined her body...

...when a horrific groan escaped me...

She did not sob or sniff, but it was like turning on a faucet and it was scary how the transparent beads suddenly rolled over her pale cheeks. Her eyes did not seem to register anything, especially not me, and remained focused on some point behind me. I ignored it or else I would lose my self-control for sure. However, the alternative wasn't better.

Her body. Her beautiful perfect body. MY BODY.

It was so...broken...it took every ounce of courage to look at her body. Mia did not help when I picked her up to free her from the shitty latex suit. Meanwhile, I swallowed the incessant barrage of curses that tortured my tongue. However, I was not completely successful. When she was naked, I sat on the edge of the bed and with my fingertips gently touched her cheek... Her reaction was slight, albeit her shivering subsided a little.

"Oh fuck...baby..." I whispered unintentionally and started my examination at her neck, which had been covered by the catsuit's collar. It was blue...she obviously had been choked, the marks left no other conclusion...and not just once... I also noticed damn BITE MARKS on her fine skin.

My gaze continued further south and the pressure of my teeth on my lower lip increased to such an extent that I tasted blood. Her usually creamy fair skin was littered with hematomas still in the development stage. *His* damned paws had been on her that much was visible. He had treated her roughly, not gently...

But not just that...

"Did he?" I leaned over and gently stroked the small round burn blisters, which were especially visible on her breasts.

I could not believe it...they were definitely caused by cigarettes.

A wave of nausea overcame me. For a moment, I was not in control of myself and tempted to kneel beside the bed to empty the contents of my stomach. So far, I had been able to suppress the intense urge — the question was for how much longer?

Here and there, dark hickeys peppered her entire body... Her legs were also covered with bruises... Her wrists and ankles had bloodied abrasion marks... I was afraid to inspect any closer. Truly afraid.

"I'm so sorry." Extremely lightly, I stroked her wounds. I tried to treat her as gently as I possibly could and no longer fought to hold back my tears, which freely ran down my cheeks.

They were sincere, important, and appropriate in this terrible situation. Perhaps it was the ultimate proof that I was still a human being who had a heart.

I could not even begin to imagine what all she had been through in those few hours and ALL BECAUSE OF ME...

I closed my eyes for a moment before forcing myself to look at her again.

"Mia...may I examine your...private area...?" Fuck! I simply could not bring myself to say pussy...it did not work — not in this context!

She did not reply nor did she look at me. She continued crying but spread her legs. THANK GOD!

Regardless that the gesture symbolized her full surrender and resignation, I suspected — perhaps even instinctively knew — she was not doing it for me, as usual, but because of the newly taught humility over the past few hours.

An overpowering sob rose in my throat at an intensity that I had not felt for more than two decades. In truth, I regressed emotionally, in part, felt like the little boy who had stood before the shards of his existence and helplessly clung to the hand of his father. It took me a while to realize I was experiencing my second existential crisis.

No, it wasn't the third because comparing the moment where my mother had killed herself to what I was experiencing right now made the moment of Mia's alleged betrayal seem RIDICULOUS. Oh fuck! It was unimaginable that I had become so obsessed with such a tiny issue. At least that was how I saw it now.

I took another deep breath before I finally knelt between her legs, yet I still hesitated before touching her knees and as gently as possible opened the smooth legs even further. I noticed that she wanted to resist somewhat, which was only natural. But some new force, one that until yesterday was unknown to her, successfully prevented her and instead, only made her moan a little.

"Sorry...fuck..." I said hastily and glanced briefly up at her while stroking the battered skin around her ankles before forcing myself to look at my favorite part of her body.

This time I not only felt sick, I felt sick as a dog and actually gagged. I barely managed to swallow the acidic liquid that had already risen in my throat.

She was bleeding!

It couldn't be true!

"Oh God!" My forehead broke out in sweat and my stomach twisted into a knot. Therefore, I quickly closed my eyes and tried to compose myself. "Fuck... fuck... fuck..." I mumbled to myself while gently stroking her lower legs. She should not think I would leave her alone for even a minute.

Once my nausea subsided a bit, I opened my eyes again.

"I have to touch you there, okay? I won't hurt you..." She was nonresponsive so I went to the sink to dampen some soft towels.

"I'll move you to the edge so I can wash you better." Carefully, as if she were made of precious porcelain, I moved her into the desired position. I placed two chairs a couple of feet apart for her legs to rest on like a makeshift gynecologist chair, which did not make me feel any better.

I knelt in front of her and tenderly wiped away the blood. Damn... I honestly had no idea if she needed to go to the hospital for stitches...

She gnashed her teeth as I touched her and although she did not move away from me, it was enough to eat away at my soul. She no longer trusted me! *Me*, who usually could do whatever he pleased with her.

Luckily, once the blood was gone it didn't look as bad as I initially suspected. Nevertheless, the pig was as good as dead! He would die slowly. I cursed myself for not following through with my original plans.

None of this would have happened had I taken him out that first time in Mia's apartment. If needed, I could have made her wear headphones and watch Bambi on TV. No, seriously, it would have been so easy. I could have used whatever pretext to get Mia out of the room and then gag the disgusting piece of dirt to muffle his death screams. Then again, my revenge would have been far more satisfying without noise-inhibiting elements. I wanted to hear his moaning, groaning, pleading, and begging. He should know what it felt like to be humble and die of fear.

Just to hear his screams might evoke the greatest orgasm of all time. But definitely the sight of his verminous blood-smeared body...

Oh...fuck!

Deep inside dwelled a total degenerate asshole and – dammit – I loved that side of me.

But all that had to wait; now it was my girl's turn. My tortured, raped, abused, helpless girl...

For a few crazy seconds, I rested my head against her thigh and actually allowed myself to lose control. The emotions overwhelmed me, yet it was better to let them run their course than wallowing in a wild panic.

It took me a while to notice the change, at which time, I no longer felt embarrassed. I simply clung to her velvety thigh and sobbed like a damn baby.

I had no right to feel sorry for myself! Only Mia had that right, which she also made use of... That was a start... I kept crying my eyes out while mumbling how sorry I was and that I had never wanted any of it to happen and that she should forgive me. I downright begged her, but it seemed she did not hear me.

As soon as I could manage, I pulled myself together even though it was damn hard because the lump in my throat simply would not go away. I cleared my throat and rose. She might not need sutures, but she definitely needed to be taken care of. I was also sure she would love to take a bath.

Putting myself in her shoes, I definitely would want all that blood and sweat off me.

"Mia? Would you like to wash yourself?" I asked quietly. "Shall I run you a bath?"

*No reaction.*

"It might do you good..."

*No reaction.*

"Fuck!" I swore under my breath and clenched my teeth. To put it mildly, it was too much for me. After all, I was basically a selfish asshole who did not care a lick about a fellow human being's psyche and all that shit.

Way too complicated, hazy, and in general, too embarrassing.

But it was about my girl...which conflicted me. Yet again...

"Okay, baby..." I said once I took a deep breath and had run both hands through my hair. "I'm going to bathe you now whether you like it or not..." And off I marched into the adjoining bathroom to turn on the water. Obviously, I didn't add bath oil. When I returned to the room, she had not moved.

Determined, I positioned myself so she had to look at me.

"I'm going to carry you to the bathtub now... Mia."

I no longer expected a reaction from her, which was what happened. She did not cringe when I gently reached under her knees to pick her up. Her little hands instantly clenched my shirt and she pressed her face against my neck. She had stopped crying, but otherwise, everything remained the same.

Anyway, the fact that she had clung to me in desperation as soon as I had her in my arms gave me hope.

It told me I was still her Tristan and she was still my girl.

Carefully, so as not to bump her head on anything, I carried her into the bathroom and set her down on the fluffy bath mat, which did not turn out to be easy at all because once again, she refused to let go of me. Eventually, I managed to pry her off while forcing myself to ignore her fragile state — or I would have gone completely crazy. For a second, I even thought about joining her in the bathtub, but quickly decided against it.

An already irritated part of me knew that whatever kind of spontaneous sex was out of the question for now. However, once again, I didn't care at the moment.

"I will lift you into the water. Hold on tight to me!"

She did not look at me as her arms instinctively wrapped around my neck. However, when she was in the water, she again would not let go of me, nor did she loosen her grip. Slowly but surely, I lost my balance.

"Baby...you have to let go of me... Fuck... Mia!" I started to panic. No mercy! She clawed at me as if letting go would ring in the end of the world. So, I had no choice but to keep her company, clothed or naked.

"Oh man!" Without further ado, I stepped into the tub in my leather pants, shirt, and shorts... Fortunately, I had left my gun in the office, what else could I have done.

I slowly lowered myself and ignored the disgusting feeling of my clothes soaking in water. The bathtub was large so it was easy to position Mia between my legs and lean her against my chest. She rested her head on my shoulder and closed her eyes while I had a hard time resisting the inner urge to grab and gently massage her tits. One look at the burn marks was enough to instantly drive away whatever sexual thoughts.

"Is the temperature okay?" I asked stupidly. *Dammit!* As if she would answer me. I turned on the hot water and grabbed the red sponge from the counter next to my shoulder.

"I'm going to wash you now, baby," I announced and began to wipe down her body gently with a weird-looking Sponge Bob sponge. I mostly concentrated on her arms and upper body, purposefully sparing her private area. To me, it seemed as if the sponge caresses helped her relax a little. Still, it could not compare to how her little body used to wriggle under my hands with satisfaction.

Ignoring the sickening burning in my chest, I raised her arms and she held on to my neck as I washed her armpits. From time to time, when I touched a particularly sensitive spot, I heard her inhale sharply. That was the only reaction I received. I could not stop myself from kissing her temples, whereupon she immediately stiffened so I abruptly stopped.

"Sorry!" I apologized hastily and felt like kicking myself.

Once her upper body was clean, I pushed her a bit down so I could wash her hair. I made sure to be gentle and careful not to touch her laceration. Her expression did not betray her emotions and as the silence continued, I grew ever madder.

The little masochistic in me wanted to know the details of what happened to her. I wanted to hold her in my arms and let her cry on my chest. I wanted to tell her I loved her and always would. I wanted to take away the pain. Or at least share it and help her cope with it. But as long as she did not let me in, I was in no position to do any of it. That powerlessness was quite frustrating and overwhelming.

When I finished washing her hair, I moved between her bent legs and cleaned her beautiful lower legs. I spent time on each toe and massaged her feet extensively. Although she tolerated it and did not flinch, she made no sound of satisfaction.

By the time the water was almost cold, I decided it was time to get out. I stepped out first and left her alone briefly so I could rip off my disgustingly wet clothes. Then I dashed into the bedroom where I slipped on black sweatpants and a white muscle shirt. I quickly grabbed a nightgown for her and made it back the moment her face slid under the surface of the water.

I cursed myself for I should have expected it and I tried not to freak out. I lifted her out of the tub and started to dry her. I slid the nightgown over her head for she still was unresponsive, but she hissed when I put undies on her. For a second time, I felt like screaming and promised myself yet again, Francesco would pay. Perhaps I'd even reciprocate in kind, two or three times as bad. Counting each wound he had inflicted on my girl and taking into consideration that she would be plagued by nightmares for the rest of her life, oh, he would pay — with his life.

When she was all set, I wanted to tuck her into bed, but once again, she stuck to me like Velcro, meaning, I had to slip under the covers with her. Now, for the first time in my life, I had no idea how to touch her in bed. When I thought perhaps I should keep them to myself, she surprised me by placing a leg over my waist and nestling her cheek against my chest...

Then she cried. The whole damn day.

# 13. The Revival

*Tristan 'In Pain' Wrangler*

Over the following weeks, her demeanor did not change. Mia simply could not find a way out of her depression.

I tried everything. For hours, I knelt in front of her, caressed her expressionless face, and pleaded with her to talk to me. I wanted to know what I could do to make her feel better. However, she remained silent and I grew more desperate.

It was like I was living with a breathing corpse.

Whenever we were in the kitchen together, she sat on my lap, motionless and lifeless, with her face buried in my neck and eyes closed. Her fists clung to my shirt or neck and never loosened, not even for a moment. It was as if that very same act might make her relive the ordeal again.

She hardly ever slept at night, mostly was awake crying. And *when* she actually slept, she had nightmares, thrashed around in bed, moaning and begging him to stop. During those incidences, it was not only once that I was the recipient of her wrath.

I could hardly bear to lie next to her and see the tears running down her pale face while she looked so pitiful and fragile. I felt like screaming.

Whenever I had to work or for some other reason, could not hold her, she merely sat in my room in her chair with Stanley in her lap, staring blankly over the city rooftops.

She always trembled unless I was around.

In my desperation, I asked Vivi, Phil, Tommy, and even Lena to talk to her. However, no one successfully engaged her in conversation, not even Vivi, who tried every day to involve her by chatting with her as if she was not...traumatized.

Over time, I felt dead and empty inside, which probably must be what my girl was going through, just much worse because all I had were suppositions. I had run out of ideas about what to do.

Even Katha tried to get through to her because she had gone through something similar during her early childhood. Even after telling Mia her complete life story teary-eyed, she did not speak a word. However, Mia had raised her hand and placed it on Katha's trembling forearm. It was the first strong reaction she had shown. Otherwise, she acted the same.

In the evenings, when I knelt next to the bed with my forehead against hers, feeling emotionally DRAINED...or tears silently rolled down my cheeks and I sobbed helplessly, thinking I would lose it at any moment, she unexpectedly placed her hand on my cheek or stroked my hair. That was all she was able to do for me. Not that I was holding it against her. I mean, dammit, none of us could imagine what she had experienced. None of us could even begin to understand what she was going through.

None of us could help her.

She also did not work, which was one of the worst consequences because Robbie called every day asking for his Mirti. It broke my heart to *always* put him off every day, saying she couldn't come after all. Her neglecting the little guy made me a bit upset with her. Not to give a damn about us I could understand, but Robbie...he idolized and NEEDED her! Even more so than me...

I did my best to distract him and spent most of my free time with him. Either I took him to the boxing gym, because he loved watching strong men spare for hours, or to train with me. Or I took him to the Alz River. We skipped stones or stared at the caged animals in the zoo. Dammit... I even tried to bake gingerbread with him, but I failed miserably. I knew I could not replace Mia, but I could make an effort to put a smile on Robbie's face as often as possible because I was now quite fond of the little bugger. So, naturally, it pained me to always see the disappointment in his eyes and his little heart breaking every time I told him his Mirti would not come again.

Otherwise, I had a few other things to take care of. In the home, I had a few conversations with the head nurse, who every time could not help herself and looked at me with affection. Had she not been a nun, I was sure she would have tossed her panties at my head. However, besides that, she had been completely thrilled and thankful that I cared so much about the tiny orphanage and had offered to renovate it. It was the least I could do. Vivi and Katha had already started the planning phase and were busy creating drafts as well as talking with Sister Carmen and the authorities so everything was set to begin in the spring.

And a few things regarding my girl had to be taken care of. I mean, dammit, I wanted HER. I was slowly running out of patience. Now that she was finally back together with me, we could have started to make our imagined future a reality. However, she simply was unapproachable. She might be present, but at the same time, she was far off in her own world. Sometimes, it felt as if I had lost her all over again, as if she no longer existed, like my heart had been ripped out of my chest yet again.

Yes...lately, a lot had happened, all of which seemed to pass her by.

By the time the first snow fell, quietly dusting the land in white, rather like my girl, silent and pale, I was so desperate I even contemplated having her committed. I had already acquired the necessary paperwork. None of the therapists who diagnosed her had success in getting through to her. And whatever renowned shrink I had flown in from around the world, all ended in disappointment.

So...the next option would be committing her. However, I knew if I took her there, she would shiver, cry and, most of all, cling to ME in desperation while silently imploring me not to leave her alone and take away her last means of protection — namely me, well, that I simply could not bring myself to do. Apparently, I managed to convey that to her every time I held her in my arms. Considering her pitiful state, there was no way would I entrust her to a stranger! Thus, the papers were shredded and recycled.

Christmas was approaching. Everything was ready, but I could not tell her. I could not *do* it because she was still dead.

Vivi was busy decorating my office, the kitchen, and even my bedroom, yet Mia merely sat silently in whatever room, obviously in her own little world. Her soul was a caged bird with broken wings... Somehow, I had to free her...show her that it was worth the courage to take up flying again. However, this required that I push her out of the safe nest, *force* her to react.

Otherwise, I might lose her completely.

One cold morning, Garrett and Georgi had a twisted idea that I immediately and vehemently rejected, yet it repeatedly popped back into my mind. It sounded so crazy it actually might work. So far, I had tried to get through to her with compassion, understanding, friendship, and even love — always unsuccessful.

That left me with one last option before having her declared incompetent and committed because she barely ate and hardly ever slept. I was worried about her health, both physically and mentally.

It could not go on like that.

\*\*\*

It was December 11<sup>th</sup> when I decided to take the extreme step. I was damned scared to do it to her, but there was no way around it. It had to be.

I knew Mia...the old one and I knew perfectly well how to push her buttons so she would — totally freaked out. The fact that I had to inflict more pain on her in order to do so certainly was necessary, but right now, it was by far the most stupid idea I could come up with. Especially, considering I could lose her for good. However, I was damn sure hoping for a different outcome!

Therefore, I had to be a total asshole. It had to be so realistic that it would convince her she could lose *me*. Because I knew it would rekindle her fighting spirit. At least, it was what I hoped.

I discussed the details with Mary. She was the perfect accomplice because my girl could not stand her. Granted, the hoity-toity slut would have been perfect for it, but on short notice, I had unceremoniously handed her to Leo — as a sign of goodwill.

Mary was stunned when I approached her with my idea, albeit her eyes sparkled with lust, which was the typical reaction when it came to my fucker. So, naturally, she agreed.

A few days before the master plan, I began flirting with her. And not exactly subtle. It was painful to feel Mia stiffen in my lap. How she held her breath every time I hit on Mary with some common come-on or when I eye-fucked her in front of my girl while making ambiguous remarks. I felt like a miserable lowlife scumbag, an unconscionable bum, a piece of shit!

I had to remind myself that her small reactions to my new tactic verified I was on the right track. However, it was not enough. I needed her to really FLIP OUT, crack her barricade with one huge bang.

So I stepped it up a notch.

I locked the old nice Tristan away in a box and released the uber-ass Tristan. Her overly pronounced jealous nature was the strongest weapon and my last chance to fight her apathy.

\*\*\*

It was evening and snowflakes silently fell from the sky when Mary and I headed for my bedroom where Mia sat in her chair busy staring at nothing. Mary wore work clothes, a flimsy pink negligee that favored her delicate curves. I was still casually dressed in a gray shirt and black jeans when I entered my bedroom and immediately pulled Mary into my arms.

Unobtrusively, I quickly glanced around the room.

As usual, Mia sat by the window. It seemed she had not even noticed us since she did not turn her head to us. I abruptly grabbed Mary's ass and she gasped. *Now,* Mia tensed, so I lifted Mary, who immediately wrapped her slim legs around my hips and held on to me.

"Whoa...sweetie...slow down..." I laughed hoarsely as she kissed my neck and then noticed Mia's head turning to look at us through narrowed eyes. Then she looked away again. DAMMIT!

I felt like such a BIG SHIT! Groping another chick in front of my suffering girl. However, given there was no alternative, it had to be.

"I'm sure you don't mind me having a little bit fun, do you, Mia baby?" I asked, sounding slightly distracted. "I mean, after all, I am a man and you won't let me fuck you anymore...so... I'll do you a favor and we'll use the bathroom... Naturally, I'll make sure I use a rubber." Fucking crap!

Just saying those words was hell on me. Imagine how she must have felt! However, all I could do was curse under my breath as I continued the performance.

And so, with Mary's legs still wrapped around my hips, I marched in the bathroom without giving my girl another look. FUCKING CRAP! If it did not work, I really was at the end of my wits! I had hoped she would lose it IMMEDIATELY...but obviously she needed a few more minutes. Hopefully, the whole drama would have the desired result!

After closing and locking the thin bathroom door, I set down Mary on the edge of the bathtub and winked at her. I took a seat on the closed toilet lid and flipped through the newspaper that I grabbed from the small side table, which always had the latest one because I needed reading material when taking a crap.

Anyway... The new Audi was out, even had a so-called turbo function. THAT would become my new baby number two.

While I read the ad with interest, I began in a smooth seductive voice, "H'm, Mary...you have no idea how long now I've been meaning to fuck you!" She grabbed the little file from the edge of the sink and began to work her long nails, looking bored.

"I wanted to fuck you the first time I laid eyes on you... OH, you're such a god!" She sounded lascivious and lustful. It was no surprise for she had years of experience as a phone sex worker. I grinned behind my newspaper.

"Then show me how great a god I am!"

"OHHH...yeah..." she gasped louder.

"Get on your knees and grab my...eh... the staff of god," I shouted across the room.

"Whoa... Tristan... IT IS SO BIG!" Mary pretentiously blinked at me in wonderment. I rolled my eyes and groan... "That's so hot. I can tell you're experienced!"

"I'm better than that corpse out there, huh? Forget about her and..." she murmured and I bent down a corner of the newspaper to give her a warning look that immediately silenced her.

"Shut up and keep blowing... Oh... yeah..." It seemed I had to take it up another notch. "Okay, that's enough," I announced hoarsely. "Now sit on the washing machine and spread your legs!" I slapped my bare forearm. "Wider, Mary... I want to *lick* you!"

"Tristan Edward Wrangler, DON'T YOU DARE STICK YOUR TONGUE IN HER!" came from outside, whereby my actual second name was revealed, the one I had carefully kept secret from the public for decades. My siblings were forbidden, under the threat of death, to mention it. It was too embarrassing!

Simultaneously, a blazing flash shot through my stomach — not anger, quite the opposite!

I was the happiest fucker on the planet! She sounded loud, desperate, and crazy. YEAH!

I froze and lowered my newspaper when I heard her firm, harsh, hysterical voice, which sounded like a lovely melody to me! I almost started crying in front of Mary! When she tried the knob and banged on the door, I flinched.

"DAMMIT, OPEN UP! So I can kill you!"

Mary looked at me wide-eyed, probably because she did not trust little Mia Angel to have such an organ or the actual courage to use it against me. I nodded proudly. "OPEN UP! STOP IT YOU TWO! DON'T TOUCH HER! DON'T TOUCH HIM! DON'T TOUCH EACH OTHER! OPEN UP ALREADY!" The knob jiggled so fiercely I thought it might break.

"You should disappear as quickly as possible while I'll distract her," I whispered to Mary and was at the door in one step.

"Baby, you'll end up breaking the knob!" I joked as I opened the door. As soon as the gap was wide enough, a small solid fist dashed in between and smacked me right on my jaw. WOW! I had not expected that!

"YOU FUCKING PIG!" I did not have to distract Mia from Mary, who instantly rushed out of the room because Mia was only focused on me as she grabbed my shirt and pulled me out of the bathroom. Wow! Unbridled rage gives a person immense strength!

"I feel like shit and you have nothing better to do than stick your fucker in some bimbo? Tell me, have you lost your mind?!" I looked down at her wide-eyed, mouth gaping. Her eyes no longer looked dead but full of life. Under the surface, blazed a raging fire, looking like despair and above all, *madness*. The latter *made* me think, but at least I could assume I was on the right track. Somehow.

I rolled my eyes...and chuckled.

"Sorry...but you know I'm a fucker..."

"You're a son of a bitch, just like all the other guys!" she hissed between teeth and dragged me over to the bed. OH, FUCK! This would be hard. She was shaking all over as she shoved me roughly onto the mattress and straddled my hips with her legs spread far apart.

Abruptly, she again hit my face with a fist. OH, FUCKING FUCK! THAT actually hurt!

"Shall I show you what it feels like to be humiliated? Shall I show you?" Clearly, a rhetorical question for she had already possessively pressed her salty lips against mine. For a moment, her sweet tongue darted into my mouth, heavenly. Next, she slapped my already slightly sore jaw with an open hand.

"Get your knife, asshole!" she ordered and got off me. Like a goddess of death, she knelt on the bed and crossed her arms in front of her chest. For a few seconds, I stared at her, stunned. She returned my gaze, iron-hard, as the fireplace's licking flames reflected in her insane-looking, glittering eyes while at the same time, seductively dancing over her delicate features. Her long hair was a mess and her petite figure trembled. The rings under her eyes, in particular, made her look demonic or perhaps even crazy...depending on your perspective.

The image of her with my knife scared me a bit. However, I had to pull this off. I had to help her even if she released everything she had amassed and kept bottled up during the past few weeks on me. FUCK! The thought caused a shiver. Nevertheless, I leaned forward and fished the knife out of the nightstand drawer, which I handed her with the blade facing me. As I watched like a hawk, she grabbed it with a sure grip. My whole body was tense, ready to spring into action should she attack me now like a wild fury. However, she merely stared at me, fiery, yet icy cold, and finally set it next to her on the mattress with a brief grin of satisfaction. Her voice was gentle. Calm. Emotionless.

"Is the big strong Tristan Wrangler scared of his girl?" Abruptly, she slapped my face again with her palm.

OH, FUCK! This time I hissed and touched my cheek. She swung one leg over my hip and settled on top of me, grabbed my shirt, and ripped it open. The buttons flew across the bed and landed on the floor, where they rolled here and there before coming to a stop.

"Take it off, you fucking horny ass!" Again, she slapped me on the same side!

"Can you switch to the other one?" I could not resist a smart remark and was immediately punished for it — naturally, the same cheek.

"Dammit," I mumbled as she pulled my shirt off. As soon as it landed on the floor, she pushed roughly against my chest. It was not forceful enough to knock me over, but I played along and fell back in the middle of the bed. Fascinated, she stared at my naked torso.

"So perfect...so...so muscular..." she breathed absently as her fingertips brushed over my well-trained hard muscles. "So pure...so...unused..." I knew she was thinking about the scars on her once flawless skin and swallowed hard when her almost wistful look broke away from my body and stared coldly into my eyes. Fuck, I would gladly trade my good skin for her marred skin!

"You are every woman's dream. I see how they all ogle you... I see how you imagine fucking them... But you are mine, ONLY MINE, and you will fuck ONLY ME! Therefore, I think we should *brand* you... What do you say, baby?" she asked suspiciously pleasant and reached for the knife. Leery, I tried to read her and fought the impulse to snatch it from her. However, as I replayed her words in my head, I realized something. How she looked and touched me, what she said... I realized she was doing to me what teeny-weenie had done to her.

It was her way of coping with the events, her way of telling me everything because she could not put it into WORDS. However, she had no problem SHOWING me. It was her way of sharing her pain with me...her way of transferring it to me. And I would accept it. Silent, wordless, motionless. I owed her that much. Besides, I did not mind physical pain, in contrast to the burden I took from her. And IT would help her to have power over me. The fact that it had to be me was *crucial* because, in the past, I had dominated her quite often and always made her the victim. Her therapy was for her to overcome her role as submissive by becoming the dominating personality.

So I gnashed my teeth as she held the blade to my throat and applied light pressure. At the same time, she leaned forward so that her lips almost touched mine. Her hair fell down on either side of my face, enveloping us.

"Will you be a good Tristan?" she whispered and increased the pressure.

I nodded and swallowed.

"Good." Satisfied, she sat up and laid the knife on the pillow right next to my head. It was quite disturbing and distracted me as she made herself comfortable on top of me wearing only one of my ancient white shirts and her dark blue hot pants.

Devoutly, she stroked my upper body while holding her head at a slight angle. It seemed as if she was memorizing its impeccability one more time. She must have realized that I wouldn't look like this ever again after her treatment. Regardless, I would willingly pay that price as long as it brought my girl back. At the same time, I clenched my fists when I remembered EVERYTHING Francesco had done to my girl.

Humming with delight, she leaned forward and brushed her soft lips along my jawline, then further down to the side of my neck, where she licked and nibbled my skin, making me shudder when I felt her warm breath.

"Why do guys always think with your dicks?" And she bit me...HARD. I grabbed the sheet to distract myself from the pain and lay still. She knew she did not have to tie me up. She also knew she could take everything out on me. She trusted me completely — finally! Many times, she had problems showing trust on her part! That, she had overcome now.

Yet I could not say the same applied to me. Although I was sure she would not kill me, I was unsure about whatever else might happen.

Oh, how our roles had changed.

It was quite aware...I would have to feel pain. It was clear she was dominating me right now and had complete control over me... But then, if need be, I would sell my soul for her.

She licked the bite mark she had left on my neck and then, as if nothing happened, her lips continued to my collarbone to nibble extensively on it. "Why are you men always so selfish? It's always about your satisfaction. Your needs?" She *BIT* the middle of my collarbone! She really sunk her teeth into my flesh. I clenched my teeth and closed my eyes as she continued to work her way down. I did not want to know what to expect down south. *Honestly!*

Once again, looking totally innocent, she played extensively and gently with my right nipple. She circled it with her tongue and sucked on it with her wonderfully soft lips until I was groaning and wriggling around on the bed, my nipple now as hard as my fucker, which was drooling.

Then it was the left nipple's turn. The one that bore my tattoo. Devotedly, she spoiled it with her mouth while tweaking the other nipple between her little fingers. My heart was beating like crazy and my forehead broke out in sweat.

"THIS here is mine. ALL OF IT!" Then she bit the nipple. I gasped because that shit really fucking hurt! She looked up at me knowingly, sporting a wry grin like the sexy devil herself. Breathing heavily, I clawed even harder at the bed sheet instead of burying my hand in her locks, as usual, to pull her away from me.

Meanwhile, Mia's fingers slid down over my stomach. Tenderly and slowly. Her grin grew wider as she stroked my hardness...to which I smiled slightly stupidly... In the next moment, she tightened her grip and literally had me by the balls.

"ARGH!" Now I *actually* clawed at the mattress and arched my back in pain.

"You think you can dominate me? NO SUCH LUCK! You can't because you are mine! As a matter of fact, I can do with you as I please...another fact, *you are my* pussy..." She whispered the fucked-up truth and squeezed harder. I almost fainted from the pain and squeezed my eyes shut in agony. My entire body was as stiff as a board.

"Fuck... Mia!" I piped up.

"Shut up, Tristan!" she growled.

"I'll...do whatever you want... BUT now, let go...Mia... Marena!" I stammered. She let go and I collapsed in relief when she slapped my already throbbing cheek again.

"Never call me Mia Marena again!" she hissed. OH FUCK! She was the perfect dominatrix!

"Mia baby...it's OKAY!" I gasped a bit more, glad when the unspeakable pain between my legs became more tolerable. After all, I was not a good slave nor was I into receiving torture. For a few more seconds, she regarded me thoughtfully.

"Are you actually aware of everything you have done to me?" she said, sounding almost weak, and suddenly, she jumped up. "You will find out what it means to feel pain and to carry those scars as a reminder for the rest of your life." With that, she pulled my shirt over her head, completely baring her upper torso in front of me. It was torture to view her marred body. I had to swallow every time I saw the round pale pink scars that were everywhere. Then she quickly fetched my pack of cigarettes and lighter from the table next to the patio door.

FUCK!

I stared at her wordlessly as she made herself comfortable on top of me again and took a smoke from the box. She slipped it between my lips and lit it.

"You look so damn sexy when you smoke. It's porn-worthy." She let me take another long drag while she eyed my lips in fascination as they wrapped around the filter. "That's enough!" With that, she grabbed the cigarette between two fingers like a pen and lowered it close enough to my left breast that I could feel the heat of the cherry all the while staring into my eyes.

"In recent weeks you constantly told me you would take responsibility for everything...that you couldn't imagine what I'd been through... So, shall I make you feel what I had to feel?" With those soft-spoken words, she VERY LIGHTLY pushed the cherry against my skin. Dead center of the heart tattoo.

"ARGH..." My body bucked and I clawed at the sheet and mattress even harder while squeezing my eyes shut and clenching my teeth. I forced myself *not* to push her off me.

"Does that hurt?" *No! I actually like it, Mia, for fuck's sake! It's like going to a spa!*

She went down another inch making sure not to burn my skin. And then, almost devotedly, she ran the cigarette over my entire upper body.

Starting with my left breast to my right one and on down to my stomach leaving behind a hot burning trail of pain. At the waist of my pants, she stopped and looked up into my tense face. She smiled in satisfaction when she noticed my torment and put the butt between my lips again.

"Have a drag!" Vigorously, she leaned forward and placed apologetic kisses along the trail she had dragged the cherry. I moaned because her soft lips were such a sharp contrast to the painful heat. Her hair tickled my sensitive flesh. Her lips elicited a quiet gasp from me.

"I hate it, Tristan..." she mumbled at my belly button and straightened up somewhat. Out of nowhere, she grabbed the knife and placed the blade between my pectoral muscles.

"I hate you because you're two-faced. An angel..." Without warning, she cut a straight line into my flesh and I pressed my lips together as I growled and tossed my head back and forth... "...and a devil," she announced as she sliced her way down. The cut burned like fire, but I managed to keep my teeth clenched and not scream.

"Yet I love you...because you have both natures." She licked the wound from bottom to top. She took delight in licking the blood with her tongue while humming, "M'm h'm!" Unexpectedly, she kissed me. Mia's sweet taste tainted with blood... Her velvety tongue not only soothed mine it conquered it.

A crazy mix!

It was so sick...and, at the same time, so unspeakably erotic...

She breathed heavily as she freed her lips from mine, then lazily brushed the blade over my pants, at which time, my eyes grew a bit wider. She grinned demonically as she saw panic flaring in them.

"Are you scared?" she asked softly with an evil smile.

"YES, dammit!" I exclaimed, provoking a humorless laugh.

"Don't be scared, baby... I would never do anything to IT." Her words only slightly reassured me because right now, I thought her capable of anything.

She opened my jeans.

"Lift your ass!" I did as ordered and she pulled down my pants. She tossed them on the floor and placed the knife next to my hips as she knelt down beside me.

Unexpectedly, she bent over my hard cock and took it deep and firmly in her mouth. I let out an unbridled groan because, for some strange reason, I was ready to come right then. She felt the suspicious twitching and muttered about my hardness.

"You better not come!" Then she sucked harder, circled the tip with her tongue while massaging my balls just as I liked it.

"God... Mia... Please... Stop!" I could barely stand it and envisioned a grandma's sagging tits and the Pope as I lay there with my eyes closed, not daring to look down to where she was tormenting me. She sat up with a grin and wiped the corners of her mouth.

"Doing what?"

Now she almost resembled my old Mia again, her eyes were alive and her smile beaming. She climbed up my body, leaned over, and kissed me hard. I moaned in her mouth as she rubbed her wet panties against my fucker.

She broke off the kiss much too abruptly, stood up on the bed, and took off the hot pants.

Then she squatted over me again, grabbed my fucker with one hand, and slowly jerked me off while lightly pushing it against her paradise. I felt her seductive velvety wetness on my tip and groaning deeply, forced myself not to thrust my pelvis upward.

My wild gaze flicked over her pale shapely body against which the licking flames of the fire danced. She looked like Satan personified. Her long full hair covered her shoulders and a few strands curled around her perfect round tits. Fascinated, I followed her pronounced waistline down to where the wet paradise was waiting for me. She lowered herself a little more so I ended up right against her entrance.

I moaned harshly since I was absolutely hypersensitive right then.

"You like what you see?" she asked mischievously. My eyes dashed up to hers and I quickly nodded eagerly and rather stupidly.

"Mia Ma..."

I had not even finished when she slapped my sore cheek again with her flat hand. At the same moment, she lowered herself all the way onto me and firmly and determinedly embraced me.

"AHHH," I groaned helplessly.

"Do not call me that, dammit!" And then she started to move on me. She threw her head back and full of passion, grabbed my hands and placed them on her bouncing tits. My hands automatically started to knead them and I gasped with her.

"Mia... BABY..." A deep groan escaped my throat as she leaned down to me.

"Yeah..." Then she kissed me while pressing herself against me. My hands wandered to her back and down to her divine ass. She kept her lips locked on mine, breathed violently into my mouth, and contracted around me as she fucked me like never before. I was shortly before coming and had to clench my teeth.

"Did you miss me, Tristan?" she whispered. "Did you miss THIS around you?" She contracted again while slightly changing the angle so that I was deep inside her.

"FUCK!" I moaned in torment.

"Did you miss kneading my tits and ass? Or my tongue playing with yours...or when I lean on your chest and shamelessly scream with lust?"

"FUCK, YES!"

Satisfied, she straightened up, ran both hands playfully over her divine body while gazing into my eyes, and placed my hands on her hips.

"No other woman can give you this. You're addicted to me... Ahhh." I tried to gyrate my hips when sweat formed on her tender skin as she closed her eyes and felt me even more intensely. "You only want my body, mainly, my pussy...you just want my...soul." Suddenly, her voice trembled slightly, so I grabbed her tighter and clenched my teeth when she opened her eyes again.

Within a few seconds, the mood tipped from absolute violent to absolute devotion.

"And it's yours. Only with you, do I feel so...*safe.*" Unexpectedly, a tear ran down her cheek and I knew my old Mia was back at last. My girl was alive again. As I held her and reverently observed her transformation, her look grew softer and vulnerable. She was so delicate and yet, even in that moment of collapse, radiated strength. Even though she had already been through so much shit.

Even with me...

And yet she was back again...and gave me EVERYTHING.

Even I had a difficult time keeping tears from gathering in my eyes.

"Only I can get that blood in your veins to boil. Only I can make you shed endless tears... Only I can let you FEEL — the intensity, the force, the depth," she whispered with quivering deep red cherry lips while rocking gently.

"Yes, baby," I whispered. Our movements almost completely died down. We simply enjoyed our deep physical and emotional connection.

Fuck... Now my tears ran freely and hers dripped on my stomach.

"Say it, Tristan. I MUST hear it!" she demanded and desperately grabbed my hands, which held her even more urgently. "PLEASE," she sobbed and gazed at me pleadingly before squeezing her eyes shut in obvious torment. She must have given up hope of ever hearing those words from me again, even though by now, she should know perfectly well what my feelings for her were.

Or not?

Oh, FUCK!

"I love you, Mia baby!" The words left my mouth with fervor. She sobbed and shocked, ripped her eyes open and stared at me as if she could not trust her ears.

I pulled up one corner of my mouth into a weak smile, typical of my girl.

"Now don't start crying again just because an asshole like me fell in love with you a second time," I whispered oh-so-softly and moved my hands up so they could cup her rosy cheeks. Swiftly, she bent down and her cracked lips ravished mine. Her hands held my face as her tongue battled mine. My fingers clawed at her back before I pressed her closer and straightened up. I wanted to be as close as possible to her. As her hands disheveled my hair and her breathing mixed with my moans as I pulled her even closer, she bit my lip.

Abruptly, I pulled her back by the hair and whispered hoarsely near her full lips as she started to move again and rode me as hard as if there would be no tomorrow.

"I love you, Mia baby... I've always loved you. I did not want to admit it, but I am lost without you. Please, stay with me...please..."

"Yes, Tristan," she moaned devotedly. At any moment now, I would come like never before... Then again, I could feel she was ready too — both of us trembled all over.

"I am yours, Tristan Wrangler. Always have been and always will. Now come together with me, baby," she gasped...and contracted around me.

We came violently, like never before...and thus sealed our groans.

# 14. Heavenly Awakening

## *Mia 'Free' Angel*

The air around me was fresh and a bit chilly...even though the body below me was more than warm. In fact, it actually felt rather hot. A sluggish smile played on my face when I detected his smell emanating from his smooth skin. He smelled of SEX. Good old wild sex...

My smile grew more pronounced when I realized he was still in me. Although it was flaccid, we obviously had been united the whole night. My legs had fallen asleep and as I stretched them, I lay on him with my full weight. AHH...it felt wonderful... As I blissfully snuggled my cheek against his chest to listen a bit to his quiet breathing and slow heartbeat, I noticed...

Abruptly, I sat up and in shock, covered my mouth with both hands as I stared blankly at the deep cut that ran down the middle his perfect upper body. My memory was confused...images flashed through my mind...

*My hand holding a flashing knife... my lips around his fucker... my fingers on his body... the cherry of a cigarette ... over his skin... his hands desperately clinging to the sheet...*

Frantic, I looked around the room and squinted as I whispered, "No!" I sobbed and repeated "No!" when I realized what I had done to him. I quickly raised my eyes and almost felt sick when I saw his face. He had a bruise on one cheek and I noticed my right hand was throbbing...

At that moment, images from yesterday mercilessly flooded my mind. Flashes of me threatening and even hurting him, *my* Tristan...

In a panic, I shook my head as the memory gradually returned without sparing me even the slightest detail. Like his expression when I caused him pain. Or his arms, which he had simply tensed and kept motionless on either side of his body. Or his knuckles, which turned white from clenching his fists so hard. Or every pained gasp... every gnash of his teeth...

*The knife that I had used to cut him, to mutilate his flawless skin with, to hurt the body I loved so much... his blood that I had licked...*

OH, GOD! I felt sick!

Panicking, I swung my leg off him when I felt the urge to sob loudly and, most of all, hysterically. Most likely, it would wake him. However, before I could crawl out of bed, his arm whipped forward and wrapped itself firmly around my hip. Pulling me back onto the mattress so that I landed on my back, he held me tight.

"What's going on?" he asked, sounding equally sleepy, amused, and upset. As my tears ran freely, I simply shook my head as I looked at his stubbly cheek that had turned black and blue.

"Are you crying?" He frowned sleepily.

"No," I squealed, wiping away my tears. "My eyes are sweating!"

He threw me a skeptical look, leaned over, and brushed his nose over mine.

"Okay, baby," he said wryly.

"No," I shrieked again. "Nothing is okay! I mistreated you!"

He raised his head and rolled his eyes. "I challenged you."

"Regardless, I shouldn't... I shouldn't have done that!" Gently, he looked at me and brushed the hair out of my face.

"That was your therapy, Mia! It's not like I didn't have a chance to fight back," he said in my defense and leaned his forehead against mine. "I'm glad it helped, so incredibly glad. I honestly was afraid I had lost you again..."

Although his last words promptly gave me a guilty conscience, they also touched me and I covered his face with both hands to caress his beautiful features. Just to show I was here for him again.

"I could not...Tristan...I simply could not find my way out. Everything was black and gray. All I could think about was him. And what he had done to me... All I saw was him... I could not find you..." I whispered.

"I know... which is why I pretended to fuck Mary... I planned to shock you out of your state."

I squeezed my eyes shut. "I'm so sorry, Tristan... I did not mean... I did not mean to hurt you like that... I did not mean to do to you what he did to me..." I could not go on talking as my brain was yet again overwhelmed with the endless loop of horrible images from the last few days. Panting, I resisted it — yet, as usual, in vain.

"Baby, I'm here!" I quickly opened my eyes and looked straight into Tristan's green-brown compassionate depths. He pulled me against his chest and as his fingertips danced over my upper arm, gently continued talking.

"You do not need to apologize. It is what you needed and I made myself available to you. Considering everything I put you through, it was the least I could do." Feeling his deep even breaths and being so close to his warm skin slowly calmed me down. I shook my head and gently touched the encrusted cut on his chest.

"This here...should never have happened...it will leave a scar."

"I know..." He stretched out beside me and spooned me. His lips brushed my neck.

"The scar will be my constant reminder that I can never treat you like I did in the beginning. It will always remind me to stay in the light..." he mumbled next to my skin as his fingertips traced my side. Sighing, I completely relaxed under his tender touch.

This here was what I had been fighting for. This here was MY Tristan. Old or new, it did not matter — he was mine.

"I don't mind you showing your bad side in bed. You know it turns me on."

He laughed roughly. "I know...and you know I'm still going to do that...but unlike in the past, I won't humiliate you." His fingers brushed over my stomach and their tender touch soothed me. It felt so good... Tristan was always there for me... And he had already sacrificed so much for me... He was my shining hero that I could count on... Never again would I be alone or without his protection.

At last.

I closed my eyes and snuggled up closer to him.

For some time, I silently enjoyed the feeling of his caressing fingers. However, something was still bugging me... There was one more thing to clear up in order to make it perfect. Granted, I could feel it with each of his touches, still, I needed verbal confirmation.

"Were you serious about what you said yesterday?" I whispered almost silently and took his big hand in mine. I raised it to my lips and brushed them over every inch of his palm. He was gently kissing my neck and I could feel him smile.

"You know perfectly well I don't joke around with those words, Mia baby." Reassured, I grinned against his hand.

"Will you say it again? Right now, it feels as if I heard it in a dream."

I was convinced he was rolling his eyes, then he pulled me back by the shoulders so I came to rest on my back and we could look at each other. Luckily, he lay on the battered side of his face as he smiled gently at me. He had never seemed more beautiful to me, which said a lot.

"I love you, Mia baby...actually, I have loved you the whole time. Even when I hated you, I always loved you. I simply didn't show it. But, I DID feel that way and always will. At one time, I even tried to tell myself otherwise, but it didn't work... So, I ignored my feelings, which doesn't mean they went away."

"Meaning, you caved?" I asked softly and caressed his temples, high cheekbones, pronounced jaw, and the dimple in his masculine chin. Finally, he shook his head and snorted.

"I'm a selfish bastard, so, eventually, I got it in my head that it would be better for me to show you my feelings for you instead of fighting them." His green-brown eyes literally glowed with passion. "Mia, I want...to spend the rest of my life with you. I want to grow old together with you. I want to live with you and our three children in the boonies, in a log house with a damn vegetable garden right outside the kitchen window. I want all our dreams to come true... We've already waited or rather, wasted way too much time. Basically, it's only about one thing; I want to be able to do this here every night before falling asleep with you in my arms." He raised his hand and mimicked me by running his smooth fingertips oh-so-gently over my eyebrows, cheeks, nose...

"I'm so sorry...baby... I'm so very sorry. I was such an...*asshole*..." he breathed close to my face. His eyes showed deep regret, anyone could tell.

"No, Tristan." I placed a finger over his full lips. "Since I'm not allowed to apologize, the same applies to you! Besides, you don't have to...everything is fine now...and that's the only thing that matters." Smiling, I removed my finger, leaned forward, and replaced it by gently placing my mouth against his.

"Better than good," he hummed against my lips. I laughed cheerfully and reclined again. My belly seemed to be full of butterflies dancing the samba or rumba because suddenly I was immensely happy.

There was so much for us to discuss.

"Now what?" I linked our fingers and rested them between us.

Tristan frowned slightly. "We will move in together..."

"WHAT?" I screamed. Suddenly I grew dizzy, everything seemed to spin. The darn little beasties in my belly were no longer content with merely dancing; they were now doing pirouettes that would make Russian Cossacks proud.

Tristan rolled his eyes. "Baby... I told you I WANT YOU ALL TO MYSELF! So, don't act all shocked now... I've already got everything worked out. Okay...there are a few, how shall I say...*conditions*...that you might not like."

"And those would be?" I asked somewhat grudgingly.

"I refuse to stay in this city. It is not good for you and what is not good for you is not good for me! I want us to have a NORMAL life, actually, quite an ordinary one. I guess there comes a time in every person's life when they should choose to live normally just to finally get some damn peace and quiet. Besides, I want to be certain you're safe. And that is not possible here. Too much has happened in this damn place. You understand that, don't you?" I was gnawing my lower lip.

"But the children's home..." Tormented, I stared at him for my heart felt like it was breaking... "*Robbie*..." He smiled softly, somehow reassuringly. However, he seemed a bit nervous and glanced away.

"We never said we'd have our own..." he whispered and at first I did not understand his meaning...but then...it hit me like lightning. Goose bumps covered my body and my heart started to beat fiercely. My face took on a noticeable radiance.

"YOU WANT TO ADOPT ROBBIE?" burst out of me.

Relieved, Tristan laughed — like he had been worrying about me vetoing his suggestion.

"I've been bugging Sister Carmen and the authorities for months, however, me being a felon poses a problem...

Granted, it is my criminal record and it happened during my youth, now, basically, I'm a successful businessman and quite the civilized citizen. Besides, I support many charitable organizations and lately, even this stupid state... And since you have a degree in social education, are young, financially secure..." I was about to interrupt him as I certainly was not that, but he placed a finger against my mouth and continued... "...and work at the home; so in essence, are already HIS caregiver, we will be shown leniency. We merely have to take care of a few more things...but, by next spring, we could... Whoa, Mia!"

"AAAAAAAAAAAAAAAAHHHHHHHHH," I yelled and flung myself at him. Then I sat on him and kissed him, his whole face...basically everything within reach of my lips. Bruised or not bruised, I simply was too happy. This man always surprised me, amazing!

He not only wanted me, he also wanted ROBBIE! Now, after all, I still would end up with both.

"I love you, Tristan Wrangler. I love your generosity. I love your compassion! Your passion, I even love your hardness because, with me, you are also soft and gooey. I love your fighting spirit, your courage, simply everything about you! I love you so much...everything little bit about you!"

I could not stop sniffling, which didn't seem to bother Tristan. Carefree, he simply laughed and held me tightly while I kissed him. This had to be how it felt in heaven.

Everything I had ever hoped for he made come true.

My fight had been worth it. Once again!

I remained on top of him as my initial shock of joy subsided.

I snuggled my face against his neck and enjoyed his fingers brushing over my skin, causing goose bumps to break out here and there.

"Mia..."

"H'm?" I smiled contentedly.

"That night...the one before that shitty morning, why didn't you tell me the truth?!" OH, GOD! He sounded quite insistent. I squinted and clung tightly to him, not wanting to think about that cruel time.

"I was a coward because I was used to being intimidated by my father and knew what he was capable of. I had to put up with his manipulation for 17 years... You can't simply turn it off. I was really...scared," I whispered against his skin and stroked his hairline.

He remained silent for a while.

"What about afterward? When I was in jail? You could have called me...wrote to me...establish contact SOMEHOW... You obviously had no problem staying away from me — all those years..."

"God, Tristan..." I replied and sighed. "I missed you so much. Every day. Every damn minute and each *second!* And I did write to you, about a thousand letters — honestly, they would make up a whole book — but I never sent one because I knew you hated me. I had hoped you'd start a new life without the turkey and her loony parents. It was my intention not to cause you any more harm... And I was scared — of you. I felt like you never loved me when I saw your initial reaction, it was like we never existed. All I saw in your eyes was mistrust. You *immediately* gave up on us...as did your siblings... I felt so ashamed, so certain...I would never be good enough for you..." I kissed his neck. "Besides, you see what you get for sticking around me...nothing but trouble... My mother... Francesco... Patrick..." I continued in a broken voice.

"Yeah..." Tristan growled and his hands briefly stopped caressing me. "It really took me by surprise. Who knew your FUCKER of an UNCLE was a big scumbag like your father... He won't be invited to family get-togethers!"

"There you have it! All because of m..."

"Oh, give it a rest!" he snapped. "I don't want to hear that shit! Your problems are my problems. I'm certainly capable of handling them. Francesco is already in the process of being dealt with."

"What?" I sat up and looked at him, shocked. He grimly looked back. "How?"

Now he was grinning, but not in a friendly way.

"You've met my masseuse Babette... Well, in her spare time she's a contract killer. Actually, the way we met is quite a crazy story..." He rolled his eyes. "So...since I know where teeny-weenie goes for massages...and it so happens the owner is one of my clients...everything fell neatly into place. Next time he goes, Babette will massage him and accidentally break his neck, but not before she lets her sadistic side have some fun with him... I mean, I would rather do it myself, you have no idea how much, but..." He stopped me again when I tried to voice my protest by placing a finger on my mouth and stared at me with deadly sparkling eyes. "But I *won't do anything* that might *somehow* endanger our future. Besides, I figured you'd have a problem with his blood sticking to my fingers. Babette was quite excited to be given the opportunity to slowly and painfully take someone's life. Especially since I told her what he did to you! Oh, you cannot imagine... Anyway, I also have Leo to consider or he might bury us somewhere in the woods. I have no desire for that to happen." He shrugged.

I stared at him.

Actually, I should have been appalled that he was having my ex-lover killed. But I hadn't been Francesco's first or last victim and I only got away with my life because Leo had wanted me. Otherwise, I'd be dead now...and he would torment more women, women who did not have someone like Tristan to look after them, that I was sure of...

"Okay," I said weakly and rested my face against his shoulder. "Let's never mention it again."

"H'm," Tristan replied as he continued stroking me. My lips brushed lazily over his neck. Despite the previously discussed subject, it was a moment of perfect harmony — the moment I had fought for, yet, at the same time, still felt quite fragile.

In some bizarre way even more so than usual.

"I'm so scared, Tristan," I whispered and snuggled closer to him, even wrapped a leg over his hip.

"Why?" He increased the pressure of his hold, pulled me close, and buried his nose in my hair.

"I'm afraid everything will be ruined again."

"That won't happen as long as you trust me!" Now, he sounded a little annoyed, for which I could not blame him. I raised my face and looked into his deep clear eyes. "From now on, I will always keep you informed."

"Good." His lips brushed gently over mine. He wanted to leave it at that, but his mouth felt just too good to me...and his hard fucker was pressing urgently and longingly against my stomach. So, I lustfully licked my tongue over his lower lip, which made him grin.

"Ah...once again insatiable, Miss Angel?" he teased. I chuckled and laughed loudly as he suddenly swung me around so that he ended up between my legs, which automatically wrapped around him. "It's nice to see this side of yours has not changed a bit." His perfect mouth slowly explored my neck. I smiled, stroked his luscious hair, and wriggled beneath him just how he loved it.

Considering what I went through, I shouldn't enjoy sex all that much...but this here was Tristan and I knew he would NEVER harm a hair on me! Quite the contrary! He loved me...and it was his actual unconditional love that would make me whole again.

"Sleep with me, Tristan Wrangler, and show me how much you love me," I whispered.

"Your wish is my command, as always, Mia baby. I am completely at your disposal." With that, he unexpectedly thrust deep into me and kissed me gently...

He never kissed and loved me like that...

\*\*\*

Once we showered and dressed, we decided to return to reality.

It was as if the entire time, I had looked through the thick bottom of a jam jar. I was shocked to see Christmas decorations already and that it had snowed. It felt so unreal. I had been under the impression it was still autumn!

What else had I missed?

Tristan held my hand as we entered the kitchen.

"Good morning, my dear slaves," he joked as he pulled me into the room. All eyes were on me. They saw Tristan and me holding hands and noticed the shy smile on my face, to which I promptly turned bright red. Timidly, I waved at Lena, Garrett, and Georgi.

"I'm back," was all I managed to say before everyone crowded around me for a hug, which greatly annoyed Tristan.

It was almost too much — but only almost. Tristan made sure to keep a sharp eye on Garrett's and Georgi's fingers so they wouldn't get lost in forbidden zones.

But then there were also remarks about his bruised cheek. Although he remained composed and didn't let on about yesterday evening's incident, I knew on the inside he was furious. Anyway, I was lucky, otherwise, I would have died from embarrassment.

By the time we finally sat and had breakfast together, Mary entered the kitchen and gave me an annoyed look, which I coolly ignored. Everyone made sure to keep the conversations light and voiced their anger at the snow. I, on the other hand, looked with fascination through the glass at the flakes while Tristan eagerly stuffed me with Nutella rolls.

At some point, the others left us alone to do their own things. Lena and Georgi (who lately were smitten with each other!) went shopping, Garrett left for the train, and Mary had an appointment at the spa.

When everyone was gone, I grabbed the phone to call my sweetheart — my first act as a fully functioning human being.

\*\*\*

I spent every free minute with Tristan. When I was asleep in his bed with nightmares, I clung to him and I consulted a therapist about what had happened to me. I could not yet go back to work because every now and then, I thought about Francesco, thoughts that always overwhelmed me and regularly sent me into a lethargic state where I was no longer responsive. Only Tristan was able to pull me out of such flashbacks, which thankfully increasingly lessened.

Still, I talked often with Robbie on the phone and visited him as much as possible, but I was not yet able to return to my job. However, I made progress on a daily basis and before I knew it, it was December 21st.

Satisfied, I sat on Tristan's lap and relished our cozy togetherness after the busy breakfast with everyone. I sat perpendicular to him with my legs dangling and my face snuggled against his shoulder.

He smelled so good... H'm...

"We should leave soon," he announced after glancing at his Rolex.

"Excuse me?" I really didn't want to go anywhere. Especially not *leave soon* because it meant we had to go *outside* and it was cold outside...white...and wet!

"It's Christmas in three days, baby..."

"I haven't bought a single present!" I noticed and stood up in shock. How could I have been so absentminded?

"There's no need for any damn presents. You don't have to measure up to anyone's expectations but yours! Besides, we won't be spending Christmas here anyway!"

HUH? "We won't?" Grinning, he brushed a strand of hair from my face because, for the first time in a long time, I left my hair untied.

"Nope," he answered nonchalantly as he lifted me from his lap.

"Where are we going instead?" Tristan straightened my sweater, which had slipped off my shoulder and gave me an unusually nervous look.

"We're spending Christmas at home with my dad... ALL OF US."

While I was still digesting the new information, he pulled me into my old room where an opened red suitcase was lying on my bed. Okay?! Mister Sex God casually leaned against the closed door and with an annoyed gesture of his hand, indicated I should start packing. I did as told and used the time to needle him with questions.

"Every year, I spend Christmas and New Year's Eve at home with my family."

"On Gran Canaria?" My eyes must have filled with a wistful glow as I pictured the sea...palm trees...WARMTH.

"No..." Tristan shook his head and the palm-vision transformed into a cold winter landscape. "We kept the old house. My father commutes from there to work. Winter time, he usually spends on Gran Canaria, but the whole family spends Christmas and New Year's Eve here." He took a deep breath once he had voiced the last words rather reluctantly.

"The whole family?"

"H'm, um..." Tristan came up from behind and hugged me.

"What about Robbie?" I wanted to, no, I *had to* spend Christmas with him..." God, I didn't even have a present for him..."

"Baby." He tried to interrupt, but my guilty conscience got the better of me. "No, Tristan, that won't work! You have to go without me! I won't leave him alone during the holidays. I cannot do that to him!" I resolutely closed the suitcase.

"Mia!" Tristan caught me by my hips as I backed away from him.

"What?" I snapped, annoyed.

"I'm well aware you would not celebrate Christmas without him." I froze and stopped resisting his hands, which pulled me back to him.

"WHAT?"

"Can you pack your things now? He's waiting for us to pick him up."

Confused, I shook my head. "Sister Carmen..."

"Gave her permission."

"REALLY?" I grew more excited.

"Yes..."

"And the authorities?"

"I don't give a fuck about." Tristan laughed as I attacked him, showering him with happy kisses.

"We're going on a real vacation over the holidays? Together with Robbie?" *Like a family?* Which I dared not say. Tristan rolled his eyes.

"No, Mia, it's a fake vacation. Now hurry up!"

***

Once my state of happiness ebbed, we packed my suitcase and Tristan led me out of the club and back into the real world, where everything was covered in layers of white while dreamy falling snowflakes added increasingly more. Fortunately, Vivi had already laid out the appropriate clothes for winter temperatures. In my mind, I thanked her as I pulled the collar of my thick beige coat closer together.

We laughed, joked, exchanged endless unnecessary kisses, held hands, and enjoyed life as we drove to the children's home to pick up Robbie. I was so excited, I could not sit still in my seat, which greatly amused Tristan. He slowed down in the cleared parking lot and between big piles of snow, called his siblings to check if they were on the road.

As soon as he came to a complete stop, I hopped out of the car, instantly slipping and nearly landing on my butt. I skidded over the iced-over path, on through the small garden gate, and as I arrived at the front door and was about to open it, it flew open.

I saw twinkling blond strands and quickly crouched down in time to catch the little man who flung himself at me screaming, "MIIIIRTIIII!"

He hugged me with a steel grip. I did the same, pressing his small firm body against me and sniffed his fragrant hair...while I wept inside.

"Hello, my little darling," I mumbled and kissed his silky soft cheek. He snuggled his warm face in the crook of my neck and remained silent, simply clung to me as I got up with him.

Sister Carmen joined us outside and smiled warmly at me as she handed Tristan an old scuffed suitcase. I unobtrusively wiped tears from my eyes and gave her wrinkled cheek a peck. She truly was a good woman who devoted her life to children. Still, you simply could not take a child from a home for a vacation over the holidays, but somehow she and Tristan had managed just that. He refused to tell me how.

"Thanks." She caringly patted my arm.

"Robbie and you belong together. And with this beautiful man at your side, Robbie suits you even better. Right?" She poked firm fingers in Tristan's cheek! He was decent enough to blush and I laughed.

"We'll be back in two weeks as discussed," Tristan said to the friendly woman with compassionate eyes and accepted Robbie's passport and a note from the home, simply a matter of safety so we couldn't be accused of kidnapping the child. Then again, he looked so much like Tristan it was unlikely anyone would think he was not *his* child. Seeing them standing next to each other always amazed me.

"Just take care of those two," she replied and stroked Robbie's hair again, who was still clinging to me.

"With my life," Tristan assured her with a slight bow and gallantly kissed the back of her hand. Well, Tristan even managed to get a nun's panties wet for his lips had barely touched her skin when she turned as red as a tomato and the old woman's eyes glazed over. With my free hand, I squeezed her rather sturdy figure while she muttered to Robbie to behave himself.

Then the three of us went to the car — and even though it actually happened, it felt unreal again.

Tristan was stowing the luggage in the trunk when the little one started bombarding him with questions as to why he didn't have snow chains on the tires.

"Because I drive an Audi!" *Like that explains it, Tristan.* However, Robbie apparently seemed satisfied with it.

Tristan had bought a Superman car seat, especially for this occasion, into which I strapped Robbie. He could not stop grinning from ear to ear and excitedly clutched his little yellow Sponge Bob cuddly toy in his hands. But then he spotted Stanley next to him on the back seat and in no time the cuddly toy was replaced by the tiny black dog. Immediately, Robbie's face received a thorough cleaning, whereupon the little boy squealed with joy while trying to push the dog away. It was simply too cute, especially since Stanley usually did not like kids. However, the first time I had taken Stanley to the children's home, those two were love at first sight. No other children were allowed to come near him — but Robbie was different.

Finally, Stanley simply crawled onto Robbie's lap and closed his huge eyes, obviously content despite the constant petting and babbling.

I sat sideways in the passenger seat and handed Robbie something to drink, then took off his shoes before I got comfortable. Under usual driving conditions, the commute would have taken a little more than an hour, but we had to drive slower since the roads were icy and slick.

For once, Tristan was not in a hurry. He maneuvered his battleship easily through the dense city traffic and onto the highway. His hot long fingers were on my thigh, his thumb caressing me in a circular motion as he talked to Robbie. It was incredible to note that even those little, almost incidental touches, made my heart go pitter-patter. I smiled and linked fingers with him. Then I raised them and kissed his knuckles, immediately earning such a beautiful smile that I nearly fainted.

"Why are we driving such a big car? Why are you driving so slowly? Why is it snowing anyway? How cold is snow? Why do you always look at Mirti so funny? Do you want to eat her? Can I have an ice cream? Or a chocolate bar? I'm thirsty! I have to go to the bathroom! Trisan...sing with me... Why not? Mirti always sings with me... Okay ... we'll sing five little ducks... Trisan, sing louder... LOUDER!"

Yes...that was how our trip proceeded.

Tristan and I did not have to talk much since the little chatterbox in the backseat provided plenty of entertainment. And lo and behold, Robbie eventually got Tristan to sing along... Here was my Mister Sex God, interacting with little Robbie and, best of all, seemed to be enjoying himself. It came naturally to him like the boy was already part of his life...

Although he really had to watch his dirty mouth, he never got impatient and kept answering whatever silly questions... It seemed he had spent a lot of time with Robbie for they were familiar and complemented each other like a well-rehearsed team. Almost like father and son.

Three months ago, when Tristan Wrangler and I had met again, I never would have thought that someday he'd sit next to me and sing *The Fox* wholeheartedly.

It did not seem fake or embarrassing, but simply harmless fun as it should always be.

Tristan and I had found our place in life. Together. With Robbie between us.

However, when we encountered a traffic jam, the little Pavarotti eventually grew tired and fell asleep. I played soft music and passed the time tracing the lines on Tristan's hand. It still seemed like a miracle to me that I was allowed to touch him and he actually liked it. This breathtaking man was all mine and nothing would separate us again.

Smiling broadly, I eventually fell asleep. It showed a great amount of trust because, usually, I was unable to sleep when someone else was behind the wheel... However, with Tristan, it was different. I placed my life in his hands without hesitation.

\*\*\*

I awoke as I was lifted out of the car by familiar arms. I opened my eyes to find myself staring at the place where my life had ended so terribly eight years ago.

In front of the Wrangler's house in that small hoity-toity community of mansions.

I was instantly wide-awake when I recognized the area and looked around. Not much had changed; the front gardens still were meticulously maintained. Grinning Mary's and other crap was displayed. The houses outdid each other with Christmas decorations; reindeers, Santa Clauses, and snow made everything look like a fairytale world. The street was empty except for a luxury car parked in a driveway here and there.

Although all that white was blinding, the snowflakes falling from the sky and covering everything made it seem quieter, almost peaceful. I noticed the spot I was presently standing on was where I had collapsed and where Patrick had picked me up.

"Oh, God..." I mumbled and stared at the big yellow house.

"You can say that again." It was then that I realized Tristan had not moved from my side and was staring down at me with a funny look on his face. Suddenly he whispered, "I remember it as if it happened yesterday. I can still see the expression on your face...that look you gave me...when I told you I hated you... Your eyes... I could tell you loved me, but I DID NOT WANT to admit it. It made it easier for me to accept that there would never be an US." His jaw clenched at the memory.

I could also still see that handsome young Tristan who had stolen my heart with one open smile yet also with hate blazing in his beautiful eyes. That repulsive way of keeping his distance from me, which had hurt so much. Without being able to suppress it, a sob escaped, which I tried to muffle with Tristan's jacket.

"Mia!" He sounded impatient.

"It's almost over..." I grumbled into the downy material.

"Whoa, baby... I already forgave you! When will YOU forgive yourself?" he asked somewhat annoyed.

"Never," I muttered honestly and dejectedly. He sighed and I felt his cheek resting against my head.

"Well, we're alike. Call it poetic justice. Because I can never forgive myself for the way I treated my girl these last few months."

"Pffff..." I managed to say before the swift opening of the front door and a multi-layered clothed Vivi rushing towards us caught me off guard. She hugged both of us, screamed for joy in my ear, and annoyed Tristan by ruffling his hair. He ALMOST lost it. But only ALMOST. He barely managed to keep it together.

God...he was SO SEXY when he pulled himself together, he made me all tingly and hot. I wanted him to take out his anger on me...obviously, in bed. However, that was not possible.

Tom joined Vivi and then Phil and Katha came outside. Her belly literally resembled a basketball that Phil obviously admired. Katha was glowing and for the first time in her life, seemed at peace. It was quite an unfamiliar sight and it only enhanced her womanly beauty — as if that was even possible!

Everyone greeted me warmly, which rather confused me. The last time we saw each other, they had been pretty reserved. I was downright shocked when Phil hugged me and whispered in my ear, "Well, finally here?" I knew he didn't mean we were late and sighed in relief as I hugged his big build and whispered, "Yes, finally."

Overly careful, as if handling nitroglycerine, Tristan lifted the sleeping Robbie out of the car while the others took care of the luggage. I loved to watch as he handled the boy like the little being was a priceless fragile egg. Clearly, the kid had Tristan Wrangler wrapped around his finger. But that was no surprise given the little one's eyes.

Startled, he woke up when the cool air hit him, but immediately calmed when I stroked his cheek and whispered that everything was alright.

At first, he was a bit shy with all the new people and hid behind me once Tristan set him down in the hallway. Then, uninvited, Phil put Tristan's old boxing gloves on him and instantly became his best friend. We took our coats off in the entryway and left the suitcases there so we could first have a cup of tea in the kitchen. The others had made the house ship shape. Only David was missing. He probably had to take care of a project on Gran Canaria...

I quickly relaxed in the old environment and in the end, was happy to be here. Just like Robbie. His enthusiasm for whatever mundane things infected all of us.

He already knew and adored Vivi and since Katha shared her cookies with him — everything was A-Okay.

Phil promised Robbie that he'd give him the best training of his life and Tommy pretended to fight with him over Vivi. In their own way, they all were good people. The naturalness and warm-heartedness that welcomed the little boy into the family touched me. Naturally, this was not lost on him and it didn't take but 20 minutes for him to feel at home.

I was so moved that I shed a few tears. Obviously, Tristan noticed who silently stepped behind and hugged me tightly while he rested his chin on my shoulder and the two of us watched the image of harmony and happiness that Robbie so greatly deserved.

All this, Tristan had made possible, first for me and then Robbie.

"Your mother would be so proud of you. Of all of you — you are such an extraordinary family. But especially of you..." I whispered after a while and ran my fingertips over the back of his hand. He sighed deeply and showered my neck with tender kisses. A remark from him was not necessary, feeling his smile on my skin was enough and satisfied, I smiled.

In the evening, the boxed Christmas decorations were brought up from the basement. The women started decorating the house while the men took Robbie to cut a Christmas tree out in the woods. Tristan couldn't refrain from commenting when I frowned. "What were you thinking, baby, we never buy a tree, hell no! This is a fucking tradition! Don't you know that movie with Chevy Chase?"

"Well, just make sure to check the tree for squirrels before bringing it into the house!" I replied with a grin. He promised and became annoyed when he heard Katha ordering him and his shoes to vacate the living room immediately as she reclined on the couch like some grand dame. Then she started bossing Vivi and me around...

*"No, that garland has to be lowered a little, a bit more, yeah, that's it, and now a little more to the left...oh no, that won't do, put it back!"* Kind of like that. I couldn't help wondering how many more cookies the woman could stuff herself with before she burst or ruined, regardless of the pregnancy, her wonderful figure for good. At least she was somewhat tolerable as long as she could satisfy all of her pregnancy cravings. However, if the macadamia nut cookies ran out, she mutated into a fury Phil confided in me. As a result of being let in on a secret, I always peered anxiously at her bowl in order to refill it or get out of the line of fire in time and shove Vivi into it. She was better acquainted with Katha and knew how to handle her mood swings.

By the time the men returned with the tree, Katha was asleep, exhausted from giving instructions. Thus, we were able to take our time decorating the fir while sipping mulled wine, just a bit...or we might have grown rambunctious and woken Katha!

Robbie, who was lifted by Tristan, even put the tree topper on. He was so proud!

Around nine, I put the kid to bed. Considering he was on vacation, staying up that late was an exception.

Meanwhile, he brushed his teeth while yammering nonstop about Trisan promising him we would go sledding tomorrow and that he was looking forward to it and that Trisan had a very big sled. And that Trisan bought him new gloves and that Trisan let him help carry the tree... To be blunt, Robbie was even more smitten with Tristan than I, which said a lot!

As soon as I put him in the guest bedroom and his head touched the pillow, he was gone.

And here I had my reservations about making him stay alone in a guest room. But it was adjacent to Tristan's former bedroom with a connecting door, through which Robbie could come and sleep with us in case he was scared. THEN AGAIN, probably only under heavy protest from the other adult!

But my concerns were unfounded: Robbie was exhausted and was slumbering with a blissful smile. For a few minutes, I looked at his relaxed angelic face, took a deep breath, and went into the adjacent room.

Tristan's old room.

The room in which I had spent the happiest hours of my teenage years. Nowadays, it was pretty empty, but still the same sanctuary with the desk and cupboard still standing in their old places. The furniture was still polished to a high gloss so that the light of the lamp reflected — as did the parquet. That wooden floor on which I had landed unceremoniously the few times he had pushed me out of bed because no one was allowed to know anything about our relationship... I strolled around the room and reminisced. Dreamily, I stared at the desk where I had sat sobbing as I immortalized us in the picture of the clearing. The wardrobe, in which he had made room for my things and first revealed to me HOW MUCH I actually meant to him... Finally, I went to his sanctuary, where he had shown me what happiness was, as well as where he had tickled, kissed, fucked, and loved me.

Sighing, I stroked the golden-colored pillow and silently reminisced while suppressing a few melancholy tears. I recalled the first morning I woke up in this bed, when he had already been deep inside me and robbed me of my mind — when he made it clear that I was and would always be THE BEST. Now, I finally believed him.

"You simply were unspeakably alluring," suddenly, a slightly rough voice came from behind me. I shuddered when I heard the underlying promise.

"How could you possibly know what I'm thinking?" I mumbled, not turning around and continued staring at the bed.

"I'm not...really sure, but..." His imposing body stepped up behind me and every fiber of my being was electrically charged. His hand touched my hip, then moved forward and stroked my stomach while gently pulling me backward. His lips caressed my ear. "Sometimes I think I can read your thoughts." He kissed my neck and began to play gently with my skin. I let my head fall back against his shoulder while I enjoyed our closeness and smiled.

"I think so too..." I hummed. His second hand joined in and both slid up my stomach to gently grab and knead my breasts.

"I also know what you're thinking right now, Miss Angel..." His words and voice alone gave me goose bumps. As usual, my sex god knew what he was doing.

"Oh, yeah?" I lazily rubbed against him and sighed softly as his thumbs caressed my nipples.

"Uh-hm... I think you want to relive old times..." I smiled wider and felt his hand moving...way too slowly to the waistband of my pants. Determined, he went for my snail.

"Definitely..." I mumbled and then moaned softly as his finger slid into me...

# 15. New and Old

*Tristan 'Daddy' Wrangler*

OH FUCK!

I just had déjà vu...

So here I laid – the early morning light illuminating the balcony door – and right next to me was my girl. Like when I was 18 and she, 17 — and as much in love now as back then.

Basically, the only thing that had changed was our age.

She was lying on her back with her face turned to me, her long eyelashes casting shadows on her flawless cheeks. A slight smile graced her full lips.

The dark circles under her eyes revealed her restless nights these past few weeks, albeit last night, for the first time, she did not wake up screaming. I hoped she would eventually move on, yet, at the same time, I feared that might never happen. Having been through such a terrible ordeal that would probably always be with her, she had to learn not to constantly recall it and not let it ruin the rest of her life. She had to drown out negative memories with new positive ones, which were presently succeeding.

It had been a good decision to bring her back here and make her recall the beautiful chapters of our past! To appeal to the young woman she had become in this bed.

I was so relieved I could not resist bending over her and oh-so-tenderly brushing my lips over her lightly reddened, slightly opened mouth. She softly sighed my name and smiled wider. The delicate noise immediately was noticed by my morning boner, which, naturally, twitched in response.

"Fuck..." I knew she was bare-ass naked under the light cover. I knew what was waiting for me there... "Oh, fucking fuck..." Tormented, I rubbed my face with both hands and closed my eyes. However, my mind had definite plans and would not leave me alone until I acted on them. Images of her legs wrapped around my body, her hands in my hair, her lips on mine...

The only thing missing — the taste.

I grinned devilishly as I crawled under the cover to give in to my urges. They say the most important meal of the day is breakfast. In that sense, I guess a bit of pussy would certainly hit the spot.

It was pitch-dark under the cover and she mumbled something as I gently parted her legs at her knees and lay down between on my stomach. HA! I could sleep every night in this spot and use her pussy as a pillow — a warm, wet, scented pillow.

As always, she tasted fantastic as I slid my tongue between her labia. She lolled lazily and moaned oh-so-softly.

Just like years ago when I had woken her up by sticking my fucker in her...

I grinned and lightly blew against the warm flesh.

"Wow..." she murmured while shivering noticeably. I felt her hands sluggishly reaching for and burying themselves in my hair. She was awake, my signal to get going.

"M'm," I hummed directly against her sensitive skin for I knew she loved my voice... Always...especially when I teased her, making her body spasm from ecstasy. Then again, my voice was quite rough and simply sounded sexy. Especially when waking up...

Happily, I slowly circled my tongue around her clit while making sure not to touch it. Her hips instantly twitched and she used my hair to try to guide me to the desired spot. Naturally, I did not give in...

"Oh, God...already, before breakfast!" I stroked her sensitive spot and her hips jerked. Then I slid my hands under her divine buttocks and began kneading them in rhythm to my licks. The time for torturing was over. Now I wanted her to climax as quickly as possible...because I really had the urge to thrust into her... and I planned to do that just prior to her coming. Did I ever mention that I loved to time my first thrust into her exactly at the moment she had her orgasmic explosion?

She ruined my plan when she suddenly tensed and painfully pulled my hair — away from her pussy!

"OUCH!" I complained as she started to stammer.

"Uh...Robbie...sweetie... W...what are you doing here?"

"What's Trisan doing under the covers?" I heard him ask innocently, yet could not refrain from snorting, annoyed. *Well...what do you think I'm doing down here...having breakfast!*

She hit my head as a warning.

"Um... uh... well..." Grinning, I blew a little.

"Um..." She shoved me roughly away as I tried to stop laughing. Let her explain it to the little one. "I lost an earring and Tristan is searching for it..." I rolled my eyes at her weak excuse, knowing the little shit could see right through Mia.

"But Mirti, you're not wearing earrings!" Frustrated, she snorted. I could FEEL her blushing. She was as hot as a stove, so I decided to help her out somewhat because breakfast had flown out the window. I stripped off the ring I always wore on my thumb, yet I did not deny myself the opportunity to kiss her clitoris longingly one last time. As a goodbye...

"Uh, not an earring..." She lightly slapped my cheek.

"She meant to say ring!" I remarked and got up on my knees...presenting the ring to Robbie. I still had shorts on...but not Mia, who shrieked as the covers slid off her and quickly rolled out of my bed and out of sight...right where she had landed eight years ago. I knew she would love to kill me on the spot, which only amused me more.

Robbie immediately dashed toward me in his Superman pajamas and enthusiastically, threw himself on the bed.

"It IS BEAUTIFUL!" He took the ring from my hand and examined the simple clunky silver ring in detail.

"Yeah, it is. My dad gave it to me. My brothers and I have similar ones." *And he will get one when the time is right.* I patted his head and leaned across the bed to face Mia. Seeing her freezing on the floor while giving me a murderous look made me laugh.

"Need a blanket?" I held it out to her, but couldn't refrain from commenting again. "I had no idea you still liked to sleep on the floor and, come to think of it, how's your as...eh, butt?" She quickly grabbed it from my hands and grumbled.

"HA, HA, Mista Wrangler. I'm laughing so HARD!" She wrapped it around herself and ended up looking like a worm. "I'm going to take a shower now! ALONE!" She awkwardly struggled to her feet, almost fell again as she stumbled over her cocoon, and then disappeared into the bathroom with her last bit of dignity.

Dammit, this was not how I imagined the morning proceeding. A full house did not offer many opportunities for togetherness — naked togetherness. I had imagined we'd end up together in the shower, sweaty and naked, and I would soap up her divine body after kissing every inch of her tender skin, followed by her washing my fucker with her mouth. I was quickly ripped from my daydream when Robbie, who was now jumping up and down on the bed, landed on me, almost knocking the air out of me.

"LET'S GO SLEDDING! LET'S GO SLEDDING! LET'S GO SLEDDING!"

Prepared for his next jump, I quickly caught and tossed him into the pillows.

"We are going to go sledding all right!" I tickled his little body until he nearly peed himself from laughing so hard...

Then I held him tightly against me like a little bundle, whereby he tried to wrestle free even though he didn't stand a chance. His hands pushed against my chest. As he accidentally touched the cut, he instantly stopped laughing and glanced up at me in amazement. His green eyes immediately showed concern. I eased up on him and set him on my thigh, where he traced the crusted wound with his index finger.

"Where did you get that?" he asked bluntly.

I gnashed my teeth and smiled at him. "Someone I love hurt me, but I'm strong and can take this person's pain."

"Was it Mirti?" His eyes widened in shock and I hastily denied it.

"No! Mirti would never hurt me... It was somebody else – somehow – and it's not as bad as it looks... It'll heal soon." *And as long as it helps her get over her mental anguish, I'll take on whatever pain.*

"Why do you have such an ugly picture here? What is it?" Thankfully, Robbie let it go at that moment and instead traced the lines of the woman's hand breaking the detailed heart that shattered into chunks. His little smooth fingers tickled my skin. I took a deep breath as I contemplated an apt reply.

"You know... There was a time when I thought my heart was broken in two. I was in a great deal of pain. That was when I got this tattoo." Thoughtfully, I stroked my chest. "But now it's whole again, thanks to Mia." Robbie's compassionate doll eyes widened.

"But you cannot live with a broken heart!" I laughed because, fuck... the little bugger took everything always so literally... Sure... He was six years old... But then, he was also right...

"You're quite right. But now that you and Mirti have entered my life, my heart can heal again. Anyway, let's go get ready!"

***

Once in his room, I rummaged through the suitcase's entire contents to find suitable clothes for him to wear while I was bombarded with questions, even about why my pee-pee-man was standing earlier this morning and if it hurt. I told him straight out that every man had that dilemma...it was just part of waking up. Whereupon he made sure his was not standing at attention at that moment. I rolled my eyes and finally came across a blue sweatshirt hoodie and baggie blue jeans, which most likely would look sharp on him.

Grinning, I dressed him as he continued bombarding me with questions like why Mirti had been as red as a tomato and whether I had tickled her. Nothing got by the little guy — I really had to watch what I told him.

"Mirti was red because she felt hot... That's it. Now let's go brush our teeth."

"I don't want to!" Robbie pouted with his arms crossed in front of his chest. In his hoodie, he looked like a little gangster...the only thing missing were gold chains.

"Don't you want to knock women dead with just your smile?"

"How am I supposed to knock someone dead with a smile?" I laughed.

"Well, not literally... I mean make them like you."

"I'd rather knock them dead, girls are stupid and annoying anyway, but not Mirti," he replied honestly. I grinned.

"You're right, but try it anyway, at least then they won't annoy you. Here, it is easy...simply make sure to slightly pull only one corner of your mouth up...you see...like this..." I demonstrated my patented crooked smile. He tried his best to mimic me and looked like a bad dude! The girls would be eating out of his hands!

"That's it pal and if you want them to do ANYTHING for you...and I mean ANYTHING... like give you their chocolates and more... well then, do this..." I smiled, showing my pearly white teeth and provocatively tilting my head. Robbie watched in RAPT fascination and when he finally imitated me, I almost cracked up laughing.

"Yeah...you're definitely the uber Casanova! Now, you also have to brush one hand through your hair... And all this won't do you any good if you have crappy teeth! Yeah, yellow teeth look shi...uh...bad and will mess it all up!" I ruffled his soft hair and stood up for I had been squatting in front of him the entire time.

"Uber-ca-sa-no-va... What does that mean?"

"THAT, Robbie, are guys who can conquer the world by using only their charm."

\*\*\*

Whether Mia was decent or not...I opened the bathroom door and walked in with the little bugger. She was no longer showering – too bad – but in the process of brushing her teeth in nothing but black underwear... OH, FUCK!

*Acute hot pants alarm!*

My inner voice screamed at my fucker to keep it together for I was in no mood to explain to Robbie why he looked *so funny* again...

Unfortunately, her time alone had not had the desired effect of calming her, no, she actually seemed angrier. When I stepped next to her in front of the big mirror and silently mouthed *WOW*, I saw her roll her eyes and give me the cold shoulder. Robbie squeezed between us and expectantly looked up at us.

"What?" I asked, amused as I squeezed toothpaste onto my toothbrush.

"Well...how am I supposed to make sure I have a great smile WITHOUT A TOOTHBRUSH?" He looked at me as if I was a bit dense. Mia snorted.

"That's just like you to not pack everything..." She stepped around me, careful not to touch or look at my distracting body, and hurried out of the room. Robbie watched her, amazed.

"She is getting you a toothbrush, pumpkin..."

"I can't be eaten," the little guy countered and chuckled.

But...in fact... with his rosy skin, fragrant hair, cute face, and determined character, you wanted to eat him up. He was simply too...cuddly... Fuck, I was mutating into a woman when it concerned him!

"You are sweet and gooey like a pumpkin!" I rolled my eyes, unable to believe the feminine drivel that came out of my mouth. The little guy seemed just as surprised.

"Oh, I get it!" He grinned at me and winked conspiratorially.

Mia returned and behaved normally toward Robbie.

"Here, sweetheart!" She squeezed child's toothpaste onto a new toothbrush and he happily started to brush his teeth. In the meantime, he sneaked looks at me, imitating every one of my moves. I could not stop grinning, which was not lost on my girl. Incidentally, I pierced her with a look through the mirror and q-u-i-t-e accidentally brushed her tit with my knuckles as I reached for the comb.

She gnashed her teeth and shot me a look that could kill. I grinned innocently and raised an eyebrow questioningly, then bent down to spit out toothpaste and rinse my mouth. Robbie immediately copied me if he was my shadow.

I straightened up while Robbie was still leaning over the sink. Seemingly absentminded, I rubbed my abdominal muscles as I leaned with my ass against the large bathroom counter. I noted with satisfaction how Mia's eyes narrowed when she stared at my hand and this time, I did not suppress a grin.

"I'm starving now, especially since I couldn't finish my breakfast earlier..." I patted my stomach exaggeratedly.

"H'm!" was her reply and then she tried to grab the comb from my hand. I kept my grip on it and could not keep the amusement out of my eyes as she glared at me obviously pissed off. She pursed her lips and pulled harder, but I did not let go — instead, I raised a brow and puckered my lips, to which she rolled her eyes, but her blushed cheeks betrayed her...

Slowly, she stepped around Robbie, who was busy gargling with water so she would not have to let go of the comb. She was gripping the plastic item as hard as I was. Of course, I was much stronger and eventually maneuvered her so her breasts pressed against my chest merely by raising the comb straight into the air. She giggled because we looked stupid.

"Kiss me," I whispered and raised my arm a little higher.

"Robbie!" She could no longer remain serious and broke out in laughter. Seeing her blush was too cute.

"Yes, that's his name...now kiss me anyway!" I glanced sideways at the kid, who was busy in a sword fight with his and my toothbrush, imitating the sounds of a lightsaber from Star Wars.

I took it a step further and ran my hand up her spine. Firmly and determinedly, I grabbed her neck before I let up and gently massaged it with my fingertips. I knew she loved it...

My girl had no choice but to snuggle against me and close her eyes while almost purring like a happy kitten. Having successfully turned her brain to mush, I leaned down and gently brushed my lips over hers. Our hands clasping the comb slowly lowered.

She smiled against my lips and I ran my fingers through her hair, feeling the damp abundance...but before I could intensify the wonderful game, Robbie tugged on my pants and brought me back to reality.

"Let's go sledding! Bite Mirti later!"

I grinned at her perfect cherry mouth and gave her a brief chaste kiss. Then I broke away from her, at least when it came to my lips, and glanced down at the little spirited pumpkin.

"How about pancakes first?" And off he ran to the kitchen, faster than an eye could blink.

\*\*\*

Two hours later, we were finally dressed and ready to go. I was a bit disappointed because Mia was bundled up in an insulated black winter jacket and snow pants, so I could not see any of her incredible curves. Then again, her look reflected the same because her x-ray vision didn't work on my pants that hid my butt. I actually saw her pout as I bent over into my car's trunk to take out the sled my brothers and I had raced down hills with when we were kids.

For a fleeting moment, I paused in the process and sighed as I saw myself at the age of five. My mother had always joined us, enjoying lots of fun with her little men. Snowball fights and sledding, we could have done that every day. Cheering and rejoicing. The time was carefree and happy but soon would never be again. The memory abruptly ended the moment Mia placed her hand on one of my ass cheeks and squeezed it firmly. I gasped and grinned from ear to ear, even flexed my ass for her, to which she chuckled as she leaned her forehead against my back.

"LET'S GO SLEDDING! SLEDDING, YIPEE!" Phil and Katha were pulling up in their big bronze-colored Mercedes with Robbie in the rear seat. I set down the sled and straightened up when I heard his singsong voice coming through the open window. I grinned at my girl, who regarded me through shining eyes.

"I love when you lift heavy objects," she whispered to me.

"Is that so?" I closed the trunk and leaned casually against my car for a smoke. "Well, that definitely excludes you."

"Well...I'm sure I'll gain some weight again." She wiggled under my arm so that it ended up around her shoulders. Incidentally, I lit my cigarette and stowed the lighter and pack of smokes back in my jacket pocket before pressing her against me. Fascinated, she watched me take a drag and casually exhale smoke rings.

"God... although smoking is not healthy, you look SO damn sexy, it would be a crime to prohibit you..." she whispered dreamily and I rolled her eyes. In the next moment, she suddenly robbed my mouth of the nice nicotine. "BUT pumpkin is coming and you're a role model!" Without hesitation, she threw my just-lit cigarette into the snow. Before I had a chance to let her have it with a proper curse, chatty pumpkin was already there. Sometimes...she went too far — actually to the point where I felt like exploding, especially when I was not properly satisfied and the object of my desire was moving so seductively before my eyes. It also turned me on when she acted so confident. Fucking crap!

To get the naughty thoughts out of my head and calm down, I left Mia with my family and headed for the cable car ticket booth. I had to go all the way to the station and wait in line. It was beautiful weather, which was why the snow was blinding me since I had forgotten my sunglasses, pissing me off even more. We were not the only ones who had the grandiose idea to take the gondola up to Hochfelln while enjoying the cloudless view.

As I waited in line, quite bored and trying not to let the glances of every female of every damn age bother me, I heard it — damn giggling. Such silly giggling only absolute hoity-toity sluts can manage... To make matters worse, I recognized the voice. Oh, what I would have given if I could have ignored it, but that was absolutely impossible...

"Tristan Wrangler?" I turned around and rolled my eyes.

Damn, there were two sluts — blondie and blonder. No idea what those pussies and their fancy silicone enhanced busts names were, but they definitely belonged to the Eva Eber Fan Club.

"Oh... Hi, uber sluts," I replied casually and shoved my hands into the pockets of my white ski pants.

"OH, GOD, it's really you!" They grabbed each other's hands and almost jumped around for joy like two teenagers confronted by the school jock. As much as it annoyed me, that basically was the case except I was a few years older now and had upgraded to god. Those kindergarten days, in which those two still clearly belonged, were history for me.

"How are you, Tristan? It was terrible what had happened back then... We did not think you'd ever show your face around here again..." blondie mumbled and I could tell by her expression that she was upset with herself for not putting on enough makeup. Unfortunately, no makeup in the world could make up for an ugly soul...

"I come here every season," I said with a shrug and was glad it was my turn to buy totally overpriced tickets.

I was about to disappear after purchasing the tickets when blonder's hand dashed out and grabbed my upper arm. I stopped in disbelief and eyed her excited expression with a raised eyebrow.

"Don't leave yet..." she mumbled, obviously intimidated by my expression for she let go of me. I was about to point out that she had a HUGE ZIT on her nose when I heard an angry trembling voice, "Tristan!"

I was abruptly whipped around and my girl's lips pressed hard against mine.

"Wow... Mia..." I mumbled into her mouth as her nimble tongue brutally raped mine. She made me moan hoarsely as her hands slid down my back and grabbed my ass possessively, just like I usually did. Her behavior downright screamed: MINE!

I grinned against her lips and was only too happy to play along as she demonstrated her rights of ownership once and for all right in the sluts' faces. I felt like laughing but managed to restrain myself. At some point, she ran out of breath. She broke away, gasping, her lips bright red.

"You remember my girl, right?" I slipped an arm around Mia's waist as she wrapped BOTH arms around my stomach and glared combatively at the sluts.

"Uh, yep... yeah... hi... Turk..." blondie's eyes widened when mine narrowed. "Uh, Mia Angel! Right? It has been a long time!" she said.

"Hi," Mia replied sweetly. "How are you?" It was obvious she enjoyed hugging me in front of them knowing they were envious since they had the hots for me. Considering how they had treated her in the past, I could sympathize and buried my nose in her cool hair.

"Doing pretty good...so you two are still..."

"LET'S GO SLEDDING," could be heard from across the hall and I rolled my eyes as the little guy slammed full speed into my leg. Blondie and blonder simply could not close their mouths and Mia could not stop grinning complacently. "When are we going? The track starts over there!" Robbie squeaked and Mia chuckled.

"Right, sweetheart." She ran her hand over Robbie's red knit hat and played with the pompom on top. I noticed both blondes had the same realization. But that usually happened when anyone saw Robbie and me together.

"You have a child?" Their voices sounded even more hollow than usual. Mia tensed a bit as Robbie looked at the two women as if they had lost their minds.

"Robbie, say a proper hello to the ladies!" I acted like a dad would and relied on his good manners, which I was sure Mia had taught him.

Robbie eyed them skeptically with one raised eyebrow. Considering his expression, he could have been my son. But then, he held out his hand and smiled crookedly. "Nice to meet you!"

I almost choked, trying to suppress my laughter as they blushed and hesitantly shook his little hand. The little

Casanova was actually making them feel self-conscious and Mia chuckled loudly, probably because she thought the same thing.

"Like father like son, huh?" she remarked with a grin and grabbed Robbie's hand. "So, have fun..." She winked at them and we left them standing there dumbfounded to join the rest of the Wranglers in the cable car to travel up the fucking mountain. And who had to schlepp the damn sled around all this time? Me, of course!

However, the satisfied look on Mia and Robbie's faces as they stood in the cable car and watched the passing scenery outside the window as we were transported up the white landscape made up for everything.

And by everything, I meant everything.

\*\*\*

At our stop at the halfway station, we left Katharina the Great behind in a café, who was only too happy. The rest of us started to climb the little hill that was suitable for sledding. The spot was only used by beginners and a few other sledders, so there was plenty of room for fun. Mia gave up after walking a bit uphill and collapsed exhausted in the snow, sighing theatrically.

"I'll stay behind. You all go ahead and have fun without me. I'll die if I have to take another step!"

Since Tommy was carrying Robbie, I handed the sled to Phil, grabbed my girl, tossed her over one shoulder, and schlepped her up the mountain while listening to her screams. Leave her behind, nonsense! She must have had a momentary lapse of reason! A little punishment might make her snap out of it, so I slapped her ass.

Once we were on top, we stood there looking a bit stupid as we realized our sled was not big enough for all seven of us. I thought about putting the two boys next to us out of commission and borrowing their sled, but I knew Mia would never tolerate such behavior.

So, I decided Robbie would go with Phil and Vivi first and I used the time to have a smoke. When Mia glanced at me sideways, I acted absolutely innocent.

"Now what? He isn't even around!" I said in my defense and she rolled her eyes.

This time, Robbie had to get up the hill on his own and was bright red by the time he arrived.

I immediately put him back on the sled and after Tommy got on, I gave them a hard push –Tommy the pussy – screamed like a little girl!

Mia and I remained behind alone. I laughed when I saw Robbie making a fuss about having to walk back up again, so Tommy and Phil played rock, paper, scissors to determine who would carry him. Now we were up to 10 runs! I found the whole shit took way too long and looked at the little boy who stood next to us.

"Hey," I said as I squatted in front of him. Mia urgently tugged at my jacket.

"Tristan, leave the boy his sled!" Fuck, how did she know what I was after? The little one looked at me suspiciously, so I smiled as I pulled out a bill.

"Here, five bucks...if you let us use your sled." The little shit was already greedy for he pursed his lips and countered, "Twenty!" he demanded coldly.

*"Twenty bucks?* Damn, that's highway robbery!" I complained as he crossed his arms in front of his chest, a sure sign he would not budge.

"Okay, you greedy sh...mutt..."

"Cool!" The boy grabbed the bill as he handed me the sled rope.

When I turned around and presented my new acquisition, Mia threw me a look that said I was crazy and had totally lost it.

"What?" I asked innocently as I set the sled down in front of her. "I'm a shit that has very little patience and, from the looks of it down there, before they make up their minds, my balls will have frozen. The boy will get his sled back as long he runs after it all the way down the mountain...so, come on...take a seat!" I wanted to help her onto the vehicle, but she stiffened.

"I don't want to!"

"Why not?" She squirmed around a bit while rolling her eyes in a cute way.

"I've never sledded down a mountain!" I stared at her, confused.

"You've never... WHOA! FUCK! WE CAN'T HAVE THAT!" Before she knew what hit her, I had her sitting on the wooden slats right in front of me.

"No, Tristan! I'll end up...steering us into a tree!" She clung to my left and right upper thighs and pressed backward against me. I laughed and moaned in unison because her ass was pushing against...that certain part of me that she loved so much and it her.

"There are no damn trees to worry about...so relax! I'll take over the steering, just put your feet up on the bar!"

"What bar?" she asked skeptically and stiffened even more as I systematically placed her legs the way I wanted them.

"God, Tristan... I told you it was best if I stayed behind," she joked weakly and held on tighter. "HOLD ME!" she ordered, panicking in the next second, and I wrapped my arms around her stomach with an *M'm*.

We must have looked stupid because the boy who was still clutching his hard-earned money in his fingers laughed his greedy little ass off.

"Okay, baby...here we go!" I pushed off and she clenched her jaw.

It was slow going as the slope was not all that steep and I had to push a few more times for us to finally gain A LITTLE momentum.

"This isn't so bad now is it, baby?" I grinned next to her ear and kissed her cheek. Although she chuckled softly, which was a good sign, she did not relax whatsoever as we went down the white slope at a snail's pace. I was about to push off again when I heard someone call my name. Actually, I should have known better as it was unmistakably the voice of some hoity-toity chick. Regardless, something made me look in the general direction and I could not resist a *holy SHIT!* The two blonde sluts, blondie and blonder, stood off to the side with their coats, sweaters, T-SHIRTS, and BRAS pulled up, flashing their bare TITS at me!

I caught myself too late, staring with a gaping mouth at the quite unfamiliar indecent picture for such a family-oriented place where parents were sledding with their kids. By the time I finally closed it, it was too late, my girl had seen everything... Unexpectedly, she pushed with all her strength against my chest so that I ended up flipping backward off the sled and landed in the snow. Just then, the sled gained momentum.

"Fuck, dammit..." I swore as I scrambled to my feet, covered in lots of white crap, just to see Mia panic and start screaming.

"Tristan, I DON'T KNOW HOW TO STEER!" Well, she should have mentioned that earlier!

Anxiously, I watched her racing downhill toward the only ski jump on the damn slope. I knew the only thing left for me to do was pray. The sled squealed as it rushed down the ramp with her and flew a good 6 feet into the air.

To me, it looked like it was in slow motion — quite impressive!

"FUCK!" The sled continued on its way while Mia screamed and crashed butt first into the soft white snow. I was already on my way. If I hadn't been so worried, I would have laughed so hard, tears would have spilled. I hope she was not hurt.

By the time she cumbersomely got to her feet, everyone had rushed to her side, helping to steady her and knocking snow off. I elbowed my family aside and put an arm around her.

"Baby...are you okay? Did you hurt yourself? Do you have a headache? Are you feeling sick? Should I get a doctor?' She brushed a few strands from her face. Her breathing was labored and she gave me a DEADLY glare.

"Don't touch me!" Abruptly, she grabbed Robbie by the hand and started to walk down the hill with him.

"WOW! That was quite a stunt..." My siblings still had moist eyes from laughing so hard. I too chuckled as I replayed the pictures in my mind. It really had been awesome! However, since she was really pissed, I hurried after her and Robbie.

"Mia, wait up!"

She increased her pace.

"Wow, Mia! STOP RIGHT NOW!" She sped up, almost to the point where she was dragging Robbie. Even running, I did not catch up with them until we were at the station. Even then, I was lucky there wasn't a cable car there to take them down without me.

"Damn, woman!" I grabbed her upper arm and she whirled around, flashing her angry eyes. I would have loved to pin her against the wall, kiss, and then fuck her; unfortunately, Robbie was still clutching her hand, who glanced back and forth between us, obviously confused.

"Robbie," I said sternly, but not harshly, for I was NEVER unkind to him. "Plug your ears!" He immediately obeyed as he had to do so a few times prior to today and began humming a song. When I was sure he could not hear us, I pulled her a bit away from him — only for her to cross her arms in front of her chest.

"I couldn't help it...I did not expect it and those tits were right in my *face!"*

"THOSE WEREN'T TITS. THEY WERE UDDERS! Udders you've already had your hands on and who knows what else," she hissed combatively. I was powerless against the laughter that escaped me.

"Seriously?!" She ALMOST smiled but continued glaring at me.

"That's not funny. It hurts when you look at the...the...udders of others... Is it really necessary?"

"I'm a fucking man who reacts to optical stimuli...and when some tits..."

"Udders, Tristan," she promptly interrupted. I rolled my eyes and heard Robbie's voice happily start up, "A little man stands in the woods." "Udders...are presented, it's merely an automatic reflex. It was so unexpected!" She once again narrowed her eyes and I realized she had no intention of *calming down*.

"So you *did* stare at them?" I grabbed my hair with one hand and took a deep breath to keep my own anger in check, which was slowly but surely reaching its boiling point. After all, I was not exactly a peaceful fucker and I did not care for being screamed at when, in my opinion, it was unwarranted.

"Mia Marena," I growled...warningly.

"WHAT?" she immediately snapped.

"Don't be so fucking jealous! You have no reason!"

"Okay," she merely said.

"Okay, what?"

"Okay, I believe you, but I'm still annoyed! There's no law against that!" She gave me one last angry look before she turned her back to me and pouting, waited for the fucking cable car. She continued ignoring me and for a few seconds, I stood there helpless and eventually sighed.

"You're making too big of a deal out of it."

"Pfff..." she merely voiced and continued to ignore me.

I remembered to let Robbie know it was okay to remove his hands from his ears and lit a smoke before joining my siblings, who were approaching. Vivi and Katha joined Mia, who had picked up Robbie to name the surrounding mountains. I watched the, at first glance, seemingly peaceful scene through narrowed eyes when Phil and Tommy patted my shoulders.

"WELL, let's see how tonight goes..."

"What do you mean?" I raised an eyebrow.

"We wanted to check out the club that just opened here..." Tommy rubbed his hands together and grinned with anticipation. Oh, well... I had actually had enough of clubs, once and for all... because I basically wanted peace and quiet.

"You guys go right ahead," I said, bored, and flicked my butt away. Then I buried my hands in my pockets because I had given Mia my gloves and it was cold as fuck.

She gave me a little look as I huffed in annoyance. I nodded at her in a way like your place or mine. Immediately, she rolled her eyes and looked away to continue talking with Katha, Vivi, and Robbie, who was currently glued to Katha's stomach, trying to hear the baby.

"We're supposed to take your girl with us without YOU?" Phil asked sneakily and then tried to breathe life back into his freezing fingers. He too had sacrificed his gloves...

"Why are you taking my girl along?" Tommy and Phil snorted ironically.

"Hello? Do you think Vivi will go clubbing without Mia? She's been on her ass this entire time!"

"Who is going to watch Robbie?" Dammit, I really didn't like the idea and I sure as hell wouldn't let Mia go to a club without me.

"Dad should be home tonight."

"Fucking great!" I mumbled as I ran my fingers through my hair... "I guess we'll go CLUBBING!"

# 16. Jealousy

*Mia 'Provocative' Angel*

I ignored Tristan the entire drive home — not only in the cable car, even in the car I barely looked at him.

To be honest, I had had enough because, recently, I had been tormented with feelings of doubt, which increased with every hour. Because, considering Tristan was already so horny around me, how did he behave with other women? He could have kept that earlier stupid comment to himself. Why did he talk to them anyway?

Yes, he was an insanely desirable man — whereas I, in comparison, was the mousy type. I could enter a room with him and I would be overlooked as all eyes are on him. Whatever women were present usually started to drool and sharpen their fingernails in case he got close enough for them to dig their claws into his flesh. He was well aware he had the charisma of a gigolo and made sure to use it to his advantage to get his kicks from the female sex. He had perfected this game and enjoyed it immensely.

In this regard, he limited it to only one player, me. However, what if he eventually got bored and thought about involving someone else now that we had pretty much cleared whatever hurdles there were? I was sure there were plenty of temptations at his SEX club that he kept secret. How long could he resist all that bare flesh once he was bored with me?

I stared at him from the side and devoured his stunning profile. The prominent eyebrows, straight nose, full pink lips, that expressive chin with its little dimple in the middle... my eyes narrowed. Somewhere, I had heard that men with dimples tended to stray.

The whole sex club thing disturbed me more and more because one thing had become clear to me over the last few days; that was not the way I wanted to continue our life. Not because of Robbie, mainly because of me. Tristan had taught me to think more about myself. Mission completed! I knew over time, I could not handle him being around women who would not be shy about coming onto him. Wife or no wife. Child or no child.

In this regard, I did not trust him.

"I want you to give up the club!" The words escaped before I had finished the thought and shocked, I covered my mouth.

"Excuse me?" Tristan still seemed pissed about my earlier rebellion. The fact that I was the only one who could get away with it slightly helped me rein in my anger.

His nostrils flared slightly when he faced me and, in an absolutely beautiful and equally arrogant way, looked down at me like the uber god himself.

*Time to stand up for yourself, Mia! Come on! What the fuck did I teach you for?* Tristan would have said if he had been in a better mood.

"I have kept my mouth shut long enough, believing I could put up with anything when it regarded you, but I cannot, okay? I'm the only one you're supposed to see naked. Meaning, you have to get rid of the other women!" I nodded twice and stuck my chin out in defiance.

"Say, Mia Marena, are you on something? If so, make sure you refrain from doing so in the future..." That bum!

"Sure, there's a new drug on the market that's called, Tristan Wrangler... Apparently, it kills off all brain cells..." He ignored my sarcastic remark.

"I already told you that I built up that business with my own two hands and I assumed you understood that I couldn't just give it all up for you..."

"Okay! As you wish! Is that better? I don't give a rat's ass what you're doing, okay? And if you fuck all of them, why, yes, naturally, it's your business, so sorry I even opened my mouth..." I had no idea why I had to make a scene now and throw all that at him instead of keeping my mouth shut. To make matters worse, I started to sob...

Abruptly, he hit the brakes since we had arrived, then jumped out of the car and slammed the door so loudly I flinched in my seat. Disappointed, I watched him walk aggressively to the house and quickly wiped the tears out of the corner of my eyes.

God! How did this come about? The last thing I wanted was to quarrel with him.

"Shit, shit, shit!" I pounded my head against the dashboard each time I said it and then straightened up when I felt a headache coming on. As I touched my forehead, I witnessed a very attractive and well-preserved David Wrangler exiting the house and unexpectedly pulling his son into an embrace.

Restraining himself, Tristan did not push him away but patted his father's back while exchanging a few words. David had not changed. His dark hair was slightly longer, he had a three-day beard, and was deeply tanned. Other than that, he radiated the calm and serenity he had always displayed. Together with Tristan, who was grinding his teeth, strolled back to the car and opened my door.

"Well, if it isn't Mia Angel," he greeted cheerfully as I got out.

"Hello, David!" Somewhat self-conscious, I held out my hand, which he grabbed and pulled me close into a tight embrace.

WOW! Tristan looked right through me with his chin held high, but still wordlessly pulled me against him once his father released me. His hands felt cold on my skin and every fiber of my being sensed how angry he was. God...honestly, I was so intimidated right then, I wondered if it would be better if I were not alone with him in a room.

Then, thankfully, the others arrived. Everyone greeted and happily hugged each other and Robbie was fascinated by David's many gorilla stories. They liked each other from the start — which was natural. It was hard not to like David or Robbie for that matter.

While the men, with Tristan in the lead, grabbed a bottle of aged whiskey that was always in stock in the cupboard and poured snifters, Vivi started to pull me upstairs. She was excited that I could fit into her clothes now and pressed a gold dress with a V-neck and black stockings into my hand. I looked at her as if she had gone crazy.

"Tip number five thousand: Show him your goods! At every opportunity!" she remarked.

As I heading to our room to grab suitable underwear, the men came clattering upstairs and made themselves comfortable in Phil's old room. It was right across from Tommy's room, which we were in. However, by now, it was hard to set foot in because clothes and accessories were strewn everywhere.

David and Robbie had fallen asleep on the couch, Phil reported — which was a miracle considering the noise the guys were making.

When I noticed the bottle was already half empty, I glanced at the clock in amazement. Shit! It was only eight in the evening and we had only been home half an hour! Well, we'd see how the evening progressed!

"Come on, one more round!" Tristan persuaded them as I passed the door and I clenched my jaw to keep from commenting.

They left the door open so we could overhear their conversation, which was mainly about cars and business. At nine, when we three girls were in the bathroom putting on our makeup, their topic abruptly changed.

"Do you remember...what's her face...Irina? Who firs' blew you and 'en me?" Tristan slurred, directing the question at Tommy. Vivi and I froze and shocked, stared at each other in the mirror, I with mascara in my hand, she with her rouge brush.

"Did he just say that, really?" I asked quietly.

"YESS!!!!!!!!!" Tommy growled. "Damn...man...remember...that full bush..."

"That's why we insisted...on blow jobs..." I heard the guys clink glasses and watched Vivi literally blow a fuse.

"I'll kill him!" she hissed and aggressively applied the rouge.

"Thankfully, Philip would never think of it." Katha grinned and touched up her perfect lips.

"WAIT," just then, the aforementioned man yelled loud enough for the whole house to hear, to which I could well imagine how he was holding Tristan and Tommy back. "Once, MAN, I had a broad with TITS, SHIT, I COULDN'T GET HER NIPPLES IN MY MOUTH!"

"SON-OF-A-BITCH!"

"NO, REALLY MAN! I've never again seen ones that big...not even when Katharina's are standing at attention!"

"Mia...has the best tits..."

"NOPE, small but nice is much better..."

"And Mia has the tightest pussy!"

"Katharina has the best figure and biggest tits!"

"But Vivi is the most flexible!"

"Now imagine!" Tristan stammered on while we girls thought about the best agonizing way for our men to die. "All THAT in one!"

"Yeah," all three shouted and clinked glasses again. "THAT WOULD BE THE PERFECT WOMAN!" We were finished...and our nerves were stretched thin.

"Tris...do you remember...when I was deflowered — us two with that ditzy cow? To make Katharina jealous...?"

"WHOA! Okay! THAT'S ENOUGH!" I yelled, and the three of us marched next door to find them peacefully assembled while Tommy was in the process of uncorking the second, third, or whatever number bottle. It was hard to say as numerous empty ones lay strewn about and it smelled like a distillery. They looked at us as if we were ghostly apparitions and then even dared to ask, "What's up?" followed by a belch. Naturally, that was Tristan's contribution.

"We can *hear* you!" Katha crossed her arms in front of her chest.

The guys' mouths were gaping. "You can *hear* us?"

"God, you're so dense!" Vivi replied. "How could we not with the way you guys are roaring? You're welcome to stay here and continue your juvenile banter, but we're going PARTYING!" She grabbed Katha's and my hand and pulled us downstairs, where she called a taxi.

In her black jeans and the same-colored see-through top with a sequined top underneath, high boots, a several foot long chain, and smooth red hair, she would be the star of the evening.

Katha, however, given that she was pregnant — wore a pair of jeans and a snug gossamer pink sweater and her hair tied up. Even though by her standards, she was underdressed, she looked stunning — like a supermodel Barbie version.

I was pulling on a few curls I had thanks to Vivi when we heard the taxi pull up. However, we had no chance to get in because the ape-men came running downstairs hollering and ran straight outside to snatch our taxi away from us. Meanwhile, they were laughing their asses off...*idiots!*

Snorting, we waited 20 minutes for the next taxi to arrive, which took us to the club that had recently opened just outside the city. In the distance, we could see colorful spotlights illuminating the establishment as well as a throng of people waiting in line, which must have been much shorter half an hour ago. So now, all partygoers were there, who probably did not have such idiots as friends.

Annoyed, we got out ahead of the large red brick building and walked toward the club.

"Mia..." I heard a loud soothing, yet attractive voice call out. I merely rolled my eyes and turned toward the intrusion.

Tristan and his three brothers were standing off to the side. All had their backs to us and were, um...peeing...in the snow!

"What?" I asked, enraged and my two companions also became aware of their friends.

"Come here, baby...I have something for you," Tristan shouted over his shoulder and I went over, grumbling.

"What is it?" I stopped at a safe distance because Tommy and Phil were still doing their business. And everyone always talked about girls going together to the bathroom!

"Ha-ha," Tristan laughed and nudged Phil with his shoulder. "Now the 'I' is fucked up... Need a hand? I can still piss!"

"What the hell are you guys up too?" Besides me, Katha was completely stunned and disgusted.

"We write...your names...in the snow...but... Tris has the shortest...it's unfair," Tommy replied cheerfully. They were quite crazy! Or quite drunk... Such idiots! Well, that's men for you!

"You guys are so nasty!" Vivi replied, frowning, and that was when I received a tap.

"Mia? Mia Angel?" I turned and looked into two friendly dark brown eyes.

"Martin!" I called out and barely noticed Tristan whipping around. Not thinking anything about it, I wrapped my arms around Martin's neck and hugged him tightly while quietly squealing in his ear. It felt good to see him again and, to be blunt, I was excited.

"For fuck's sake..." Tristan hissed. "I have to piss faster..." he complained to Phil, who had finished and was laughing at him.

"What are you doing here?" Martin and I asked simultaneously as we let go of each other.

"This is my club!"

"I'm here for the holidays," we spoke in unison. The girls were all ears.

"Your club?" they asked and Martin nodded proudly. "Yep! I opened it three months ago... If you don't feel like standing in line, please fol..."

"Forget it!" Tristan shouted, cursing that he still was not done. It was my chance — for he would not let me go.

"Okay!" I grabbed Martin's arm and pulled Vivi along.

"Mia! NO! NO! NO! NO! WOMAN, WAIT UP! FUCK!" I ignored him and we disappeared through a side door into the interior of the club. I had no idea what had gotten into me, but I wanted to push him to the limit! Phil and Tommy were also unsuccessful in stopping their girls. And so, we found ourselves in the VIP lounge, toasting a great girls night out. Paul, Stefan, Jared, and Ludwig were also there and greeted me warmly. It was good to see the boys again as well as being out with Vivi and Katha – who, naturally, drank only non-alcoholic cocktails – and I let loose knowing Robbie and Tristan still belonged to me anyway. It felt great to be out and around friends as — *myself*. Previously, I had never experienced anything like it, so I decided to enjoy the evening fully even though I was already longing for Tristan.

However, considering our recent argument, I guess a nice evening out with my old sweet Tristan was out of the question. Especially since I had run into Martin and greeted him in such an intimate way, not to mention leaving with him. Instead, I would have to put up with the old psycho-lover who was also quite drunk. Therefore, I preferred to stay here, hoping it would not take him long to calm down...and drank...*a lot*... I had no idea a martini was so tasty — in a mixed drink.

An hour or so later, I was not really sure, everything was spinning...and I really had to go to the ladies room or my panties would be wet (for a change, not because of Tristan) and ruin the expensive leather seats. I elbowed my way through the dancers on not so steady legs and ALMOST made it to the restrooms when a hand dashed out and grabbed my wrist. With a jerk, I was spun around and bumped against a chest, *his chest*, for his scent betrayed him. In the next instant, he pulled me into a quieter corner, the chill-out lounge.

"Okay...what are you up to...? Can you tell me where you've been hanging out? I've been looking for you everywhere..." He had me pinned with his arms on either side of me and I stared up at his beautiful face. HELP! He was so sexy...all in black...like Satan...with similar glowing eyes.

"Had ya looked for me, ya would hep found me... Tha's an ol' peasan' sa'ing," I slurred with a heavy tongue.

"Damn, Mia!" His eyes widened. "You're totally shitfaced!" he deduced brilliantly.

"No..."

"Yes!"

"No!"

"Yes!"

"Maybe a little." I measured with forefinger and thumb.

"No, no, not a little... You can't fool me, woman..." he growled. Ahhh...he leaned a little forward...so he could brush my temple with his nose... The tension built, even stronger than usual. It throbbed again between my legs...drunk or not drunk.

"Is not so bad...o?"

"Of course it's...bad...when I'm not with you...but you hanging with some mutt..."

"Martini is nice and no mutt!"

"That's only because he wants to fuck you... Just like me, by the way..." He removed a hand from the wall and stroked my waist. His fingers were much surer than his slightly slurred speech.

"You have not come across likable udders yet?"

He grinned and chuckled softly. "Sure! Yours!" I pushed him away from me, which was easier than usual because he was also somewhat unsteady on his feet.

"I DON'T HAVE UDDERS," I shouted. The people around us stared at me and immediately subjected them to closer scrutiny. Tristan rolled his eyes and swayed as he ran a hand through his hair.

"Who cares what they are called...yours are the BEST...baby... I'm not interested in other udders, tits, or boobs! Get it in your head and give it a rest already!"

"Lick me!" I hissed and quickly slipped past him.

"Tell me when and where and I'll be there...!" He bellowed indignantly, but I had already taken off. I still had not gone to the bathroom and I was so angry, I almost slapped Martin when out of nowhere, he grabbed my upper arm.

"Hey, signiorita...will you honor me with a dance?" I turned around to see Tristan making his way through the throng of partying bodies like a black shark. In my head, I even played the appropriate music, which gave me déjà vu and I slightly panicked.

"Sure!" I answered and pulled Martin onto the dance floor to our right.

I hastily glanced over his shoulder at Tristan as I started to move. Tristan stood off to the side clenching his fists. I winked at him! He cocked his head, crossed his arms, and surveyed his surroundings, looking for a victim!

OH, HE WOULDN'T DARE!

A triumphant smile crossed his face when he noticed a little red-haired chick in a plaid mini skirt with inflated breasts standing off to his left. He pursed his lips, shoved a hand into his pants pocket, and as he ran his right hand through his hair, he started to stroll casually toward her. Suddenly, he no longer appeared drunk and I began to worry! As if she had felt the presence of this sex god standing behind her, she turned and froze as soon as she saw him. Her eyes widened and roamed over his body with fascination before coming to rest on his exquisitely masculine, mischievous, attractive face. She smiled shyly and blushed deeply as he spoke to her. I saw his beautiful lips form words. I saw the auspicious twinkle in his eyes, which he should only have for me, and I clung tighter to Martin's upper arms.

The song changed to *Chica* by *Culcha Candela*.

Martin pulled me closer.

"You know, Mia, I still like you the way I always have." He whirled me around so that I lost sight of the two. My stomach knotted up in anticipation and I felt like dying. What if he disappeared into the bathroom with her? Surely, he would not do that to me, would he?

"Yes, yes, thanks...Martin." With all my strength, I guided us back to a spot from where I could make out Tristan among the many people. Relieved, I noted he had merely pulled the chick onto the dance floor. However, his hands were holding her waist, which invitingly gyrated under his grip, while his eyes were glued to her cleavage. He skillfully moved his hips, his belt buckle reflected the flashing strobe light...and then he moved in a little closer — in fact, there was not even an inch of space between them.

NO! DON'T YOU DARE RUB YOUR FUCKER AGAINST HER! NO, NO, NO!

*He started to rub!* She clung tightly to him and I could see her disgusting lips moan.

AAAAAAAAAAAAAAAAAHHHHHHHHHHHHHHHH! DAMN, DAMN, DAMN!

As I move by an empty cup, I grabbed it and threw it in his direction. Bull's eye! YIPEE! Right smack against the back of his head and I quickly ducked. Tristan flinched...

He casually spun her around so she had her back to him and then gave me a deadly look. I swallowed as his hands provocatively moved up her body.

Inch by inch.

"WHOA!" I cried and in the next moment thought, HE CAN KISS MY ASS!

I took my eyes off him and smiled at Martin.

"Martin...you're so muscular... I like men who keep their bodies in shape, yet are so easy-going!" Confidently, I stroked his upper arms before I linked my fingers behind his neck, then pushed against him and started to move my hips against his. It got hard and he was panting softly.

I could almost feel a pair of green-brown eyes shooting me deadly looks and grinned. Then I licked my upper lip and slowly raised one leg...up Martin's hard thigh and wrapped it around him.

"Oh, God, Mia!" he sighed and pressed against me. Again, I risked a glance over his shoulder as I rubbed against him and immediately squinted when I realized what Tristan was doing. His no longer seemed amused, but rather determined...with his magic hands hovering right over her scantily wrapped balloons for a few seconds.

"NO!" I mouthed, but he grinned coolly. Then he grabbed them! My inner voice screamed hysterically as I pressed even closer against Martin and briefly looked around.

Vivi and Katha were standing off to the side, looking upset and wildly gesticulating while shouting "CUT! STOP! NO! CUT!" Across from them stood Tommy and Phil, both pumping their fists in the air while cheering me on. "GO! GO! GO! GO! GO!"

Meanwhile, I was so angry I could have cried with rage, but I did not... Instead, I let my hands slide down and grabbed Martin's bubble butt in the way I usually did with my divine piece of ass over there.

Tristan froze for a moment in disbelief, then almost aggressively, spun his submissive victim to face him and mesmerized her for a bit with his wry smile as he held her hips before he leaned toward her. He made sure to look me directly in the eyes as he stopped his lips an inch above her collarbone.

I pierced him with a look, even tossed grenades at him, and slashed him with knives, scratched up his much too beautiful face, and cut off his fucker.

Tristan merely grinned when he saw the murderous intent flare in my eyes and continued...

He licked her skin.

With HIS TONGUE!

*That did it*!

He was desecrating MY TONGUE! SO BE IT! Then I would desecrate HIS HANDS and go to the forbidden zone. I smiled at Martin and felt a bit guilty about using him in that way, but I was way too angry to turn back now.

He grinned self-consciously and, regrettably, quite cute as I removed my leg from around his hip. I glanced at Tristan and winked at him...as I was about to touch Martin's manhood...

Tristan pushed the poor woman away and my heart immediately pounded in my chest as he charged toward me like a crazy madman.

Oh, oh — Tristan had gone into fight mode... Perhaps I had taken it a bit too far, but then who knew how much farther he would have taken it!

"You should not have done THAT," he hissed as he towered a head above me and ripped me out of Martin's arm, who was dumbfounded and made no move to interfere.

"I could say the same to you!" I replied and tried to wriggle out of his grasp while I bit my lip. However,

Tristan was relentless — naturally. When he set his mind on something he made sure he got what he wanted.

"You resist *me*, yet *him* you touch?" Tristan glared down at me, looking incredulous with a vein on his temple throbbing dangerously.

"As you can see!" I shouted and Martin was about to intervene when Tristan must have had it. In one fluid motion, he grabbed me by the hips and had me up over his shoulder before I knew what happened. I felt a bit sick as I was too far up in the air and the alcohol did its thing.

"Tristan, put me down!" I beat on his back, but he merely made his way through the crowd while paying no attention to me, the screeching woman on his shoulder. Martin remained behind staring after us, while I indicated to him not to interfere. That I would handle my freaked out psycho-lover on my own...somehow, which I always did anyway.

I twisted around to see where we were going and almost panicked when I saw the sign for the restroom! Just then, I remembered that I still had not gone pee and suddenly, my bladder felt as if it was ready to burst if I did not relieve it soon.

"DON'T YOU DARE! LET ME DOWN! TRISTAN! YOU FUCKER!" I bellowed loudly and tried to grab a corner that we were walking around, but Tristan was stubborn. He slapped my ass and growled, "Shut up!" in reply. My heart pounded harder against my chest. I was so mad... SO MAD at him...and at the same time, SO aroused.

The ladies' restroom was filthy... The floor was littered with toilet paper and two women stared at us in shock as Tristan opened a yellow stall door and slammed it shut behind us. It was rather cramped, which was why he set me down on the toilet seat.

"Let me go right now!" I tried to kick him and nearly fell off the toilet as I lost my balance. He steadied me by my hips.

"Stop it or do you want to end up in the shitter?!" he hissed and glared at me from below. His clenched jaw and still throbbing vein in his temple indicated he was at least as angry as I was. Oh...it was going to be rough! After all, right now, I was facing my psycho-lover. My drunk...stinking drunk psycho-lover... Yet at the same time, he had never been more erotic! What was he up to? His eyes were so dark, so meaningful, then there was the bulge in his jeans, which said it all.

"Don't you dare fuck me now, Tristan Wrangler!" I warned, which was exactly the wrong thing to say.

"Shut up!" Abruptly, he set me on the floor.

"AHH!" I shrieked as he roughly pushed me face-first against the stall wall.

"Tristan! NO!" I squirmed, but he pressed harder against me so that my ass rubbed his crotch favorably. Then he hissed indignantly in my ear and started to fumble impatiently with his pants. God...could I have been any wetter? Could my heart race even faster?

"Stop struggling!" He bit my earlobe.

"YOU are behaving like an ass and you still expect me to put up with something like this? TAKE YOUR HANDS OFF ME, Tristan!" Unconcerned, he slapped my ass.

"Enough with your screaming, woman! It won't do you any good anyway!" I felt indignant when I felt his fingers push my panties aside as his knee spread my legs further apart. I put more energy into my struggle, squirmed more forcefully, and even managed to kick him so hard that I was able to push him away from me, which was only because he was drunk. "Stop it!"

That was the only way I could catch my breath. As I tried to get to the door, he grabbed both my hands and raised them over my head so that my back pressed against the stall wall. Previously, he had just been toying with me...my present absolute helpless state made that clear to me. His eyes were blazing, burning me. His beautiful face spoke of lust and he was panting as wildly as I was.

We stared at each other for a few seconds, dueling with only our eyes.

Then, without warning, he leaned in and kissed me hard. Imperious. His lips were hard, his tongue still supple.

I moaned in his mouth because this was the most exhilarating thing I had ever felt or experienced. Seemingly, to be taken against my will by the man I loved. It was intoxicating and surreal; his relentless body, his domineering touches, his piercing looks — the danger combined with the knowledge that he would never seriously hurt me and always stop if I really did not want it.

His fingers unerringly slid between our bodies to my crotch where they began to massage me.

"AHHH," I moaned into his mouth and bit his lip — so hard I tasted blood.

Panting, he jerked back and glared down at me in disbelief before he raised his hand, which stopped spoiling me to wipe the blood slowly from his lip. Unexpectedly, it dashed forward, grabbed both cheeks, and pressed my mouth together.

"You bit me!" he hissed.

"You were slobbering all over her!" I countered. "Now let me go! I don't want to fuck you now!"

For a moment, he eyed me thoughtfully, probably gauging whether I actually meant it. Then, that diabolical smile spread across his pretty face, which I knew too well and which equally caused my body to tremble, my legs to weaken, and my breath to catch in my throat from all the tension.

"But I *will* fuck you. You're my Mia baby...my slut...my girl..." Suddenly, he swung me around again so that I couldn't see him. I slammed against the stall wall and groaned. "And...I want to fuck the woman I love more than anything fucking else...be deep inside you...all the way... I want to hear your moans, your screams... I want to hear you scream my name repeatedly with your damn seductive cherry lips..." Helpless, I had to accept his fingers pushing my panties aside and exposing my dripping wetness. I felt so vulnerable and it was...phenomenal. "NOW...my dear

Mia Marena... NOW... I'm going to do just that...and nothing can or will ever stop me! Not even...YOU!" Although it was only a game and I was quite drunk, those words registered in my mind and, whether I liked it or not, caused fear.

REAL fear.

As soon as I stiffened, he immediately paused. A tender finger brushed my hair out of my face and his voice no longer sounded psychopathic. "Don't take this shit seriously, Mia baby, okay?"

That was enough to make my heart pound fiercely in my chest again and I was reassured everything was damn fine. "Shut up, Tristan..." The breathless whisper was enough to make him chuckle softly near my temple, which he then kissed tenderly only to grabbed me much rougher.

Promptly, he placed his fucker against my entrance. As I wiggled around and tried to push him away again, I accidentally pushed him inside and groaned.

"It makes me so hot when you resist," he growled in my ear and abruptly grabbed my forearm...twisted it around to my back so that it tugged slightly but did not hurt. I knew he would never seriously hurt me, which was why I enjoyed the whole thing without showing it.

"Me too..." I gasped as I struggled a bit to keep up my part of the game, basically resisting. He laughed harshly and oh-so-gently brushed my sweaty hair over my shoulder.

"You should stop, baby, or you might hurt yourself. You can never win against me anyway, which you don't want anyway." Now he pushed deeper into me, while at the same time, twisting my arm a little bit more, to the point where it hurt so that I had to clamped down with my teeth and surrendered — for the time being. Then I felt him pull out and push his tip a few times in and out of my entrance to rub himself...

"Good girl," he whispered and out of nowhere, thrust forcefully into me all the way while releasing my arm.

"AHHH," I groaned helplessly...and braced myself against the wall...he was in me, deep...as always...oh-so-deep...so wonderfully deep. I threw my head back, pushed my butt against him, and felt him inside me. Every vein... EVERYTHING!

"Fuck...you're killing me...!" He took my hands and with linked fingers, braced our hands against each side of the stall as he slid out and for almost an entire second, lingered like that. His fingers grabbed mine tighter. I felt the strength of each of his movements. Whether it was with his hands, chest, or hips...

"I love you so much, Mia..." He buried his nose next to my throat and kissed my neck... Then he thrust into me again, but so hard, the walls shook.

"GOD, Tristan!" I couldn't help but moan for it was too intense...so powerful...then he started fucking me hard while holding me so tightly that I could not move an inch.

"You. ARE. THE. ONLY. ONE. For. Me. DO. YOU. Feel. This?" He circled his hips as he lightly nibbled my neck and pulled me even closer against him. "All. Others.

Don't. Mean. Shit. To. Me. Mia. Baby." He sounded strained...well, he was, in fact, I felt the same.

"I. Am. Scared. You. Eventually. Get. Tired. Of. Me... Ahhhh!" He hit my G-spot and grinned against my skin. "With. All. That. Competition. Around."

Suddenly, he was out and spun me around. All I saw was glowing dark-green-brown as he cradled my face in both of his hands and looked at me seriously.

"You think so...not really...do you?" He was out of breath, yet still tried to speak. His fucker twitched as it pressed against the thin fabric of my dress at belly height... I too was contracting and dripping...barely able to think, and here he was asking me questions...NOW?

"Can you first finish fucking me?" I asked curtly and raised one leg, wrapping it around his waist as I clung to his forearms, hoping he would grab me when I raised my other leg.

"WAIT!" he exclaimed, hindering my other thigh from wrapping around him. "Do you *really* think I would ever desire any another woman other than you?"

Oh, my, God... What happened to his anger? His aggression? What happened to the raging glow in his eyes? Everything had given way to sweet devotion and I knew my Tristan was back and the psycho-lover, ancient history. However, I could not grieve for him because I adored ALL of Tristan's personalities.

"You have lots to choose from..." My anger had long ago gone up in smoke. My voice trembled suspiciously and tears puddled in my eyes... How could I stand here all horny and discuss such an issue with him? And in a disco club? "I'm not...such a hottie," I added and bit my lower lip when his eyes took on an almost...sad look.

"Baby..." He leaned his forehead against mine and completely overpowered me with that intimate gesture we liked to share. A tear broke free and ran down my cheek. "How many times? YOU are the best... Fuck... I love you and once I love someone, well, dammit, it's forever... There NEVER was another and there NEVER will be another for me!" He kissed me tenderly and I kissed him back as passionately as I could while I clung to him more tightly... To feel his heart and soul because it was good to know that he felt the same way I did. As unsure as I always felt, I required repeated confirmation from him.

"I love...you also...so much..." I mumbled and ran my tongue over his lower lip. He released my thigh and instead, grabbed hold of my knee to wrap my leg around his hip. He kissed me and robbed me of my senses as he lifted me up effortlessly. I felt the hard muscles of his upper arms under my hands and moved them up the sides of his neck to bury my fingers in his disheveled hair. I pulled on it...while I loved him...more than everything...

His fucker entered me as if on its own – our bodies were perfectly tuned to each other, even mental guidance was not necessary – and we both groaned. Tristan broke away from my lips and gazed deeply into my eyes as he slowly and gently thrust in and out of me, and then he said something that made me dizzy.

"I'll give up the club. The decision was made some time ago."

# 17. Our Future

*Tristan 'Sexy' Wrangler*

Finally, it was Christmas Eve Day and, fittingly, everything was white and covered in a fresh thick layer of snow. We spent half the day outside and had fun building snowmen and snowwomen. Naturally, the women had nipples and the men boners... And despite everyone having a bad hangover, our outing ended in an epic snowball fight.

It the afternoon, we all took a nap to catch up on sleep. Robbie lay between us on my holy sanctuary and made himself comfortable. I almost grew jealous when Mia stroked his face as he slept and not mine...but that would have been stupid. Actually, it felt good to see the little pumpkin feeling so at ease between us. He literally emitted an aura of peace, which he so greatly deserved. Then he smacked his lips and hugged me. I thought it a bit weird that he slept at all considering he bugged us all day long because he could not wait for the handing out of the presents. He had bounced around like a Superball while shouting, "Presents, presents, presents!" Who could be angry with him considering it was his first real feast with a family, he more or less could be as silly as he liked.

We men continued dozing as Mia crept out of bed to prepare Christmas dinner.

I had begged for a very special meal – where I would have my lips between her thighs – and she was gracious. This year's Christmas feast would be her legendary paprika chicken. I was damn glad she did not care to abide by some generally accepted crappy tradition for we were not a conventional family by nature.

By the time I woke up still a bit dazed, the whole house smelled of delicious paprika, mulled wine, cinnamon, and chicken. A rather strange scent for Christmas. I let Robbie sleep because it would have been a sin to wake him. I quietly put on my sweatpants and, bare-chested, strolled downstairs. Still sleepy, I rubbed my eyes and, as always, looked around the room for Mia. I found her in the kitchen standing in front of the oven dressed in a black wool dress and red apron.

"What's in the oven?" I unexpectedly embraced her from behind, whereupon she gasped, and I placed two kisses on her neck before sniffing it like the randy mutt that I was so often. She giggled and I too had to grin.

"Stanley," she said with a straight face and I rolled my eyes as cute laughter burst out her. As if she had called him, which, in essence, she had, he came running and jumped happily up my leg. To the ankle. Since I was now quite fond of the little furry slobberer, I squatted, scratched his small velvety belly, and checked out what was baking in the oven.

Trays of cookies... COOKIES! When was the last time I had homemade goodies? The answer came swiftly and it was equally destructive and sad: when my mother had been alive. I recalled bits and pieces about how she used to whirl around the house before Christmas, transforming it into a true wonderland. "I found this handwritten recipe in a cookbook..." Next to me, Mia gnawed her lip as I stared blankly into the oven.

"It was my mom's recipe." Her fingers, which gently and knowingly ran through my hair, were unspeakably comforting. Without a word, I got up and pulled her close, hugging her tightly, and leaned my face against her delicate neck for a few seconds. I liked the smell of freshly baked cookies... Mixed with my girl's scent, it was perfect and distracted me from all negative thoughts, which inevitably rose during this time of the year.

At Christmas, I always became so fucking sentimental.

"Out of the way!" Vivi bumped into us as she whirled by – causing us to separate – and tossed something into the trash before scurrying back into the living room. I watched her and frowned at the picture that presented itself. The living room resembled a beehive it was that busy. Vivi fussed about here and there, adding ornaments and shiny balls so meticulously, I was surprised she did not use a measuring tape... As usual, Katha was reclining on the couch, eating and busily bossing around my dad, Phil, and Tommy, giving those poor pissers quite detailed instructions on how they should set the table. They seemed a bit unsure and appeared rather sweaty as they nearly trampled over each other in their attempts to please Katha.

Wimps!

I had no interest in being roped into that work and decided to, unobtrusively, put some distance between me and the war zone.

"I'm going outside for a smoke," I whispered to Mia, giving her a kiss under the ear and grinned as she knowingly rolled her eyes before I tiptoed out.

FUCK! It was cold! However, ten horses could not drag me back inside to grab a blanket off the couch, thus coming near Katha. I'd rather freeze my fucker off. I had smoked not even half a cigarette when I was already shivering and my nipples were frozen hard. So, I went back inside.

Robbie had now woken from his comatose sleep and was hopping excitedly around the living room. My girl was busy taking the delicious smelling, crumbly things out of the oven. I was sneaking back into the kitchen when Vivi caught and stopped me by holding onto my waistband.

"Not so fast, my friend!" She purposefully and angrily waggled her manicured index finger. I rolled my eyes. "Grab the vacuum cleaner and get to it!"

I was no longer amused when she finished that awful sentence.

"Are you crazy?" I had not cleaned anything since I was twenty-one! When I heard giggling from the kitchen, I yelled, "Baby, that's not funny!"

"Oh, but it is!" she remarked while chuckling. Funnily enough, not five seconds later, Vivi was pushing the vacuum cleaner towards me with her chubby hand.

"Get to it!" I rolled my eyes as I accepted the hellish machine. Once the noisy thing was running, I cursed.

What a dull job! Pushing it forward and backward even though there was no dirt, but me saying so did not matter. Oh, no... Apparently, I was the ass here. Thankfully, wherever I went (with my friend the vacuum cleaner) the noise drowned out whoever spoke and I was spared Tom's and Phil's stupid remarks.

Once I made it to the kitchen, Mia hopped up and sat on the sideboard. She dangled her legs like a little girl and her longing doll eyes grew darker the longer she watched the play of my muscles as I played fucking housekeeper. As I was about to push the damn thing back out of the kitchen, she suddenly grabbed my waistband and pulled me back.

"You're SO SEXY when you vacuum!" Her eyes glowed mischievously. In the next moment, I felt her soft lips on mine and her delicate hands running through my hair.

WOW! If she reacted that way when I performed such a meaningless task as vacuuming, I might do it more often. Grinning, I wrapped an arm around her waist as I deepened the kiss and moved my hand to her ass. She squealed and slapped my bare chest when I squeezed. Much too soon, she pushed me away with reddened cheeks and swollen lips and, taking a deep breath, I resumed vacuuming.

\*\*\*

At some point, everything was actually finished.

Christmas music was playing, the table was abundant with food, and the colorful sparkling tree was lit by candles.

Robbie sat between us and his eyes sparkled with excitement as Dad recited the prayer and thanked my mother for taking care of us and for making this evening possible. We would not be here if it were not for her nor would we be the people we were today. As always, Vivi sobbed like a baby so that Tommy had pulled her close while we all listened to my dad's words.

Overall, the atmosphere was...*peaceful.*

I felt balanced. Happy. As if at last, I had found my place in life. Right here — next to this little boy and wonderful woman, who was in the process of raising her hand to stroke my neck. Before she could touch me, I caught her hand and kissed the palm, pressed her tender skin to my face, and silently thanked my mother for this moment, for the life that would finally come true because I was sure she would have wished it for us — wherever she was now.

We did not *eat*; *we gorged ourselves,* and in between, talked about our plans for the next few days because we had much to do.

Robbie finished eating first and could not wait for us to do the same. He was as restless as could be, squirming around on his chair, and for a moment, I debated taking my extra-sweet-time, but my conscience would not let me take out my sadistic streak on him. Besides, the food was too delicious for it not to be wolfed down, even the smallest crumbs.

When all bellies were stuffed, Mia, Robbie, and the women disappeared upstairs while we retrieved the gifts from the basement and spread them under the big tree. My dad rang the stupid little bell whose tone I had heard as a kid once Santa Claus had visited our house. The loud clatter of Robbie's feet immediately followed as he stormed down the stairs at the speed of light.

He looked like a damn angel in his black pants, gray shirt, and stylish black vest, all of which accentuated the green of his eyes nicely. Although Mia had tamed his wild hair with a comb, his bouncing around made it stand up in all directions. I was quite familiar with the dilemma and it was years ago when I had given up fighting the chaos on my head.

"WOW, SO MANY GIFTS!" On his knees, he skidded to the tree. Grinning broadly, I followed, then sat cross-legged on the floor, and glanced at the staircase when I heard Mia coming down.

If Robbie was an angel, she was a saint. Her long brown hair now fell in shiny curls over her shoulders. I loved running my fingers through her thick silky strands, only to grab them the next moment... I could almost feel them under my tingling fingertips.

The tight dark-green knee-length dress greatly accentuated her curves, which offered the perfect adventure land for my hands and lips. I would kill to see that contented smile that always spread across her beautiful face when she saw Robbie and me together. Such an absolutely breathtaking smile, and, it was only for me... MY SMILE from MY girl. And as for Robbie, I would gladly share with him.

It was like a revelation as she floated down the stairs and I was glad my beautiful swan finally belonged to me.

Absolutely idiotically, I grinned at her. She smiled shyly back and bit her lip because, for some reason, she was as smitten with me as I with her. OH FUCK! She looked innocent and hot at the same time. Only this woman was able to radiate such mixture.

I held out a hand to her, as I could not wait to touch her. She immediately grabbed it and with her back to me, settled on my crossed legs.

"M'm," I hummed against her tender neck, then brushed her hair aside with my nose and kissed the fragrant skin. She embraced my arms that I had wrapped around her stomach and trustingly leaned against me.

The brief sweet moment was...well...let's say...ruined, when Robbie plopped down on Mia's lap with a thud, whom she embraced with her arms, first getting her wind knocked out, followed by a giggle. I found it just as funny and simply wrapped my hands around both of them.

The others finally arrived and searched for places to sit after my dad handled out the mulled wine. Mia sipped from my glass while Katha and Robbie had to make do with punch that was not spiked. After Vivi and Tom joined us and the others sat on another couch, the youngest, in this case, Robbie, was allowed to hand out the presents.

Luckily, Lena had been in charge of the presents, whereby she had oftentimes ignored my suggestions, albeit I was reassured, all would go well. The others seemed to feel likewise. In the last few years, they used to make sour faces once they had unwrapped their presents. To this day, I still have no idea what was so bad about sex toys.

Vivi and Tommy received books. *Always those Grain Eaters* and *Is life Better on a Grain Diet?* Phil was still amused an hour later. Also a grain crusher, a so-called grinder.

Katha was given a family pack of her favorite cookies and a voucher to see a personal fitness trainer so she could get her figure back once she gave birth. Curiously, she seemed to know which was my present to her and glared at me. And here I really had fought to get my way because Mia and Lena had been against it. The *I told you so* look my girl threw me, spoke volumes.

Phil and Tommy were given a men's trip to a dude ranch in the American Wild West, where they would ride horses over the prairie herding cattle. Tommy was as happy as a clam because he really loved the outdoors and – like all of us – a big Bud Spencer and Terence Hill fan. Phil had mixed feelings about the whole affair. He was not keen on being separated for so long from his blond poison.

My dad got a brand new SLR camera from Mia and me, as well as a Moleskine notebook, that way, he could properly photograph and document his monkeys.

Robbie almost peed his pants as he unwrapped the pair of boxing gloves I had promised him. From Dad, he received clothes, how typical, naturally brand name items — and a new super-high-tech bike. From Phil and Katha, a remote-controlled car, Vivi and Tommy gave him wooden blocks, whereupon he asked if the cubes were to start the fire in the fireplace. Then he opened his Christmas card, which held the absolute surprise: two tickets to see a Klitschko fight, obviously from the VIP lounge, and a personal *meet and greet*. From that point on, the little pumpkin could barely sit still. He ran around and hugged everyone before happily clinging to Mia. She tried to hide her tears, but she could not fool me.

Then it was our turn to unwrap the rest of the presents. Among them was a treat yourself vacation to the Maldives, which was why it was now Mia who almost freaked out with joy. She was also given a self-defense course by my brothers so she could defend herself against me. I rolled my eyes and assured the others Mia was in no need of such for she now had no problems grabbing me by the balls. Actually, in the long run, I was more worried about me!

I received the usual aftershave, the camera I wanted, and a VERY ABSTRACT image of Vivi that she had painted herself. To me, all it looked like was splashes of piss-colored yellow. When I eyed it suspiciously from all sides, looking somewhat disgusted, she burst out laughing. Apparently, she read my thoughts for she emphasized she had painted the picture with organic *paint* and nothing else!

Phil and Katha would treat us to dinner in MY restaurant, which I acknowledged with an ironic huff and quickly wrote out a couple of vouchers, each one for a free fuck before I no longer owned the club.

Katha tried to throw herself at me like a woman gone crazy, but thankfully, Phil held her back despite lots of protests. Like he would even redeem it...he was in seventh heaven with his blonde Barbie lookalike since she had first allowed him entrance and he almost died of muscle soreness!

Stanley was not overlooked either. The bone in front of him was longer than he was and decorated with a nice red bow, which he was sniffing skeptically.

Eventually, all but one, my girl, had received their presents.

And when everyone was happy, so was my empty-handed girl as she sat on my lap stroking my forearms — as if *she* would have been overlooked! She merely took pleasure in the joy of others. Robbie and Grandpa David played with the new remote controlled car, trying to chase Stanley with it. Tommy and Vivi snuggled together, engrossed in their books. Phil was stroking Katha's stomach while whispering filth in her ear, whereupon she even stopped eating her cookies occasionally and burst into laughter.

"Baby," I whispered in Mia's ear and ran my nose through her hair.

"H'm?" she replied dreamily.

"Did you think I'd forget my girl?" I grinned and kissed her temple.

"Oh...um, your love is your present to me," she answered deadly serious. I rolled my eyes.

"That's not a damn present, it's the only thing I can return for your mere existence. But I have something else for you...it's quite big...and didn't fit under the tree."

NOW Mia straightened up and faced me.

"You do? What is it!? she asked, completely taken aback.

"Nothing special..." I shrugged and lifted her off my almost asleep legs.

"Nothing special? Well, where is it?" Confused, my girl scanned the living room only to find nothing but a mountain of wrapping paper in which our family was buried.

"Follow me," I answered with a grin and took her hand.

"Where are we going?" Mia asked excitedly.

"To where we belong." I leaned down and gave her a little kiss...then I pulled her to the hall closet.

# 18. Our Dreams or the Happy Ending

## *Mia 'Not Poor' Angel*

"Tristan, where are you taking me?" We drove along a winding bumpy road through the forest. To the left and right of us were dense fir trees whose boughs were laden with snow. It was a miracle that the road had been plowed at all.

Although it had been more than eight years, somehow the forest seemed familiar. Still, I was not sure because the road had not been here back then. But, if I was not mistaken, we were actually heading for the clearing. Perhaps Tristan would give me a clue, which was stupid of me to think because the man loved keeping me in the dark.

As he was doing now. He merely raised a prominent eyebrow and looked arrogantly down at me.

"Why do you think I'm dragging you out here to the middle of the forest? I'm going to tie you up, rape, stab, and bury your body!"

"HA-HA! I might have believed that three months ago, but now, you've done away with your intimidating psycho-killer personality. The tiny fact that you love me makes you harmless, baby." As if confirming my words, I gripped the arm he was using to hold my thigh with and rubbed my cheek against it like a cat. Which I was when I was with him — just to mention it. "I knew we would be happy someday, Tristan. It was simply a matter of time. If there's any justice at all in this universe, then a happy ending was inevitable." His grip on my thigh tightened while the thumb traced little circles.

"Because you're my girl," he said softly and kissed my hair. I sighed pleasantly and leaned against him. Yes, his girl, *h'm*.

"We're going to the clearing right?" I tried again.

"WHAT!" he exclaimed indignantly. "What makes you think that? What clearing do you mean? I don't know of any damn clearing!"

"Don't act all daft!" Still, I could not help but laugh as I punched his shoulder, only to rub my aching hand as I leaned back in my seat to peer out at the snowy nocturnal landscape. "But I LOVE to..."

"I know..." I could only roll my eyes at his typical arrogant response. Thick white flakes were falling from the sky, but since Tristan's car had all-wheel drive, it was no problem getting through the ever-thickening snow.

I thought about us being a family soon. A real... Sure, we had to get some bureaucratic crap out of the way like see a judge, go to the notary, and the youth welfare office. I had to prove I could be a good mother to Robbie. And since I was already vetted by the youth welfare office and all my colleagues had only good things to say about me, it should not be complicated. The normal way to adopt Robbie was to first take him as foster parents and about a half a year later, start the final paperwork.

Tristan had already done some preliminary work. Not just the way he behaved when around the child, but especially in relation to the adoption itself. He had informed himself and talked to the administration of the children's home. He even hired a good adoption lawyer and bribed the judge so everything would be fast-tracked.

"We're going to the clearing!" Whether it was snowy or not...eight years later or not... I recognized the forest, at least where the road went slightly uphill and the undergrowth was less dense. The huge uprooted tree still lay in the same place.

"Did you actually put in a road to here, you tree-killer?"

Tristan only grinned mysteriously as we rounded the last corner and...the dirt road came to an end. We had arrived at our destination.

"WOW! YOU DID NOT DO THAT!" I yelled in the small interior of the car and Tristan winced. Tears immediately came to my eyes and ran down my cheeks.

NOW, he looked at me, uncertain, unbuckled himself, and ran his knuckles over my cheek.

"You don't like it?" he whispered softly, almost anxiously.

I jerked my head around and stared at him, shocked. At his beautiful lovely face, for which I would kill every day to see.

"You question if I like it?" I remarked, sniffling. He used his thumb to wipe away my tears as he continued giving me an uncertain questioning look. I cupped his face, leaned my forehead against his, closed my eyes, and inhaled his indescribable smell.

"That is awesome... You're crazy! You make all my dreams come true one by one. Please don't wake me up! Please don't burst the bubble... Just tell me it's true!" Now he smiled. I did not see it, but I literally felt the tension leaving him.

"You'll realize it's true as soon as you've seen our bedroom." He gave me a quick peck on the lips and got out, came around to open my door and help me out.

Trembling, I grabbed his hand and stood there for a brief moment, soaking it in.

The clearing had been enlarged. The creek still bordered the left side, albeit it was frozen over now... The willow, now covered in snow, was still there — albeit taller and even more impressive looking. Behind it, instead of a small red tent, there was a...oh no...cute, two-story Canadian-style log house.

"Our first home together," I whispered weakly, at which Tristan laughed as he picked me up and carried me through the open waist-high garden gate from which a snow-covered wooden fence ran on either side.

I was sure I had secretly died and gone to heaven.

***

"If you say *my God, Tristan* one more time, I swear I'll shut you up by sticking my fucker in you, baby," my personal god warned as we entered the upstairs master bedroom.

Everything was so overwhelming! I simply could not help myself.

Obviously, the room was not yet furnished and our footsteps echoed loudly. The kitchen, however, was almost completely finished. It had an L-shaped cooking island, a custom painted lilac-colored sub-zero refrigerator, which looked intimidating, buffed to a shiny gloss. Then there was a state-of-the-art oven that appeared to be more like a fancy supercomputer, which was why I was hesitant to touch it. I guess I would have to study the manual first before I could use it. I was too distracted by the splendor around me to give it further thought.

The cooking island separated the kitchen from the living room, which was spacious enough to feature a dining table, a cozy couch corner, fireplace, and much more. Ecstatically,

I already envisioned the place completely furnished and decorated and could not wait to start. The natural light that illuminated the place gave it an unspeakable homey flair all thanks to the wall facing the back yard, which was made entirely out of glass instead of logs, after all, this was Tristan Wrangler's house. It offered a great view of the extravagantly covered terrace and large garden, which formerly had been the clearing and now featured a jungle gym including a slide, a sandpit, and two swings. Here and there, doghouses were placed. The entire area was fenced and could be accessed via two garden gates. Going through one gate brought you to the parking area, which would still receive carports, and the other went downhill into the forest and to the stream, where we had made love eight years ago.

In addition to the living area, which was floored in rich dark parquet, the first floor also had a guest room, a pantry next to the kitchen, and a small bathroom with a luxurious shower. However, the best thing was... I could open the kitchen window and there it was! A raised bed for herbs! Tristan had really thought of everything and forgotten NOTHING.

When I saw it, I screeched, sprang at him, and kissed him... just like I did with the fireplace...the wooden patio complete with stone barbecue, the stairs, because they were made of a beautiful warm cherry wood...the *two* children's rooms, both of which had their own balcony and floor to ceiling windows. All of it was simply dreamlike.

Like the marble bathroom with three sinks, two toilets, a glass-enclosed shower center stage, and the big corner spa bath, which blew my mind!

Of course, one wall was also made entirely of glass so you could lie in the bathtub and look out at the forest. However, when privacy was desired, the glass wall and windows had electric shutters that could be operated and individually adjusted with a push of a button. The same went for the floor heating. Hanging lamps were nonexistent, only built-in ceiling lights and wall lamps provided light, besides a beautiful acrylic glass aurora, whose intensity could be controlled by turning the dial on the wall switch.

The rooms were still unpainted because Tristan thought that I would want a say in the choice of colors.

GOD! Like I CARED! This was OUR DREAM HOME in our DREAM PLACE! It was fucking perfect!

At some point, we arrived at the bedroom, which, of course, the back wall was also made of glass and opened onto a huge balcony. But when I noticed the other walls and even the ceiling were entirely mirrored, I simply could not or did not want to resist one last "Oh my God, Tristan!"

As if he had been waiting for just such a faux pas, he raised an eyebrow and stopped abruptly. He had insisted on carrying me for the first tour of our house and did it as if I weighed nothing. Now he lowered his face to me.

"You had to say it again... I thought you understood my clear warning, Mia Marena!" As he whispered in my ear and ran his nose through my hair, I shuddered. I stared up into the mirror and whispered bravely.

"Well, let me have it!"

"I'm looking forward to it...but, you know it won't be gentle, right?" With one jerk, he had me on my feet and looked smugly down at me with his arms crossed in front of his broad chest.

OH my, Tristan! My belly grew tingly under his intense gaze.

"I would not expect any less considering it's the christening of our bedroom or are you now doing things half-assed, Mista former psycho-lover?" I countered teasingly and bit my lower lip.

Tristan was struggling not to laugh as he reached out to stroke a strand of hair gently behind my ear.

"Then on your knees...*slut*..." he whispered slowly, deliberately, and dark, which was in total contrast to his loving touch. I shivered again...suppressing a grin because, while he named me such, I clearly saw his love for me radiating in his increasingly darkening eyes. I was unable to move, frozen in his gaze.

"Baby, you really need to be quicker following my orders!" Roughly, he grabbed my upper arms and shoved me down on my knees.

For a moment, he stared at me, seemingly completely satisfied.

I watched his back in the mirrored wall opposite me and could not believe this broad-shouldered, strong, sex god actually loved me as he stood in front of me in our house. Our house. I wanted to reach out and pull him close by the hips to free his fucker, but he slapped my fingers away.

"Oh, oh... Miss Angel, did I say you could touch me? You really are a bad girl.. just cannot resist me, huh? Do I have to take appropriate action?"

"Appropriate action?" I repeated, confused.

"Take off your sweater, Mia Marena, THIS INSTANT!" he breathed lazily, but I knew he could act quite differently if I did not obey quickly enough. So, I did as ordered and slipped the dark-green sweater over my head. At that moment, I was so glad we had changed clothes before leaving for our ride over here. My dress would have been more than impractical. Tristan took that one last step that separated us and grabbed the fluffy material from me. One of his hands slid over my neck as he slowly circled me. The footsteps of his heavy boots echoed through the room. Fascinated, I watched in the mirror in front of me as he stopped behind my kneeling figure. He crouched down, made eye contact with the reflection before brushing the hair from my neck, and ran his lips from my shoulder to under my ear, where he kissed me gently. I leaned slightly against him and sighed softly and confidently, to which he smiled at me through the mirror with demonically sparkling eyes.

"Hands behind your back, baby," he whispered in my ear before tracing its contour with his tongue, whose skillful touches made me shiver in my innermost region.

I obeyed and felt the soft fabric of my pullover binding my wrists. As soon as he finished, he grinned diabolically at me in the mirror and slid his long fingers between fabric and skin, to make sure it was not too tight.

I moved my wrists in an attempt to break free and immediately realized I had no chance. I bit my lip hard; Tristan reproachfully clucked his tongue and reached forward to free it... As a thank you, I lightly bit his index finger, licked the tip with my tongue, and noticed with satisfaction how his breathing rapidly increased.

"You're just asking for it, aren't you, baby?" he whispered playfully against my neck and tapped his hand against my cheek.

I gasped softly and felt the wetness pooling between my legs. I had to close my eyes for I was unable to resist the scorching look staring at me through the mirror in front of me. Instead of answering, I turned my head and bit his neck. He gasped and stood up abruptly. He walked around to face me and patiently waited until I opened my eyes again and glared combatively at him.

"So, Mista Wrangler, what will you do now?"

Since I said it with a grin on my face, he replied by raising an eyebrow challengingly and undoing his belt slowly right in front of my nose. I wistfully watched his long talented fingers, wishing they were already in me and teasing me to my first orgasm. But that was not going to happen soon because I knew what Tristan would stuff my mouth with... Anticipation made my heart beat faster for I loved to tame him with my lips.

As soon as the button was free, he teasingly pulled down the zipper. He enjoyed watching my breathing increase and me watching his teasing hands. He took pleasure in increasing the tension to the point where I could barely stand it and I was about to shout at him to finally get a move on.

When his pants opened, his fingers slid in and I saw him grab it and slowly start stroking his hardness. However, he did not take it out and thus denied me any visual fun — the sadist!

"Tristan!" I accusingly whimpered and squeezed my thighs together because the throbbing grew stronger and stronger. Reproachfully, I took my eyes from his jerking hand and looked into his amused yet lustful expression.

"I could come in my pants right here and now without you even having a chance to touch or even look at it. And then we would go home again where I cannot fuck you because of the little rascal." His voice was rough, hoarse, and most of all, nasty! My jaw dropped as he uttered this extreme cruelty, then my eyes narrowed and flashed lethally.

Now, unable to restrain himself, he burst out laughing and threw his head back.

"Oh, baby...you should see your face!"

"Well, at least you're having fun! I thought you wanted to shut me up?" I remarked snappishly.

Faster than I could blink, he made good on his threat and was hard, deep, and throbbing in my mouth. My favorite fucker! I choked and tears welled up in my eyes, but I immediately enclosed it, never wanted to let go of it, and circled its tip with my tongue. He pulled back a little only to slightly push back between my lips.

We both groaned.

"OH, FUCK... Baby... I LOVE YOU!" Tristan gasped... "Look at how horny you look!" Unexpectedly, he grabbed my hair with both hands and turned my head so I could watch us in the mirror.

I grew even wetter when I recognized the beautiful self-confident woman in the white tank top and tight black jeans kneeling helplessly on the ground with her hands bound behind her back, head thrown back with the hard cock of a sex god in her mouth as he dominated her by hold her hair and moved his hips to pleasure himself.

Delighted, I closed my eyes as he took what he needed... At the same time, I noticed how careful he was not to strangle me because Tristan was an indescribably considerate lover. Albeit, at first glance, it might not look that way. I always came first and he was well aware that I loved to submit to him. Kneeling in front of this beautiful man and being completely at his mercy made me feel beautiful and aroused me just as much as him. We connected in a way that was only possible through sex.

However, if he sensed his game growing too much for me, he would switch roles with me in a heartbeat and submit to me. That was what I loved and adored about him. It proved his true greatness and masculinity.

His fingers massaged my scalp and caused one shiver after another to run down my spine. His suave dirty talk made me forget the here-and-now as I sucked with my eyes closed like there was no tomorrow and fully enjoyed it.

"Fuck... Fuck... Fuck... I'm ready to squirt on you and I want you to watch... Open your eyes, baby!" I groaned as I looked up at his dreamy muscular body and met his dark aroused gaze. Seeing his expression was enough to make my snail feel the onset of my climax. He was not even touching me! Merely his words and actions brought on the tingling sensations and caused my imagination to run amok.

"Keep your eyes open! Forget it, baby..." he hissed and started to fuck my mouth more urgently, whereby he clenched his teeth so hard, the sight of his pronounced jaw muscles and pained expression almost made me come.

Forcibly, my eyes darted to the mirror and watching us as I pleasured him while on my knees was better than any porno and gave me another rush of excitement. Helpless, I whimpered and he groaned loudly in response. I was on the verge of the ultimate leap...and here he had not even touched me yet. THAT was Tristan Sexy Wrangler as he lived and breathed.

My desperate sounds around it must have done it for he withdrew from my mouth and left me panting heavily while staring as if hypnotized at the graceful play of his movements. Especially when the white liquid shot out of him staccato-like and shamelessly landed all over my breasts. Oh...yes... He loved to soil me, *mark* me, completely let go. Then again, THAT was typical.

Just before his last squirt, he quickly grabbed my hair and shoved it again between my lips –while gazing deeply into my eyes – and swallowed greedily. I adored his tormented look when he came and completely lost control.

Tristan turned me on so much.

One last time, he rubbed his divine fucker back and forth so every last drop landed in my mouth because he was strictly opposed to wasting sperm. I grinned devilishly before I ran the tip of my tongue over the little opening on his glans, whereupon he flinched and uttered a quiet "Fuck!" from overstimulation. He rolled his eyes, took it from me, and tucked it out of sight, closing his zipper. And here I would have liked to play with it some more.

"YOU ASS!" I cried out, finally making him laugh.

"I just soiled you all over like some degenerate ass and here you are complaining that you cannot clean it up..."

I glared at him, obviously pissed, and did not answer.

"Do you know I love and adore your sick twisted mind?" he continued a little softer. Then he abruptly picked me up by the waist, my hands still bound, and placed me with my back to the wall before dropping to his knees RIGHT BEFORE ME.

"Would you like to bind my hands, Mia baby?" he asked as he slowly opened my jeans and pulled them down my thighs.

I only stared at him with greedy starved eyes and lifted one leg after another so he could free me from my pants. Without being told, I watched the arousing image in the mirror across from us; a dark-clothed sex god on his knees in front of me...running his big hands up my smooth legs and then in one smooth movement, ripped my black thong off me. Seeing the movements of his pronounced muscles as he ripped the piece of clothing from my body was immensely erotic.

"Oh...God," I stammered and threw my head back.

"I love you... Since the first moment," he whispered on my oh-so-sensitive wet flesh and I knew it was not meant for me but my snail. I rolled my eyes even though the same applied vice-versa for she loved him too. With nimble hands, he placed one leg of mine over his shoulder. I could not take my eyes off him as he ran his tongue between my labia with glowing eyes.

Seeing his head between my thighs was the most beautiful picture on earth.

My breathing was fast and my heart pounded wildly in my chest. It was like in the old days when he had playfully chased me, Turkey, across the clearing outside. I might have ended up landing in icy water, but that place symbolized our beginning where now – years later – we again were drawn to this holy refuge. However, now our home stood in this place, where I had been allowed to spend the best days of my life. The first was the last day of our former life some eight years ago.

And the second was the first of our new life.

Some time ago, it had ended in this place.

Now, we would start over again here.

And in the way EVERYTHING had started.

With sex.

Oh, yes, sex with Tristan was breathtaking! Each time was a surprise, each time a little different, but always passionately. No wonder it was the most intense and beautiful way people who loved each other united. There was nothing wrong with that.

"AHHHH," I sighed through the empty room for Tristan's velvety tongue was phenomenal. I accidentally heard his hoarse growling.

"Oh, fuck... you're coming at any moment now..." he stated. "Just one touch with the tip of my tongue and you'll explode... Should I? I love you and you know I would do it for you, Mia baby. Only for you, of course, only you — totally unselfish." He was annoying me since his questions were nothing but a delay tactic because he couldn't help but DRIVE ME CRAZY!

Not once could we have normal sex without some games. Although actually, I loved those games, which I would never admit, not even when threatened with death, I now wished it would be quite banal, along the lines; man licks woman, woman comes. Finished...

I would have slapped him if my hands had been free and if I had enough air in my lungs, I would have screamed at him. But since neither was possible, I gave him one of my deadliest glares. He interpreted it right on the money and grinned mischievously before leaning forward and once, hard and mercilessly, flicked the tip of his aforementioned talented tongue on my yearning spot.

I exploded...screaming...his name... Through blurred vision, I observed in the mirror how sensual it looked when his strong beautiful hands – which I could always rely on – held me when I came and prevented me from collapsing from ecstasy.

We were in our first house where we would spend the rest of our lives.

And it would go on as it always had.

We had been there for each other through a variety of storms and we would continue doing so.

The real fucker and his Mia baby. To fucking eternity.

Amen.

# Epilogue

*Tristan Wrangler*

The summer was ending and some tree leaves were already turning and floating to the ground like swaying drunks.

We were celebrating Robbie's seventh birthday, but as I urgently needed a little time for myself, I went up to the third floor to my photo studio that overlooked the roof.

Over and over again, I read the innocent-looking computer printed lines and still refused to understand their urgent meaning.

It could not be true!

Sighing, I raised my gaze and let it wander over the clearing where my wife and son played catch on the green grass.

In a funny chef's hat, Phil managed the grill. Stanley sat next to his huge feet not moving an inch, slobbering, waiting for something to fall. Katharina, the uber-mom, followed her little shit as it crawled across the patio. Lena had finally admitted she had a fondness for a certain

Russian, Georgi, and was also pregnant and damned happy to have such a huge belly. I had paid them a handsome severance pay and fired them on the spot before Leo could get his greasy hands on them, just as I had done with Mary and Garrett, the latter had gone back to his family, while Mary disappeared from my radar.

Anyway, everything that had had a purpose in my life for so long was now completely unimportant. Even Mia seemed a bit faded next to *her*.

Tommy sat with Vivi and, like an idiot, grinned down at the little dark-haired curly head Vivi was stroking. It was the head that I had first held in my hands and had looked down on its wrinkled red face. She, who, besides Robbie, was Mia's and my pride and joy. Simply pure perfection.

I had everything I ever wanted or needed and so much more... I was...*happy.*

Eline Belle, my little angel with the big chocolate brown eyes, rosy cheeks, and the most beautiful cherry lips I'd ever seen, was the symbol of beauty. Because she resembled my girl – who was actually my wife but to me, always my girl – like they were two of the same. So, one thing was clear; I could not hold her long enough in my arms and lull her to sleep. When her lips turned into a little angelic smile, I knew I had done everything right. For hours, I could watch her lying on Mia's stomach, smacking her lips while eyeing me curiously. Shit, I was able to make funny faces for her, which those like Tristan Wrangler were not supposed to know! I did not speak to her — I *purred.*

Never had my hands been that gentle or my heart that wholesome than when dealing with that precious being.

During Mia's pregnancy, I had driven her mad because, if it had been up to me, she would not have taken a single step unsupervised. Of course, my girl had vehemently refused to be treated like an infant.

This smaller version already acted like typical Mia.

For example, when she gripped my index finger in her iron grip and looked dissatisfied when nothing came out, she sucked on it...never gave up, never shouted, never complained, she just kept going.

My eyes were quite moist again when I returned to the here and now and watched Mia and the little boy chasing her.

Again, I noticed what I was holding in my hands and thinking of the note pushed everything else into the background. The letter in my hand was crumpled because I had clutched it tightly as I made a fist. With some effort, I forced it flat again, then, exhausted, leaned back against the glass before holding it up to read the black letters for the thousandth time.

They blurred in front of eyes and made me relive another memory.

Prior to this letter, I had received one two weeks ago.

*"Tristan Wrangler..."* it started off... Innocent sounding, one would assume...

*"Oh...how I loved to say your name... And I enjoyed the envious looks of other women even more. It was really*

*great to be by your side even if I only imagined that you heard me. I am sorry for never seeing more in you than your looks. I wanted to tell you this first."*

Naturally, I immediately knew who sent the letter regardless that it was in my mailbox one morning without a stamp or return address. Only *one* slut had told me my name sounded so sexy.

What did that slut want from me? Had her mind not registered my last words to her?

*"I'm sure you're wondering why I'm bothering you after all these years."* No shit! *"After all, you said you never wanted to see me again. You told me you knew from personal experience that I'd eventually have to answer for my actions, at which time, it would already be too late. You were the meanest person ever. But all that has become clear to me now, which is why I would pay you back in kind for your honesty even if it made me hate you for so many years. So now it's time for me to be truthful for once. It's my last chance to ease my conscience.*

*I have a brain tumor that has already metastasized. I am writing you these lines from my hospital bed. I don't want your pity, I simply want to make amends, and you're the first on a long list of people I am asking this of...*

*There is something you need to know."*

When I read those words, deep within me, I knew what would come, which was bad because when I started the letter I was sitting with Robbie in the living room at our round dining table. He sat across from me and was busy drawing. Compared to when I met him, he already acted quite grown up.

His lower lip was pushed out and to the side, his increasingly darkening hair hung in his eyes, and he repeatedly tried to blow it away before groaning in annoyance and turned his attention back to the drawing. As if spellbound, I watched him tightening his grip on the pencil as he became more and more agitated because his hair would not cooperate. Suddenly, he raised his head and our eyes met. Green looking at green-brown.

"What is it?"

"Nothing!" Okay! It did not require a response and suddenly I was eager to read the next lines.

*"You do not know what it meant to me when I learned from my sister (Mary) that out of everyone, you had adopted Him."*

And so I had confirmation and everything began to spin wildly as I tried my best to decipher the words that followed even though my vision blurred and my heart pounded in my ears like a jackhammer. *"You are one of the few people in this world who still has a good heart even if you are constantly trying to persuade us otherwise. That too became clear to me later on.*

*Your heart probably always knew...it found him among all the children in the world, showed you the right path...to Robert, who is your son."*

The last letters were completely distorted. However, it was not so much due to my teary eyes but because she had cried when writing the note and smudged the letters. I read the lines over and over again only for my mind to become even more confused.

"Dad?" The child – *my child* – who was unaware of anything and busy painting a picture of our happy family, asked me as if he had done so forever, "Why are you crying?" Fittingly, about two months ago, out of nowhere, he had started to call Mirti and me, Mom and Dad. Even back then, I was so overwhelmed, my heart tightened in my chest, but now I managed to suppress the sob rising in my throat, closed my eyes, and shook my head. I was utterly overwhelmed.

"I'm not crying because I'm sad...but because I'm happy, come here, pumpkin!" I finally mumbled once I had composed myself and smiled down at his open beautiful face.

He did not have to be told twice. As was his nature, he hopped with full speed onto my lap. I gave him a little peck on the temple as he snuggled in my arms as if it was the most natural thing to do. He smiled at me and patted my cheek almost disparagingly, albeit sympathetically, before pulling his drawing material closer to finish his work of art. In the meantime, he was babbling and I unobtrusively inhaled his scent.

Maybe on a subconscious level, I always knew.

And most likely Mia and her patented Tristan radar had also immediately sensed that he was part of me. That was why she immediately felt connected to the little shit and had no other choice than to succumb to him since that was how she felt about his father.

Of course, a DNA test was required despite my intuition for I wanted to be absolutely certain — once and for all.

*** 

Now I held the results in my hand.

*A paternity match — 99.9998%.*

The paternity was proven... it said so in black and white.

Of course, at the exact moment I came to terms with it and took a deep breath, Mia glanced up at me. Our eyes met and no words were needed for she understood immediately — as always. Her footsteps faltered and she sobbed wide-eyed as her hands darted up to her mouth. Her gaze flashed to Robbie, who was running toward her. He took his chance and grabbed her legs with a loud, "Got you, Mama!" She went down on her knees in front of him and did what I had been thinking about all along: She laughingly showering him with kisses and his boisterous giggles drifted up to me and lifted the corners of my mouth.

A humongous weight fell from my heart.

She would ALWAYS take my side. She was my girl and would ALWAYS remain so!

Still, on the inside, I almost died when I had to confess to her how I had a hand in Robbie's creation...

***

We had put Eli to bed as soon as she had her extensive titty snack and then gone downstairs into the illuminated living room.

Tired, I merely sat there waiting for her to question me about the letter I had received. It had been addressed to *TRISTAN WRANGLER* and she was aware I had read it by now. Not to mention my grumpy behavior and determined stare naturally told her that something was absolutely wrong — because now I looked at Robbie through different eyes.

Naturally, as long as the kids were awake, she restrained herself, but as soon as night fell and Eli was asleep, she no longer tiptoed around the issue.

"What's wrong with you, baby?" She forcefully pulled me to the beige couch and pushed me down into the pillows. I smiled weakly even though I felt my throat closing.

"Aren't we pushy, huh?" I joked playfully, but my smile faltered as soon as she straddled my lap with her legs wide apart and pressed a soft kiss against my lips.

"No matter what it is, just tell me! What did it say?" Her warm brown eyes radiated genuine affection and boundless love. That was my girl, my wife, my everything. She was the most emphatic person I knew. She would have understanding for me. She would not push me away. Not after everything she had endured to get to this point. Each of us had learned not to let the past destroy our future! Painful!

I raised my hands and cupped her flawless face while stroking my thumbs over her cheekbones. I wanted to remain silent for a while longer... Just for...

"Tristan! Tell me!" she urged, for patience was certainly not one of Mia's virtues, especially when it regarded me. Like a coward, I closed my eyes to escape her curious stare and was amazed that she did not pry them back open.

I took one more deep breath, squeezed my fucking ass cheeks together, and goddammit, told her:

"It happened shortly after I was released from prison..." I opened one eye just enough to peek at her expression. She looked open, innocent, beautiful, and adorable, she did not deserve this! Fucking shit, she had no idea what I was hinting at! Fuck! I quickly closed my eye again and continued. "I partied quite a bit at that time, trying to forget, to repress. I wanted to feel nothing. I did not want to...EXIST." I opened my eyes again to see if she at least had an idea where my confession was going. But confused, she simply frowned and continued to look at me naively and questioningly. DAMN!

"Through her, I met Mary..." Her expression instantly darkened and I quickly continued. "She was her sister, which I found out in hindsight. Her name was Victoria and she was, to put it bluntly, absolutely obsessed with me. Every night, she and some junkies I met through Pete sat in my tiny room and got on my nerves. Oftentimes, she was too fucked up to make it home, so that was when she crashed at my place. I may be an ass but I don't put a half-dead woman out on the street, right...baby?" The fingers that fondled my neck turned to ice. As did her expression. It seemed she finally understood why I was confessing and inside, braced herself for what was to come.

I continued forcing myself to look at her as I stroked and held her tight.

"I must have downed a crate of beer together with a bottle of whiskey, smoked 20 joints along with 10 lines of coke... I was not squeamish when it came to drugs as you may recall." Her now wide-eyed aggressive stare said not to dare make up some damn excuse and come out with the truth. So, I quickly continued my report. "Anyway...like every night, I was sitting like some little pussy, looking at the pictures of us in the clearing. Maybe I even cried, I don't recall, in any case, I was the lowest most disgusting broken wreck you can imagine. Suddenly a hand stroked my chest. I imagined it was yours. I swear, Mia, I was actually hallucinating, and you were so damn hot and beautiful, and I was missing you so fucking much. I needed you like I needed air to breathe; all I wanted was you...and then it all happened so fast. I don't quite recall how it came about! But all of a sudden, the slut was on my lap...my pants were undone and I stuck him in her..."

Mia sharply inhaled and pulled back with a jerk.

"You fucked her...?" she asked breathlessly. Damn tears came to her incredulous eyes.

"Yes," I admitted firmly not avoiding her scorching look. What else could I say? Actually, the slut had taken advantage of my fucked up state and raped me. The next morning, I thought it had been a bad trip! To me, that shit never happened! But what difference did it make what I said, fact was, I *had* done it. End of discussion. Fuck!

"You told me you hadn't had any sex!?" And therein lay the problem, not to mention, her voice had that slightly shrill sound again, which never meant anything good.

And here I hadn't even come to the good part yet. She wanted to move away from me, but I was selfish and continued holding her tight. If I released her in her current state, she'd run away — go hiking through the woods or something. That was her way of torturing me whenever we argued. And I would sit here on the couch, worrying myself to death, over and over again.

"Baby, please...please, listen to me..." I pressed my face against her fragrant neck and felt her pulse throbbing against my nose. "I did not want to fuck her... I did not want her on me...and do those things with her that are only ours..."

"Why are you telling me this? STOP IT!" she screamed, losing it, and forcefully tried to get away from me. I held her even tighter.

"I know...I know, Mia baby... but you MUST know! Having had sex with her, I never wanted to see her again. So, since I rejected her, she conceived a treacherous plan for revenge to destroy me. When that did not work, she even tried to kill herself in front of my eyes, so I had her committed. I never heard from her again and was glad to have learned another lesson. I believed that fucked-up part of my life would have no consequences for me...but it HAS some!" She immediately stopped struggling and instead, grabbed my face to examine it closely from all angles.

"What do you mean? Did she pass a disease to you? What did she do?" I shook my head in resignation when I saw her innocent eyes flash so much concern for the asshole that I was.

"No, don't worry about me." I gently brushed her hair from her face. "Everything is fine with me."

"So what consequences are you referring to, Tristan? Spill it!"

"She got pregnant by me!" I dropped the bomb and kept on yapping like I had not noticed her suddenly paling. "And this morning, when you went for your checkup, I read the anonymous letter — from her! Karma has fucked her, like it does everyone else, because she's dying...and she wanted to tell me something important before that happened: Robbie is her son...and it is possible I'm his father."

At first, she did not react at all, merely stared at me with her mouth gaping. Tears made their way down our cheeks and she shivered. Disbelief and shock were written in her face.

"That cannot be!" she eventually whispered breathlessly. But the moment she uttered the words, her eyes clearly widened again. And she looked at me like she was seeing me for the first time in my life. "It *can* be! Of course!" she whispered again before she ogled me for a while and I felt like I was charred, impaled, lynched, killed, and murdered. Suddenly, she wiped her tears away and straightened up.

"Please, let me go?" she asked somewhat composed. I eyed her suspiciously and did not move an inch.

"Will you run away?" I inquired straight out, throatily. Once again, she seemed quite amazed.

"No!" she replied as if I was completely stupid. "I need fresh air," she added and I forced my taut arms open so she could leave. No matter how incredibly difficult it was for me, I had no choice when she needed distance.

So, I let her go, rested my head in my hands, and listened to her push open the patio door and step outside.

"Fuck, fuck, fuck," I whispered to myself...

"What's going on?" I suddenly heard the sleepy voice from my little crapper and looked up. He stood on the upper landing with his Spongebob firmly clutched to his chest. He was wearing his old Superman pajamas, which he simply did not want to part with, so the pant legs only reached his knees and the sleeves only to his elbows, which did not bother him.

"Sometimes, I'm an idiot, that's all." I forced myself to grin as I gestured for him to come to me.

Willingly and barefoot, he padded down the stairs and snuggled up next to me on the couch. Like Mia, he lifted my arm and wrapped it around his little shoulder. He was nicely nestled in and I could not help but play with his soft strands — not much longer now, and he might think he was too old for this. It was effeminate, but I had to take advantage of it while he was still so affectionate. I kissed his hair as I stared at the black screen of the television.

"Why does Eli always slobber so much?" he asked after some time when I thought he had long since fallen asleep, making me laugh... Fuck, I had asked myself the same thing when I had changed her shirt for the third time one day.

"Because she's little and needs to learn how to control her body."

"Is that why she always pees when you change her diapers?" OH, MAN! The little boy always managed to make me laugh.

"Yes and I'm sure Mama does it better..."

"What can I do better?" I heard her soft voice asking from behind me. I turned slightly and saw a red-eyed Mia looking down at me. OH, FUCK! I had sworn to always make her happy and now, here I was doing the opposite — again!

"Everything," I answered honestly, visually begging her not to move farther away from me. I needed her right now... URGENTLY SO! I ALWAYS needed her! She was my slut. She was my girl. My Mia baby... Everything I ever wanted from a woman united in one goddess.

My girl sighed softly and smiled weakly. Seemingly calm, she relented, completely unselfish and strong — raised her hand and stroked a few strands from my forehead. I smiled too when she leaned down to me and pressed a tender longing kiss to my lips, which I returned with all my heart.

"UGGGHHH! You're always SMOOCHING." Robbie made us laugh again and at that moment, I once again realized that Mia would stand by me *no matter* what.

With her by my side, I truly was the damn luckiest shit in the world.

Without hesitation, I pulled her over the back of the couch so that she landed with her head in my lap and laughed. Mia put an arm around Robbie and tenderly caressed my cheek with her other hand. As she gently traced my face with her fingertips, she smiled dreamily and Turkey-like while I scratched her neck and reverently took in her unruly beauty. I still could not believe she was FINALLY my wife and the mother of my children.

We had come a long way, but now we had made it — reached the goal line at last.

Rage had turned to joy.

Desperation to happiness.

Greed to satisfaction.

Longing to desire.

Domination to humility.

And hatred to love.

And so, they actually loved each other for the rest of their lives and if they have not died yet, they still fuck to this day.

# The fucking end

# ACKNOWLEDGMENT

Four years!

That is how long I have been accompanying Mia and Tristan now and this END especially hurts. I know you feel the same for you have grown as fond of them as I have.

For me, it is an extremely dramatic END...

THEREFORE, CAUTION! I MAY BECOME MELODRAMATIC, CRASS, AND CORNY, BESIDES, IT COULD BECOME EMBARASSING, BUT I"LL JUMP OVER OF MY SHADOW AND SAY IT ANYWAY BECAUSE IT IS DEAR TO MY HEART. (Like when I write my stories.)

So... *dramatically clearing of throat*

*When* my message has been understood and maybe has helped a little – in whatever way – I'm happy, and every day you prove to me that is the case.

There are still damn Mias and Tristans in this world! People who are trying to do the right thing! Not because they expect something in return but because they are still aware of what is right. They are fighting for fuck's sake, for the good in this world and, fucking crap, that damn well gives me hope for a better future.

Against abuse. Against oppression of the helpless. Against damned corruption and fucking money, which is being worshipped while common courtesy is lost sight of. Against mankind's unspeakable cruelty that he is capable of.

For respect, compassion, decency, and love!

These are the driving forces in my novels because they are the driving forces in my life. That was what my father taught me despite this shitty world before he left us.

I will always try to approach people with an open heart and a smile on my lips, and I thank you for having shown me the same courtesy at the beginning of this series. Really!!!!!!!!!!!!!!!!!!!!!!!!!!!!!!!!!!!!!!!!!!!!!!!!! !!!!!!!!!!!!! !!!!!!!!!!

They still exist. Good people.

Of course, my parents first come to mind. I would be nothing without them. And then there is my sister, you cannot imagine what a great person she is, I'm so proud of you, Vicki!

And of course my husband who, YES, Tristan was oftentimes modeled after. He does not mince his words, he does not pretend, he's a goddamn Russian – even back in school everyone was scared of him – yet here he is, the first one to fight for those who are weaker or help a granny across the street. Although, she might think he is going to steal her purse. Yes, simple fucking prejudices! A person's appearance can be so deceptive and I thank you, Alex, for allowing me to peek behind your mask.

Think of Robbie and then imagine my son. (Robbie was modeled after my son, be it age, behavior, appearance, or his effect on other people). He wraps everyone around his little finger, especially me — I don't have to say more about the most precious person in my life, do I?

Sofia. The strongest woman I have ever met is also my best friend and, dammit, because she is so damn strong, she will follow her love to Australia. Although I am wholeheartedly happy for her, I cannot help but die a thousand deaths. Why couldn't you have fallen in love with a fella who lives in Europe? Oh no? Of course, your damn soul mate has to live on the other side of the world. So, as you know, there are times that I hate you for leaving, but I know we will pull through it together ;)

Anke...and Peter... The family one would look for. I don't know, perhaps it's crazy, but it really feels like you're my parents (I know Anke, you're killing me right now, but I don't care *I am giving you the tongue!) You merely want the best for me and you're such good people! Together we can and will accomplish anything! I love you!

And so, slowly the whole APP Verlag is becoming a big family: first, there is Babels (my soul slut, my sister, my favorite East German, and one of my best friends. Baby, you are like me, just older and wiser, and I thank you for standing by me through thick and thin as well as for telling me it's shit when it's shit!), Bella (I do not have to say much about her, except that I'm really happy to have you and that I love you and that I still feel bad about throwing that dog toy into the Chiemsee — will you come back next year anyway?), Mandy (up, down, feel like vomiting, but at least I'm not alone and I thank you for helping me no matter with whatever book or problem!), Nicky! (grrrrrrrrrrrrrr, lol)

I love our Verlag and YOU GIRLS!

But also Berenike, Tina, Nicole, Melanie, Mel, Kerstin, Natasha, Steffi, Rita, Susanne, Heike and many, many other wonderful people whom I met on the internet. I have so much to be thankful for, it's hard to put it all into words. The list is endless and includes each and every one of you.

\*\*\*

And now, stop crying because the Always on Saturday series is over! \*wiping away a tear\*

Every end is a beginning!

Rotzi, will soon make his debut and, considering you already loved Tristan...blow your mind. I promise...

Until then, give the Tristan series reviews as much as possible! Let's have one last blast! <3

He's just mumbling: Bye you sluts (HE even seems somewhat sad) and maybe... someday... in 10 years or so... they'll make another appearance... (NO, a sequel is NOT planned!!!! However, what do you think about more insights into the Wrangler family, including baaaaaaaaaaaaaaad Tristan?)

Whatever! Merry Christmas (this is my only true present to you!) Thank you for everything.

Yours, Don Both

# Exclusive Excerpt FROM:
# rock or love

"All the senseless screaming and constant jumping around. The useless smashing of guitars and vulgar SPITTING! Women-despising-Satanists. Hotel room vandalizing art performers. Motorcycle traffic light ignorant! Drug addicted devourers of women!" These are rock stars in the eyes of the country's most feared chaperon.

Hannah Amalia Hawking meets her toughest client: Spank Ransom, aka Mason Hunter. Self-proclaimed sex god, proud turtle owner, and world-famous ruffian rocker, whom she must turn onto the virtuous path because his mother fears for the reputation of her only beloved offspring. Grudgingly, Hannah takes on the hopeless case without having any idea what she is getting herself into.

However, the sexy lout has made it his mission to convert *her* instead... Of course, in his own oh-so-special way, which is far from G-rated, shockingly bewitching, and far from good *manners*.

His offer: hours of nocturnal games for daytime etiquette training.

Ultimately, however, both have to make a choice between

*Rock or Love.*

Coming soon …

# 1. I blow good = I love God

Dear God! Why did I look like this?

I was forced into too tight jeans — according to my sister, tube jeans. Even though I could not stand pants because I believed they were inappropriate for women. However, that was not the worst.

It was my T-shirt, which was literally glued to me like a layer of skin and mercilessly revealed every little contour.

Usually, I only wore beautifully ironed, high-necked, bright-white blouses. Yet here I was wearing a black top with the golden glowing phrase, I BLOW GOOD. Since I vehemently refused to learn English (after all, we lived in Germany!), I had no idea the meaning of the bright letters on my chest.

Magda and Rose, my dear little sisters, who were responsible for this horror, laughed every time they looked at me. Although I had been quite skeptical, they had assured me it meant, I LOVE GOD!

As it corresponded with my belief, I finally wore it full of pride and fervor in spite of its unflattering cut.

Besides, my hair was down! It fell over my shoulders in obstructive auburn waves, which usually were smooth and pinned up. Now the loose curly locks constantly obscured my field of vision, so I tried with one strong exhale to blow them out of my face.

"What have I gotten myself into?" I mumbled for the thousandth time and glanced at my youngest sister who happily steered her yellow mini through heavy traffic.

"We're going to have so much fun! I'm sure of it! Maybe you'll find your true love or at least get laid!" Magda chirped in her much too piercing voice, which caused my temples to throb slightly.

"No thanks! I'm good without sex, just fine. It's completely overrated anyway. And who needs men in this day and age? We women are quite capable of living good lives without those belching, ball scratching, much too loud creatures. Without them, the world would be much better off. Believe me," I replied dryly, as usual.

"But the world is nothing without Spank Ransom!" my middle sister stated from the rear seat as she enthusiastically wiggled around. Her golden curls appeared as she squeezed forward between Magda and me. For the last few hours, her expression had been the same; her blue eyes were wide-open and glowing like those of a kid on Christmas. Her cheeks bore reddish spots, which suggested she was more than excited...

I rolled my eyes because I knew how they behaved when it came to this particular subject. Magda giggled in the way women giggle when they think of a two-legged photogenic sex symbol.

"Oh, yes, a world without Spank Ransom would be dreadful and boring...simply monotonous..." Magda reached her hand back, which was eagerly slapped by Rose. Their gazes fused in the rearview mirror.

"WE WILL SEE HIM TODAY!" Magda cried out. Irritated, I snorted and pinched the bridge of my nose with two fingers. However, it would have been better if I had covered my ears because the second round of hysterical screeching started.

"YESSSSSSSSSSSSSSS! And I'm sure he's going to fuck his microphone stand!"

"And he'll moan into the microphone!"

"Maybe he'll wear one of his torn muscle shirts."

"WOWZA, YEAH! Pierced nipple alert! And he'll stroke his sexy hair!"

"YESSS, and...and...and...he'll lick his lower lip!"

"He will put on his bedroom look... ooh, I almost came just thinking about that I-want-to-fuck look!"

"LANGUAGE!" I reminded them in between and was ignored.

With every passing second, they grew louder and younger sounding — even though they were already behaving at the level of 14-year-old adolescents the entire evening. And here their actual ages were 19 and twenty-two.

"MAYBE HE'LL LOOK AT ME!"

"IF HE LOOKS AT US, HE WILL LOOK AT *ME*!" Rose straightened her voluminous curls in her compact. I had had enough for they were at it like that the whole trip, so I put an end to their wishful thinking!

"He will *not* look at *either* of you! The stadium holds 80,000 people and *if* he happens to notice you, I'm sure he'll try to get to safety as fast as possible. Because he'll see right away that you're obsessed with Satan and are totally nuts!" I threw in a bit louder than usual for their pseudo teenage posturing really went on my nerves.

Their eyes immediately broke contact and looked at me threateningly.

"Now listen up, Han!" Magda hissed like a pressure cooker — never a good sign.

"Hannah! Magda, my name is Hannah!"

"Who cares!" Unimpressed, she even hissed a notch higher. "When I love something, well then I love it *wholeheartedly!* And I *love* this band! I think they make great fucking music that contains really important messages. I find Spank hot, and unless you are a lesbian or totally without taste, you'd also find him hot! Hot, hotter, Spank Ransom! He simply is the most beautiful man on this planet! He has a voice like velvet and fire and he can move his oh-so-salivating inspiring body like a god! Besides, we have been waiting *five years* for him to give a concert here! FIVE YEARS! SO LET US HAVE A LITTLE FUN EVEN IF YOU DON'T UNDERSTAND! WHAT'S SO DIFFICULT?" Her hissing had turned into that familiar murmur whispering through her teeth, which she always brandished shortly before losing her composure.

"Are you finished now?" I asked calmly.

"YES!" Obviously furious, she looked back at the road and started venting her anger by blowing the horn like a madman at the standstill traffic in front of us. "Fucking idiots!" she screamed shrilly. "Why is nobody moving? We're already running late, dammit!"

"Could you please watch your language? Your behavior is unacceptable!" I energetically reprimanded.

"NO!" She threw me a burning look. On the rear seat, Rose giggled because she always got a kick out of our boisterous discussions...

It was not hard to argue with Magda. Her temperament equaled that of a rabid mule, whereas Rose's was that of a lamb, or rather a sloth, so to speak. Nothing fazed her quickly — as for my part, I was even harder to get a rise out of. As a certified chaperon, I had acquired a thick skin because I always worked with the hardest cases. However, if I ever got angry, watch out!

At the moment, however, I was miles away from it because, for me, it was rather amusing to see Magda getting even more worked up, cursing, honking and getting a bright red head, which did not become her.

Yet a good half hour later, my mood had turned nonetheless, for the concert was supposed to start in 33 minutes and we still had to RUN to Olympia Hall. And I was wearing five-inch heels in which I had a hard time walking in under normal circumstances. The paving stones did not exactly help either. I was certain that by now I had colonies of blisters on my feet. Hopefully, they would not turn into Americans.

In front of the entrance, the crowd was really bad. On one hand, it was good I had not eaten before because my stomach was empty when I was half-crushed by the masses. On the other hand, my vision started to blur, which was probably due to the oxygen escaping me as I was almost crushed by a wild horde of insane women.

Add to that constant screaming in severe tones: "SEX ON TWO LEGS! SEX ON TWO LEGS!" Just to avoid a misunderstanding, it was the name of the band.

"We cannot let go of each other," Magda announced. I wanted to laugh because I thought it impossible and was abruptly proven right. She was about to grab my hand when the crowd pulled her along and I was unable to grab her.

"Don't worry! I'll meet you at our seats," I shouted at her and caught her worried look. However, the opening band started to play its first notes and Magda's black and Rose's blonde head disappeared into the jumble of people.

At the same time, some of the girls and even a few of the poor men around me *started to* scream *even louder* and charged. As I was tossed back and forth, I thought about calling out that it was only the opening band, but I didn't think anyone would have heard me anyway.

"Hey, please! Careful! Watch out!" I said, outraged as someone was about to stomp on my feet again. My attempts to defend myself with my elbows remained relatively unsuccessful — I was simply too small, not to mention, wobbly on my legs... Why didn't I take my umbrella along for self-defense?

Inevitably, I crashed... The last thing I recalled was hitting my forehead against the railing and landing on the floor near a barrier.

\*\*\*

Great!

Did I mention I abhorred everything rock and roll and its genre?

The senseless screaming and constant jumping around. The useless smashing of guitars and vulgar SPITTING! Women-despising-Satanists. Hotel room vandalizing art performers. Motorcycle traffic light ignorant! Drug addict devourers of women!

In my opinion, that was a rock star's life work and I had no idea how someone could become such a human being — maybe they were born that way. In boots with open shoelaces and long hair!

That was not my world. I lived for completely different ideals — at least I HAVE some!

I had no idea what I was presently doing or where I was...

Especially when I opened my eyes and found myself on an uncomfortable green gurney. My head was throbbing, just like fifteen years ago when I drank alcohol for the first and last time. As I looked up, I flinched in shock because I saw a girl sitting next to me on the gurney. Apparently, she had never heard of Clearasil or water because her pus bumps literally popped unwelcome into my line of sight.

"Oh, you're awake?" she asked, grinning and baring her braces with food scraps for later. I think she had spinach for lunch.

Shaken to the core by the cruel sight, I sat up and immediately cradled my head, which felt quite dizzy and *from* which a cold pack fell directly into my neckline. Suppressing a sharp cry, I quickly fished it out and the girl with the impure skin kindly took it from me.

"It appears so," I answered as soon as I remembered her question. Unfortunately, after a while, I gradually remembered everything else. "Where am I?" I asked the girl with the unfortunate skin condition.

"In the hospital room on the lower level of the stadium. You're lucky a security guard saw you get run over."

"Ah," I said, not at all thrilled. Unexpectedly, the girl's eyes lit up.

"Hey, you know what, we're in the VIP area and could go looking for the band's dressing room!"

"No thanks!" I replied curtly and stood up. My sisters must be worried about me by now, besides, someone had to keep an eye on them.

Braces girl seemed flabbergasted. *"No thanks?"* she repeated in disbelief. "What do you mean no thanks? We're near the sexiest man in the universe!"

I rolled my eyes. Another one of those lamebrain women — evidently I was in the immediate vicinity of a hive.

"Feel free to pretend I'm looking with you," I offered and headed for the door. "Okay then, have fun!" I wished politely for manners were always a must.

\*\*\*

Even as I left the sickroom, I felt uncomfortable pressure on my bladder, which unequivocally let me know nature had to take its course.

I was in need of a restroom!

Now where on earth would I find one in this maze of tunnels? I decided to start searching as my need grew more urgent with every second. I found it difficult to suppress the telling sounds such emergency brings forth. Basically, much uhhhing and ahhhhing. Not to mention almost breaking my ankle every other step. I was tempted to break off my heels and toss them in the nearest trashcan. However, Rose would wring my neck because they were her favorite shoes.

Just when I thought I would have to leave a nasty puddle in the tunnel, I noticed it; the sign that looks the same worldwide, a lady in a housewife dress.

Almost delirious from my full bladder, I stormed through the door full force and froze as soon as I realized it was *not* a clean-kept toilet but a dressing room.

Just then, from a door to an adjacent room, an Adonis of a man stepped in completely naked as God had created him with water pearls all over his body. He was drying his hair with a black towel and I could not see his face. *What* I saw, however, was oversized and totally distracting from the rest of the world.

*His feet!*

I hated feet!

Then my gaze wandered up.

My indignant gasp was obviously overheard because he dropped the towel and glanced around confused. Then it dawned on me *who* I was facing and an emphasized gasped followed.

It was none other than *Sex on Two Legs*' lead singer. I had to admit, the name hit the nail on the head. For that, or better said *he*, was actually sex on two legs. Although I had no prior experience in this regard, my womanly intuition told me that was the case.

Smooth, shaved all over, muscular, sex on two legs.

Tattooed, stunning, bad boy, sex on two legs!

Self-confident, misogynist, idiot, sex on two legs!

He grinned mischievously when he noticed my gaze wandering over his athletic, tattooed, and pierced body while lingering in certain places.

His voice was velvety, but what he said belied it and totally confused me.

"Yea...keep eye-fucking me and I might actually get a boner. OOH! He just twitched. Did you see it?" I could not believe his words as he pointed to his penis, which truly twitched and bit by bit straightened out. Now, the owner's gaze wandered over my body and stopped not between *my* legs but on my T-shirt. He dramatically raised an eyebrow.

"Nice. Honestly, do you?"

Flabbergasted, I peered down at my top and then back at the shocking area of his crotch. I simply could not stop staring. It grew even bigger and harder. I was sure he was aware of how infinitely embarrassing I found the situation. However, instead of ending it, he made it worse. He stood there in front of me not caring about being completely naked with an almost full erection. Then again...he really did not have to be ashamed of his body as it bespoke of discipline and hard work.

"Are you purposely wearing no bra? So your hard nipples are pleasantly visible? Damn, I have to say they sure look great!"

HUMPF! He certainly does not beat around the bush! And here Magda and Rose had literally begged me not to wear a bra. Naturally, my hands flew up to cover the so-unabashedly mentioned place.

"Excuse me?" I barely managed to part my teeth for steam was about to burst from my ears. "Did I just hear you right?"

The arrogant Adonis obviously ignored me and sauntered over to the buffet set up in a corner of the rather small room and popped open a can of cola. As the cool liquid ran down his gullet, I felt like I was in a commercial for that caffeinated drink, which, by the way, was almost nothing but sugar and the reason I categorically refused its enjoyment. I stared spellbound at his Adam's apple and muscular tattooed neck.

And sweet Jesus, I was in the mood for cola!

*Now!*

As he crumpled up the empty can with one hand and let out an extensive loud belch, I flinched. Good God! He behaved like a Neanderthal! Even though the specimen here was unusually hairless...

"I believe you heard right, babe. I said you have great NIPPLES!" He winked suggestively.

"Babe?" I repeated, incredulous. My desire for the sugary solution instantly vanished out of fear of getting diabetes. "I kindly ask that you communicate with the appropriate vocabulary to me. Your language leaves much to be desired and, PLEASE, cover yourself. Perhaps you have not noticed, but you're in the presence of a LADY!"

Now he burst out laughing. It was melodic and boisterous.

"Ladies do not wear shirts with the phrase 'I blow good!'"

"What?" I stared at him, perplexed. "It means 'I love God'!" I mumbled to myself, to which he laughed harder. The man laughed so hard he had to hold on to the buffet table with both hands, which provided an incredibly stimulating picture. His back was in no way inferior to his front and it was just as smooth...

"Okay, so let me get this straight," he said once he calmed somewhat, "You're not a crazy groupie who is going to jump me now? You're not here to have wild SEX?"

"No, I am certainly not!" I replied indignantly. "I was looking for the restroom!"

"Oh! I can help you with that, but the door stays open!" His eyes glowed with amusement.

All I could do was stare at him. Of course, merely as a precaution to be certain HE did not suddenly fall over ME. Because his penis sure looked like it was about to. I wondered how such a monster could even mate with a woman without seriously injuring her.

"Yes, a man's cock sure is interesting, isn't that so? If you want, you can touch him."

"Don't you dare bring that THING closer to me!" I yelled shrilly. "Any chance you can put it away in a pair of underpants, which is, in my humble opinion, where it belongs?" I had a hard time not shielding my eyes with one hand.

"He does not belong in underpants," he countered immediately. "He belongs in a woman!" He said it as if it was the most natural thing in the world and crossed his arms in front of his broad chest. I noticed the tattoo that crisscrossed along his right arm in a dark pattern. It continued on to his shoulder and neck and I blushed when I saw it running down his right side to get lost in the impressive groin area.

"You're not going to rape me?" Overall, he did not come across as someone who would attack me, but his erection and the wild unrestrained behavior made me seriously think.

He smiled haughtily. "I don't have to resort to raping a slut, don't worry." I sharply inhaled. How dare he! I guess I should not feel as if I was addressed considering I was a virgin and pious, but being called by that title was an outrageous impudence.

"I'm ending this conversation now," I announced. "Meeting you was quite uncomfortable; nonetheless, I wish you a successful evening!" I turned away with my head held high and started to march toward the door.

However, I did not get far for in the next moment he called out in full fervor, "Fuck this!"

Then I felt him grab my upper arm and turn me around so that suddenly he was uncomfortably close. I actually could get lost in his cheeky glittering golden-brown dark speckled eyes. From this distance, I noticed his skin was absolutely smooth without any blemishes whatsoever. It was intimidating when a man had such a complexion. The feeling his touch triggered was also intimidating. It was as if a force was emanating from them, one that made even my bones pulsate in whatever area he touched. The corners of his mouth raised and his full lips smiled down at me. It was almost charming, but I was not fooled.

"I thought you had to use the shitter?" His beer reeking breath swept over my face and yanked me out of my stupor.

"Have you heard of chewing gum? Damn, that's horrible!" Disgusted, I pinched my nose closed with two fingers. His eyes flashed mischievously and a strand of his chaotic locks fell over part of his forehead. On the sides, he kept his dark brown hair razor short. His wild hairstyle matched the rest of his wild appearance. My fingers twitched and I jumped when I realized I had almost reached up to brush the strand from his smooth forehead.

His stirring gaze wandered over my face and finally stopped at my lips. He licked his smooth lower lip and I eyed his pink tongue that emerged while an unfamiliar heat spread within me.

He would not just kiss me now, would he?!

"Don't you dare! Don't even think it..." was as far as I got because at that moment, he actually dared to lower his face and forcefully placed his lips against mine. Initially, I was petrified. All the emotions coursing through me were nothing like I had ever experienced. He braced one hand on the door behind me while the other firmly held my waist and pressed me against him. Or was his body pushing against mine?

He was so warm, so hard, so NAKED!

I had no idea what I should do for my emotions were far too contradictory. He, on the other hand, seemed to know perfectly well what *he* needed to do to break down my barriers.

His tongue brushed over my lower lip and, embarrassed, a little sigh escaped me as I felt how velvety it was. My little faux pas had made me open my mouth, which, obviously, he took as an invitation, one I had never planned to give him!

His lips curled, most definitely into a triumphant grin, but it did not detract from his outstanding kissing talent.

Before I could prevent it, the curious tip of my tongue touched his, sending electric shock waves through my entire body that eventually caused the area between my thighs to throb. At about the same time, any sense of logic and decency, all of which I was so proud of, departed my mind and some previously unknown part of my subconscious mind fought its way to the surface.

It was as responsible for me lifting both hands and clawing his wet full hair as it was for me shamelessly rubbing my crotch against his impressive hardness, which promptly elicited a throaty surprised moan.

He had not expected me to make such a move.

My heart was trying to burst out of my chest. My breathing became urgent and mixed with his soft gasps.

Suddenly, I no longer cared about his breath because the taste of the sweet coke mixed with the nasty bitter aftertaste of beer was phenomenal. The taste buds in my mouth danced the samba.

I never thought one kiss could trigger all that and be so consuming. Not to mention, I was totally surprised it was enough to make me light-headed.

I could not remember my name, completely forgot I was searching for a restroom, and men like him, I abhorred abysmally.

That was probably because the man who was presently muddling my mind must be the best kisser in the world even though, in my experience, I had no one to compare him to.

Unfortunately, or should I say, thank goodness, he took it a step too far, which sent my logical mind into overdrive. At that moment, his hand ran up my stomach and his long fingers suddenly grabbed and squeezed my breast as he let out a raspy, clearly primitive sound from the depths of his throat.

So, finally, FINALLY, I did what I should have done all along.

"You're a boor!"

With all my strength, I pushed him away by his broad shoulders and in the next instant, my flat hand slapped his baffled-looking face.

*SMACK!*

He stared at me, astonished and breathless, as his long tattooed fingers slowly touched his sore cheek.

I, on the other hand, wordlessly rushed past him into the room he had come out of with the hope of finding a toilet next to the shower. I was lucky.

Of course, I locked the door and was careful to cover the seat with toilet paper before sitting down to relieve myself. I made sure to take my time for I expected he would eventually have to go on stage.

And that was the case. As soon as I heard the door slamming, I cautiously peeked into the room. He was gone.

Only his wonderful scent still lingered in the air. As if on its own, my hand raised and my fingertips brushed my still tingling lower lip.

The kiss had been amazing, whereas all else should be forgotten. I prayed I'd never see that primitive Neanderthal again after the concert.

However, I had sinned, so my prayers went unanswered ...

# 2. Down with the sickness!

By the time I finally managed to fight my way through the hall to my sisters, I was actually carrying my killer high-heeled shoes. Our seats were practically right next to the big stage. Exhausted, as if I had hiked a day through the jungle, I dropped onto the uncomfortable plastic chair, slipped the things back on, and breathed deeply.

Rose and Magda were busy watching the remaining technicians walk across the stage. They were holding hands and seemed too excited to notice I had risen from the dead.

Luckily!

After all, I still felt a bit vulnerable from the previous ambush. I could still feel his long fingers on my skin, which, on one hand, I felt degraded and dishonored, yet, on the other, somehow...*different*.

I did not like that the boor made me feel *different*. But he had. Thinking back at those few minutes in the dressing room when his lips had been on mine, made my blood boil, whether I wanted it to or not.

As soon as my pulse returned to normal, I was able to face my surroundings. The stage was round and a sparkling black drum set bearing the huge inscription *SEX ON TWO LEGS* was elevated. To the right and left of it, two catwalks lead out into the now impatiently screaming crowd, presumably to bring the musician closer to his fans or to give the Neanderthal in him an opportunity to mess with even more innocent women's heads. One of them was only seven feet away from us. I felt a bit leery sitting right next to one of those catwalks and hoped he would not recognize me if he walked down it. To be certain and less inconspicuous, I made myself as small as possible in my seat.

Good God! Now I was as brain dead as my sisters! How would he identify me among 80,000 other people? My paranoia was horrendous! I needed to focus on calming down so my blood pressure would finally return to normal. I also strongly urged myself to forget what had happened. Otherwise, my sisters might discover something was wrong. And they would take my HEAD off if they ever found out I had lived their most intimate dream.

ME...

And here I had not even wanted it!

Greedily, I looked at the water in Rose's hands and pulled on her short black skirt to get her attention. Reluctantly, she took her eyes off the stage to let the disturber have it when she registered it was me and relief flashed across her face. As she dropped onto the seat next to me and even though it was very rude, I grabbed the water from her hand and emptied it in one gulp.

"Thank God you're here! We were worried you had flown the coop!" she said in a voice much too deep for a woman.

"As if I stood a chance!" I mumbled derisively.

"What took you so long?"

Now also Magda noticed me, took her place beside Rose, and leaned forward to eye me from head to toe.

"Yeah, where the fuck were you and why does your hair look so weird? It's disheveled. And your lips are swollen?" Magda pushed Rose out of the way and came so horribly close to my face to examine my mouth that I shrank away. Her gaze also traveled to my forehead and lingered there, surely because blinking bold red letters announced:

I had kissing sex!

Automatically, I rubbed my forehead.

"OH, PLEASE, Magda. Stop your cursing... I... I slipped and fainted." Rose gasped in shock, Magda, however, remained skeptical.

"LOOK AT THIS!" I raised my straight bangs to expose the unsightly bump on my forehead as proof.

"OH!" Now Magda also looked sympathetic.

"I was taken to a hospital room." My sisters' eyes widened. "But it wasn't anything serious." I made a dismissive gesture and pressed the cool cup against the bump. Considering I liked my head just fine on my shoulders, I left out everything else that happened. "It merely took time to get out of there and to you here. All these crazy people here are somewhat scary!" I said, shrugging, and leaned back exhausted while closing my eyes

"Oh, sweetie, and we left you alone!" Rose brushed a strand of hair from my forehead and I slapped her fingers.

"I can take care of myself just fine, thank you!" Incidentally, I was rummaging in my purse for my earplugs, which I carry almost everywhere, after all, my impeccable hearing, up to the high-frequency ranges, was sacred to me and in this country, construction sites were on every corner.

However, my earplugs were immediately ripped from my fingers and without further ado, carelessly tossed into the crowd.

Rose laughed her dark laugh, probably due to my expression, and tossed her corkscrew curls over her shoulder. Meanwhile, I looked at her grimly as I thought, not for the first time, how the man that ended up with her would be a poor schmuck and a lucky guy at the same time. Rose had inherited all of our mother's beauty, the golden blonde hair, tall figure, to perfect proportions. Amongst us three, she had the biggest breasts for which Magda had always envied since she was as flat as a board. Besides, Magda was also the shortest of us girls, but she had the biggest eyes and was of the most extroverted character.

As for their self-confidence, my sisters were on equal footing. Both were not lacking. They knew they were intelligent and beautiful in their own way. Magda's slender face was framed by a modern bob, while Rose's features were softer and more classical — as was her haircut. Presently, her body was dressed in a short black skirt, same-colored tights, glittering top with batwing sleeves, and adorned with lots of chains and jewelry. Her pantyhose apparently had not been washed on the gentle cycle for there were runs and holes all over. Dreadful. I had offered her a new pair of mine, but all I got in return was the finger.

Magda, on the other hand, had squeezed into a dark blue corset dress with laces. She combined this with an undamaged pair of pantyhose and numerous bracelets.

Both looked like rocker chicks, which, incidentally, they were. All day long, they listened to nothing but that genre. Preferably songs by Sex on Two Legs. By now, I was sick and tired of Spank Ransom's growling voice and I did not want to see his face either! After all, every time I entered my sisters' room I was stared at from all the walls by that, in my opinion, empty-headed expression, which regularly made my flesh crawl and blood boil. The posters scared me and caused one or two nightmares!

When it came to him, my sisters behaved like two little girls instead of adults! However, most likely, he was used to driving women insane simply with one look, even if it was only from a poster... Now that I had met him, I could somewhat sympathize with that fascination for he had also mesmerized me with his frivolous way. It was hard for me to admit that and I was glad when suddenly, the main light dimmed and the stage lit up in bright red.

Various strobe lights flashed through the hall in random, uncontrolled patterns, illuminating it in all kinds of magical colors. Soon, it grew pitch black and, in anticipation, the entire crowd fell into a hushed silence. I swear a pin dropping could be heard.

A burp in the microphone broke the tension and everyone screamed!

The music started, led by heavy drums and then an electric guitar... It was rousing, I had to admit it, whether I wanted to or not.

*"Can you feel that?"*

...a deep male voice, apparently symbolizing pure sex, breathed into the microphone!

*"Oh shit..."*

Unfortunately, the words went directly to my private region. Presumably, that was how he sounded when entering a woman...

*"OW WAHAHAHAHAHAHA!"*

...he suddenly bellowed into the microphone. Then fireworks lit up the hall and the crowd went wild as Spank Ransom jumped onto the now lit stage. Everyone was out of their seats, bobbing up and down while holding their arms up and slightly waving their hands back and forth.

"What an ape!" I rolled my eyes and crossed my arms as the crowd around me whipped itself into a frenzy.

He made more primate sounds while next to him, his blond guitarist hopped around like Rumpelstiltskin and his bear of a drummer banged his instrument like a maniac. However, they were rather secondary.

I could not help but take a closer look at *him* as he gripped his microphone with both hands. He drove Magda and Roses absolute out of their minds when he started to rape the microphone stand to the beat while continuing to produce disgusting sounds.

My God, why couldn't my sisters love Richard Wagner?

The rocker wore tight black leather pants and boots with laces undone, over which I was sure he would stumble, possibly even hurt himself or others, quite irresponsible in my opinion. He also wore a tight torn dark muscle shirt that showed more than it covered. Leather straps snaked around his pronounced tattooed forearms. A thick silver chain dangled from his neck, his hair – disheveled. His slender hips – adorned with a couple of studded belts – moved to the beat of the music as if he'd learned it professionally. All the while, his charisma was incredibly erotic, I could not deny that.

And when he started to sing...to actually *sing*...not bellow...it felt as if his voice was pulling me into another world...

*Drowning deep in my sea of loathing*
*Broken your servant I kneel*
*(Will you give it to me?)*
The crowd screamed. "YESSSSSSSSSSSSSSS!"
*It seems what's left of my human side*
*is slowly changing in me*

*(Will you give it to me?)*

Now, the crowd freaked out completely and my heart beat much faster. Annoyed, I noticed my right foot bobbing to the beat, so I quickly put both hands on my knee and pushed on it.

*Looking at my own reflection*
*When suddenly it changes*
*Violently it changes (oh no)*

His voice grew stronger and I shuddered from the timbre relentlessly blaring through the hall. I felt the bass in every fiber of my being, my whole body tingled and vibrated. The leg continued to do what it wanted, even my other one had a mind of its own and would not keep still.

*There is no turning back now*
*You've woken the demon within me...*

And then he looked at me!

I was so shocked that I almost choked on my saliva. His eyes were burning my eyes — he was literally devouring me. And he saw *me!* He knew where I was sitting and talked to me through his song. His voice was breathtaking and went down like honey...when he was not yelling. I sat there with a petrified heart and tears eventually came to my eyes for whatever reason, even if I did not understand a single word he was saying.

He grinned contentedly, licked his full lower lip, then turned his eyes from me and, as the refrain repeated itself, stretched out both arms with palms facing up in an effort to get the audience to sing along. They were putty in his hands.

*Get up, come on, get down with the sickness*
*Open up your hate and let it flow into me*
*Get up, come on, get down with the sickness*
*You mothers get up, come on, get down with the sickness*
*You fuckers get up, come on, get down with the sickness*
*Madness is the gift that has been given to me!*

Meanwhile, the song was pulling me along and my body swayed as my head nodded uncontrollably. His flowing movements mesmerized me. He was at home on stage. You could clearly see how comfortable he was and how much he loved to make the women squeal and kneel in front of him, willing to do anything for him. He and his well-toned body were one. A powerful weapon mixed with his rousing full voice!

*I can see inside you, the sickness is rising*
*Don't try to deny what you feel*
*It seems that all that was good has died*
*and is decaying in me*
*(Will you give it to me?)*

And here I still had the frightening feeling he was talking to *me*!

*It seems you're having some trouble*
*In dealing with these changes*

*Living with these changes*
*Oh no, the world is a scary place*
*Now that you've woken the demon within me*

The crowd was no longer calm. They jumped around and jostled each other — basically completely flipping out. Already, the first panties and bras were tossed onto the stage! He took an item, rubbed it between his legs, and then yelled into the microphone.

"Don't kill yourselves over it, you horny motherfuckers!" He waved it over his head and flung it back into the crowd. I saw a bunch of hands frantically trying to grab it and rolled my eyes. Disgusting!

The song ended with a loud bang and Spank Ransom jumped a good three feet into the air, apparently having fully exhausted himself. Finally, he landed on his knees in a good old rocker pose, while to the right and left of him red fireworks exploded.

Then he stood up in one smooth provocative move and like a predator, sauntered over to his microphone stand as his bandmates rang in the first deep beats of the next song.

"Fuck you all!" He gave the audience his two middle fingers and smiled demonically as he was cheered on like he was a god. Granted, his grin was something...

"Do you want to go crazy with us?"

"Yessssssssssssss!"

"I asked, do you want to go crazy with us?"

"YESSSSSSSSSSSSSSSSSSSSSSSSSSSSSSSSSSSSSSS!"

"THEN DO IT, YOU CUNTS! Maybe this is YOUR LAST CHANCE!" he shouted into the microphone before the next song started and a laser show almost stole my vision.

Honestly, I could not take my eyes off the boorish yet intriguing man who was *walking* and jumping, if not to say *prancing* around like a *great* ballerina on stage...while constantly raping whatever inanimate object by rubbing his crotch on it — which, by the way, each time made both of my sisters WHIMPER. He constantly grabbed his impressive package and made suggestive movements with his tongue, which obviously he had mastered. Some women in my and other rows even fainted, like in some weird domino set up, and I thought I was in a bad movie when one after the other had to be carried out.

Rose and Magda were no longer with me and had their eyes glued to him, *unblinking*, and I was sure they had to be dried up.

Since he had not looked at me again, I thought I was safe, which, unfortunately, I was not. As he announced the end of the show with a particularly nasty grin and made his way with the microphone onto the catwalk and over to our row of seats, I sensed wickedness.

"Well, soon the party will be over...but we're going to have one more blast... And for this song, I need female support...without her a good fuck simply is not a good fuck!"

Apparently, the crowd knew which song would come now for I heard several people already screaming.

"CLOSER! CLOSER! CLOSER!"

"Yeah! You're right on! The closer the better!" Shocked, I backed away as his glowing eyes flashed at me again like lightning.

Magda and Rose were holding their breaths as he jumped off stage and leaped across the barrier to prance toward *me*. All the while, he was flanked by six bodyguards or else he would have been swallowed up by women like Ramses was by the Red Sea.

"TAKE ME! TAKE ME! TAKE ME!" Whatever females within 20 feet screamed at the top of their lungs and I feared the sudden deafness threatening me for so long would now set in.

And then he was there – *right in front of me!* – smirking arrogantly. Now Magda and Rose stood there frozen with mouths gaping. I was probably the only woman of those 80,000 present who was standing there facing him with her arms crossed in front of her and giving him an irate look.

"Under no circumstance! No... AHHHHHH," I shrieked as he bent down, grabbed my thighs, and swung me over his shoulder! WHAT?!

"I have caught my prey, people! UGA, UGA," he joked and I felt his hand slap my behind.

"How dare you!" I exclaimed, only to hear him laugh as he carried me off. "I'm not a piece of meat! You really are a Neander... UGH!" With a jerk, he sat me down on a type of throne that had been placed center stage.

Meanwhile, he had switched from a hand-held microphone to a headset...

When he looked at me, his eyes glowed with such desire and anticipation that, at that moment, I knew I was lost. Completely lost...

CUT!

*Rock or Love - Coming soon!*

# **About Don Both**

Don Both, aka Bethy Zimmermann is 30 years old. Her parents are from Prague in the Czech Republic. At the age of 12, her class held a short story contest where she discovered her true great love — writing. During her schooling and vocational training as a nanny, she wrote throughout the day and drew comics at the same time. At first, she created animal stories, family stories, fantasy stories ... As she grew older, her novels and male protagonists became hotter and hotter and she discovered her other great love: eroticism.

In 2010, she took the big step and went public with her novels. Through her cheeky, provocative, and extraordinary writing style, she quickly gained an enthusiastic fan base. At the time, the young woman won several competitions and prizes — for example, "Best Fanfiction Author" and "Best Erotic Story".

At the time, her husband's health was declining and the company where she worked as a baker's assistant went bankrupt. Practically overnight, the small family became Hartz 4 recipients (Welfare, unemployment program). In dire straits, the desperate mother discovered Amazon Self-publishing and with their last money published "The unholy Book of Tristan Wrangler". It was a smash hit. What every author dreams about. It has become a bestseller that has since grown into one of the most widely read eBooks on the German market.

Since then, she and her two best friends founded A.P.P. Verlag (publisher), which includes more than 30 successful authors. In the meantime, she became acquainted with the media. Several newspapers wrote articles and she was on television.

Privately, the curvy dynamic woman is committed to animal welfare and the fight against body shaming, while trying every day to do something good. She loves yoga and resides with her cats, her super sweet German Shepherd dog, husband, and son in a small Bavarian town.

www.ingramcontent.com/pod-product-compliance
Lightning Source LLC
Chambersburg PA
CBHW070347260626
47161CB00001B/53